SHE COULDN'T RESIST

"Marry me, Emma. Please." Did he sound too enthusiastic? She must think him a lunatic. But it would be a sensible decision on her part. Charles tempered his voice. "Our marriage would solve so many problems. We'd get rid of these London idiots. My nieces would get a mother and you'd get a home of your own. Your father could marry Mrs. Graham without disturbing your peace." He grinned at her, leaning closer. "And I'd get the lovely opportunity—many lovely opportunities—to produce an heir. What do you say?"

Emma's stinging slap was eloquence itself.

The Naked Marquis

SALLY MACKENZIE

ZEBRA BOOKS
Kensington Publishing Corp.
www.kensingtonbooks.com

ZEBRA BOOKS are published by

Kensington Publishing Corp.
850 Third Avenue
New York, NY 10022

All Kensington titles, imprints, and distributed lines are available at special quantity discounts for bulk purchases for sales promotion, premiums, fund-raising, educational, or institutional use.

Special book excerpts or customized printings can also be created to fit specific needs. For details, write or phone the office of the Kensington Special Sales Manager: Attn. Special Sales Department. Kensington Publishing Corp., 850 Third Avenue, New York, NY 10022. Phone: 1-800-221-2647.

Zebra and the Z logo Reg. U.S. Pat. & TM Off.

ISBN 0-8217-7832-3

First Printing: March 2006
10 9 8 7 6 5 4 3 2

Printed in the United States of America

For Mom and Dad,
and Kevin and the boys, of course,
and for Ruth.

And with thanks to Elin
for the bachelor's buttons.

CHAPTER 1

Why the bloody hell did Paul have to die?

Major Charles Draysmith stood on the broad gravel drive, rain dripping down his neck, and stared at the immense sandstone facade looming before him. He did not want to go inside.

He had lingered in London as long as he could, meeting with the solicitor, with Paul's bankers, taking care of all the details of the succession—and hating every bloody minute. Every "yes, my lord" tore another piece of his life from him.

Thanks to an anonymous Italian thief, he was now the Marquis of Knightsdale.

A gust drenched his greatcoat, sending more rain cascading down his neck. He couldn't stand out here forever like a great looby. Aunt Bea would be along shortly with the carriages and her servants and her overfed cat to prepare for the house party.

God. Tomorrow a horde of aristocratic young virgins and their mamas would descend on Knightsdale. Dread clawed at his gut, and his palms started to sweat, just as they had before every battle he'd fought on the Peninsula. He wanted to turn and run.

He stepped forward and banged on the door.

"Good morning, my lord."

"Is it a good morning, Lambert?" Charles let the butler take his wet hat and coat. It had been ten years since he'd last seen the man—since Paul's wedding. Lambert had new lines around his mouth and eyes, and his hair had thinned.

Doubtless the man noted changes in him as well, Charles thought. He'd barely been out of university when he'd last been home; now he was thirty, aged by the blood and dirt of war.

"Have someone look after my horse, will you?"

"Certainly, my lord. Is Lady Beatrice with you?"

"No, I rode on ahead. I—what is that racket?" Charles swore he heard the rumble of distant artillery.

"I believe it is Miss Peterson, my lord, with Lady Isabelle and Lady Claire."

"What the hell are they doing?" Charles started for the stairs. The noise was coming from one of the upper floors.

"Skittles, my lord. In the long gallery."

Skittles, Charles thought. *How can the girls be playing skittles? They're only infants.*

He heard another rumble and then shrieking. Was someone hurt? He started running, taking the stairs two at a time. The long gallery, if he remembered correctly, had a number of heavy, marble busts of past Draysmiths. If one of them fell on a small child . . . And was that barking? A dog, too? Whatever was this Miss Peterson thinking? He had assumed Nanny and the governess—*was* her name

Peterson? He hadn't thought so. He would have remembered, surely, as that was the vicar's name. He had assumed his young nieces were in good hands. Apparently he had been mistaken. Well, this Miss Peterson would shortly be finding herself seeking other employment.

He reached the long gallery just in time to see a small black and white terrier crash into the pedestal that supported Great-Uncle Randall's bust.

Emma Peterson leapt to steady the statue just as a man bellowed from the stairs. The surprise of hearing a male voice almost caused her to knock over the ugly sculpture herself. Surely Mr. Lambert would not have let a bedlamite into the house?

"What the bloody hell do you think you are doing, woman, letting that animal run loose? One of your charges could have been crushed."

Emma stiffened. Who was this man, to come here, cursing and criticizing? She pushed her spectacles higher on her nose. Did she know him? His voice sounded slightly familiar. If only he would come closer.

What was she thinking? She should be wishing him back downstairs and out the door. He was not overly tall, but his broad shoulders and general air of command indicated he was used to getting his way. What if he proved threatening? If she shouted, would anyone hear her in time to come to her aid?

"Prinny didn't mean any harm, sir." Brave Isabelle faced their intruder with her narrow shoulders back, though she did step closer to Emma.

"Course he didn't mean any harm." Little Claire threw her arms around Prinny's neck. "You're a good dog, aren't you, Prinny?"

Prinny barked and licked her face.

"Prinny? Good God, Prinny! He may be a good dog, miss, but he doesn't belong racing around in here."

"Sir." Emma was pleased that her voice did not waver or crack. She pulled herself up to her full, if insignificant, height. "Sir, I must ask you to leave. Immediately."

"*You* must ask *me* to leave? Madam, I shall be telling *you* to leave in no short order."

Emma swallowed. Lud, he was coming closer. "Isabelle, Claire, come here, darlings."

The man stopped. "Isabelle and Claire?"

"Yes." Emma raised her chin.

He was close enough for her to see him clearly now. His face was sun-darkened, his curly brown hair cut ruthlessly short. He was older, stronger, more assured than the man she had last glimpsed from a distance at the late marquis's wedding, but she knew him. She could never forget those eyes—clear blue, like lakes, with dark rims. Charles Draysmith, the boy she had idolized and the man she had sighed over, had returned to Knightsdale.

"*These* are my nieces?" Charles stared at the girls. The older one—Isabelle—looked to be about nine years old. She was thin with straight, wispy white-blond hair, high cheekbones, and Paul's green eyes. The other one still had the plump curves of babyhood, but she was no longer an infant. She had his own wildly curly hair.

Claire, the little one, put her small fists on her hips—an action he'd swear he'd seen Nanny do countless times when he was a boy—and jutted out her chin. "Are you a bad man?"

"Claire!" The woman frowned. "This is your Uncle Charles, the new Marquis of Knightsdale."

Charles studied the governess. How did she know who he was? Well, the servants should have been expecting him—he'd sent word that he and Aunt Bea were coming—so it wouldn't have taken a genius to deduce his identity. But she had not known who he was at first or she would not have ordered him out of the house. She had bottom, he'd grant her that. She'd stood her ground in the face of his bellowing. Many an army private had blanched when on the receiving end of his temper.

She was only a few inches taller than Isabelle, but she did not look at all childlike. Not at all. He jerked his eyes higher to study her face. Dark blond hair, the color of warm honey and even curlier than his; a sprinkling of freckles; golden-brown eyes, fringed with long, dark lashes . . .

"Runt?" He swallowed a shocked laugh of recognition. Surely this could not be Emma Peterson, the vicar's daughter, the skinny little waif who used to follow at his heels like a lost puppy? The other boys had taunted him, but he hadn't had the heart to turn her away. "Your pardon. I mean, Miss Peterson. Surely you are not the girls' governess?"

"No, my lord. The governess, Miss Hodgekiss, was called home suddenly to care for her sick mother. I am merely filling in while she is gone."

A delicate flush colored her cheeks. She did not meet his eyes. His gaze sharpened. His gut told him Miss Emma Peterson still harbored a shred of hero worship for him. Interesting. She was an attractive armful. Perhaps she would prove to be the solution to his problem. What if he asked her to marry him? He could certainly do worse. If he got her consent before the bloody house party, he wouldn't have to spend the next few days running before the matrimonial hounds.

Charles felt Claire tug on his sleeve.

"Miss Hodgekiss is afraid her mum might die." Big brown eyes stared up at him. "My mum died on a mountain in It-lee."

"Italy. Your mother and father died in the mountains of Italy." Charles had to clear his throat. He had never much liked Cecilia, Paul's wife. He'd thought her beautiful and shallow, like so many of the society misses. He tangled his fingers in Claire's curls and glanced at Isabelle. The girls did not look grief-stricken. Not surprising. From what his friends the Duke of Alvord and the Earl of Westbrooke had said, Paul and Cecilia had not been doting parents. They'd spent most of their time in London or at someone else's country estate.

"Are you our papa now?"

"Claire, don't be a ninny!" Isabelle scowled. "Uncle Charles doesn't want us. He wants his own family."

Charles heard Miss Peterson draw in a sudden, sharp breath. He, too, felt as if he'd been kicked in the gut. True, he hadn't given the girls much thought—hell, he'd thought they were still babes in arms—but that wasn't at all the same as not wanting them.

"I'm your uncle, Isabelle. Your papa's brother. So you are my family, and this is your home. Claire is right—I am like a father to you now."

He smiled, seeing some of the tension leave the older girl's shoulders. Surely he could be as much a father to his nieces as Paul had been.

"Tell me about your dog—Prinny, did you call him? He doesn't look much like our Regent." All

Charles could see of the small white and black dog was its stubby tail and hind legs. The rest was wedged between the wall and Great-Uncle Randall's pedestal. "Hey, sir, get away from there!"

Prinny stopped scrabbling at the base of a pilaster, sneezed, and padded over to investigate Charles's boots.

"Prinny's Miss Peterson's dog, Papa."

"Claire, dear, Lord Knightsdale is your uncle, not your papa."

Claire's lower lip stuck out. "But I don't want an uncle—I want a papa!"

Charles knelt so his face was level with Claire's. He saw the uncertainty and fear behind the stubbornness in her eyes. He'd seen those emotions in the eyes of so many children in Spain and Portugal. Claire was the child of a wealthy English family, but she was still a child.

"Some people might get confused if you call me Papa, Lady Claire. And it wouldn't be nice to forget your own papa, would it?"

Claire's lower lip trembled; her small arms crossed tightly across her chest. "I want a papa. Why can't you be my papa? And Miss Peterson can be my mama."

Charles felt as if he were teetering on the edge of a precipice. One false step and Claire would dissolve in tears.

"What if you call me Uncle Charles in company and Papa Charles in private?"

"In private?"

"When it's just you and I—and Isabelle and Miss Peterson. Would that be acceptable?"

Claire chewed her bottom lip, then grinned and threw her arms around Charles's neck. His arms came around her reflexively to keep from being knocked backward.

Claire's skin was baby soft. Her curls tickled his jaw. Her breath, as she kissed his cheek, smelled of milk and porridge. He felt an odd melting sensation in his chest.

"That would be 'ceptable, Papa Charles," Claire said, before she turned to hug Prinny.

Ah, so he was not so much different from the dog. Were all children so free with their affection? He glanced at Isabelle. No, he thought not.

"You may call me Papa Charles, too, Isabelle, if you'd like."

"I am nine, Uncle. I am not a baby anymore."

"No, indeed." He wished she were. Her body was too straight, too stiff. She reminded him of his young privates before their first battle. Nine was too young to be all grown up.

"Do you suppose I might borrow Miss Peterson for a while? I should like to have a word with her."

"Of course," Isabelle said.

Miss Peterson appeared to be suppressing a smile. Good. He definitely wanted her favorably disposed toward him.

"Isabelle, would you take Claire back up to the nursery?"

"Yes, Miss Peterson."

"Can we take Prinny with us, Mama Peterson?"

Charles bit his lip to keep from laughing at Miss Peterson's expression. She clearly was uncomfortable with Claire's new name for her but did not want to hurt the little girl's feelings.

"All right, as long as you make sure he doesn't annoy Nanny."

"Prinny wouldn't 'noy Nanny, would you, Prinny?"

The dog yapped twice and licked Claire's face.

"See, Mama Peterson? Prinny is a very smart dog."

"Yes, well, he can also be somewhat excitable."

"Nanny likes Prinny, Miss Peterson," Isabelle said. "She only pretends to be annoyed by him."

"I don't think she was pretending when he knocked over the flowers and soaked her dress, Isabelle."

"But he didn't mean to do that." Claire stroked Prinny's ear. "He just wanted to smell the big red rose."

"Just be certain he stays away from Nanny's flowers this time."

"Yes, Miss Peterson, we will. Come on, Claire."

Claire's high voice carried across the gallery as she skipped toward the stairs. "I think Papa Charles will be a splendid papa, don't you, Isabelle? He has very nice eyes and his hair is as curly as mine."

Charles grinned, looking down at Emma. Her cheeks were flushed.

"I apologize, my lord. Claire is still very young. I'm sure her manners will improve."

"Oh, I'm not offended. My hair *is* wretchedly curly—much like yours." He let his eyes wander over her curls. She had tried to tame them, pulling them back off her face, but a number had escaped. Her blush deepened in a most attractive manner. "And I cannot object to having nice eyes—do *you* think them nice, Miss Peterson?"

"My lord!" Her face turned an even brighter red.

He smiled, offering her his arm. "Shall we repair to the study? I would appreciate your telling me about my nieces. As you may have guessed, I've not kept up with their lives."

She hesitated, then laid her fingers on his sleeve.

They trembled slightly, and he put his hand up to cover them. They were so small, so delicate. She had not struck him as delicate when she was a child—she'd been struggling so hard to keep up with him and his friends, he supposed. But she was not a child any longer. His eyes slid over to contemplate her bosom. No, not at all. And her lovely breasts certainly were not small, though he'd wager they were exquisite. A delectable handful, though covered by a very boring frock at the moment. His fingers itched to loosen her buttons and reveal the wonders she was hiding.

Sudden lust made a part of him, never small, grow significantly larger. He averted his eyes and repressed a smile.

His future suddenly looked much brighter.

Emma walked with Charles down the stairs to the study. Her emotions were disordered. She had been angry and frightened when he had burst upon them, but once she had comprehended who he was . . . well, she didn't know what she felt.

She should still be angry. She had been angry these past four months when he had failed to make the short trip from London to visit his nieces. Not that the girls had missed him—they were used to neglect, more's the pity. But Emma admitted to herself as she walked down the long staircase that *she* had been disappointed in him.

Oh, he had come briefly, for just a handful of hours, when the marquis and marchioness were laid in the family vault. But he had hurried back to London before the last prayer had faded, and he had not visited since. Why? What had happened to the man? Had the war changed him so drastically? Surely the boy she'd known would not have ignored his nieces in such a manner.

She remembered the day she'd met him. Remembered? Lud! She treasured the memory, recalling it whenever she felt lonely or sad or discouraged.

She had been six years old. Her father had just taken the Knightsdale living, and she missed her old house, her old playmates, everything familiar. Loneliness was a throbbing ache in her middle. She'd found a nice log by the stream that ran though the woods near the vicarage, and had settled down to cry until she had no tears left. But crying only made her stomachache worse.

And then Charles had come whistling into her world. She'd heard him before she saw him. She would have hidden away, but she was too exhausted from her tears. He'd stopped in front of her and put his hands on his hips.

He was only four years older than she, a skinny boy with curly brown hair, but he had seemed like a god in the wood's still, leaf-sifted sunlight. He had made a noise of disgust and then had pulled a grubby handkerchief out of his pocket.

Buck up, he'd said as he'd scrubbed her face. *Stop blubbering. You don't want everyone to think you're a baby, do you? Come on, you can help me look for salamanders.*

She had fallen in love then, and she had never quite fallen out.

She looked down at his hand where it covered hers. He was not wearing gloves—nor was she. The warmth and weight of his palm and the touch of his strong, slightly callused fingers did odd things to her breathing. She had the shocking urge to turn her hand and weave her smaller fingers with his.

He was beyond her touch. She knew it. She had always known it, even when she had stared at him in the woods twenty years ago. He had been the son and brother of a marquis—now he was the marquis, and she was just the vicar's daughter, as common as a buttercup in the Knightsdale fields. Still, she had tagged after him like a puppy, happy for some scrap of attention. When he'd left for school, she had cried again—and again the tears had not helped the empty ache in her middle.

And then her mother had died and she'd had her sister, Meg, and her father to care for. No time for silly romantic dreams.

She glanced at Charles's profile as they reached the entrance hall. No time, perhaps, nor sense in it, but she had dreamed anyway.

She'd been sixteen when he'd last been home. Not yet out. Too young to be invited to his brother's wedding ball, but not too young to desperately want to attend and perhaps dance with Charles.

She had done the most daring thing—the only daring thing—of her life. She had slipped out her window, through the woods, and up to the terrace. She'd hidden in the shadows, watching the men in their white linen and black eveningwear, the women in their jewels and colorful dresses.

She had seen Charles come out onto the terrace with a London lady. Emma had stared at the woman. Her dress had clung to every curve and dipped precariously low over her full breasts. She'd been amazingly, shockingly beautiful. And then Charles had taken the lady in his arms and kissed her, his hands roaming freely over her body.

It had made Emma feel very odd—breathless and uncomfortable. Embarrassed and wicked and . . . fluttery and hot. She had hurried back to the vicarage as if Satan himself were after her.

She'd seen that kiss in her dreams a thousand times, but in her dreams, she was the woman in Charles's arms.

Well, she should be cured of that affliction now. She took her hand off his arm as they entered the study. The servants did their best, but the room still smelled of old fires and dust. It had been more than a year since the marquis—the former marquis—had visited the estate.

"Miss Peterson, I apologize if I startled you just now." Charles gestured for her to take a seat by the fire. She preferred to remain standing, forcing him to stand as well. He threw her a puzzled glance. Emma gripped her hands before her.

"My lord, it has been four months since your brother and his wife died, leaving your nieces orphans. Why have you taken so long to come home?"

Charles shrugged one shoulder. "Home?" His mouth tensed and he looked down at the desk. When he looked back up, his face was emotionless. "The girls were in good hands. I spoke to your father at the funeral. Nanny was here and the governess as well. Why would they care to see an uncle who was a stranger to them? And I truly thought they were still infants."

"How could you have thought that? Isabelle is nine years old and Claire is four."

"I was only twenty-one, a young man on the Town, when Paul had his first child. Beyond the disappointment that he had not managed to get an heir, I didn't think much of it. And then I went to war. The little one—Claire—wasn't born when I left for the Peninsula."

"And do you intend to leave them again, now that you've seen them?"

Emma could see from his expression that was exactly what he had intended.

"You can't, my lord! The girls have lived long enough in the care of servants. They need a relative in the house. You heard how much Claire wants a papa! Isabelle, too, though she is too reserved to say so."

"And what about a mama, Miss Peterson? Surely the girls need a mama as much, or more, than they need a papa?"

"Well, of course they need a mama, but there's no one available at the moment to fill that position."

"No?" Charles grinned suddenly. "How about you?"

Emma felt as if all the air had been sucked out of her lungs.

Charles bit the inside of his cheek to keep from laughing. Miss Peterson's jaw had dropped like a rock.

"It's the perfect solution, when you think of it, Miss Peterson. The girls need a mother, as you yourself have pointed out. They know you and like you—and you live nearby, so you'll have the comfort of your own family at hand."

And I find the notion of bedding you distinctly appealing. Charles smiled, trying to imagine how Miss Peterson would react to *that* statement. But it was true. He hadn't thought of her in years, yet to see her now, to have her standing just inches from him . . . Perhaps it was the contrast—his memories of her as a little girl with her very grown-up figure. Whatever it was, it was distinctly erotic. He shifted position, turning away from her slightly to hide his reaction.

It was the perfect solution to his problem. Neither of them would be inconvenienced. It was not as if he had to spend a vast quantity of time with her. He had no desire to live at Knightsdale. He'd find something useful to do in Town and just come down from time to time to work on his responsibility to sire an heir.

Yes, he'd come down to take her to bed. To strip that ugly frock off her lovely body. To bury his face in her soft, shapely breasts. To . . .

He turned abruptly to the desk. His breeches were getting distinctly uncomfortable.

"What could be better, Miss Peterson? You don't have a beau, do you?"

"Well, no, but . . ."

"And pardon me for saying so, but you *are* a bit past the usual age for marriage, are you not? As I remember, you are twenty-six, four years younger than I."

"Yes . . ."

Charles glanced at her, noting her heightened color and heaving bosom. Especially her heaving bosom. He jerked his eyes up to meet hers. Behind her spectacles, gold sparks smoldered under deeply furrowed brows.

Perhaps he should not have pointed out that she was firmly on the shelf, but surely it must be a factor in her decision. It was unlikely she would have a better offer—or indeed, any other offer.

"I don't intend to be in your way, you know. I'll spend most of my time in Town. You'll only have to put up with my occasional visits."

"Why bother to visit at all? You've been able to keep yourself away all these years."

Charles coughed into his hand. Surely she saw the obvious? He looked at her again. Her arms were tightly crossed under her glorious breasts. She lifted one of her brows. How could he not have noticed before how delightfully they flew up at one end? Or how kissable her mouth was, even drawn into a tight line as it was now.

Would it soften if he put his lips over it?

"There is the matter of an heir."

"What?" Both eyebrows flew up and then slammed back down. "What do you mean, exactly?"

The ice in her words was an interesting counterpoint to the fire in her eyes. Charles realized retreat was probably advisable, but he had gone too far into enemy territory. He had to brazen it out now.

"An heir. I'll need one, now that I am the marquis. And I can't very well get one if I'm in London and my wife's in Kent, can I?"

He ducked as a small china dog flew by his ear and shattered on the study door.

CHAPTER 2

"Am I interrupting?"

Three orange plumes poked cautiously around the door, followed by gray sausage ringlets and a very round face with Charles's clear blue eyes.

"Not at all, Aunt Bea. Please come in."

Emma blinked and adjusted her spectacles, her haze of anger replaced by an equally fiery sight—the rotund form of Charles's Aunt Beatrice, stunningly attired in a dress of broad red and orange stripes, its neck cut so low Emma feared the woman's sizable breasts would escape the confines of her bodice. A necklace of diamonds and rubies glittered on the vast expanse of her chest.

"Are you going to introduce me to your companion, Charles?" Lady Beatrice pushed aside the china fragments with her foot and raised her lorgnette. Two enlarged eyes inspected Emma.

"Certainly, Aunt. This is Miss Emma Peterson, the vicar's daughter. Miss Peterson, my aunt, Lady Beatrice."

"Lady Beatrice." Emma curtsied. "I'm pleased to—oh!"

Emma gasped and jumped to one side. Something had brushed her ankle.

Lady Beatrice laughed, a rich, musical sound that seemed to come from deep inside her.

"Don't be distressed, my dear. It's only Queen Bess."

A large orange cat leapt onto the chair by Emma and curled up to fill the seat. It looked like an oversized muff—an angry, oversized muff, Emma thought, noting how the cat glared at her before turning to clean her paws.

Charles laughed. "I'm not certain Prinny will approve of the queen, Aunt."

"Don't tell me you've invited that fat fool, Charles. He most definitely was not on *my* guest list."

"Nor is he on mine. No, I mean Miss Peterson's dog."

"You have a dog named Prinny, Miss Peterson? Splendid!"

"He's actually my sister's dog, Lady Beatrice."

"Ah. Well, then, I look forward to meeting your sister." Lady Beatrice moved farther into the room. "Is there a reason we are standing, Charles? Some infestation in the furniture, perhaps? Not lice, I hope? Or fleas? Poor Bess does hate fleas."

"As far as I know you—and your cat—don't have to fear the furnishings. Can't speak with complete authority, of course—I just got here myself. I was waiting for Miss Peterson to sit, but she has been disinclined to do so."

"Oh, well, I am not so disinclined—though I did just sit all the way from London. Now that you're the marquis, Charles, you'll have to see to the carriages. Thought my teeth were going to be rattled from my mouth—I swear I felt every rock on the road."

Lady Beatrice settled gracefully on the settee,

quite a feat, Emma thought, for someone of her impressive girth.

"Come, Miss Peterson, take a seat, do. You'll give me neck strain if you don't, and I'm sure poor Charles here needs to take the weight off his feet. Bess will move for you, won't you, sweets?"

The queen paused in her ablutions long enough to look in Lady Beatrice's direction, then went back to applying her tongue to the area under her tail. Emma averted her eyes.

"Just give her a little push, Miss Peterson," Lady Beatrice said. "Bess is sometimes a mite stubborn."

Just like the Thames is a mite wet, Emma thought. Queen Bess did not look eager to move. Emma certainly was not eager to get her hand clawed.

"Allow me." Charles's arm brushed hers as he reached for the cat. She felt the accidental contact as if a shock had passed between them. He was so close, she could feel the heat of his body and inhale his clean, male scent of soap, leather, and linen. She watched his broad, capable hands gently scoop under the cat's middle, and remembered the feel of his palm and fingers.

She hoped he didn't hear her sudden, sharp intake of breath or notice the way her body stilled. She stepped back so quickly her heel caught on her hem and she had to steady herself on the edge of the desk. When she looked back at him, he was delivering Queen Bess to his aunt's waiting lap.

His aunt's eyes were firmly fixed on Emma. Emma swallowed a nervous giggle. Lady Beatrice glared in much the same way as her cat.

"Thank you, Charles. He is quite the hero, isn't he, Miss Peterson?"

Emma smiled slightly and edged back to the

now-vacant chair. She tried surreptitiously to brush off the orange cat hairs before she sat. She glanced at Charles. He bowed and grinned.

"I try my humble best, Aunt, to save damsels in distress from dragons—and tabbies of all descriptions."

"Hmm." Lady Beatrice stroked her cat and studied Charles. Emma tried not to fidget when the woman's eyes examined her. "Does this damsel have a particular need to be saved, Charles?" Her tone was lazy, but Emma detected an icy undercurrent.

"Not that I know of, Aunt." Charles shoved his hands in his pockets and leaned against the mantel. His voice was sharp. "Why do you ask?"

"I am not accustomed to hearing crockery shatter as I prepare to enter a room."

Emma studied her hands clasped in her lap and hoped her cheeks weren't burning as brightly as she feared.

"I believe I said something with which Miss Peterson disagreed."

"Really? One wonders what conversational topic could possibly provoke a gently bred young lady to heave the knickknacks about."

Emma decided that it was past time to flee. "I believe I should be getting back to the girls, my lord, Lady Beatrice. I'm sure they've worn Nanny out by now."

"Don't go, Miss Peterson," Lady Beatrice said. "I've hardly met you."

It was not a request. Emma sank back into her chair. "There's really nothing at all interesting about me, Lady Beatrice."

Lady Beatrice raised one eyebrow. "That is what I am trying to determine, Miss Peterson."

"Aunt, leave off. Miss Peterson is kindly filling in

while Miss Hodgekiss, Isabelle and Claire's governess, attends her ailing mother."

"I see. And she is staying at Knightsdale?" Lady Beatrice paused. Her blue eyes raked Emma from head to toe. "How . . . convenient."

Emma sat a little straighter in her chair. Surely the woman could not be insinuating . . . No, it was impossible. No one had ever accused Emma—no one had ever considered accusing Emma—of anything other than perfectly proper behavior. She must have misunderstood Lady Beatrice's inflection.

It was hard to misunderstand the hard look in the older woman's eyes.

"Miss Peterson and I were just becoming reacquainted when you arrived, Aunt."

"*Reacquainted*, Charles? So you and Miss Peterson had a . . . relationship of some sort?"

"No." Emma hoped she had not shouted the word, but from the way the older woman's eyebrows shot up, she was afraid she had. She surged to her feet. She was going to leave this room now, whether Charles's aunt liked it or not. "Lady Beatrice, I can assure you . . ."

"Please don't, child." Lady Beatrice waved a heavily bejeweled hand in her direction. "Sit down. I apologize if I offended you."

Emma sat but remained on the edge of her seat, ready to leave at the first insult.

"I am not accustomed to such treatment, Lady Beatrice. I hope it will not be repeated."

Lady Beatrice chuckled. "Got claws, do you? That's good. So, then, tell me why you threw the"—Lady Beatrice looked over at the shattered pieces on the floor and shrugged—"why you heaved that gewgaw at the door."

Emma flushed. "It was a dog, Lady Beatrice."

"Ah." The older woman rubbed the queen's ears. "Bess here would probably agree with you—she doesn't care for dogs herself. I do find it odd you apparently associate with a live version of the creatures, if you despise the beasts so much you feel compelled to rid the world of canine gimcrackery—gimcrackery, I might add, that does not belong to you. You did say Prinny was a dog, did you not?"

"Yes." Emma looked to Charles for help. The wretch had his hand over his mouth, muffling his laughter. "I didn't mean to break the figurine."

"No? What did you mean to do?"

"I was aiming for Lord Knightsdale's head."

"Of course. Charles?"

"I merely asked Miss Peterson to wed me. She declined."

Lady Beatrice blinked. "I see. A simple 'no' would not have sufficed?"

"Apparently not."

Emma wanted to scream—from mortification or frustration, she wasn't sure which. "Lady Beatrice, I do apologize. I really can't explain my reaction."

"Then don't attempt to, dear. Some things are inexplicable—and others become clear with time. It remains to be seen into which category this little event will fit. You did say you have met before?"

Charles chuckled. "Miss Peterson and I were childhood playmates, Aunt. I saw her again for the first time in years just shortly before you arrived."

"Years, Charles? How many years?"

Charles shrugged. "A few. At least ten. Probably more like twenty."

Lady Beatrice stared at Charles. "You haven't seen

Miss Peterson since you were a child and yet you just asked her to marry you?"

Charles shifted his weight and cleared his throat. "Yes."

Lady Beatrice shook her head. "Miss Peterson, my apologies. I completely understand. Next time I suggest a heavier object at closer range."

Charles watched the ladies chat. Lambert had brought in tea and cakes—and a saucer of cream for her highness.

"You did say you are staying in the house, didn't you, Miss Peterson?" Aunt Beatrice helped herself to the largest cake.

"Yes. Miss Hodgekiss left suddenly last week, and I thought it best that I move up here to help Nanny. She is getting on in years."

"Indeed. And your family can manage without you?"

Emma paused, and Charles leaned forward. Had there been a shadow in her eyes?

"Oh yes. My sister is seventeen, so she no longer needs—nor wants—my daily supervision."

"Hmm. And I believe your mother died many years ago, didn't she?" Aunt Bea brushed a few crumbs off her bosom.

"Not long after Meg was born." Emma smiled, but Charles saw the shadow again. "I raised Meg and kept house, but, well, things change. I can easily afford to teach the girls until Miss Hodgekiss can return."

Charles watched Emma nibble a piece of cake. She had a nice mouth—a full lower lip, a slightly bowed upper. Kissable lips. He watched the small pink tip of her tongue dart out to capture an errant crumb—

and felt heat flood a certain part of his anatomy. He could imagine lovely things for that tongue to do.

"Don't you agree, Charles?"

"Hmm?" He tore his eyes away from Miss Peterson's lips to find Aunt Bea staring at him. "I'm sorry, Aunt. I'm afraid I was woolgathering."

Aunt Bea snorted. "Is *that* what they call it now? In my day—"

Charles glanced at Emma's bewildered expression. "Aunt, could you save us all our blushes and just repeat the question?"

Aunt Beatrice glanced at Emma also.

"All right. I was trying to persuade Miss Peterson to join our little house party."

"An excellent suggestion!" Charles beamed. Trust Aunt Bea to come up with such an inspired notion.

"But Lord Knightsdale, I couldn't possibly join your guests."

"Why ever not, Miss Peterson? You would be a lovely addition."

"But I'm the governess."

"Pshaw! The temporary governess." Aunt Bea offered the queen a morsel of cake. Her highness sniffed carefully, then tilted her nose up, rejecting the treat. "Your birth is impeccable—father's the son of an earl, if I remember correctly."

"The *fourth* son of an earl," Miss Peterson said.

"No matter. Blood's blue enough."

Miss Peterson clattered her teacup into its saucer. "Blue enough for what?"

"For the *ton*, Miss Peterson." Aunt Bea popped the cake Queen Bess had declined into her own mouth. "I don't suppose you ever made your come out?" The question was muffled by cake crumbs.

"No. When I was seventeen, Meg was only nine. I

didn't want to leave her, and my father wasn't interested in having me go to London. I suppose we could have gotten one of his sisters to sponsor me, but it didn't seem worth the trouble."

Aunt Bea nodded, her plumes bobbing. "Lady Gromwell, the countess, and Lady Fanning, the baroness. Perfectly acceptable." She reached for another cake. "You did say your sister is seventeen? Did she also decline a trip to Town?"

"Yes. Father offered her the opportunity. Lady Elizabeth, the Duke of Alvord's sister, was making her bows—Meg could easily have gone up with her." Miss Peterson sighed, shrugging slightly. "Meg isn't interested in gowns and furbelows, I'm afraid. She'd much rather be out mucking around in the fields, looking for plants to add to her collection."

She paused, gazing into her teacup. Charles saw the shadow in her expression again. Her mouth tightened.

"And things were a little . . . unsettled at home."

What was bothering the girl? He wanted to see only laughter in her eyes—or sparks of anger and passion—not sadness.

"Sounds as if your sister could stand a little polishing, Miss Peterson," Aunt Bea said. "I suggest we include her in the house party, Charles. It will be a perfect opportunity for her to ease into the *ton*."

"A splendid idea, Aunt. And Miss Peterson will be here to show her the way of it."

"Lady Beatrice, I don't think . . ."

"No, we insist—don't we, Charles?"

"Definitely. I will escort you home today, Miss Peterson, to present the invitation in person."

"But . . ."

"Come, Miss Peterson," Aunt Bea said. "I'm certain

your father cannot object. He must be happy to see his daughter—his daughters—acquire some social polish."

Miss Peterson abandoned her teacup and sat up, her nostrils flaring, fire back in her eyes. "Lady Beatrice . . ."

Aunt held up her hand. "Now, Miss Peterson, don't be tiresome. What possible objection can you have to a little enjoyment? Some cards, a picnic or two, a ball? All unexceptionable pursuits."

Miss Peterson's chin jutted out much like Claire's. "I will need to attend to the girls."

"Of course, but not every instant of the day, surely. Nanny can keep an eye on them in the schoolroom, can't she?" Aunt Beatrice looked at Charles.

"Certainly." He grinned. "She's looking after them at the moment, in fact. And it's not as if they are babies. Isabelle struck me as very responsible."

"Too responsible," Miss Peterson said. "And she needs to keep up with her lessons."

"Which she shall." Charles saw victory within his grasp. "I shall visit the schoolroom and assist, as long as you don't want me to instruct in watercolors. I can't paint—or draw—at all."

"Umm . . ."

"It's decided, then." Aunt Bea snagged the last cake. "Go get your bonnet, Miss Peterson, and Charles will drive you over now."

"But . . ."

Aunt Bea made shooing motions with her hands. Miss Peterson looked at Charles. He chuckled at the confused mix of frustration, anger, and resignation on her face. And anticipation? Surely there was a glimmer of anticipation as well? He suspected it had been a long time since Miss Peterson had let herself have any fun. Maybe she had never allowed herself pleasure.

Charles was determined to change that. He found he would dearly love to give her pleasure. Glorious pleasure. Hot, sweaty pleasure. Late night and early morning pleasure.

He watched her lovely derriere swish as she stalked out of the room.

"Settled on her, have you?"

Charles shrugged, turning back to his aunt. "You've been nagging me incessantly to wed ever since we got word Paul had died. Miss Peterson will do."

"You have many ladies to choose from."

"All of whom I've seen before."

"Ah, but they are much more interested in you now that you are the Marquis of Knightsdale."

Charles felt his stomach twist. God, that was one of the things he hated most about the bloody situation—the toadying. People who could not be bothered to notice mere Major Draysmith stumbled over themselves to greet Lord Knightsdale.

"That is part of Miss Peterson's charm, Aunt. I don't believe she gives a fig for my title."

Emma forced herself to walk calmly down the stairs. She was still fuming. The gall of the man! To come here after all these years and suggest she marry him. She'd swear he hadn't even recognized her when he'd first seen her in the long gallery.

He just wanted a breeder. She was certainly not going to offer herself up so the Knightsdale dynasty could continue one more generation. The way she felt now, she'd happily terminate the line immediately. With her bare hands.

She paused on the second-floor landing, gripping the handrail so tightly her knuckles showed white. She took a deep breath.

She was angry with herself as well.

Why couldn't he be ugly—cross-eyed or pockmarked or hunchbacked? Why did he have to be the one man who haunted her dreams?

She put her hands on her flushed cheeks. He had haunted more than her sleep. Even awake, she had dreamed of him, of the kiss she had seen.

She had invited him into her bed the very night she had rushed home from his brother's wedding ball.

Lud, it was true. Papa's proper daughter had climbed into bed, blown out the candle, and summoned up her memory of Charles on the Knightsdale terrace. But in her thoughts, he was kissing her, not some anonymous London lady. She had tried to feel his lips moving on hers. Would they be warm or cool, moist or dry? She had imagined his arms around her, his chest against hers, his hands on her— She squeezed her eyes shut. She would *not* think about just where she had imagined his hands.

Now he had asked her to marry him. She could discover exactly what his lips felt like. What his hands . . .

Enough! She could not marry the man just to test the accuracy of her imagination, could she? No. Certainly not. Such a thought was ludicrous in the extreme.

She continued down the stairs.

She had almost died in the study when his eyes had seemed to trace the line of her lips. She could barely keep her attention on Lady Beatrice's words. The man should be forced to wear a blindfold—those clear blue eyes were dangerous to women. He had probably lured countless society ladies into his arms with them. Well, she would not be another victim—no matter how much she would like to be.

"Miss Peterson—so prompt. Splendid."

Emma looked down. Charles was standing in the hall, grinning up at her. Her heart lurched before she could take it under firm control.

"It does not take long to put on a bonnet, my lord."

"No? I defer to your greater knowledge—I have never attempted the task."

"I don't doubt you've much experience with taking *off* a bonnet, however!"

Emma bit her lip. Where had that come from? She'd never had trouble minding her tongue in the past. She stared straight ahead as she stepped out the front door, but she heard Charles's warm chuckle by her ear.

"Ah, Miss Peterson, do I detect some words left unspoken?"

"I have no idea to what you might be referring, my lord."

"So you are not intimating that I have removed more than a lady's bonnet?"

Emma felt a hot blush surge up her cheeks. She had not fully realized that she *had* been accusing him of more thorough feminine disrobement until he said the words. But she certainly was not going to admit it. Some lies were necessary for self-preservation.

"Of course not, my lord."

He laughed, a deep, warm sound. "Oh, Miss Peterson, I can see we are going to have a wonderful time together. May I call you Emma?"

"Certainly not."

"Splendid. And you must call me Charles."

"My lord, did you not hear me? I did not give you leave to use my Christian name."

"Well, Emma, I am very sorry, but I am taking that leave. One thing I learned in the war was to ask nicely, but if something is crucial for survival, take it—politely, of course. And I do think using your lovely name, Emma, is crucial to my survival."

Emma could not think of a single thing to say. She was certain her mouth was gaping open—and it opened even farther when she felt his broad, warm hands around her waist, lifting her to sit in his curricle. He climbed up next to her and grinned, tapping the bottom of her chin with his index finger. She shut her jaw so quickly she heard it snap.

To add to her confusion, the curricle's seat was extremely narrow. Charles's side, hip, and leg were pressed tightly up against her. They were amazingly hard—like rock. She shifted, trying to put more space between them. He shifted with her.

"My lord, you are crowding me."

"Charles, Emma. You know my name is Charles. You used to call me Charles when you were a girl."

"And you will not hear it on my lips now, my lord. I, at least, have some inkling of decorum."

"Hmm. Perhaps I can persuade those lips."

Before Emma had the slightest idea what Charles planned, she felt his mouth on hers.

Her eyes closed, whether to shut out the shocking sight of his face so close to hers or to better feel the touch of his lips, she couldn't—or wouldn't—say. It was the briefest brush—dry and cool—but she felt it all the way to her toes. It started an odd fire burning in her stomach, a fire that had smoldered in her dreams but had never flared to life. A fire she feared would consume her.

Lud, was she in trouble!

* * *

Charles chuckled and moved back to his side of the seat. He would have preferred to spend more time exploring Emma's mouth, but the horses were restless and Emma might soon recover enough from her shock to slap him senseless. Not to mention the fact that they were in full view of Knightsdale's many windows. Was Aunt Bea peering down at them? Or little Claire?

He didn't care. He grinned, feeling a ridiculous urge to laugh. He had not felt this lighthearted in years—certainly not since he'd left for the Peninsula. Definitely not since he'd gotten word of Paul's death. Even when he'd just come down from university and was racketing around London, he had not felt this pure, carefree joy. He'd thought he'd been living a wonderful life then, acquiring some town bronze, but too many mornings after a night of debauchery, the bronze had felt more like rust.

He took a deep breath of cool English air, drawing in the scent of new-mown grass. Maybe he had not felt this way since boyhood when he'd had a whole glorious day before him to fill with fishing and riding and playing at Robin Hood or Knights of the Round Table—often with the girl beside him tagging at his heels. He chuckled. Who would have guessed he would ever feel more than annoyance for the little curly-headed pest he had nicknamed "Runt."

"What is so amusing, my lord?"

So Miss Peterson was going to be on her high horse, was she? He glanced at her. Yes, she had her little nose tilted in the air.

"Did you know the other boys called you 'Shadow'?"

"What?" She turned to look at him. "What are you talking about?"

"When we were children. The other boys called

you 'Shadow,' because you were always following me around."

"Oh." She was looking off at the scenery now, a faint blush coloring her cheeks.

"I didn't call you that, though. I didn't mind your following me."

"You called me 'Runt.'"

"Well, you were little. You are still not very tall, though some areas of your person"—Charles allowed his eyes to rest on her well-shaped breasts— "have grown considerably."

"My lord!" Her cheeks were flaming now. Charles braced for a slap.

"Your hands, for example," he said, laughing. "I'm sure they are larger. Your feet, too. Your lovely, um, ch—"

Emma sucked in her breath, making the relevant anatomical features swell invitingly.

"—chin has grown since you were a young girl as well."

"My lord, you are so . . . *slippery.*"

"I beg your pardon?" Charles tried for his best innocent expression. "I'm sure I don't know what you mean."

"Yes, you do! I can't quite grab hold of you. I think I know what you are saying, but then somehow I don't. You are as slippery as a trout."

"Sweetheart," Charles said, his voice suddenly husky at the erotic possibilities her artless words conjured in his mind, "anytime you would like to grab hold of me, please do. I will be happy to accommodate you. If I were a trout, I would be delighted to swim in your tight, wet, um . . . ." Charles swallowed, reining in his imagination.

She threw him a puzzled, but wary, glance. "You're doing it again."

Charles reminded his body to behave itself. His voice was clearer this time. "I'm doing what?"

"Don't look so innocent. You meant something else, didn't you?"

"No."

"Yes, you did."

Charles grinned. "Well, perhaps."

"Tell me."

"Oh, no, Emma, my love. I most certainly will not tell you. I'll show you—but only once we are married."

Charles chuckled, imagining he could hear her teeth grinding. He looked ahead to the familiar stone building where he had spent so many hours learning Greek and Latin from Reverend Peterson.

"Will we find your father at home?"

"Yes."

Charles noted the sudden chill in Emma's tone. What was this about? "And your sister?"

Emma shrugged. "Meg is probably out grubbing in the dirt somewhere. If Father and—" She paused. Her nostrils flared, her mouth forming a tight line.

"And?" he prompted, pulling the curricle to a stop.

Emma's chin raised and she straightened her shoulders, like a soldier readying for battle. All teasing thoughts left his mind. He was quite certain he had found the source of Emma's shadows.

". . . and Mrs. Graham," Emma said. "Mrs. Harriet Graham. She's a widow. She helps with the church, arranging flowers and such."

"And?"

"And what, my lord?"

"And why does the thought of Mrs. Harriet

Graham, widow, make you stiffen up like you've swallowed a hot poker?"

"I don't know what you mean."

"It can't be the simple fact that she helps with the church, can it?" Charles watched Emma's downcast eyes. "You said 'Father and. . . .' It's the 'and' that's the problem, isn't it? Is this Mrs. Graham a harpy of the worst sort?"

Emma shook her head. "Of course not. Mrs. Graham is a fine member of the congregation."

"But perhaps not such a fine member of your family?"

"Are you going to help me out of this curricle or do I need to leap down?"

"I'll help you, sweetheart." Charles came around and took her by the waist. He didn't slide her down his body as he wanted to, nor did he pull her against him when her feet touched the ground. But he didn't let her go immediately either. He enjoyed the curve of her waist under his hands too much.

To his surprise, she didn't pull away. She stood quietly, looking down, her eyes hidden by her bonnet.

"Emma, are you all right?"

"Yes. Of course." She glanced up at him, then stepped back. He let her go. "I'm sorry. Come this way."

He followed her inside. The smell hit him first—the smell of learning, of old books, leather, paper, and ink. He had breathed in that scent so often when he was a boy struggling with his Latin declensions. He had breathed it at university, also, but this was better. This was home. Emma's papa had been a kind master. Strict, demanding, but always encouraging. Charles had worked hard to please him.

He had been guilty of wishing Reverend Peterson

was his own papa. Perhaps that was one reason he had tolerated Emma. He had thought of her as a little sister.

He certainly did not think of her as a sister now.

Emma stopped outside her father's study and knocked deliberately.

"We have company, Papa."

"Please, come in."

Emma pushed the door open. Charles froze on the threshold.

Reverend Peterson had aged in the past twenty years. His hair was gray; his cheeks, slightly sunken; the bones of his face, more defined. Charles knew this. He had seen the man just four months earlier at Paul's funeral. But to see him here, in this study— this room should have been an eddy where time and age did not come.

"My lord," Reverend Peterson was saying, standing. "It is good to see you again. We are all happy you have come home to Knightsdale."

Charles grinned. "Finally. Thank you for not saying it."

Reverend Peterson's smile had not changed. His lips curved only slightly, but his eyes twinkled over his spectacles. "I would never presume to criticize a marquis."

"Out loud."

The vicar's lips twitched, and the corners of his eyes crinkled. "I was just eager to see you in the neighborhood, my lord." He turned to a small woman who'd been sitting in a chair next to his desk. "May I present Mrs. Harriet Graham? Mrs. Graham is relatively new to Knightsdale, my lord, but she has been a very active member of the parish."

"Mrs. Graham." Charles took the woman's hand.

He could almost feel Emma bristle. She was still standing stiffly by the door.

"My lord." Mrs. Graham smiled calmly up at him. He liked her immediately. She had a pleasant, comfortable face with warm brown eyes and hair that had once been brown but was now streaked with gray. *So this is the harpy.* She looked like a normal, middle-aged woman, not a candidate for evil stepmotherhood.

"Reverend, I've come to extend an invitation to both your daughters."

Emma watched Charles take Mrs. Graham's hand. She had not been surprised to find the woman in the study with Papa. Lud, she practically lived at the vicarage. Maybe she would, if Meg moved up to Knightsdale for this house party.

Emma bit her lip. No, she truly could not see Papa breaking God's law, living in sin with a woman—even a jezebel like Harriet Graham.

"A number of ladies will be in attendance who are Miss Margaret Peterson's age. My aunt, Lady Beatrice, thought this might be an excellent opportunity for your younger daughter to get her feet wet in the social pond, as it were, and in familiar surroundings with her older sister to guide her."

"And who will guide her older sister?"

"Papa, I am not a complete cabbage-head. I will do very well."

Emma saw Charles's eyebrow rise, and she flushed. Perhaps her tone *had* been a bit sharp.

"I didn't mean to imply that you were, Emma, but you have not been to London, either."

"I've been to plenty of local assemblies."

"Yes, I know, but . . ."

Emma glared her father to silence.

"Do not worry, sir." There was a slight note of humor in Charles's voice.

Emma turned to glare at him. He ignored her.

"My aunt will be present, and it will not be a very strenuous gathering. Just a few picnics, a ball. Very relaxed. I believe the Duke of Alvord and his wife and sister will be there, as well as the Earl of West-brooke, so the ladies will see a few familiar faces."

Reverend Peterson nodded. "The duke's sister, Lady Elizabeth, is Meg's particular friend. I see no objections, do you, Harriet?"

Emma gritted her teeth as Mrs. Graham nodded and murmured her concurrence.

"The guests should begin arriving tomorrow," Charles said, "so I'll send a carriage to fetch Miss Margaret Peterson in the morning, shall I?"

"That would be splendid, my lord." Papa looked at his older daughter. "Emma, you must have some things you need to pack. You didn't plan for social activities when you went up to take Miss Hodgekiss's place."

"No, and I'm not planning on attending many social activities now—I will still be spending most of my time with the girls."

"But not all your time," Charles said. "Why don't you pack your things now?"

Emma did not want to pack anything. She crossed her arms, ready to tell them that, but she caught Charles's eye before she spoke. Something in his expression warned her she was on the verge of a childish tantrum. She closed her lips.

She was twenty-six, not six years old. Such behavior was beneath her. She drew a steadying breath.

"I suppose that is a good idea. I won't be long."

"Would you like some help?"

"No, Mrs. Graham. I am quite capable of managing on my own." Emma glanced at her father and saw the reproach in his face. She flushed. "But thank you for the offer. I'll just be a minute."

It did not take much more than a minute to pack. Her wardrobe was not extensive—most of it was already at Knightsdale. She hurriedly bundled a few extra dresses into a valise. She stopped, a hand on her ball gown. Should she bring it? No. Ridiculous. Her fingers slid over the silky fabric. It had been such a waste of money. She had never worn it.

She could wear it now, at the house party.

No. She wouldn't go to the ball . . . would she?

She closed her eyes, remembering Charles and that London lady on the terrace ten years ago. She'd been too young to go to that ball. She was not too young now. . . .

She grabbed the dress, stuffed it in among the rest of her things, and left her room before she could change her mind.

Charles put her valise in the curricle while she said good-bye to her father.

"Should my ears be burning?" she asked after he had helped her into her seat.

"Emma, your father would not talk about you with me and Mrs. Graham."

"I'm sure he talks about me to Mrs. Graham." Emma stared ahead, waiting for Charles to defend the woman. He said nothing. She should say nothing, too, but words were clawing at her throat, demanding to be free.

She had no one to confide in. She couldn't talk to Meg. She had tried once, but Meg was too young.

She didn't understand. And the other ladies she knew were too old. Well, and she didn't want to air her dirty laundry. But Charles had been witness to her bad behavior.

What *was* the matter with her? First she had lost her temper and thrown that trinket at Charles, and now she'd just acted like a rude child. Perhaps she was ill. Her stomach certainly felt unsettled.

If Charles had been serious about his marriage proposal, he must be congratulating himself now that she had declined his offer. She was turning into a shocking shrew.

If only Mrs. Graham would move back to where she had come from. If only things could be normal again.

She looked over at Charles. He raised an eyebrow.

"Is the danger past?"

"What danger?" Emma frowned. "What are you talking about?"

"You've been sitting there growling and flexing your hands. I feared you might explode at any moment."

"I was *not* growling. How absurd!"

"You were."

"I was not. I don't even know how to growl."

"Well, it sounded like growling to me. Would you like to tell me what the problem is?"

"No." Emma pressed her lips together. "There is no problem."

Charles sighed. "I imagine it has something to do with Mrs. Graham, but frankly, I can't fathom what it could be. She seemed like a perfectly normal, respectable lady to me."

"Well, she's not!" Emma grabbed Charles's arm and shook it. "She is shameless. Brazen."

"Mrs. Graham?"

"Yes."

They rode in silence for a few moments. Emma tried to get control of her temper. She was shaking inside.

"All right, Emma, I give up. The thought of Mrs. Graham as brazen boggles my mind. I know it is indelicate to ask, but I'm asking anyway—what did she do?"

"I found her in the study kissing my father." Emma could see the scene as clearly as if it had just happened, yet it had been two months since she had walked in to talk to her father and found him sitting on the settee with Mrs. Graham. Emma always made a point of knocking now.

"And . . . ?"

She looked at Charles. He raised his eyebrows.

"What to you mean, 'and'?"

"And what else? You saw your father kissing Mrs. Graham, and . . . ?"

"Isn't that enough? And I didn't actually *see* him kissing her, but it was quite clear that is what he'd been doing. Her hair was disordered and the neck of her dress was loose."

"I see. So they were expressing affection for each other. Perhaps strong affection. It has been—what?—seventeen years since your mother died?"

"I don't know what difference that makes."

"Has there been a procession of 'Mrs. Grahams'?"

"Of course not. My father is a man of God."

"Precisely. So perhaps he is ready to take a wife again and has found he cares for Mrs. Graham."

"He is too old to marry." Emma dug her fingers into Charles's arm. The thought of Mrs. Graham moving into the vicarage in truth . . . It had always been just her father and Meg and she. No one else. That was the way it was supposed to be.

"Sweetheart," he said, taking the reins in one hand and gently loosening her fingers, "your father cannot be very much more than fifty. He is not too old."

"But I don't want a mother."

"And I'm sure Mrs. Graham knows that. You are twenty-six and Meg is seventeen. It is not beyond the realm of possibility that you will both be married before the year is out—at least, I hope you will be. To me. Your father will then be all alone. You should be happy that he has found Mrs. Graham."

Emma dropped her hold on Charles's arm. She'd known he wouldn't understand. How could he? He was a man, after all.

"I'm not getting married."

He smiled, turning his attention back to the horses. "Perhaps not. That is your choice. You must allow your father the same freedom."

"But you don't understand. He's my *father.* He has a duty to his family."

"He's a man, too, sweetheart."

Emma looked down at her hands. "I thought he loved me and Meg. Why does he need *her?*"

"It's a different kind of love, Emma. Have you no understanding of a man's needs? Of a man's wants?"

Emma shook her head. What could possibly be more important to a man than his children? She had tried so hard to keep the house as it should be, to be a mother to Meg. What had she done wrong? What was lacking?

"No," she said, "I don't. I don't understand at all."

"Then, my love, permit me to show you."

CHAPTER 3

This kiss was different. The first one had been a light brush, cool and dry. This was hot and wet. Charles's mouth slanted over hers; his tongue traced the seam of her lips. She gasped and he slipped inside.

Who would have thought such a thing possible? She had certainly never conceived of the idea. She should be disgusted—but she was not. Not in the least.

There were so many sensations. The fullness of his tongue in her mouth. The slight friction as he swept through her. The shifting pressure of his lips. The smell of his shaving soap and skin.

His tongue withdrew and she whimpered. He surged back into her and she moaned. She grabbed his arm again so she wouldn't fall out of the curricle.

Lud. Her body throbbed in places she blushed to consider. Her heart pounded. When Charles finally, gently, let her go, she shuddered and blinked up at him. His magical lips were smiling, but there was a hunger, a blue flame in his eyes—a flame that must reflect the fire running everywhere under her skin.

Is *this* what she had seen on the Knightsdale terrace so many years ago? Surely not. The woman would have spontaneously combusted, just as Emma was certain *she* would at any moment.

"What did you just do to me?"

"Not everything I'd like to, sweetheart."

Emma looked delightfully dazed. He felt rather dazed himself. If his horses hadn't protested the long inaction, he wasn't certain when he would have stopped. And he definitely had to stop. An open carriage on a public road was not the place to initiate a virgin into the joys of lovemaking.

"Sweetheart, next time we do this, it will *not* be in a curricle with two prime bits of blood threatening to bolt."

"Next time? There will be a next time?"

"Oh, definitely. As soon as I can manage it."

"My lord!" Her brain must have finally emerged from its sexual stupor. A hot flush turned her cheeks a very becoming pink. She straightened her spectacles. "I am certain this is most improper."

"Most, I'm sure." He grinned. "But oh, so delightful."

She turned to face squarely forward. "I believe we should be returning to Knightsdale."

Charles obligingly gave his horses their office to start. "Don't you think you should call me Charles now, love? The 'my lording' seems a trifle disingenuous. We have just been somewhat intimate, after all."

"I'm certain we have not."

"No? Well, what would you call it? I did have my tong—"

"My lord!"

"If you do not wish me to describe in detail everything we just did, I think you'd better call me Charles. Not that I would mind describing it."

"My lord, please!"

"Please continue? I shall be delighted to. In fact, perhaps I shall also say exactly what I would like to do the next time I have the pleasure of putting my tong—"

"Charles!" Emma shouted his name, grabbing his arm and shaking it.

"See? That wasn't so difficult, was it?"

She pressed her lips together. "I believe I would prefer to finish this trip in silence."

"Splendid. I shall entertain myself contemplating all the lovely things we can do together the next time we have the opportunity."

Miss Peterson did not rise to the bait. Charles contented himself with imagining what it would be like to strip each article of her clothing slowly from her lovely body. He had a very good imagination. He shifted on the curricle seat. Too good an imagination. He had better turn his mind to less elevating thoughts.

Emma made a small sound, a cross between a hiss and a moan. He glanced at her. She was scowling at her hands. Where had her thoughts wandered now? Hopefully not the same place his had—he wanted her smiling, not frowning, when she pictured them together. More than smiling. Groaning. Writhing with need.

"Don't care for your style of glove, my dear?"

She grunted. "My father did not do *that* with Mrs. Graham."

"Ah. If you say so."

"He couldn't have—could he?"

"I hesitate to point this out, love, but your mere presence on this earth would indicate that he could."

Her hand flew to her lips. "Surely that is not how children are conceived?"

Charles swallowed his laughter. "Not exactly, but it does have something to do with the process."

"How much?"

"Ah, love, how I long to show you." He laughed at the annoyance in her eyes. If there'd been a china dog handy, he would definitely have felt it cracking over his head. "Think of it as the opening bars of the waltz, sweetheart. There are quite a few more steps to be completed before the dance is over."

"Miss Peterson!"

The call came from a man up ahead. Charles studied the fellow as he rode closer. He had a terrible seat—stiff and awkward. But then the nag he was astride was a sorry specimen as well. Showy, but with terrible gaits. Obviously bought by a man who knew nothing of horseflesh.

"A friend of yours?"

"An acquaintance—Mr. Albert Stockley. He's renting Mr. Atworthy's house while Mr. Atworthy is in Town." Emma nodded and smiled as the man drew up next to them. "Good afternoon, Mr. Stockley."

"Miss Peterson." Mr. Stockley bowed stiffly.

Charles liked him even less on closer inspection. He was just as showy as his horse. Small and wiry, he wore his mud-colored hair fussed into some stylish arrangement and his shirt points so high he risked poking out his watery blue eyes. His nose and lips had the perpetually pained expression of someone who smells something bad—or expects he will smell something bad in just a moment. He looked to be one of those tiresome small men who always have something to prove.

"Mr. Stockley, have you met Lord Knightsdale?" Emma was saying.

Charles definitely did not like the way Stockley's gaze sharpened when he heard his title.

"No, I have not." He bowed in Charles's direction. "A pleasure, my lord."

"Stockley." Charles inclined his head slightly. He was delighted to see Stockley's eyes narrow.

"Miss Peterson," Stockley said, "I had been going to call on you at Knightsdale, but now that his lordship is in residence, I assume you have moved back to the vicarage."

"Well, actually—"

"Miss Peterson has kindly offered to stay and help with my nieces while their governess is away attending her ailing mother."

Mr. Stockley frowned. "Oh? Is that completely proper, my lord? Not that I wish to criticize, of course, but Miss Peterson is an unmarried lady. She needs to guard her reputation."

Charles felt Emma stir at his side.

"You need not be concerned," he said. "My aunt, Lady Beatrice, is in residence. She will see that I keep my animal instincts under control."

"My lord, I did not mean to imply—"

"Excuse me, but in case it has escaped your notice, *gentlemen,* I am still sitting in this curricle."

Charles smiled—Emma sounded quite annoyed.

"Mr. Stockley," she said, "I appreciate your concern, but you may put your mind at rest. I am in no danger from his lordship's 'animal instincts.'"

"No, of course not. I didn't mean to imply . . . I know your virtue is unassailable. . . . Well, I just wished to discover if you would like to go for a drive tomorrow afternoon?"

"That would be lovely, however—"

"However, Miss Peterson will be busy tomorrow afternoon, Stockley. I'm hosting a house party, and she has consented to attend, when her duties as temporary governess allow, of course. My guests should be arriving tomorrow—you're quite welcome to come, if you'd like."

Stockley smiled, a sudden odd eagerness in his face. "I would be delighted to attend, my lord." He bowed again. "I look forward to seeing you both tomorrow."

Charles was quite pleased to see the man's back, even if he looked like a scarecrow on a job horse.

"Stockley's an odd fish," he said. "Do you know anything about him?"

"I believe he has some connection to shipping—he's only been in the neighborhood a few weeks. He seemed a perfectly amiable gentleman, until just now, that is. Really, my lord, I do not enjoy being discussed as if I were not present."

"I don't like the man."

"Well, that was rather apparent."

"Has he been buzzing around you?"

"No, he has not been 'buzzing' around me. You are being absurd."

"Hmm." There was something off about Stockley. Charles didn't doubt the man was interested in Emma, but there was something more, something twisted in his regard. He planned to keep a close eye on him. "There is something you should know, Emma."

"What?"

"You are definitely in danger from my animal instincts."

* * *

Emma was relieved to reach Knightsdale. She was hoping to retreat to her room for a short while to gather her composure before she sought out the girls for lessons. At least she could trust Isabelle to have walked Prinny. She was such a responsible girl.

"Miss Peterson, you have company," Mr. Lambert said as she crossed the threshold.

"Entertaining already, Miss Peterson?" Charles raised his eyebrows, a smirk hovering on his lips. "I am so glad you are treating my house as if it were your own."

"My lord! Please. I'm sure there's been some mistake. Are you certain the individual asked for me, Mr. Lambert?"

"Four individuals, miss."

"Four?"

"Four ladies, miss. Older ladies. Lady Beatrice is entertaining them at the moment."

"Oh." Emma slapped her hand over her mouth. "The Society. This is the second Tuesday of the month, isn't it?"

"I believe so, miss. Lady Beatrice has requested refreshments. Perhaps you could join the ladies in the blue drawing room?"

"Certainly. Thank you, Mr. Lambert."

"The Society, Miss Peterson? Are you some wild-eyed reformer?"

"Hardly, my lord. I would like to discuss issues, but the other ladies never get beyond the latest gossip." She sighed. This was exceedingly awkward. "I do apologize for the intrusion. Since I was staying here, I thought it would be easiest to have the ladies meet at Knightsdale. I didn't mean to presume."

"No, no, I would love you to consider Knightsdale

your home. What is the name of this society I am hosting de facto?"

"The Society for the Betterment of Women."

"My God."

Emma thought the ladies sounded a bit more animated than usual as she approached the drawing room door. She glanced at Mr. Lambert, who was still hovering nearby. He cleared his throat.

"Lady Beatrice requested refreshments."

"Yes, you said that."

Charles chuckled. "Broke out the sherry, did she, Lambert?"

"And the brandy, my lord."

"*And* the brandy? I suspect you will have some inspired discussions this afternoon, Miss Peterson. How long have they been at it, Lambert?"

"The ladies arrived shortly after you and Miss Peterson departed."

"Ah. So plenty of time to get well and truly foxed."

A burst of raucous laughter erupted into the hall when Emma opened the door. She stepped over the threshold cautiously.

"There she is. Come in, Miss Peterson. Let Lady Bea fill up your glass—uh, cup." Mrs. Lavinia Begley, the squire's wife, sat—well, sprawled, really—in a chair facing the door. Her nose was two shades redder than normal, and her face was definitely flushed.

Charles's aunt looked over. She had changed into an apple green and jonquil striped dress with a diamond tiara. The tiara had slipped slightly so it was in danger of sliding over her eyes. She pushed it back and smiled.

"Yes, do come in, Miss Peterson—and you, too, Charles."

Emma glanced around the room. The regular Society attendees were all here—Mrs. Begley, the Misses Farthington, and Miss Blanche Russell. She had tried to get the younger ladies of the neighborhood interested in Society meetings, but so far she had not been successful. Mrs. Begley, who was comfortably over fifty, was the youngest of the group besides Emma.

"I'm very sorry, Lady Beatrice. I forgot about the meeting—and I never would have invited the ladies here if I'd known you would be in residence. I mean, I never meant to impose. . . ."

"Don't get yourself in a pucker, Miss Peterson. I've enjoyed making Mrs. Begley's acquaintance and reminiscing with Miss Russell and the Misses Farthington. It's been too long since we've enjoyed a comfortable coze, hasn't it, ladies?"

Miss Esther and Miss Rachel Farthington, twins who had made their come out when the Prince Regent was an infant, nodded in unison.

"Yes, much too long." Miss Esther had a green ribbon threaded through her sparse white locks.

"Since poor Paul's wedding." Miss Rachel's red ribbon unfortunately accentuated the pink of her scalp.

"No, Rachel, remember . . ."

". . . we didn't go to the wedding. That's right."

"Because you were sick."

"Had a touch of dyspepsia."

"Which I caught from you the next day."

"Would you care for some more inspiration, ladies?"

The twins nodded and held out their teacups for Lady Beatrice to pour another dollop of brandy.

"And you, Miss Russell?"

Mousy Miss Russell hiccupped and nodded. Well, at least the spirits had put a sparkle in her watery eyes, Emma thought.

"Come in and join us, Miss Peterson, Lord Knightsdale." Mrs. Begley took the bottle from Lady Beatrice and helped herself. "There's still some left."

"Oh, sister, there's the new Lord Knightsdale." Miss Rachel elbowed Miss Esther so hard a little of the liquid in her teacup splashed out.

"So it is."

The two elderly ladies stared at Charles.

"He's gotten big," Miss Esther said.

"I remember when he used to get into all sorts of mischief."

"And Miss Emma, she was always following him around."

"Think they'll make a match of it?"

Emma assumed the twins thought they were whispering. Since they were both more than a little deaf, their whispering was only slightly quieter than their regular speech.

Miss Esther nodded. "Smelling of April and May, I'd say."

Emma bristled. She was afraid if she looked at Charles, she would find him grinning.

"They'll make nice-looking babies, don't you think?"

"Yes, indeed. Lovely babies."

Emma heard a choked laugh behind her. "Wonderful babies," Charles murmured. "Many wonderful babies."

She felt an odd trembling in her stomach. Perhaps *she* had a touch of dyspepsia.

"Aunt, I believe these ladies would make brilliant additions to our house party, don't you?"

"Yes, indeed. Splendid idea, Charles." Lady Beatrice held up her teacup. "What say you, ladies? Who's for a house party?"

The ladies—even Miss Blanche—raised their cups high.

"A house party," they said. "Huzzah!"

"I believe I'll go check on Lady Isabelle and Lady Claire," Emma said.

"Were the girls well-behaved, Nanny? Down, Prinny! Shh, you idiot dog. Whatever are you wearing?"

Prinny, attired in a doll's red bonnet and cape, yapped and danced around Emma's skirts.

"Course we were behaved, Mama Peterson." Claire frowned at the dog. "Come back, Lady Prinny, it's time for you to go to the ball."

"I thought ye said that dog was yer sister's." Nanny took a mutton bone from behind a battered copy of *The History of Little Goody Two-Shoes* on the schoolroom shelf. "Here, ye heathen beast, go chew on this."

Prinny grabbed the bone and brought it over to where Claire had arranged her dolls. Isabelle was curled up in the window seat, reading.

"He *is* Meg's dog."

"Don't look like it to me." Nanny adjusted her spectacles and tucked a few stray strands of white hair back under her cap. "Looks like he's making himself right at home, I'd say."

Emma watched Claire try to tie a small cart around Prinny's waist.

"Don't worry, I'm sure he'll go home quite happily when Miss Hodgekiss comes back." Emma hated to disturb the girls. Isabelle looked so engrossed in her reading. Perhaps sums could wait for another day. "How is Miss Hodgekiss's mother? Has anyone had word?"

Nanny grunted. "Better, I believe."

"Well, see then. You won't have to suffer Prinny's presence much longer. I am sorry about the flowers."

"Oh, I don't mind him, not since I got some bones from Cook." Nanny pursed her mouth and looked at Emma. "I'm just wondering if yer making yerself at home, too."

"Nanny!" Emma's stomach dropped to her slippers. "What are you saying?"

"Nothing bad, miss, so ye can wipe that look off yer face. I'd be happy if ye married his lordship. The girls like ye. And they need a ma. Why, Lady Claire's been talking about Mama Peterson all afternoon."

"Nanny, you know how Claire is."

Nanny chuckled. "Aye—a bossy little devil."

"Exactly. And much as I feel for her, she can't arrange other people's lives to suit her wants."

"Why not?"

"Why not?" Emma hardly knew what to say. She stared at the older woman, who shrugged.

"If Lady Claire wants what's best for everyone, why not?"

"Best for everyone? Nanny, the marquis just arrived this morning. I barely know him—nor does he know me."

"Oh, pish! Ye've been in love with the boy forever."

"I have not." Emma knew the words came out a little too forcefully—she didn't need to see Nanny's smirk to tell her that. A hot flush ran up her neck.

"I watched ye follow him around when he was a lad."

"I was a child—younger than Isabelle."

Nanny grinned. "And was ye a child when ye spied on him at his brother's wedding ball?"

Emma closed her eyes. Perhaps this was all just a bad dream and when she opened her eyes, she'd see her room at the vicarage.

"William, the footman, saw ye hiding in the bushes."

Emma was going to expire from embarrassment. No wonder Charles had thought she'd be eager to marry him.

"No, I'm sorry. Marrying Lord Knightsdale is clearly out of the question. He is having a house party and will find a suitable bride from the selection presented, I'm sure."

Nanny made dismissive clucking noises. Emma looked over and saw Isabelle staring back at her.

"That one worries too much," Nanny said softly.

Emma nodded. She walked over and sat down next to Isabelle on the window seat. Claire was still happily playing on the floor. Prinny had his head on his paws, a look of resignation in his eyes, as Claire tried to tie a bow on his tail.

"*Could* you be our mama, Miss Peterson?"

"Isabelle." Emma gently pushed the girl's soft blond hair off her forehead. She suddenly remembered her conversation with Charles on the way back from the vicarage, how she had said she did not want a mother. She did not, now. But she had wanted one desperately when she was Isabelle's age.

"Isabelle, I would love to be your mama, but it isn't that easy."

"Why isn't it?"

Emma looked at the girl's small, serious face. How could she explain? When she'd been nine, she had not understood about men and women. She thought about Charles's kisses in the curricle, how they had made her feel. She was twenty-six and she still didn't understand.

"Isabelle, I would love to be your mama, but then I would have to marry your Uncle Charles."

"Don't you like him?"

Emma took a deep breath. "I don't know him well enough to know if I like him or not."

"Is there someone else you would rather marry?"

"Isabelle." Emma was afraid she saw where this conversation was headed. "No, there is no one else—now. But I might find someone else, and then I couldn't marry him if I were married to your Uncle Charles."

Isabelle smiled. "That's not a problem, then. Molly, one of the upstairs maids, says if you haven't found a man by your age, you aren't going to find one. So you can marry Uncle Charles."

Emma was tempted to quiz Isabelle to determine which of the upstairs maids Molly was so she could strangle the cheeky girl.

"Your Uncle Charles may find a girl *he* would rather marry, Isabelle. That's the point of this house party, you know."

"No, I'm sure he won't like any of them better than you. You are beautiful, Miss Peterson."

No one had ever called Emma beautiful before.

"Thank you, Isabelle." Emma touched the girl's cheek. "Just keep an open mind, will you? I'm sure any lady your uncle marries will love you and Claire."

"Mama Peterson, look!"

Emma turned to see Prinny tearing toward her, wearing a purple bonnet now and dragging a small cart with two of Claire's dolls inside. Emma laughed—and heard the wonderful sound of Isabelle giggling.

"What have you done to that poor dog?" Charles asked from the doorway.

"Papa Charles!" Claire scattered her toys as she

leapt off the floor and ran to her uncle. He caught her up and swung her high while she screamed and laughed.

"Now don't get Lady Claire all stirred up, my lord."

"Nanny." Charles lowered Claire to put her down, but the little girl wrapped her arms around his neck and buried her face in his cravat. Emma saw his eyes widen slightly, and then his lips slid into an odd little smile and his arms tightened around his niece.

"See," Isabelle whispered, "Uncle Charles will make a wonderful papa."

Emma heard the longing in Isabelle's voice, and it went straight as an arrow to her heart. She swallowed sudden tears.

Perhaps Charles would make a wonderful father—but would he make a wonderful husband?

"Would you care for more peas, Miss Peterson?"

"No, thank you, my lord."

Charles leaned back in his chair and observed Miss Peterson sample her turbot. Something odd was afoot. He had come to the schoolroom to invite her to take dinner with Aunt Beatrice and him. She had tried to decline, but Isabelle of all people had urged her to accept. Now Emma was concentrating on her meal as though it were an epicurean feast.

It was not. Charles sighed, taking another forkful of dry fish. Good, honest English cooking—edible, but not quite what his impending house guests would expect from a marquis. He didn't want to offend Cook, but perhaps she'd be happy to have some help in the kitchen. Certainly Alvord or Westbrooke, if they valued their palates, would lend him the services of one of their chefs for the duration of the house party.

"Haven't had food like this in ages," Aunt Bea said, frowning down at her plate.

"Bland food will settle your stomach, Aunt."

"Bah—I don't want the stuff. Just pour me some more Madeira, will you, Charles?"

"I will not. I have just finished loading a carriage with drunken ladies—I do not want you more bosky than you already are."

"I can hold my liquor."

"You are certainly holding a vast quantity of it at the moment, so we will not add to it, I think." Charles hoped she did not take an opportunity to admire herself in any mirrors. Her green and yellow ensemble was making *him* queasy, and he had not downed several bottles of brandy.

"You'd better have thrown some chamber pots into the carriage as well, Charles. Don't doubt if several of the ladies will cast up their accounts, especially once the coach starts swaying."

"Yes, that thought had occurred to me."

Emma put down her fork. "I am sorry, Lady Beatrice, for presuming to invite the Society to meet at Knightsdale. I never would have done so if I had realized how, um, inopportune it would be."

Aunt Beatrice hiccupped. "Nothing inopportune about it, miss. Had a wonderful time—hadn't seen the twins or Blanche in ages. Liked Lavinia, too. Don't think the ladies will be feeling too lively in the morning, though. Doubt they'll be the first of the guests to arrive."

She reached for the wine bottle. Charles moved it.

"When are your guests arriving, Lady Beatrice?"

"Charles's guests, miss. That's the point, don't

you know? Find Charles a wife. Needs to get himself an heir. Don't want the title to pass to Cousin Aubrey. That idiot would probably scream if he found a woman in his bed." Aunt Bea leaned closer. "You want to know what I think? I—"

"Aunt Bea! I am quite certain we do *not* want to know what you think."

"Well, I'm sure it's true." Aunt Bea stabbed a portion of turbot and waved it at Miss Peterson. "You could save us all a significant amount of trouble, miss, if you would just agree to marry Charles now. He's quite a catch, you know."

"Aunt!"

"Lady Beatrice!"

Aunt Bea tasted the fish. "Bleah! Terrible." Her fork clattered on her plate. She leaned close to Emma again and nodded at Charles. "Clean those spectacles of yours, girl, and look at the man. That's no Cousin Aubrey sitting there. I'm sure he'd make getting an heir quite an experience. Am I right, Charles?"

Charles was afraid his face was as red as Miss Peterson's.

"If you'll excuse me," Miss Peterson said in a strangled voice, getting to her feet, "I really must . . . I'm feeling a trifle . . . ."

"Hot?" Aunt Bea said to Miss Peterson's fleeing back. "You should be feeling hot, girl. Think of the shoulders on the man. The legs. The thighs. The—"

"Aunt Bea!"

She stopped and looked at Charles.

"You didn't have to yell, Charles. Thought you was used to plain talk, but I swear you're blushing more than Miss Peterson."

* * *

Charles untied his cravat. He had finally poured Aunt Bea into bed—well, he had turned her over to her long-suffering maid to deal with—and had found his own bedchamber.

"That will be all, Henderson. I won't need you anymore tonight."

"Very well, my lord."

He watched the door close behind his valet. He wanted to be alone. Needed to be. Needed to come to grips with . . . this.

He looked around the room at the dark paintings, the heavy furniture, the huge bed. God. He gripped the bedpost so tightly, the carved ridges dug into his fingers. He shouldn't be here. This was his father's room. Paul's room. It was never, ever supposed to be his room.

Poor Paul, having to move in here when he was only fourteen. Father had died of impatience in an inn yard, screaming at a post boy who'd moved too slowly for his tastes. The innkeeper had been most apologetic, but Charles had understood completely. He'd made avoiding his father's short temper and sharp tongue a high art. It was one reason he'd roamed the countryside so much.

And he'd been only the second son, hardly worth Father's notice. Paul had borne the brunt of the marquis's attention.

But at least Paul had been ready for the title. Well, not ready, perhaps—who could be ready to take over such vast holdings so young? But Paul had been bred to the job—he had known from the cradle he would be the marquis. It was Paul's fate, Paul's destiny. Not his.

He stripped off his shirt and flung it across the room.

He remembered that afternoon at White's as if it were yesterday. He'd been sitting with Robbie, the Earl of Westbrooke. They'd been celebrating their small role in bringing together their friend James, the Duke of Alvord, and his wife, Sarah. Charles had been rolling a mouthful of port on his tongue when the messenger found them.

"Major Charles Draysmith?"

Dread knotted his gut. He knew from the man's stern, serious face and solemn tone that his life was about to change irreversibly. He swallowed quickly.

"Yes? I am Major Draysmith."

"I am sorry to inform you, Major, that the Marquis of Knightsdale and the marchioness have had a tragic accident."

Damn, damn, *damn.* He flung away from the bed to stare out the window at the dark expanse that was Knightsdale. There was no moon; the clouds were as thick as his feelings.

In that moment, when that damn messenger had told him Paul was dead, he had stopped being himself. His plans, his future, his identity all were stripped from him. He'd become the Marquis of Knightsdale. All that remained were the legal details. The heretofores and thereinafters.

He snapped the curtains closed. He ripped off his stockings, his breeches, his drawers. He would have liked to have ripped off his skin. Escape this room, the title, all the unwanted responsibilities.

He couldn't. Knightsdale was his duty now— unsought, unwanted, but still his duty. If the army had taught him anything, if the years of mud and blood had imprinted anything on his soul, it was duty. It had become his one constant in the madness of battle, the long marches, the days of hunger, thirst, exhaustion. Duty had carried him through the

Peninsula, and it would carry him through here in England, too.

Unbidden, the memory of Claire crept into his thoughts, the sounds of her happy squeals when he had picked her up in the schoolroom, the feel of her baby-soft arms around his neck and her small body, light as feathers, in his hold.

Well, perhaps it was more than duty.

He stretched. And there was Miss Emma Peterson. Bedding her would certainly be more than mere duty. He imagined her stretched out, naked, on his sheets. Yes, she would definitely make this room, this bed, more appealing. He chuckled. At least one unruly part of his anatomy was quite inspired by the thought of her lovely curves.

He climbed into bed, forcing his . . . mind to ignore its desire to have Miss Peterson present. She might not be quite so delighted to see him.

He should have gone to her immediately after dinner to apologize, but he suspected she would not have been happy to speak to him just then. She'd needed time to regain her composure. Truth to tell, so had he. It was going to be a very interesting house party if Aunt Bea remained so frank. He made a mental note to lock up all the brandy.

He would talk to Emma in the morning, before the guests arrived. She was an intelligent woman. She would see the wisdom in their marriage. It was obvious she cared for Claire and Isabelle. Well, anyone would love Claire—she was a sweet baby. Isabelle, with her serious reserve, was harder to reach, yet she had been sitting close to Emma, leaning into her and whispering in her ear when he had come to the school-room earlier.

And their marriage would have benefits for Emma

as well. Charles smiled up at the bed canopy. Though Reverend Peterson hadn't said a word, Charles was certain he and Mrs. Graham would be happy to have Emma out of the vicarage.

She was twenty-six. It was past time for her to have her own home, her own family—and he was more than happy to provide her with those things. More than happy. He would especially enjoy teaching her how delightful an activity family-making could be.

If her response to his kisses this afternoon was any indication, it would be quite an invigorating exercise.

CHAPTER 4

Charles was in the middle of a very satisfying dream. Emma Peterson was in his bed. Her honey-blond hair was spread over his pillow; his hands were spread over her glorious breasts. Her fingers stroked his arm. Hmm. Another part of him was aching for her lovely fingers. She slapped his shoulder, and he paused. He had never played those games before. . . .

"Papa Charles, wake up!"

Charles's eyes flew open. He was staring into Claire's face, only inches from his nose.

"Um, Claire." Charles was very conscious of being stark naked under his sheets. He'd have to make a point of locking his door if the little girl had a habit of sleepwalking. "Is there a reason you are here?"

"'Course, Papa Charles. You have to come quick. There's a ghost in the nursery."

"Now, Claire, you've probably just had a bad dream. Did you tell Nanny?"

Claire shook her head, sending her curls bouncing around her small face. "She's screaming too loud."

Nanny? Calm, no nonsense Nanny? "Why is Nanny screaming?"

Claire rolled her eyes and slapped his shoulder again. "I *told* you. There's a ghost. Mama Peterson sent me to get you. Now hurry up, Papa Charles. You need to catch the ghost."

"Right."

Claire resorted to tugging on his arm. There was no time to pull on his breeches—nor did it look as if Claire was going to allow him the privacy to do so— so he yanked the sheet off the bed and wrapped it around his body. He grabbed a cravat pin to fasten his makeshift toga as Claire pushed him out the door.

They encountered Aunt Bea in the hall wearing a puce dressing gown with gold tassels, a scarlet nightcap, and a very pained expression. Queen Bess, looking equally annoyed, swished her tail at Aunt Bea's feet.

"What in God's name is all this racket? Can't I be left to die in peace?"

"Apparently no one is resting in peace tonight, Aunt—and if you hadn't gotten so deep into the brandy bottle, you wouldn't feel near death now."

"And I suppose you've never been jug bitten?"

"Jug bitten? I'd say you were more than jug bitten."

Claire tugged on his arm again. "Come *on*, Papa Charles. The ghost will get away."

Charles went with Claire. Aunt Bea and Queen Bess followed behind.

"*What* did Claire call you?"

"Never mind."

"That's quite some ensemble you're wearing."

Charles grunted. It was difficult to move quickly— his legs kept getting tangled in the sheet. And stairs were impossible.

"How do you ladies manage?" he asked after he'd tripped for the fourth time.

"Better than you, obviously. Oh, get out of the way and let me pass, will you?"

"What if there is a ghost?"

"I'm sure it has been scared away by now. I can hear Nanny caterwauling from here."

They finally reached the nursery. Miss Peterson—dressed in a long white nightgown with a neck to her chin, Charles noted in disappointment—was trying to calm Nanny. Isabelle stood nearby, holding Prinny.

"I brought Papa Charles, Mama Peterson," Claire said.

That was the last coherent statement for many minutes.

Nanny looked at Charles and screamed. Queen Bess looked at Prinny and hissed. Prinny looked at Queen Bess and howled.

Aunt Bea took one look at the scene and put her head in her hands. "My God," she muttered. "Tell me I'm hallucinating. Please."

Prinny, barking wildly, charged at Queen Bess, who fluffed up to twice her size and tried to climb Charles's toga. Charles, considering himself a gentleman at all times, grabbed his sheet to keep from parting company with it and tried valiantly to withhold the many phrases that begged to be uttered as her majesty's sharp claws dug into his skin. He was not completely successful, as he surmised from Claire's round eyes and indrawn breath.

"Ooh, Mama Peterson, Papa Charles said a bad word."

Emma dove, capturing Prinny's hind legs and treating Charles to a glimpse of a well-turned ankle before he heard an ominous ripping and felt fur and air on his own ankles.

"Aunt, come get your blo—blasted cat."

Aunt Bea uncovered her eyes. "I knew you must have nice legs, Charles. See, Miss Peterson? No need for false calves with those legs."

Charles couldn't tell if the heat he was feeling was from mortification or fury. "Madam, corral your animal."

"Really, Charles, we are not on a battlefield. Well, perhaps we are a bit, but you can lower your voice. You're scaring her highness."

"I will do more than scare the f—"

"Charles! Remember, you are a gentleman."

"—feline if you don't pick her up *now!*"

Aunt Bea scooped Queen Bess off the floor and held her next to her face. "There, there, puss. The evil man didn't mean it."

"Didn't I just," Charles muttered. He took stock— his legs were exposed, scratched and bleeding, but all his essential parts were covered. As were, unfortunately, all of Miss Peterson's. She *was* staring at his legs, however.

"Oh, my lord, your poor legs. I'll just get some warm water to bathe them, shall I?"

The thought of Miss Peterson bathing his legs caused the skirt of his now-short toga to bulge in a remarkable way. He could see Aunt Bea opening her mouth to remark on it.

He turned to Nanny. At least she had the grace not to ogle him.

"Can someone tell me what this is all about? Nanny?"

Nanny wrung her hands. "Oh, my lord, I was never so frightened in all my life. I thought I heard a noise, so I got up to check on the dear lambs and I saw something in the hall. I screamed, and it floated over the floor and vanished right there." She pointed at a spot near the schoolroom shelves. "I heard its chains creak and rattle, I did."

"I see." Since Aunt Bea continued to hold Queen Bess, Miss Peterson had let Prinny free. The dog was sniffing around the spot Nanny had indicated. "So, you saw the ghost vanish just where Prinny is now?"

"My lord?" Nanny looked confused.

"There," Charles said. "Where Prinny—Miss Peterson's dog—is."

"Miss Peterson's dog? Oh! Excuse me, my lord." Nanny disappeared into her bedroom and came out a moment later wearing her spectacles. "Ah, that's better. Aye, I think it was exactly where the dear doggy is now."

Charles stared at the old woman. "Nanny, why did you scream when I came upstairs?"

"I thought ye were the ghost returned, my lord." She looked at him closely. "Ye do have a rather odd, um, outfit on, do ye not? Is it a costume? Were ye at a masquerade, then, dressed as one of those Roman gents?"

"No, Nanny." He glanced at Miss Peterson. She was studying the floor by her feet—her very nice feet, Charles noted—and making odd little choking sounds, but at least she had thought to don her spectacles. "Did you see this apparition as well, Miss Peterson?"

"No"—she tried valiantly to stifle her laughter—"my lord." She swallowed. "By the time I left my room, it, uh, it had vanished." She grabbed her sides and bent over, whooping with laughter.

"I am so delighted you find the situation amusing, Miss Peterson."

Emma waved her hand at him, obviously unable to spare the breath to speak. Tears ran down her cheeks.

"You do look extremely funny, Charles," Aunt Bea said, "though I believe Miss Peterson's reaction might be a trifle overdone."

"Pardon me, Lady B-Beatrice," Emma said, going off into howls again. Isabelle and Claire were giggling as well.

"Hmm." Charles surmised that the "ghost" had been a figment of Nanny's imagination. Still, he could not ignore the fact that even though Miss Peterson and the girls were amused, Nanny was not. She tried to smile, but her eyes and mouth were tense.

"If you ladies feel you can finish out the night up here," Charles said, "we will find you sleeping accommodations downstairs tomorrow. Would that be acceptable?"

Miss Peterson finally got hold of her emotions. "Certainly, my lord. We will be fine."

"Aunt, we do have room downstairs, do we not?"

"Yes. It will be a bit crowded—most of the bedchambers will be taken with the house party guests—but I'm certain we can find the space."

"Splendid. Then I wish you ladies good night."

Charles picked up the torn end of his sheet, gesturing for Aunt Bea and Queen Bess to precede him down the stairs. As he reached the first turn, he heard Nanny's voice.

"Mercy, Miss Peterson, but his lordship *does* have nice legs."

* * *

Emma hung her last gown in the wardrobe. Her ball gown. It was silly to have packed it, and yet . . .

She never should have bought the cloth. It had been shockingly self-indulgent. A mad extravagance. That was it. Madness had come over her when she'd seen the blue satin in Mr. Ashford's store. She'd had to have a length of it. Well, even Meg had liked the color— said it reminded her of the afternoon sky in early autumn. That had been—what?—four years ago.

Emma ran her fingers over the silky fabric, tracing the dress's narrow bodice, high waist, and straight skirt. Well, perhaps buying the cloth had been understandable, but letting Mrs. Croft, the village mantua-maker, make this dress had been lunacy. What had she been thinking? What had Mrs. Croft been thinking? The dress was much too revealing for a vicar's daughter, especially one who was firmly on the shelf. The fabric barely covered her breasts and clung like water to everything else. She had been shocked when she had tried it on.

Shocked—and entranced. The woman who'd looked back at her from the mirror had been a stranger, a sophisticated, voluptuous, glorious stranger.

She'd hung the dress at the back of her wardrobe, never to be worn. Looked at, perhaps; dreamed about, definitely; but worn? Never.

Until now. Emma gave the gown one last pat before closing the wardrobe door. She would wear it at the house party ball. It was sadly out of date and would doubtless look quite ordinary among all the London finery certain to be on display, but that could not be helped.

Would she look like the woman she'd seen in the mirror four years ago? No. She would not delude herself. She'd spent four more years on the shelf—she was quite dusty now—and in any event, she was sure she must have embellished the memory. To think that she could be that beautiful . . . absurd. The woman in the mirror was the sort Charles would admire, the sort who thought nothing of letting men put their tong— Emma flushed and took a deep breath. The sort of woman who knew all about kissing.

She was definitely not that sort of woman.

She sat on the window seat, the morning sun warming her back. Her new room was not much larger than her room on the nursery floor, but it was more lavishly appointed. The bedstead, instead of simple beech, was mahogany, and the wardrobe, washstand, and desk were far nicer than even those in her room at the vicarage. And this was one of the smallest bedrooms, left for last-minute guests such as herself. Nanny and the girls were in a larger room across the hall.

She closed her eyes, letting the heat of the sun relax her neck. She had not slept well last night. There had been that ridiculous incident with the ghost. Why hadn't she realized Nanny did not have her spectacles on? She felt so stupid. But she had thought there was an intruder in the nursery, and she could not risk the girls' safety. So she had done the only thing she could think to do—she had sent Claire running to get Charles.

She smiled, remembering his outfit. He had looked so funny. Funny and incredibly attractive. Nanny and Lady Beatrice were correct—Charles had nice legs. Wonderful legs. Not that she had ever seen a pair of bare male legs before, of course. And not just his legs had been revealed to her interested gaze. His arms, his neck, his shoulders, part of his chest. He'd looked just like a statue of a Greek god, except he was alive. Warm. Flesh and blood.

Suddenly the sun streaming in the window was too hot. She moved to the chair on the other side of the room.

What was the matter with her? Was she sick? She'd spent all night dreaming of Charles. Well, she had dreamt of him before, but now she had so many more details. More, but not quite enough. She did not know how he *felt*. She flushed. How wanton—she wanted to touch him. To be touched by him. To feel his arms around her. To run her fingers over his muscles, the hair dusting his chest. Was it soft or wiry? And his skin—all that glorious skin—how would it feel under her fingers?

She had dreamt of his kisses also. The first one, the quick, tantalizing brush, and the second, the hot, wet second kiss with his lips and mouth and tong—

She fanned herself with her hand. Her body felt extremely odd thinking of that kiss. She had actually *throbbed* in a most unusual place last night. The same location felt distressingly damp at the moment. Damp and, well, needy.

Perhaps it was time she married. She had not seriously considered it before, but, as Charles had said, Meg was now seventeen. Certainly her father no longer needed her. He had Mrs. Graham, and, though he had never said so, Emma was convinced he would be happy to have her move out of the vicarage. The only way she could do that was to find a husband.

Perhaps marriage would also cure her of her new . . . yearnings.

But she wouldn't marry Charles. She couldn't,

even though it appeared that he and his aunt had selected her. She'd thought she'd expire from embarrassment at dinner last night. Lady Beatrice was too plainspoken for her own good—or Emma's good. Surely she would not say such things once the house party arrived!

No, Charles had only suggested she wed him because he didn't want to be bothered courting some society miss. That would change today. Today he would have a selection of attractive young ladies near at hand. He would not have to exert himself in the slightest. He could sit in the drawing room and have them parade past, as if he were choosing a new horse for his stable. There were certain to be any number who were willing to sell themselves for a title.

She was not one of them. Definitely not. And anyway, it was ludicrous to think Charles would want an aging spinster once he surveyed all the younger possibilities.

She went back to the window. Her new room had a good view of the broad front drive. It was empty now, but in a few hours it would be filled with traveling carriages bringing their sacrificial women. Surely a selection of unattached men would also be in attendance. Charles could choose only one of the ladies—there would have to be a few extra males available.

Perhaps one of those could care for her—for herself, not her breeding potential. It might be possible. In any event, this was the closest she would ever come to a Season and the London Marriage Mart.

She would take this opportunity to do a little shopping.

* * *

"Meg." Emma had seen her sister arrive and hurried downstairs to meet her.

Meg was scowling. "You are evil, Emma," she hissed under her breath.

"Meg! Why ever would you say such a thing?" True, Emma had not expected Meg to be enthusiastic about the house party invitation, but still—it was a wonderful opportunity for her to get some social experience.

"You're the one who put this house party bee in Papa's bonnet, aren't you?"

Emma choked. "Papa doesn't wear a bonnet."

Meg was not amused. "You know exactly what I mean. Did you or did you not come to the vicarage and invite me to this ridiculous house party?"

"I believe Lord Knightsdale extended the invitation. And the party is not ridiculous. You can stand to move among the *ton* a bit."

"Don't split hairs. You were there, weren't you? You could have prevented the invitation. And I don't want to move among the *ton*. The *ton* is a collection of mutton-headed coxcombs and spoiled chits. I want to be out in Squire Begley's north field. I found a very interesting patch of— Lud, what is that?"

Emma turned to see Lady Beatrice approaching. She was attired in a stunning gown of mulberry and pea green today, with an assortment of ostrich feathers waving among her gray curls.

Meg definitely looked stunned. Her eyes widened and she darted a disbelieving look at Emma. Emma frowned at her, willing her sister to have the manners not to comment on their hostess's unusual fashion sense.

"Lady Beatrice, may I introduce my sister Meg?"

Meg curtsied. "Thank you for inviting me, Lady Beatrice."

"You are very welcome, dear." Lady Beatrice turned to Mr. Lambert. "Have George take Miss Margaret Peterson's bags up to the yellow bedroom, will you, Lambert?"

"Certainly, my lady."

Lady Beatrice smiled and turned back to Meg. "You know, I have wonderful plans for your sister."

Emma stiffened.

"You do?" Meg grinned. It was obvious she had noticed Emma's discomfiture. "What might those plans be?"

Emma prayed for the floor to open and swallow her, but, wonders of wonders, Lady Beatrice contented herself with an arch look.

"It's a bit premature to say."

Emma allowed herself a small sigh of relief.

"But it does involve—"

"Lady Beatrice, um, did you sleep well last night?" Interrupting one's hostess was rude, but Emma was certain strangling her was a greater solecism. Still, the selection of last evening's events as a change of topic was not inspired. Lady Beatrice frowned.

"No, indeed. I barely slept a wink, what with that spectral disturbance and my wretched head. Do not drink brandy, Meg. At least not in excess."

"Brandy? Spectral disturbance?" Meg murmured while Lady Beatrice rubbed her forehead. "Perhaps this will not be such a boring gathering after all."

"Hush."

"What did you say, dear? I'm afraid I wasn't attending."

"Nothing, Lady Beatrice. I'm just happy that last night's events turned out to be nothing significant."

Emma saw Meg's eyes were bright with questions, but fortunately Charles chose that moment to appear.

"Good morning, ladies. Did I hear you say this is your sister, Miss Peterson?"

"Yes, my lord."

Charles took Meg's hand. "A pleasure to meet you, Miss Margaret. The last time we encountered each other, you were still in leading-strings."

Meg rolled her eyes, but she did smile. "Please, Lord Knightsdale, call me Meg. No one calls me Margaret."

"Meg, then. I believe you'll find your dog in the nursery."

"My dog?"

"Prinny," Emma said. "Your dog, Prinny."

"I don't know why you insist Prinny is my dog, Emma. I may have named him when he was a puppy, but you're the one he thinks he belongs to. Probably because you're the one who remembers to feed him."

This was a familiar argument. Emma took a deep breath and tried to sound calm.

"You know Prinny's supposed to keep you company on the long rambles you insist on taking. He's your protection when you are out in the fields alone."

"Hmm. Have you told Prinny this? On the odd occasion he comes with me, he's off chasing rabbits. I don't want him with me. He tramples the specimens."

"Specimens?" Charles asked.

"I'm very interested in plants, my lord."

"My lady, Mr. Stockley is arriving," Mr. Lambert said.

"Ah, the beau." Meg grinned at Emma. "It will be rather hard to avoid the man if he's a guest also, won't it, Emma?"

"The beau?" Charles raised an eyebrow as Lady Beatrice went off to greet her new guest.

Emma would gladly have wrung her sister's neck. "It's nothing, my lord. Meg is only funning." She shot Meg a look that warned of dire consequences should she pursue this topic. Meg ignored her.

"Mr. Stockley has been a frequent—or should I say constant—visitor at the vicarage since he moved into Mr. Atworthy's house. I've missed stumbling over him since Emma came up here. He's quite smitten."

"I see. Then I am so glad we encountered him on the road yesterday and invited him to join the party."

"Yes, it was quite fortunate, was it not? Come, Meg, I'll help you settle into your room." Emma grabbed Meg's arm and fled upstairs.

"What was that about?"

"What was what about?" Emma looked around Meg's room. It was slightly larger than her own.

"That gallop up the stairs. I'm rather out of breath."

"I'm sure I don't know what you are speaking of."

Meg's room faced the back of the house. She had a very pleasant view of the gardens and the lake.

"Emma, what is going on between you and the marquis?"

"Nothing!" Did she really squeak when she said that? Surely not. "Why would you think anything was going on between Lord Knightsdale and me?"

"Emma, I may be socially inexperienced, but I am not stupid. You are usually as staid as an archbishop, but downstairs just now you acted as if you were waltzing barefoot over hot coals. Would you care to explain?"

"No. I mean, there is nothing to explain. I'm merely the temporary governess."

"Oh? And where are the children?"

"What?"

Meg put her hands on her hips. "The children. Governesses usually take care of children, do they not?"

"Oh. Oh, yes. Isabelle and Claire. You know them, Meg."

"Of course I know them, dear sister. If you are their governess, even only temporarily, why are you not governessing?"

"Good point. I'm leaving now. Welcome to Knightsdale."

Emma closed the door on Meg's laughter.

So Stockley was taken with Emma, was he? For the first time Charles was happy to have a title so he could shove it down this twiddlepoop's throat. He watched the man take out his quizzing-glass and examine a large flowered urn by the door, going so far as to lift the lid and peer inside.

"Looking for something, Stockley?"

The little fop jumped, making the vase teeter on its pedestal. Charles steadied it.

"My lord, you startled me. I was just admiring this fine workmanship. Is it from the Ming dynasty, do you know?"

"Haven't the foggiest. You're interested in crockery?"

"Art, my lord. Art. Yes, I am very interested in all things valuable—statuary, paintings, jewels."

"Indeed?" Charles wondered if he should lock up the silver. What had Emma's father been thinking, letting this bounder over the vicarage threshold?

What had *he* been thinking? He'd invited the fellow to Knightsdale, hadn't he? He would just need to keep an eye on Emma. A very close eye. It was his duty as her host.

"Charles, the Society ladies are here."

"Right. Coming, Aunt." Charles turned back to Stockley. "I hope you enjoy your stay at Knightsdale. Do you need help finding your bedchamber?"

"Oh, no, my lord. I'm quite capable of finding my way." Stockley's lips twitched and he bowed.

Charles watched him mount the stairs.

"Aunt, you didn't put Stockley in a bedchamber near Emma, did you?"

"Of course not, Charles. What kind of a ninnyhammer do you take me for? I switched his room with Miss Russell's this morning, when we moved Miss Peterson down from the nursery. He's at the far end of the east wing. Wouldn't want him mistaking his door in the night, would we?"

"Definitely not."

Charles stood by a window in the study, looking out at the gardens and the lake. All the guests had arrived. It was certainly an odd collection. Well, the husband-hunting mamas and their daughters and the assortment of unattached gentlemen were not so unusual. It was the addition of the ladies of Emma's Society that made the guest list interesting. Add brandy, and the *ton* might never be the same.

"Charles, did I just see the Farthington twins in the corridor?"

Charles smiled as Robbie Hamilton, the Earl of Westbrooke, slipped into the study.

"You did indeed."

"Gawd. I need brandy. Where do you keep the stuff?"

"In the case there—if there's any left. Just be sure you don't let the twins catch a scent of it."

Robbie paused, his hand on the cork. "Brandy and the Farthington twins?"

Charles laughed. "Teacups full. I found the entire Society for the Betterment of Women—minus Miss Peterson—awash in my drawing room. Had to pour the ladies into my carriage to get them home."

"The thought boggles the mind." Robbie filled two glasses and handed one to Charles. "Besides the inebriated elders, how have you found things, my friend?"

"Well, I believe." Charles sipped the amber liquid, savoring the warmth that slid from his tongue to his chest. "It appears Paul invested wisely, so as far as I can tell I've got adequate funds. I straightened that all out when I was in London."

"That's a relief. And the estate itself?"

Charles shrugged. "Coles, the estate manager, seems competent. I just got here yesterday and I've had other, um, affairs to attend to. I've promised to give him some time tomorrow morning."

He frowned, looking into his glass, swirling his brandy slowly. He felt the solid weight of Robbie's hand on his shoulder.

"You know you can call on me, if you need to."

Charles nodded. "I know, Robbie." He clasped Robbie's arm briefly. "I know."

Robbie grinned. "I just have more experience with this peer business. And running an estate, of course."

"Of course."

"Did Coles have anything else to say?"

"Just that I take it Paul was pretty much an absentee

landlord after he married Cecilia. Coles has been rather blunt in expressing his hope that I intend to be in residence more frequently."

"Cecilia did like London."

"And apparently any estate other than Knightsdale."

Robbie sprawled into one of the chairs by the fire. "She needed society's constant attention."

"Leaving her children with very little of hers."

"There is that. But many children grow up with only the servants to raise them. I daresay I didn't see my parents above five or six times a year—and I don't suppose you spent much time with yours either, did you?"

"No." Charles joined Robbie by the fire. "I didn't want to see my father. You remember his temper."

Robbie nodded. "And your mother?"

Charles sighed. "Not so different from Cecilia."

"And did you mind?"

"Not that I can recall. But my nieces"—Charles took another sip of brandy—"the little one calls me Papa Charles."

"What's this?" a man said from the doorway. "Are you a father, Charles? My felicitations—though it might be advisable to acquire a wife before you begin to fill your nursery."

"James!" Charles stood to greet the Duke of Alvord. "How is Sarah?"

"Quite well, thank you."

"Expecting the next duke, I hear," Robbie said.

James grinned. "Perhaps."

"Really?" Charles offered James the brandy bottle. "This calls for a drink."

"Just be sure you've shut the study door, James. Charles tells me that the Farthington twins are partial to brandy."

"Really? I never would have guessed. And was that Miss Russell I saw examining the statuary upstairs?"

"Most likely," Charles said. "Did she have a small man with her?"

James's eyebrows shot up. "Never say Miss Russell has a beau?"

Robbie laughed. "This is definitely going to be an interesting house party if that's the case. Did you know Charles got the ladies drunk?"

"I did not get the ladies drunk, Robbie. Aunt Bea did that. I wasn't even home when they broke into my brandy."

"I see." James grinned. "Or rather, I don't see. Who is the little man who is courting Miss Russell?"

"Mr. Albert Stockley, and he is not courting Miss Russell. I found him examining the vase in the entry hall on his arrival and thought perhaps he had joined Miss Russell in appreciating Knightsdale's art."

"Think Stockley might be somewhat light-fingered?" James asked.

Charles shrugged. "Perhaps. I don't like the man."

"So why did you invite him?" Robbie frowned. "Isn't he the coxcomb who's renting Atworthy's house?"

"Yes. Do you know anything about him?"

"Can't say that I do. How about you, James?"

"No." James grinned. "I've had my mind on other matters."

"I bet you have." Robbie rolled his eyes. "The Alvord ladies fled to Brighton to give your, um, mind the opportunity for complete concentration."

"Had to do my duty, after all, and see to the succession. And you'll be happy to hear that Aunt Gladys, Lady Amanda, and Lizzie are back in residence. Lizzie is joining the house party tomorrow."

"So is little Lizzie also joining the pack of young misses baying after the new marquis here?"

"I don't believe Lizzie is interested in Charles, Robbie."

"And I'm not interested in any of the young ladies," Charles said.

"You're not? So why have you collected this school of ballroom barracudas? I swear I saw Lady Dunlee and Mrs. Frampton glaring at each other in the hall. If you are not the bachelor morsel to be tossed into their jaws, who is?" Robbie put up the hand that wasn't holding his brandy. "It ain't going to be me."

"Well, it can't be me, can it?" James said. "And if Charles here is unwilling . . ."

"No. I'm too young for a leg shackle."

"There are other unattached men present," Charles said, "so you need not fear."

"Oh, no? I am not so certain. If the ladies can't have a marquis, they may pursue a mere earl. No, I shall have my valet check my bedchamber thoroughly for any stray misses before I retire each night, and I will carefully avoid all secluded areas of your lovely estate." Robbie took another sip. "Perhaps I'll just attach myself to your Aunt Bea—she'll have no trouble routing any encroaching misses, and I understand she's quite free with the brandy bottle."

"A splendid idea, Robbie," James said. He leaned back in his chair. "However, I still don't understand why you invited all these people here, Charles, if you have no interest in selecting a bride. I'm quite certain that lovely Lady Dunlee and charming Mrs. Frampton did not drag their delightful, marriage-hungry daughters down to Knightsdale for the scenery—unless, of course, the scenery included the sight of you slipping the Knightsdale engagement ring on one of their progeny's fingers."

"Yes, I understand that. I thought I was in the market, but I've already found a suitable bride."

"Oh? And who might this paragon be?" James asked.

"Miss Emma Peterson."

"The vicar's daughter?"

"Not only the vicar's daughter, James," Robbie said, chuckling. "Shadow."

"Shadow? Who? Oh, yes, I remember. The little girl who used to dog Charles's steps when we were boys. That *was* Miss Peterson, wasn't it?"

"And if you haven't noticed"—Robbie grinned—"and of course you haven't, being a married man—Miss Peterson is no longer a little girl."

"Watch yourself, Robbie." Charles was surprised by the surge of annoyance he felt at Robbie's slightly leering tone. "I'll brook no disrespect of Miss Peterson."

"Oh, I always respect my elders."

"Elders? Miss Peterson is only twenty-six."

"As am I, my friend. You are the graybeard at thirty. No, I believe Miss Peterson is two months older than I—I vaguely remember getting into an argument with her on the subject when I turned ten."

"Gentlemen, let us not hearken back to our infancy." James raised his glass. "Congratulations are in order. When will you be announcing your betrothal, Charles?"

"Soon."

"At the ball?" Robbie asked. "That would be the most appropriate time. Perhaps you can keep the other ladies guessing until then so they'll leave me alone."

"Yes. At the ball." Charles remembered the sound of the china dog shattering on the study door. "I hope. There are a few matters still to be resolved."

CHAPTER 5

"If the London Season is anything like this, I am glad to have missed it."

"Meg, keep your voice down." Emma pushed her sister discreetly in the back to get her to step into the drawing room.

A sea of conversation washed over them. Elegant London ladies in fashionable dresses chatted with gentlemen in elaborate cravats and tight-fitting black coats. Emma felt more than a little dowdy. She searched for a familiar face—and saw Lady Beatrice, resplendent in a crimson gown with knots of lime green ribbons, laughing uproariously with Mrs. Begley. The liquid in their glasses looked suspiciously like brandy.

Where were the other members of the Society for the Betterment of Women? Emma spotted the Farthington twins in the far corner examining a large painting of a naked woman, a mostly naked man, and a sprinkling of fat cherubs. Miss Esther pointed to the man's bare shoulders and elbowed her sister in the ribs. At least neither lady was drinking. Miss Russell occupied a settee nearby, also without a glass or teacup at hand. Emma felt some tension ease from her neck. She did not want to entertain the Londoners with the spectacle of drunken locals.

"Just look at that gaggle of pea-gooses." Meg nodded at a group of young ladies clustered around Charles at the other end of the room. "Or is it 'pea-geese'? It's a good thing Lord Knightsdale favors short hair or his lovely brown locks would be blown into knots by all those batting eyelashes."

Emma agreed. The girls were fawning over Charles in a most disgusting manner. It certainly could not be good for his already inflated estimation of himself. Not that he wasn't an arresting sight. He was even more handsome, if that were possible, dressed in eveningwear.

He looked up. His startling blue eyes met hers across the room, and the right corner of his mouth creased up in a half smile.

She felt an odd warmth radiate from her stomach.

"And here comes your own special admirer, Emma. He must have been watching the door for you."

"My own—oh." Mr. Stockley was slithering toward her. She had never thought of him as snakelike before, but tonight he struck her as having a distinctly serpentine quality. Perhaps it was his lack of expression. Or his quiet—stealthy, really—way of moving.

Ridiculous! She had not gotten enough sleep last night. It was the odd nocturnal events in the nursery that were feeding this bizarre fantasy.

"I keep expecting a forked tongue to flicker out of his mouth," Meg murmured. "I think I'll go help Miss Russell warm the settee."

Emma resisted the urge to grab Meg's arm.

"Miss Peterson, I am delighted to see Lord Knightsdale allowed you to join our gathering. Who is watching Lady Isabelle and Lady Claire?"

Emma gritted her teeth. "Nanny is with the girls, Mr. Stockley."

"Ah, Nanny. A mature, reliable woman. You, ah, have rooms on the nursery floor with the girls and Nanny, I presume?"

The man was presuming too much. "I can't imagine why you would be interested in my accommodations, Mr. Stockley."

Mr. Stockley smirked. "I mean no disrespect, Miss Peterson. I am confident a woman of your maturity will guard her reputation closely. It's just that . . . well . . . it would not do for you to be on the same floor as our host. A single woman without a chaperone present, you understand. It might give rise to unsavory speculation. People have such small minds."

Emma could name one person with a small mind. "Sir, I fail to see why my reputation is in danger. Lady Beatrice is in residence, after all, and now the house is filled with guests. Do you think Lord Knightsdale is going to break down my door and rape me in my bed?"

"I am continually surprised, Westbrooke, at how little we know our closest friends. Who would have thought Knightsdale had taken to deflowering virgins?"

Emma flushed and turned to find the Duke of Alvord and the Earl of Westbrooke at her elbow.

"Your grace, I did not mean—"

"Of course you did not mean anything, Miss Peterson." The duke smiled at her, but his expression hardened as he faced Mr. Stockley. "However, I do wonder what your companion meant."

"Mr. Albert Stockley, your grace, and no offense

meant, of course. I was just cautioning Miss Peterson in a general way, as a friend."

"As a friend. I see." The duke looked at Lord Westbrooke. "Correct me if I'm wrong, Westbrooke, but I believe Miss Peterson is a childhood friend of Knightsdale, is she not? One would think he would make it his responsibility to see that she came to no harm under his roof."

"One would think," Lord Westbrooke agreed.

Emma had had enough. "Oh, stop it." She had been offended by Mr. Stockley, true, but she didn't need these two defending her. "I'm sure Mr. Stockley was just trying to be a gentleman. You don't need to throw your consequence around."

"Miss Peterson, you wound me." The duke's amber eyes held a definite twinkle. "My consequence is too great to be 'thrown around.'"

"Right." Lord Westbrooke grinned. "Alvord's not strong enough for the task. Gotten too soft, now that he's a married man."

"Mr. Stockley," Emma said, "as you have probably surmised, I knew his grace and Lord Westbrooke when we were all children, though they hardly acknowledged my presence then." Nor had they paid much attention to her in recent years, Emma thought. Why were they both at her side now?

"Of course we ignored you, Miss Peterson," the duke said. "You were a girl, and we were most assuredly not interested in girls at that time."

"You can thank me you were even tolerated," Charles said. He had divested himself of his harem. "These fellows would have banned you from our games."

Deftly, Mr. Stockley had been excluded from their group. The duke and Lord Westbrooke took a slight step to the side, a shifting forward, and Mr. Stockley was invisible, hidden behind their height. Nor could he participate in the youthful recollections. The circle had tightened physically and conversationally, and he was firmly on the outside. Emma watched him hover there for a moment, then turn and wander away.

"Where is your wife, your grace?" she asked.

"Resting." The duke grinned so widely he looked like a boy again. "She tires easily these days."

"Alvord thinks he's so clever he's figured out how to—"

"Robbie!" Charles nodded at Emma.

Lord Westbrooke's eyes fell on her, and he reddened.

"As I'm sure you've deduced, Emma," Charles said, "the duke and duchess are expecting their first child."

"That's wonderful news, your grace." Emma was touched that the man was so obviously thrilled. "I hope to meet her grace tomorrow."

"Charles." Lady Beatrice appeared at Charles's elbow with a hunchbacked elderly man in tow. "It's time to go in to dinner. Duke, you're the highest-ranking man here—you get to take in Lady Augusta."

"My pleasure."

Lord Westbrooke snorted. "Unlikely. Lady Augusta will jaw you to death before you've finished your turtle soup."

Lady Beatrice pointed a bejeweled finger at Lord Westbrooke. "And you, my lord, will be squiring Lady Barworth."

"Not Lady Barworth!" Lord Westbrooke's hands flew up as if to ward off a blow, while the duke and Charles tried unsuccessfully to muffle their laughter.

"Have pity, please. I'm too young to suffer detailed accounts of gout and indigestion."

"My lord, I am certain it is not as bad as that."

"You're right, Aunt," Charles said. "I believe Lady Barworth also discusses her grandchildren's ailments."

"And word has it that the youngest Barworth is recovering from the measles," the duke said, "so you're in for a treat, Westbrooke."

"Gawd." Lord Westbrooke rolled his eyes.

Lady Beatrice glared. "I trust you will behave yourself, my lord."

"Of course. I promise to try not to nod off during Lady Barworth's medical report, and, if I cannot keep Morpheus at bay for the entire meal, I promise not to snore." Lord Westbrooke grinned. "Or, at least not loudly."

Lady Beatrice grunted and turned to Emma. "Here is your escort, dear." She shook the elderly man's arm and shouted in his ear, *"This is Miss Peterson, Mr. Maxwell. You'll be taking her in to dinner."*

"What? Thinner?" Mr. Maxwell was so bent over, his face was only inches above Emma's bosom. "Sacrilege! Don't take an ounce off 'em, my dear."

Emma stepped back before a bit of drool hit her bodice.

"Maxwell, you forget yourself." Charles looked like a thundercloud.

Mr. Maxwell twisted his head to look up at him. "What? No need to get tetchy, my lord. Didn't know you had your eye on 'em." Mr. Maxwell wheezed with apparent laughter. "Man can look, can't he, without giving offense?"

"Come on, Charles," Lady Beatrice said. "Take me in to dinner. Your Miss Peterson is safe. Poor Mr. Maxwell can't do much more than look."

Mr. Maxwell gave no indication that he had heard, but Emma was certain her face was redder than Lady Beatrice's dress. She watched Charles lead his aunt across the room.

"Shall we go in to dinner?" Mr. Maxwell asked her bosom.

"I don't suppose we have a choice, do we?" Emma said, batting away Mr. Maxwell's errant fingers.

"I don't believe I've seen a dress quite like yours this Season, Miss Peterson. Who is your mantua-maker?" Lady Oldston's prominent eyes glittered with malice.

Emma forced a smile. "Mrs. Croft—a local woman."

"I see."

"How quaint—using local . . . um . . . talent. I have never tried it. Perhaps it will become the rage." Lady Dunlee permitted herself a tiny smile, small enough not to crease her substantial jowls.

"I don't recall seeing you in Town, Miss Peterson." The third gorgon, Mrs. Pelham, yawned. "You must have made your come out"—she paused artfully, brows arched, nostrils flared—"a few years ago."

"I'm certain I did not see you or your sister," Lady Oldston said. "I would have made note of it. We were bringing out dear Amanda."

Dear Amanda looked like a cross between a horse and a toad, all bug-eyed and toothy—like her mother.

"And I had Lady Caroline." Lady Dunlee stressed her daughter's title ever so slightly. Lady Oldston flushed. She was merely the wife of a baronet; Lady Dunlee was a countess.

And Lady Caroline was rounder than her mother.

She was whispering with Miss Oldston by the garden windows.

"I do think it quite magnanimous of dear Lord Knightsdale to invite the neighbors," Mrs. Pelham said. "Don't you agree, Miss Peterson? It must be such a treat for you."

Emma grunted—politely, she hoped. The ladies appeared not to expect more coherency from such a provincial as herself.

If she'd had half an ounce of intelligence, she would have made good her escape right after dinner just as Meg had, between the dining room and the drawing room. It would have been so easy. If anyone had asked, she could have claimed a need to check on the girls.

She smiled and nodded vaguely at Mrs. Pelham's next drop of verbal poison.

She would not lie to herself. She had followed the ladies into the drawing room in the hopes of seeing Charles again. How stupid could she be?

Incredibly stupid, she concluded, feeling her heart jump as the man crossed the threshold. His eyes sought hers.

Lady Oldston sighed. "Isn't it so romantic, how Lord Knightsdale looks for my dear Amanda as soon as he enters a room? He paid her marked attention in Town this Season. I was not at all surprised to receive this invitation."

Mrs. Pelham laughed. "Oh, Lady Oldston, how droll! Of course you know the marquis is only interested in my Lucinda. Not that Amanda isn't a fine young lady, of course, but Lucinda . . . well, dear Mr. Pelham has already had to turn away an earl and a viscount." Mrs. Pelham sighed. "We feel Lucinda is a bit young for marriage, but my husband might be persuaded to turn over the reins, as it were, to a gentleman as serious and mature as Lord Knightsdale."

"It is a pity about the orphans, though," Lady Dunlee said. "So inconvenient. Whomever Knightsdale marries will have to contend with his brother's brats."

"Ah, but that is what governesses are for, are they not, Miss Peterson?" Mrs. Pelham smirked.

Emma gritted her teeth. She wished the tea had been served—Mrs. Pelham's appearance could only be improved by a teacup turned over her head.

"I'm certain Lord Knightsdale expects any woman he marries to treat his nieces with kindness and consideration."

"And you know Lord Knightsdale's mind, Miss Peterson?" Mrs. Pelham asked. "How . . . odd."

"Don't let the honor of mixing with this company raise false hopes, dear," Lady Oldston said. "I understand you don't have a mother to guide you, though one would think at your advanced age . . . But, no matter, let me whisper the word in your ear—marquises do not marry governesses."

"No, indeed," Mrs. Pelham said. "If you think to angle for an offer, well . . ."

"You'll get an offer, all right." Lady Dunlee chuckled. "An offer of *carte-blanche.*"

"A slip on the shoulder," Lady Oldston said. "Necklaces, bracelets, and rings—but never a wedding ring."

"Set your sights on someone more attainable, dear," Mrs. Pelham said. "Someone like Mr. Stockley, perhaps."

"Miss Peterson."

Emma looked up. Lady Beatrice stood by the tea tray, cup in hand.

"Would you be so kind as to pour?"

"Of course." Emma would pick the tea leaves herself to get away from these harpies. "If you'll excuse me, ladies?"

"Whatever were you thinking, sitting down with that crowd?" Lady Beatrice muttered when Emma joined her.

"They sat down with me. I had no idea they were so unpleasant."

"Unpleasant?" Lady Beatrice snorted. "If they're 'unpleasant,' old Satan is slightly naughty. I imagine they didn't care for the fact Charles singled you out before dinner—Charles and his friends, Alvord and Westbrooke." She smiled and leaned a little closer. "Give me their cups, Miss Peterson. I'm feeling a trifle clumsy. Maybe hot tea down their fronts will melt their frozen hearts."

Emma smiled back. "Do be careful, Lady Beatrice."

"Very. Anyone you particularly wish me to douse?"

"I could never single one out for special attention."

"No? I could. I have never liked the particular shade of yellow Victoria Pelham is wearing tonight. Especially on her. Makes her look like an overdone lemon tart. I would be doing her a favor to urge her to change her attire."

Emma smiled. She didn't expect Lady Beatrice to follow through with her outrageous plan, but in a few moments, Mrs. Pelham emitted a most unladylike screech.

"Aunt didn't care for something Mrs. Pelham said?" Charles asked as he took a teacup from Emma.

"I believe it was her color choice that your aunt objected to."

They looked over at the ladies. Lady Beatrice had managed to spill tea on Lady Oldston and Lady Dunlee in her efforts to mop Mrs. Pelham's front.

"She's right. Yellow is not Mrs. Pelham's color."

Emma chuckled.

"Lord Knightsdale." Miss Haverford dimpled up at Charles. "Would you come and turn my pages for me?"

"I would be delighted to, Miss Haverford. I will join you at the piano in a moment."

"Miss Haverford seems like a nice young lady." Emma tried to swallow her jealousy. Miss Haverford was seventeen with lovely golden ringlets and sweet, deep blue eyes. She was also the daughter of a viscount.

"A very nice *young* lady—like Meg."

Emma grinned. "I'm not sure anyone would describe Meg as a nice young lady. Not that she isn't nice, young, and a lady, of course, but those are not the words which first spring to mind when I think of my sister."

"Oh? What words do?"

"I don't know." Emma frowned. "Intelligent. Single-minded. Stubborn."

Charles laughed. "Spoken as a big sister." He dropped his voice. "I need to have a word with you, Emma. Meet me in the conservatory when the ladies retire, will you?"

"That sounds most improper."

"Doesn't it, though? But don't worry—I want to talk about Isabelle and Claire."

"And it can't wait until morning?" Emma saw Miss Haverford sitting at the piano, waving in their direction. "I think Miss Haverford is losing patience."

"Right." Charles waved back. "No, it can't wait. Promise to meet me?"

Emma sighed. "All right."

* * *

Emma waited in the shadows of the conservatory. She breathed in the moist, warm scent of earth and growth. The thick vegetation muffled sounds, giving the impression of privacy.

This was lunacy. She should be upstairs in her room.

She heard a step on the path and faded farther into the greenery. What if someone came upon her? How would she ever explain lurking in the leafage?

"Emma?"

Charles's voice was low and male in the darkness. "Yes?"

"Ah." He took her hand and pulled her farther into the darkened conservatory.

"My lord, we were going to discuss your nieces."

"Shh. We will—in a moment. I don't want one of the young ladies or their mamas to find me."

Emma dropped her voice to match his. "I thought they had all gone up to bed."

"They are supposed to have done so, but a man can never be too cautious." Charles stepped under the branches of a tall, potted tree. "This should do."

He had not bothered to release her hand. She tugged back slightly, and he tightened his fingers, pulling her close to his body.

It was so intimate, standing with him in the moon-lit darkness, hidden among the leaves. She breathed in the scent of his soap and skin mingled with the warm, damp smell of dirt and flowers.

"My lord, this is a trifle improper."

"Hmm. Only a trifle, Miss Peterson, and not near as improper as I would like it to be."

Her brain told her she should step back, but her body refused to respond.

"What did you want to talk about, my lord?"

"Charles."

"My lord."

His mouth curved up—his lovely mouth that was only inches above hers. "If you insist on 'my lording' me, Emma, I shall have to persuade you again to use my Christian name. Do you remember how I accomplished that feat in the curricle yesterday?"

Could she forget? Her entire body from her toenails to the ends of her lamentably curly hair ached with embarrassment at the memory of his lips on hers.

"Charles, then. You wanted to talk about Isabelle and Claire."

"Hmm." He traced her lips slowly with the tip of his finger. His skin was slightly rough, dry, warm. Her lips tingled, and heat pooled low in her body. She wrenched herself back.

"Lord Knightsdale, you wished to speak about your nieces."

He grinned. "Well, yes, but I also wanted to kiss you, Emma. I quite enjoyed the sensation yesterday, didn't you?"

Emma was definitely not going to answer that question.

"Your nieces?"

Charles sighed. "I only wanted to suggest we take them fishing in the morning. We can be out to the stream and home again before any of my guests has cracked open an eye. I think Isabelle and Claire would enjoy it, and it would give me some time with them before I have to see my estate manager and then play host."

"That would be wonderful." Emma smiled. If Charles did spend time with the girls, got to know them, to care for them, he would be less likely to leave them. They needed him in their lives. "I'm certain they would love it. I doubt they've ever been fishing."

"No? That's a pity."

"But you don't need me to come along."

"Indeed I do, Emma. I'm certain the girls would feel much more comfortable having you with them. They don't know me." He gave her a lopsided grin. "And I would feel more comfortable having you there. I don't make a habit of entertaining little girls."

You used to, Emma thought. *You used to know exactly how to make anyone feel comfortable. You probably still do.* But she could see how he and the girls might feel awkward. And if she were honest, the thought of being out in the quiet of the early morning with just Charles, Isabelle, and Claire was vastly appealing.

She refused to examine exactly why that was.

"All right, my lord. What time and where shall we meet you?"

"I'll come scratch at your door. No, don't give me that look—no one will be up to see me, so we won't scandalize a soul."

"What about the servants?"

"I won't come *in* your room, Emma. I'll talk to you through your door, if that would better suit your notions of propriety."

"Very well." Certainly there could be nothing inappropriate in such a plan. She was the girls' temporary governess—and an old maid of twenty-six. "Then I believe I shall retire, Lord Knightsdale, since I will be getting up again so soon."

Emma caught the gleam of his teeth in the darkness.

"Do you still not care for spiders, Emma?"

"Spiders?" Emma swallowed and lowered her voice. She listened, but she didn't hear any footsteps approaching. If there had been anyone nearby, he or she would have heard her squeak. She could deal with worms and beetles and the general run of bugs, but she had never been able to master her abhorrence of spiders. "What do you mean, spiders?"

"One of the drawbacks of staging an assignation in the shrubbery, sweetheart, is occasionally one plays host—or in this case, hostess—to an uninvited guest. Allow me."

Charles picked a large black spider off her bodice. She yelped when she saw it—her reaction had nothing to do with Charles's fingers brushing the top of her breasts. This was, fortunately, a very high-necked dress. No chance of spiders—or fingers—going too far astray.

She had never had her fear of spiders cause her breasts to tingle in this very odd fashion.

He held the disgusting thing over her. "Shall I drop this down your back?" he asked, laughing. "I still remember how loudly you screamed—and how high you jumped—when Robbie put that spider down your back when we were children."

"Just get rid of it, please." Emma turned and backed into him, keeping her eyes on his hand. She did not like spiders.

"Of course, sweetheart." He flicked the creature off into the bushes and wrapped his arms around her waist, pulling her tightly against his body. She felt his breath warm on her neck. "Shall I brush you off to be certain no other evil beasts have decided to invite themselves onto your person?"

"I only mind spiders." Emma barely got the words out. Charles's broad right hand was moving down her skirts. Thankfully it didn't pause over the part of her that was suddenly, shockingly, hot and wet.

Her knees wobbled, but his left arm kept her securely upright, plastered against his body.

She couldn't breathe. His hand shifted to her bodice. His palm pressed against her breasts; his fingers trailed over her curves.

Her nipples hardened into aching buds.

She was certain she should be mortified to see a male hand on her dress—to feel a male hand on her dress. But the heat surging through her did not feel like mortification. She had the most shocking desire—need—to feel a male hand on her naked flesh.

She moaned.

He turned her, and she melted against him, her hands going up to cling to his shoulders. He felt wonderful, hard and wonderful. There was an intriguing bulge pressing into her belly, and she rubbed against it. If only it were a bit lower. If only it were pressed against the place she ached most.

"God, Emma." Charles splayed a hand over her bottom and pressed her even more tightly against him. Then he cupped her jaw with his other hand, his fingers stroking the sensitive skin just under her ear while his thumb gently pulled down her lower lip. Her breath released in a sigh, her mouth opening slightly. She moistened her lips. They needed his touch, too.

They got it. His mouth moved over hers, sucking, licking, teasing with fleeting, brushing contact. It was maddening. She needed more—more pressure, more movement, more . . . something. She whimpered.

The smallest request, and the wish she didn't know to make was granted. His tongue filled her mouth as it had the day before. Both his hands pressed her bottom against him, then slid up over her waist and along the sides of her breasts. They paused there before continuing over her back and up to burrow into her hair.

She needed to touch him, also. His coat was in her way, so she slipped her hands underneath it, only to encounter his waistcoat. She let her fingers slide to his back and wander lower to the satisfying feel of his pantaloons. She explored the muscular curves of that section of his anatomy.

"Sweetheart," he whispered, his voice unsteady, "this is lovely, but I'm afraid we had best stop. The conservatory floor would not make a satisfactory bed."

"What?" Emma was having trouble thinking. All she wanted to do was feel. She ran her fingers over Charles's strong bu—

She dropped her hands as if scalded. What had come over her? She pushed against Charles's chest.

"I—"

"Shh." Charles put his finger over her lips.

"But I had my hands on . . . I was touching your . . ." Emma took a great gulp of air. "I apologize, my lord, for my extreme . . . um . . ." Emma could not begin to think of words to describe what she had just done. "Well, I do apologize, Lord Knightsdale."

Charles laughed. "Don't apologize, Miss Peterson. I was delighted to have your hands on my . . ."

Emma groaned in embarrassment.

"And you may remember that I had my hands on your lovely—"

"Don't say it!"

Charles chuckled. "All right, I won't say it—this time. But I enjoyed every minute of our encounter—your touching as well as mine—and I hope to repeat the experience, but without the annoying presence of clothing and in the more comfortable setting of my bedchamber."

"Lord Knightsdale!"

"Charles. Please, Emma. Every time you call me Knightsdale, I expect to turn around and see my brother—an especially disconcerting feeling after our rather intimate encounter."

"Oh. Um. Yes. I see." Emma didn't see anything but the vision of her naked in Charles's bed. With him, bare as a babe. But he wasn't an infant. Lud, no. Her imagination could not fill in all the details of that picture, but the glimpses she had had of him when he'd come hunting Nanny's ghost helped her draw some general outlines. His shoulders. The bulge of his arm muscles. The dusting of hair on his chest. His muscular legs. His thighs . . .

She wanted to feel his skin against hers. She wanted to run her fingers over the muscled expanse that was under his pantaloons. She wanted to see the interesting bulge she had rubbed her belly against.

She was afraid she was panting. She swallowed, straightened, tried to listen to Charles's words.

"You do remember I suggested we wed? You declined—at least I believe that was the gist of your answer when you threw that china dog at my head. Would you care to reconsider your response now?"

"No." Emma was in no condition to consider anything. Her entire body ached and throbbed and . . . well, she clearly was incapable of rational thought. "No. I, ah . . . No. I believe I shall retire. To my room. Alone."

Charles placed Emma's hand on his arm and escorted her out of the conservatory. She definitely looked as though she'd been engaging in some interesting activities in the shrubbery, but he wasn't concerned her dishevelment would be remarked upon. Everyone else had retired for the night.

And, really, if they were seen, so much the better. She would be compromised and, thus, compelled to wed him. At this point, he didn't care how she got into his bed, as long as she got there—soon.

God, he had never been so close to losing control as he had been just now. If there'd been a handy couch nearby, he probably would not have stopped. Emma certainly hadn't been making any effort to bring their activities to an end.

He looked down at her as they climbed the stairs. Her chin was up, her eyes focused in front of her. She was studiously ignoring him. She looked so cool, so self-possessed—but she had been so hot just moments before. He bit his lip to stifle a moan at the memory of her lovely body against his. God, when he had felt her hands on his pantaloons . . .

He had intended only to discuss the morning fishing trip.

Right.

They reached the bedroom floor.

"Good night, Lord Knightsdale," Emma said, addressing his cravat.

"I'm walking you to your room."

Her eyes flew up, skittered across his face, and resumed their study of his clothing.

"That is not necessary, my lord." She tried to move away, but he put his hand over hers.

"Humor me."

Her eyes flashed up again, a touch of panic in them.

"Miss Peterson, please. I am not going to rape you."

"I didn't think. . . . Of course not. . . . If I gave you that impression, I apologize."

"Oh, hush. You'll tie yourself into knots. I suppose you can be forgiven some trepidation after our recent activities, but I hope you do realize I would never force myself on you."

"Of course you wouldn't."

"And you weren't exactly discouraging me downstairs, sweetheart."

Emma made a strangled sound and stopped trying to wrest her fingers from his hold.

He smiled as they walked the length of the corridor. No, taking her into the conservatory had been a corkbrained notion. He had been thinking with something other than his head—something that still throbbed in frustration. It looked as if he'd be taking a nice cold dip in the lake once he bid her good night.

They stopped outside her door, and he considered kissing her again. If he was going swimming anyway, he might as well heat his blood back to boiling. A pity she wasn't wearing a more accommodating gown. This dress had much too high a neck. Something cut lower—something that just brushed the tops of her breasts—would be much more satisfactory. It would only take a moment to push the fabric aside. . . .

"My lord?"

"Hmm?" Could he persuade her to accept his marriage offer now? Her bedchamber door was just behind her. What could be more convenient? They could plight their troth splendidly in her bed. He wouldn't need a late night dunking in a cold lake— he could dunk the most heated part of him in her lovely warm wetness . . .

"My lord . . ."

. . . many times. Once would definitely not be

enough to cool his blood. But she was a virgin. . . .
He reached up to cup her cheek.

She batted his hand away.

"Lord Knightsdale, pay attention." She shook his
sleeve. "Don't you smell smoke?"

Charles inhaled. The acrid scent of scorched linen
cleared his mind of lust. Something besides himself
was on fire.

CHAPTER 6

Charles sat on his bed, staring at the door connecting the marquis's room with the marchioness's. Or in this case, his room with Emma's.

They had been very lucky last night. One of the maids must have left a lighted candle in Emma's room. Somehow it had gotten knocked over and had set the bed aflame. The fire had not spread—he'd been able to douse it with the pitcher of water left by the washstand. He had not had to waken the household. Still, the room was uninhabitable, so he had moved Emma to the only vacant bed. The marchioness's.

The door between their rooms was unlocked. He had not been able to find the key. He could walk into Emma's room at any moment—while she was sleeping, dressing, in her bath—as she could walk into his. But he knew not to hope for miracles.

He rubbed his forehead. He hadn't slept well last night, but, unfortunately, his sleeplessness had not been due to salacious dreams of Emma.

How could that candle have been left lit and unattended? He would ask Mrs. Lambert to have a word with the maids. Such carelessness was extremely dangerous.

He sighed and climbed out of bed. The early morning chill felt good on his bare skin.

He was not really afraid that the maids had been careless. No, he was more afraid of another possibility.

What if the candle had not been unattended?

He pulled on his breeches. He had looked at this problem from every angle, and he always came up with the same answer. Someone had been in Emma's room. There was no other way that candle could have been knocked over yet not have sent the room up in flames. It would have taken only minutes for the blaze to spread from the bed to the rug to the curtains. He had seen fires consume houses that quickly on the Peninsula.

This particular fire had not been burning more than a few seconds.

God! When he had been standing in the corridor lusting after Emma's body, someone had been in her room. On the other side of the door. Someone had heard them and left, knocking the candle over in his, or her, haste.

How had the intruder left? The room had only one door—and he had been standing in front of it with Emma.

Charles ran his hands through his hair. More important, what would have happened to Emma if he hadn't kept her late downstairs? If she had been asleep in her bed?

He took a deep breath, pulling his shirt over his head. There were too many questions. Who, what, how. But at least he had Emma near at hand now. If she cried out, he would be at her side in an instant.

He scratched on the connecting door. "Emma?"

No answer.

He debated for about five seconds before he cracked the door open. The room was in shadows. He padded quietly over to the bed. Emma was there, her hair a tangle of curls spread over her pillow, her blanket pulled up to her chin. She was smiling, as if she were in the midst of a pleasant dream. He hated to wake her, but the fish would not be biting later and his guests, unfortunately, would be.

Should he kiss her awake? No, they would never get to the stream if he did that.

"Emma." He picked up one of her curls and tickled her nose with it.

She grumbled and turned over.

"Emma, sweetheart, time to get up." He gently shook her shoulder.

"Wha—" Her eyes opened. "Ack." She pulled the blanket over her head.

He pulled it back down to her chin. "Remember, sleepyhead, we're taking Isabelle and Claire fishing this morning."

"It's so early. And you shouldn't be in my room."

"I know it's early, but it's getting late if we want to catch any fish. You need to get up. Get dressed and get the girls. I'll fetch the fishing gear and meet you by the summer house, all right?"

Emma grunted.

"If I leave you, will you fall back to sleep?" He grinned. "Should I pull the covers off you and tickle your feet?"

"No, no." She frowned up at him. "I'm awake. Go away."

"You're certain? If you leave me standing outside

in the morning chill, I'll bring a big bucket of lake water up here and dump it all over you."

"I'm certain. Now go away."

Emma felt Charles's deep chuckle in the pit of her stomach. Well, perhaps not her stomach—she felt certain this odd hunger had nothing to do with eating. It had everything to do with Charles. She had no doubt he could satisfy the gnawing in her . . . gut, if she would let him.

She waited to crawl out of bed till she heard his door latch. What was she going to do? She had awakened more than once during the night, her sheets twisted into knots, her body aching in embarrassing places, her skin burning. She craved Charles's touch. She wanted to go back to the conservatory to do everything they had done over again. And then do more.

Was this lust? She'd thought only men were susceptible to that malady, but it seemed Charles had managed to infect her. She snorted. Charles had assured Mr. Stockley that she was safe from his animal instincts, but perhaps it was Charles who was in danger.

And being here, in the marchioness's room, didn't help. It was a lovely, spacious room with a lovely, spacious bed and a lovely connecting door that did not lock. She could walk in on Charles any time she pleased.

Enough. She went to the washstand and splashed water on her face. The cold felt good on her heated skin. She would get dressed and get the girls up. Prinny would want a walk. She need not fear there would be any repeat of last night's activities this morning. The girls would be adequate chaperones. And she would keep strict control of her animal instincts.

She put on her oldest dress and pulled her hair ruthlessly back off her face, stabbing pins into it to fashion a bun. A colorless pelisse and the bonnet she had been considering giving Miss Russell for her garden scarecrow completed her ensemble.

She stepped into the corridor and headed for the girls' room. She would simply refuse to think of Charles—Lord Knightsdale—as anything other than a temporary employer. She would definitely not allow herself to consider a more permanent position in his household. He did not love her. He was only interested in expediency—in her he would have a governess and a breeding female whom he could easily plant on his estate and forget about for most of the year. Well, she might be twenty-six years old, an ape-leader, but she was not desperate. Nor was she interested in a title. She would let the London girls climb over one another to grab the grand marquis's attention.

Perhaps she would see how Mr. Stockley kissed.

"Papa Charles, I've never been fishing before!"

Emma smiled as Claire ran up to Charles. He grinned down at the little girl, and Emma felt her own heart wrench. Claire wanted a father so badly—not just someone to call Father, but a man who would choose to be part of her life. Would Charles do that?

Not if he planned to live in London, only coming to the country to sow his seed.

Emma flushed at the odd feelings that thought awoke in her. She didn't know exactly how children were begotten, but she was fairly confident the procedure was closely related to the activities she had experienced in the conservatory.

Prinny lunged to greet Charles and almost dislocated Emma's shoulder.

"Do you need to keep him on a lead?" Charles asked.

"If I want to see him again, I do. Once he's expended some of his energy, I can let him off, but if I do so now, he'll be after a squirrel and we'll never see him again."

"Well, let me take him for you. Here, girls, would you carry your fishing poles so I can help Miss Peterson with Prinny?"

"Of course, Uncle Charles."

"Yes, yes, Papa Charles. I've never held a fishing pole before."

"Well, here you are, then." Charles distributed the poles and took Prinny's lead, shifting the basket for their catch to his left hand. "You know, Miss Peterson and I used to go fishing when we were children. I was a little older than you, Isabelle, and Miss Peterson was six the first time we went to this particular fishing hole."

Claire skipped along next to him. "Really? Did you catch any fish, Papa Charles?"

"I did, but Miss Peterson just caught cold." He laughed. "She fell in, and I had to pull her out."

"I believe I was pushed in, my lord."

"Well, we never did settle that, did we? Robbie insists you tripped."

"With some help from his foot!"

They walked into the woods, following a narrow dirt path. The air was cooler here and damp. A wren warbled in the high branches. Emma breathed in the sharp, clean scent of pine and the softer smell of old leaves. She heard the stream burbling over the rocks up ahead.

She had spent so many hours of her childhood in these woods, tagging along after the man who was now laughing at something Claire had said. Even Isabelle had drawn close to him.

Charles Draysmith had been only a second son, had carried only a courtesy title—one he had never used, to her knowledge—but he had more charm in his little finger than his father and brother combined. People loved Charles—farm workers, shopkeepers, the village children. Little Emma Peterson.

He had let her be Maid Marian when they played Robin Hood. Or Guinevere, ignored by the Knights of the Round Table, true, but still a part of the game. The Duke of Alvord and the Earl of Westbrooke— then the Marquis of Walthingham and Viscount Manders—had tolerated her, but only because Charles did. Mostly they acted as if she were invisible, except when Robbie chose to squabble with her. Charles had stopped more than one of their arguments and had fished her out of the stream the time she'd "tripped" over Robbie's foot.

"Here's a good spot, wouldn't you say, Lady Claire?" Charles put down the basket. Claire ran to the edge of the water.

"I don't see any fish, Papa Charles."

"Of course not! Fish are wily creatures. They don't want to be caught, you know."

"Because then they'll be breakfast!" Claire clapped her hands and hop-skipped on her toes. "Can we eat fish for breakfast?"

"Perhaps—if we catch any."

Prinny spotted a squirrel and started yapping madly.

"And if this dog doesn't scare them all away. Miss Peterson, can you take charge of Prinny while I get the girls settled?"

Emma pulled Prinny a short distance away. He barked for a minute in protest and then found something interesting to smell by the base of a birch.

"Would you like me to bait your line for you, Isabelle?"

"Yes, please, Uncle Charles."

Claire leaned against Charles, watching him work on Isabelle's fishing line.

"Eww." She wrinkled her nose. "A worm."

"Want a closer look?" Charles quickly brought the wiggling creature up to Claire's face. She squealed and danced back, giggling.

"No, Papa Charles. Worms are slimy."

"So you don't want to bait your own line? I'll show you how."

"You can show me, Uncle Charles," Isabelle said. "I'm not a baby."

"I'm not a baby, either." Claire put her small fists on her hips and stuck out her tongue at her sister. "Show me, Papa Charles."

"Lady Claire, a little more deportment, if you please!" Charles said, a note of laughter in his voice. "Whatever has your governess been teaching you?"

"Don't blame Miss Peterson, Uncle Charles," Isabelle said. "It is not her fault if Claire is bad."

"I'm *not* bad." Claire's bottom lip trembled. "Mama Peterson, I'm not bad, am I? Mother used to say I was, but I'm *not*."

Emma dropped Prinny's lead and came over to

hug the little girl. "Of course you aren't, sweetheart. And I'm sure your mother didn't mean you were, either. Sometimes adults just get a little snappish."

"No, Miss Peterson." Isabelle looked seriously back into Emma's eyes. "Mother . . . well, she said . . . she wanted a boy, you see, so she wouldn't have to have any more babies."

Claire nodded. "If she'd had a boy, she'd have done her duty."

"Papa needed an heir, Miss Peterson, and Claire and I can't be an heir."

Emma met Charles's eyes over Claire's head. He looked as stricken as she felt.

"Well, I'm your papa now, Isabelle," he said. "And I like you exactly as you are." He took Claire's chin in his fingers, leaning next to Emma to look the little girl in the eye. "And you are not bad, Lady Claire. Of course not. But you must still learn to behave. Can you imagine what people would say if Miss Peterson stuck her tongue out at my aunt?"

Claire giggled. "Mama Peterson would never do that!"

"Exactly. So you must learn not to either, at least when you need your formal manners. But I only meant to tease you before—you don't need fancy manners when you go fishing, do you?"

"No?" Claire's eyes were huge in her small face.

"No. The fish don't care. But no tantrums, mind! The fish don't like tantrums—too noisy. You'd scare them all away."

"No tantrums," Claire agreed.

Charles dropped his hand and looked at Isabelle. "I think I had offered to show you two young ladies how to bait a fishing line before we got off on all this boring talk of manners."

Isabelle smiled. "Yes, P—Uncle Charles."

"You can call me Papa Charles if you want to, Isabelle."

"No. No, thank you. I'm nine."

"And I'm thirty, goose. Nine is not very old—certainly not too old to still want a papa." Charles held out his hand. "It could be our secret."

Isabelle put her hand in Charles's, but she shook her head. "Show me how to bait the line, Uncle Charles."

"And me," Claire said, pushing closer. "Show me, too." She glanced at Emma. "And what about Mama Peterson, Papa Charles? Are you going to teach her how to put the slimy worm on the hook?"

"Oh, I taught Miss Peterson years ago, when she was just a little older than you, Lady Claire."

"Indeed," Emma said, smiling. "And he is a very good teacher."

"Are you going to fish, too, Miss Peterson?"

"No, Isabelle. I think I'll go keep Prinny company."

"Wait a moment and I'll spread the blanket out for you."

"That's all right, my lord. I can do it."

Emma took the blanket out of the basket and retreated to the birch tree. Prinny had expended enough energy that he was content to lie in the shade. She sat on the blanket and watched Charles with the children.

He would make a wonderful father, if he were only willing to stay at Knightsdale.

"Now don't get your lines tangled up, girls," he said. "I'm going to go sit with Miss Peterson and let you fish by yourselves."

"All right, Papa Charles. We'll catch lots of fish for breakfast."

"Don't catch so many I can't fit them in the basket."

"We'll try not to." Claire smiled and turned to stare at the water, as if she could will the fish onto her hook.

Charles took off his coat and sat down next to Emma. He looked at the girls.

"I guess my brother and his wife were not the best parents."

Emma sighed. "I don't know they were any different from most of the *ton*, but their daughters surely wanted more of them."

"More might have been worse. God, I can't believe Cecilia told the girls she wanted a son so she wouldn't be required to have more children."

"We don't really know she said that, my lord. Children often misunderstand. They hear pieces and put the pieces together in a way that makes sense to them, but they have a very limited knowledge of the world."

Not that Emma believed for a minute Cecilia hadn't told the girls precisely what Isabelle had said. The woman had been exceedingly vain and self-centered. Completely insensitive.

Charles shrugged. "Whatever Cecilia said or didn't say, it's clear the girls need parents now."

"Yes." Emma hesitated. It wasn't really her place, but she felt compelled to speak up. Surely now he would understand the need for him to stay at Knightsdale. "When you marry, my lord—"

"You mean when I marry you, Emma." He turned and looked at her. "The girls like you. They—" He frowned. "Where did you get that hideous bonnet?"

So, he was just now noticing how she looked, was he? Such an attentive suitor.

"It's not hideous. It's a perfectly satisfactory

bonnet, especially for an early morning fishing expedition."

"Only if you intend to use it to *catch* the fish. It might make a satisfactory net—well, bucket. You should get rid of it. In fact, I'll be happy to dispose of it for you." He reached for her bonnet strings. Emma put her hands over them and leaned away.

"You most certainly will not. Keep your hands to yourself, Lord Knightsdale."

A distinctly wicked gleam appeared in his eyes. "But I did so enjoy not keeping them to myself last night."

"Behave yourself, sir!"

"Must—"

"Papa Charles, Papa Charles, I catched a—"

The rest of the sentence was lost in a loud splash.

"Uncle Charles," Isabelle shouted, "Claire has fallen into the water and she can't swim."

Emma lurched to her feet, but Charles was far faster than she. He was in the stream with Claire in his arms before Emma had untangled her skirts.

"Claire, sweetheart," he said, "it's the fish that come out of the water, not little girls that go in."

Claire sputtered and coughed. "The fish got away, Papa Charles."

"Well, you'll catch another one, another day. And I will teach you—and Isabelle—to swim. Would you like that?"

"Yes!"

Emma finally made it to the edge of the stream. She stood next to Isabelle and looked at the two in the water. Claire could have been terrified, but she was grinning and hugging Charles tightly around the neck. He was soaked to the skin, his shirt and breeches plastered to his body.

He looked wonderful. More than wonderful. The lust of the night before surged back, and she considered joining them in the water. She needed some way to cool her heated blood.

Charles carried Claire piggyback to Knightsdale. She sat on his shoulders, chatting and laughing. She didn't seem the worse for her dunking, but he vowed to teach her and Isabelle to swim at the first opportunity. With a lake on the property, it was much too dangerous for the girls not to know how. True, Claire was a little young, but she could learn enough to save herself if she were to fall in again. And Isabelle definitely should know. He had taught Emma when she was only six.

He glanced down at the woman walking next to him. He'd given her lessons after Robbie had tripped her and she, like Claire, had fallen into the stream. The other boys had laughed at first—she *had* looked funny with her skirts spread out in the water—but he'd seen the fear in her eyes.

She had shown no fear in their lessons. He smiled. She'd been determined not to let Robbie get the better of her again.

Did she remember how to swim? His smile widened. He'd be happy to re-evaluate her skills. This afternoon perhaps, in one of the more secluded sections of the lake. She could wear her shift.

"Papa Charles!"

Claire tugged sharply on his hair. He shifted her on his shoulders as he contemplated the vision of Emma in the water, clothed in her shift. Her wet shift. Her sheer, translucent, wet shift that outlined every one of her lovely curves and teased him with a glimpse, a shadow, of the curls above her thighs. If it were chilly, her nipples would harden into little peaks under the wet cloth, beckoning . . .

"Ouch! That hair is attached to my head, Lady Claire."

"Sorry, Papa Charles, but you weren't 'tending."

"Um." He realized suddenly that his soaked breeches would reveal to anyone who cared to look exactly what thoughts he *had* been attending to. He forced his mind to consider topics that did not relate to Emma in any fashion. Estate management. Ah. That worked like a charm.

He glanced at Emma again. She was studying the ground. At least he assumed that was what she was doing—he couldn't see her face. Her hideous head-gear completely obscured her features. Perhaps a cooper rather than a milliner had fashioned the thing. It certainly did look more like a bucket than a bonnet.

He would just have to contrive some accident to rid the world of its insulting existence.

"Papa Charles, since we didn't catch any fish, what can we eat for breakfast? I'm hungry."

"Don't worry, Lady Claire," he said. "We'll just stop in to see Cook. She's sure to have something tasty."

"We can't bother Cook, Uncle Charles."

"Why ever not, Isabelle? I used to bother Cook all the time when I was your age, didn't I, Miss Peterson?"

"Yes." Emma still didn't look at him. "Well, you did by the time I met you. You were always hungry. I believe Cook called you an imp of Satan, but she gave you the best of whatever she had—the biggest pastry or the ripest fruit."

"Were you jealous, Miss Peterson?"

Emma glanced at him quickly, then turned her eyes forward. "Of course not, my lord. I was in awe of your ability to consume limitless quantities of food."

"Ah, but I was a growing boy."

"I'm a growing girl, Papa Charles," Claire said, bouncing on his shoulders. "What will Cook have to eat, do you think?"

"Perhaps gooseberry tarts. Mmm. Not exactly breakfast food, but Cook's gooseberry tarts are splendid." Cook might not be up to London standards when it came to preparing a dinner for the *ton*, but she certainly did some things well. He glanced down at Isabelle. She was too quiet again. "Have you ever had any of Cook's gooseberry tarts, Isabelle?"

"No, Uncle Charles. Mother said we would get fat if we ate tarts, and it is very hard to catch a husband if you are fat."

Charles felt his jaw drop. "Gammon! You are only nine years old, Isabelle. A few tarts will not land you on the matrimonial shelf."

"Mother said it was never too early to think about the future. It's not as if we can live at Knightsdale our whole lives."

Charles stared at Isabelle, not sure whether to laugh or curse. Had Paul not known what his wife had been telling the girls?

"I've had a gooseberry tart, Papa Charles."

"Claire!" Isabelle said. "Don't lie."

"I'm not! I sneaked into the kitchen once and took one. I didn't like it. It burned my mouth."

"Well, there's no need for sneaking anywhere," Charles said. "We shall walk into the kitchen, wish Cook a good morning, and see if she has anything for us to eat."

"Are you certain we can, Uncle Charles?" Wrinkles

etched Isabelle's forehead. "Mother said never to bother Cook."

"Of course I'm certain, Isabelle." He turned to Emma. Her head was up, her face tight with concern. "Miss Peterson, you are the governess. What do you say? Am I right that we can enter the kitchen with impunity?"

"Of course, my lord." Emma smiled, but a line still creased her brow. He'd wager that she, too, would scream if she heard "Mother said" one more time. It was wrong to think ill of the dead, but, well, he did not miss Cecilia at the moment.

"See?" he said. "If a governess says so, it must be true. Governesses never want you to do anything fun, do they?"

"My lord!" Emma put her hands on her hips. "You must not malign the noble profession of governess."

Claire giggled. "But it's true, Mama Peterson. Miss Hodgekiss never let us do anything fun."

"Didn't I let you go on this fishing excursion?"

"Yes, but you aren't a real governess," Isabelle said. There was still a note of worry in her voice.

"Well, I am a real marquis." Charles lifted Claire off his shoulders. "And I say we can go into the kitchen." He stood as tall as he could and tried to look like the Duke of Alvord did when he was his most duke-ish. "Actually, now that I think on it, this is *my* kitchen. I am the Marquis of Knightsdale, am I not?"

"The Marquis of Knightsdale!" Claire yelled. "Watch out, Cook!"

"I don't think Cook will like being shouted at, Lady Claire," Emma said.

"Very true, Miss Peterson. As they say, you will catch more flies with honey than vinegar."

Claire wrinkled her nose. "But I don't want any flies, Papa Charles."

"Don't be silly, Claire." Isabelle suddenly sounded very much the more experienced older sister. "Uncle Charles just means you are more likely to get what you want if you ask nicely and don't order people around."

"Precisely. Ordering Cook to give us food will just put her back up. We need a more subtle approach." Charles went down on one knee so he could look both girls in the face. "I've found appealing to Cook's warm heart works very well. You and I, Lady Claire, are a very bedraggled pair after our dunking in the stream. I'm certain Cook cannot resist feeling sorry for us. Do you think you can look pitiful?"

"Oh, yes, Papa Charles." Claire opened her eyes very wide and turned down the corners of her mouth. Even Isabelle giggled.

"Very good. I will let you take the lead in the pitiful approach. Now, Lady Isabelle," Charles said, turning and putting his hands on her shoulders. They felt so fragile under his fingers. "I think you might do well to spearhead our charm attack."

"Charm attack? What do you mean, Uncle Charles?"

"Well, I have noticed that you have the loveliest smile."

"I do?" Isabelle turned bright pink. Charles grinned.

"Yes, indeed. When you smile, your eyes sparkle in quite a remarkable way. I'm sure if you smile at Cook, she will let us have whatever treats we may like."

"Really?"

Charles blinked. He had been teasing Isabelle, but now that she was grinning at him, he saw that it was true. She had a beautiful smile. It lit her thin, angular face with an ethereal loveliness that quite took his breath away. He vowed to get her to smile more often.

"I think we're ready to invade the kitchen."

Somehow Emma had to persuade Charles to stay at Knightsdale. The girls needed him.

She sat on the bench at the long kitchen table and watched Isabelle and Claire bloom under Charles's attention. To have any man take an interest in them was wonderful—their father certainly never had—but to have Charles be that man was beyond wonderful. He was charming them just as he charmed everyone. Just as he had charmed her when she was a girl.

Cook had presented Prinny with a bone shortly after they entered her domain, and he was happily gnawing on it in the corner by the fire. Claire had scrambled onto the bench next to Charles. She sat close enough to touch him. She patted his sleeve and rested her head against his shoulder when someone besides herself was talking. Emma suspected she would have climbed into his lap, given half a chance.

Isabelle sat next to Emma, across from Charles. Being nine, she was too grown-up to cling to him physically, but she was clinging to him with her eyes. Emma saw a slight blush spread over Isabelle's cheeks after one of Charles's small compliments. She'd wager Isabelle was more than half in love with her uncle. An innocent infatuation, one she would soon outgrow.

Unlike Emma.

Emma sat up straighter. This would never do. Charles was charming, but he was not for her. She was going to shop among the other eligible men, she had decided. Mr. Stockley, for example . . .

No, she would not think about Mr. Stockley right now. She would just enjoy being here with Charles and the girls.

"Here, Lady Isabelle, have some more bread, do," Cook said, putting a large slice of fresh bread on Isabelle's plate.

"Thank you, Cook." Isabelle's rare smile lit her face. Cook blinked, then smiled broadly at Emma.

Emma smiled back. She wished she had thought to bring the girls here before. She'd never imagined Cecilia would have kept them from this haven with its sunny, high windows and warm smells of baking. Cook was a plain, cheerful woman, broad of girth and heart. She might not be able to make an elegant French sauce, but she could make a little girl smile.

"And may we have some jam, too, please, Cook?"

Emma had to muffle a laugh at Claire's ingratiating expression.

"Of course ye may, Lady Claire. And would ye like a taste of my lemon cake?"

"Oh, yes, please."

"I don't suppose you have any gooseberry tarts about, do you, Cook?" Charles leaned toward Cook and flashed his own ingratiating grin. This time Emma did not have the urge to laugh—cry, maybe. He was breathtakingly handsome.

"Aye—happen I do, my lord."

"Splendid! May I have one?" He looked at Emma. "And you, Miss Peterson? Would you care for one of Cook's gooseberry tarts?"

"No, thank you, my lord."

"Are ye sure, Miss Peterson?" Cook asked. "I have plenty."

"No, thank you, Cook. I don't care for gooseberries, but I will take a slice of your lemon cake, if I might."

"Not care for gooseberries, Miss Peterson?" Charles asked as Cook went to fetch the tarts. "You have no taste, I fear."

"Not everyone loves gooseberries as you do, my lord."

"Well, perhaps that is a good thing. It leaves more for me, doesn't it?"

Charles took a tart from the top of the plate Cook put on the table. Emma watched him bite into it. He had strong, white teeth, so unlike Mr. Stockley's yellowed, crooked ones. A little of the gooseberry filling squirted onto his chin and his tongue slid out to capture it. Lud, even his tongue looked strong.

People did not have strong tongues! Though his tongue certainly had felt strong when it had been in her . . .

Emma took a large bite of lemon cake.

"Would ye like some cold milk, Miss Peterson? Ye look a little flushed."

Emma shook her head no. Her mouth was too full—and she was too mortified—to get the word out. Charles looked at her and lifted one of his masculine eyebrows.

Masculine eyebrows? She contemplated banging her head against the wooden table to knock some sense into it—or at least the lust out.

"We went fishing, Cook," Claire said. "Papa Charles showed us how to put the worms on the hooks. Then I catched a fish, but I fell in and Papa Charles saved me, and now he's going to teach me and Isabelle to swim."

Cook's eyes widened when she heard "Papa Charles" and then she beamed at Lord Knightsdale. Charles's ears turned red. Good—he could stand a little embarrassment. Isabelle added to the story, her voice young and enthusiastic, like a nine-year-old girl instead of a small adult.

Charles *had* to stay at Knightsdale. He brought fun—adventure and laughter—into the girls' lives. They had not missed him before, because they had not known him. Now if he left to live most of the year in London—it didn't bear thinking of. Their hearts would break.

Emma refused to consider if it would be only the girls' hearts breaking.

"That was capital, Cook, but I think we had better be going." Charles stood, brushing crumbs from his breeches. "I'm afraid Claire and I are sorely in need of a bath."

"I don't need a bath, Papa Charles. I only have baths on Sundays."

"Or on days when you've had a dunking in the stream," he said.

Claire frowned and stuck out her lower lip. Charles laughed.

"No tantrums now, Lady Claire. Remember the fish don't like them, nor do I. Go with Miss Peterson, and she and Nanny will get you all cleaned up."

"I don't like baths." Claire crossed her arms, her face taking on a distinctly mulish expression.

"Would you like to use a little of my lavender water?" Emma asked.

It was as if a cloud had moved away from the sun.

"Yes! Then I'll smell like you, won't I?"

Emma laughed. "Yes, then you'll smell like me."

"And you smell good. Don't you think Mama Peterson smells good, Papa Charles?"

Charles grinned slowly. "Oh, yes. Miss Peterson smells very nice, indeed."

Emma swore she flushed from the roots of her hair

to the ends of her toenails. "Um, well, let's go then, Claire. Come, Prinny." She bent to fasten the dog's lead back on his collar. No use taking chances with so many strangers in the house.

Charles was still smirking as he stepped aside to let her precede him out of the kitchen. He walked with them up the stairs to the bedroom floor.

"Miss Peterson, I will see you later."

"What about us, Papa Charles? Will you see us later, too?"

Charles ruffled Claire's hair. "I will stop by the nursery when I can, imp. I have an appointment with Mr. Coles, the estate manager, and then I have to play host to all these London ladies and gents—that's why we went fishing so early this morning, so I could see you before my other duties."

"Please? You have to see if I smell as good as Mama Peterson."

Charles grinned. "For a treat like that, I will certainly try my hardest. Perhaps I can steal a few minutes before dinner. Now run along and get your bath."

Emma and the girls almost made it safely to the nursery. They would have made it easily, if Emma had not stopped to get the lavender water. As it was, they were only a few yards from the nursery stairs when two giggling young ladies emerged from a room right into their path. Prinny barked and lunged forward. The young ladies—Miss Oldston and Lady Caroline—screamed.

"Don't be scared," Claire said. "Prinny's very friendly."

Lady Caroline sniffed, her full cheeks creased into a frown, her stubby nose turned up in disdain. She bore a striking resemblance to Squire Begley's prize pig, Ivy—or "That Damn Ivy," as he was wont to call her.

"I am not scared. I just do not care for dogs, nasty, dirty things."

Miss Oldston guffawed, her lips turning back to show her sizable teeth. "At least it ain't a cat, Caro. At least you ain't swelling up, all red and itchy."

Lady Caroline turned her displeasure on Miss Oldston. "Really, Amanda, you need to control yourself. You look and sound just like a horse."

"Better than looking like a pig. If you want Knightsdale's attentions, you'd better pay less attention to his cakes and cream puffs."

"Well, he certainly isn't going to choose a skinny mare like you."

"Papa Charles is going to choose Mama Peterson."

The sudden silence that followed Claire's artless words was thick enough to suffocate someone. It certainly was suffocating Emma. Lady Caroline gaped; Miss Oldston's already prominent eyes became noticeably more prominent. Emma closed her own eyes briefly, wishing she could vanish into the woodwork.

"*Papa* Charles?" Miss Oldston said.

"*Mama* Peterson?" Lady Caroline's hard little eyes examined Emma.

"Claire, Uncle Charles told you not to call him 'Papa' in company!"

Claire shrugged. "I had to tell them, Isabelle." She looked up at Lady Caroline and Miss Oldston. "My mother and father died in It . . ."—she paused, clearly trying to get the word right—"in Italy. Uncle Charles is my papa now. And he is going to marry Miss Peterson."

"Oh, really?" Lady Caroline slowly surveyed Emma's old dress, shabby pelisse, and disreputable bonnet.

"How odd. I must have missed the announcement. Did you hear it, Amanda?"

"Lady Caroline, Miss Oldston," Emma said, "Lady Claire is only four. She has a very active imagination."

"Mama Peterson, I did not imagine Papa Charles with you on the blanket."

"The blanket?"

"We went fishing this morning, Lady Caroline," Emma said. "Lord Knightsdale wants to spend some time with his nieces, naturally, to become better acquainted with them, as he is their guardian now. And I'm acting as their governess while their usual governess is off attending to her ailing mother." Emma knew she was babbling. Really, she did not owe Lady Caroline the slightest explanation, but neither could she bear for this gossip to fly through the house party. "I was just taking the girls to the nursery to tidy up after their fishing trip. Lady Claire fell into the stream."

"I see. How kind of Lord Knightsdale to take an interest in his brother's orphans, don't you agree, Amanda?"

"Yes, Caro, very kind."

"Though I'm certain that will change once he weds," Lady Caroline said with a condescending little laugh.

"I am certain it will not change, Lady Caroline." How could this spoiled girl say such a thing with Claire and Isabelle standing right in front of her? Emma wished Prinny were as vicious as she felt at the moment. She would love to let the dog take a bite out of Lady Caroline's ample backside.

"Oh, Miss Peterson." Lady Caroline shook her head, chuckling. "Perhaps if you had made your come out, you'd be more aware of the ways of the *ton*."

Prinny would have to wait his turn. Emma wanted

to take a bite out of Lady Caroline with her very own teeth.

"I may not be intimately conversant with the ways of the *ton*, Lady Caroline, but I have known Lord Knightsdale since we were children. He would never abandon his nieces." Physically abandon them for London, perhaps, but never emotionally abandon them. If the girls needed anything, Emma was convinced Charles would see that they had it.

"And you are . . . intimately . . . conversant with Lord Knightsdale's ways?"

"No, of course not, Lady Caroline. I only meant . . ."

"It matters little what you meant, Miss Peterson. You seem to have forgotten one crucial fact—Lord Knightsdale will have a wife. I doubt any lady of the *ton* will want to take charge of his brother's brats."

"You're a bad lady!" Claire said. Emma heard the tears in her voice. Isabelle looked as white as a ghost.

"And you're a very badly behaved child," Lady Caroline said. "You'd better mind your manners if you don't want to end up in the workhouse."

Emma had had enough. She dropped Prinny's lead. Freed, the dog scrambled for Lady Caroline's expansive white muslin skirts. Since he had been out by the stream, his paws had collected a generous quantity of fine Kentish mud.

Emma grinned. Lady Caroline could scream very loudly indeed.

"We have to do something, Claire." Isabelle sat on Claire's bed. Miss Peterson had gone downstairs to join the house party; Nanny was napping. Claire was supposed to be napping, and Isabelle was supposed to be reading, but Isabelle decided this was too important to put off. "We can't let Uncle Charles marry any of the London ladies."

Claire sat up, rubbing the smooth end of her old blanket along her cheek. "Papa Charles is going to marry Mama Peterson."

"I hope so, but we can't take that for granted, Claire. I think we had better do something to make certain they decide to marry each other."

Prinny padded in and jumped onto Claire's bed. After his long romp on the morning fishing expedition and the excitement of chasing Miss Oldston and Lady Caroline down the corridor, he was exceptionally mellow. He rested his head in Isabelle's lap and let her stroke his ears.

"How do we do that, Isabelle?"

That was the question Isabelle had been struggling with ever since Miss Peterson had dragged them up to the nursery. Miss Peterson had been so angry, she hadn't been able to speak. She had stomped around and muttered and apologized in short, rough sentences for the mean London ladies.

"I think we need to see that Miss Peterson and Uncle Charles are together as much as possible."

"We can go fishing every morning. I liked that."

"No, I think they have to be alone, Claire—just the two of them."

"Why?"

Isabelle shrugged. "I'm not certain. Mrs. Lambert was talking to Nanny last week about a Miss Wendle who lives in the house where Mrs. Lambert's sister works. Miss Wendle was alone with Lord Somebody-or-other and they got married right away. I think Mrs. Lambert was going to tell Nanny more, but then she saw me and stopped."

Claire put her chin on her knees. "Mama Peterson sleeps in Mother's room now. There's only a door between her room and Papa Charles's room."

Isabelle nodded. "Maybe if we put something Miss Peterson needs—like her brush—in Uncle Charles's room, she'll have to go in there to find it."

"And let's get rid of that ugly bonnet she had on today."

Isabelle sighed. "Yes. I wish there was a way to get rid of some of her dresses—they are not as pretty as the London ladies' clothes."

"Papa Charles doesn't care about that."

"I don't know, Claire. I think men like women in pretty clothes. Mother always wanted the newest fashions. I heard her and Father arguing about it once."

"Well, if they were arguing, Father must not have liked the clothes."

"No, they were arguing about the cost, not the clothes. And when they made up, they ended up in Mother's room together." Isabelle rubbed Prinny's back. "It's a good thing Uncle Charles's and Miss Peterson's bedrooms are right next to each other. We'll try to get them together there, and maybe the clothes won't matter so much."

"All right. We can do that as soon as I finish my nap. Nanny said all the house guests were going to walk around the lake, so Mama and Papa won't be in their rooms."

Isabelle nodded, but her mind was still on the fashion problem. She wished Miss Peterson's clothes were prettier, but there wasn't anything she and Claire could do about that. But maybe there *was* something they could do to make the London ladies less attractive. She grinned.

"Let's make those mean women uglier, too."

"You can't make the fat lady uglier," Claire said. "She looks like a pig."

"Yes, but a well-dressed pig."

"Not so well dressed now that Prinny has had his paws all over her skirts." Claire leaned forward and patted Prinny's head. "Good dog."

Prinny licked her hand.

"Yes, but remember how the horsey lady, Miss Oldston, said it was a good thing Prinny wasn't a cat?"

Claire nodded. "She said the piggy lady would get all red and itchy if Prinny were a cat."

"And swollen, though it's hard to imagine how Lady Caroline could be any fatter."

Claire giggled. "Queen Bess is a cat."

"Exactly." Isabelle grinned. "And I bet she would love to see Lady Caroline's bedchamber."

CHAPTER 7

Emma was still furious when she joined the other house party guests for a stroll around the lake. She stayed as far away from Lady Caroline and Miss Oldston as she could—which meant she also stayed far away from Charles. The young ladies were swarming around him like bees on spilled lemonade.

How could those spoiled misses have said such hateful things in front of Claire and Isabelle? It was beyond her understanding. Did they think the girls were deaf? Or stupid? If Prinny hadn't muddied their gowns, Emma would have . . . what? What could she do? She was only the temporary governess.

"It is a fine day, is it not, Miss Peterson?"

She could accept Charles's offer. She'd like to see those nasty girls' faces when *that* announcement was made. And if she actually were the marchioness, she could have those two harpies tossed out on their ears.

"Miss Peterson?"

Emma blinked. Mr. Stockley was by her side, looking at her inquiringly.

"I'm sorry, sir. I was woolgathering. You were saying?"

"Merely commenting on the weather, Miss Peterson."

"The weather?"

"Yes. The day is very fine, do you not agree?"

"Yes. Certainly. Very fine."

Emma looked for someone to rescue her from Mr. Stockley's excruciatingly dull conversation, but no savior was apparent. Most of the gentlemen were clustered around the young ladies who were still clustered around Charles. Lady Beatrice and the Society for the Betterment of Women had elected to stay indoors—Emma hoped Charles had locked up the brandy. The Duke of Alvord was keeping his wife company while she napped. At least that is what he'd said he was doing, but Emma had noticed the same intent expression on his face that Charles had had in the conservatory. The Earl of Westbrooke had gone to fetch Alvord's sister, Lizzie, and Meg was probably off investigating Charles's herb garden.

"Are you enjoying your stay at Knightsdale, Miss Peterson?"

"Um. Yes. Of course. And you, sir? Are you finding your accommodations satisfactory?" He should be. Mr. Atworthy's house was comfortable but could not bear comparison with Knightsdale.

"Very satisfactory. I am much interested in grand houses, you know. The architecture, furnishings, statuary."

"Indeed?"

"Oh, yes. Have you had an opportunity to explore Knightsdale, Miss Peterson? In your capacity of governess, perhaps, or as a young girl? I understand you and the marquis were childhood friends.

Did you play in the attics or the cellars? In any odd little closets or cubbyholes?"

Mr. Stockley's eyes shone with enthusiasm. Well, Meg could get extremely animated over some twig or other. Getting excited about a house was likely more understandable than being in alt over a weed. Knightsdale was a very impressive estate.

"No, Mr. Stockley, the girls and I have stayed in the main parts of the house. And I wasn't really a child-hood friend of Lord Knightsdale—more a child-hood nuisance. You might ask Lord Westbrooke or his grace. Or Lord Knightsdale himself, of course."

Mr. Stockley chuckled. "I don't believe Lord Knights-dale is terribly fond of me."

That was an understatement. Charles looked at Mr. Stockley just as Lady Beatrice's Queen Bess looked at Prinny. With disdain. Or disgust.

"I'm certain he would give you a tour if you asked, Mr. Stockley. Or perhaps Mrs. Lambert, the house-keeper, would be willing to show you the house."

"And you, Miss Peterson? Would you be willing?"

"Mr. Stockley, I assure you I would not be a suit-able guide."

They traversed a bend in the path and came upon a clearing with a Gothic cottage. The ladies and most of the gentlemen had gone up to examine the structure more closely. Charles stood back, hands on hips, staring. He looked over at Emma.

"What the h—" He coughed. "What is this?"

"A Gothic cottage, my lord."

"I *know* it is a Gothic cottage, Miss Peterson. What I wish to know is what it is doing here." His sweep-ing gesture encompassed the trees and the lake.

"You've not seen it before, my lord?" Mr. Stockley asked.

"No, I have not."

"That is not surprising," Emma said. "It wasn't here the last time you visited, my lord. The late marchioness had it built shortly after she married your brother."

Charles grunted. "Are there any other monstrosities littering the estate, Miss Peterson?"

"No new monstrosities, my lord. All the other follies were built by your father or grandfather or great-grandfather, I think."

"Thank God for that. I was afraid I might stumble onto a replica of Prinny's Brighton stable next."

Emma expected an architectural enthusiast like Mr. Stockley to join the group exclaiming over the building, but he barely gave it a glance once he heard it was a relatively new structure. He wandered on ahead. Emma heaved a sigh of relief.

"Happy to be rid of your beau?" Charles asked.

"Shh." Emma glanced at the others, but they were still cooing over the stained-glass windows. "Mr. Stockley is not my beau."

"I am very glad to hear that, sweetheart."

Charles had not wanted to lead this parade of idiots around the lake. He had wanted to spend time with Emma. Alone. Persuading her to accept his suit. They could investigate that ridiculous cottage, for instance, to see if it had a comfortable bed and a sturdy lock. He should definitely look into that issue. One never knew when one might be caught out in a storm.

At least Stockley had finally removed himself. Charles took Emma's hand and placed it on his arm. He wanted her with him—and if she were firmly attached to his side, he could not get stuck with one of the giggling girls.

Alvord and Westbrooke had wisely dodged this treat. He would have a few choice words for them when he saw them later. Besides Mr. Stockley, the only men—and he used that term very loosely—assisting him in escorting the ladies were three beef-witted clodpolls. Mr. William Dunlee, a portly young-ster otherwise known as "Chubs," was the Earl of Dunlee's second son. Pimply Mr. Frampton—"Spots"—was the oldest son of a baron. And Mr. Old-ston, aptly christened "Toad" in honor of the bulging eyes that were a family trait, was Sir Thomas's heir. They had all attended university together and had managed to escape without cluttering their brains with a scintilla of knowledge, as far as he could tell.

Where *had* his aunt collected such an assortment of cabbage-heads? If these sprigs and giggling misses represented the future of British nobility, England was in serious trouble. Right now Chubs, Spots, and Toad were tossing bachelor's buttons at each other. Their coats and breeches bristled with the burs, and the silly young girls watching them were laugh-ing as if this was the funniest spectacle they had ever witnessed.

"Shall we stroll ahead, Miss Peterson?"

"That would be lovely."

"You must save me from these idiots, Emma," he said as soon as they had walked out of earshot.

"They are slightly juvenile."

"Slightly? I had charge of boys on the Peninsula much younger than these three. Some were not fully grown, yet they made admirable, brave soldiers."

"I imagine war has a way of maturing a person."

"Yes, you're right about that." He looked out over

the lake, remembering when he had last walked this path. He had been a little younger than the three buffoons by the cottage. Surely he had not been as inane as they?

He closed his eyes for a moment, flinching from his memories. Perhaps he had been, and not so innocently stupid, either. He'd been aimless and angry when he'd come down from university. He'd needed to do *something*—and that something often enough had been drinking, gambling, and whoring.

When James's wife, Sarah—an American and a fervent republican—had denigrated the British system of primogeniture, Charles had argued that not all heirs were like James's evil cousin Richard, ready to murder to inherit. He'd insisted he did not envy his brother.

He had spoken with complete sincerity.

He had lied.

He helped Emma navigate a tree root growing across the path.

He had never coveted the title, true, but he had envied Paul. Paul had never been aimless. Never. He had always known his purpose. At twenty, facing the shallow world of the *ton*, Charles had craved that certainty.

"If I hadn't followed James into the army, I don't know what would have become of me. I probably would have ended up a dissipated rakehell."

"Nonsense. I'm certain you would have done well at whatever you tried."

He looked down at Emma. She had spoken so matter-of-factly, as if there was no question he would accomplish any task he set himself.

"You really believe that, don't you?"

"Of course." Her clear, golden-brown eyes calmly

stared back up at him from behind her spectacles. He remembered how she had looked at him when she was a girl. That had been hero worship—this was different. This was the confidence of a grown woman. She believed in him.

Her trust was built on air, of course—on girlhood fantasies. She didn't know him. She hadn't seen him for twenty years, since he was a boy. Yet he wanted to believe she was right. He wanted her certainty next to him always.

"Marry me, Emma. Please." Did he sound too enthusiastic? She must think him a lunatic. But it would be a sensible decision on her part. He tempered his voice. "Our marriage would solve so many problems. We'd get rid of these London idiots. My nieces would get a mother and you'd get a home of your own. Your father could marry Mrs. Graham without disturbing your peace." He grinned at her, leaning closer. "And I'd get the lovely opportunity—many lovely opportunities—to produce an heir. What do you say?"

Emma's stinging slap was eloquence itself.

"Put the fish on the pillow, Claire. I think that will work best."

Isabelle stood in Lady Caroline's room, Queen Bess in her arms. Her highness had been gracious about accompanying them once Isabelle had fed her a bit of trout. She meowed now and squirmed a bit. Isabelle adjusted her grasp.

"In a minute, kitty. Claire's making you a nice snack."

"Mrrow!"

"The pillow, Claire. Put most of it on the pillow. That's where the lady's face will be."

"I know." Claire grinned. "We want to make sure the piggy lady's face swells."

"Right—but don't put too much, either. If she smells the fish, she'll be suspicious. She won't put her face down in fish smell."

"Cook said this fish is very fresh." Claire put one more fish flake on the pillow. "There. Done."

Isabelle deposited Queen Bess. Her highness paced the coverlet and then sat on the pillow, daintily consuming every fishy morsel. She searched for more tidbits and, finding none, licked her paws, yawned, stretched, and hopped off the bed, slipping out of the room.

"I think that should do it," Isabelle said.

Claire skipped to the door. "I can't wait until the piggy lady gets back from the lake."

"Let's hope she lies down for a nap before dinner."

Emma was so angry she could barely see straight. She strode blindly down the path. She heard Charles call behind her, but she ignored him. Then she heard one of the lovely young London misses talking to him. Piggy Lady Caroline, she hoped. The buffle-headed cods-head deserved to spend some time with that harpy.

She wished she'd had another china dog at hand. She would have smashed it over Lord Arrogance's head. Marry him just to solve his problems? To enable him to get an heir and get rid of his unwelcome female pursuers? The overweening coxcomb! The mutton-headed, jinglebrained fribble! And how dare he bring up Mrs. Graham? Mrs. Graham was *not* a problem. Papa would never marry the woman. He respected his family too much.

She should be home now, taking care of him. But Isabelle and Claire needed her, too. She couldn't leave them to the callous, mean, spiteful, *evil* London girls.

What if Charles married one of those girls? What would happen to Isabelle and Claire?

She couldn't marry Charles just to protect his nieces—could she?

She stumbled down the bank to the grotto. She had always loved its quiet peacefulness. She needed that serenity now to collect her composure.

Unfortunately, she was not the only one who had sought the grotto's solitude. She stopped at the entrance and stared. Mr. Stockley stood next to the statue of Poseidon. He was behaving in the oddest manner. First he pulled on Poseidon's trident. Then he tried to twist the statue's arm. He knocked on its chest and looked in its mouth. He even stuck his hand into the small pool at its base and felt around in the water. Finally he stood, dried his hand on his breeches, and shrugged, moving on to the stone wall. He poked his fingers into the chinks between the rocks.

Obviously, he would prefer to be alone. She turned to leave, but her foot sent a loose pebble skittering across the ground to bounce off the wall. Mr. Stockley gasped and whirled to face her.

"Pardon me, sir. I didn't mean to disturb you. I thought no one would be here. I'll just be going."

"No, please stay, Miss Peterson." Mr. Stockley took a deep breath and straightened his waistcoat. "I wasn't expecting . . . You surprised me, that is all." He smiled in the most offensive way. His voice suddenly had an oily quality. "Come in." He wiggled his eyebrows. "Join me."

Did the man think she had followed him? Clearly Lord Knightsdale was not the only arrogant, mutton-headed male in the vicinity.

"No, no, really, I . . ."

Mr. Stockley swaggered closer. Emma had to swallow a giggle. He reminded her of a rooster in a barnyard. Yet there was something knowing about the man as well.

"I didn't consider . . . You'd not been encouraging . . ." Mr. Stockley crooked up the right corner of his mouth. "You need a man, don't you?"

"*What?*"

"A man. You ladies are all the same. Prim and proper on the outside, but so needy on the inside. Especially ladies such as yourself."

"Myself?" Emma was certain she squeaked. She took a step back, but Mr. Stockley stopped her by putting a hand on her arm.

"Yourself. How old are you—thirty?"

"Twenty-six." Not that her age was important, but she didn't want four extra years added to her total.

"Twenty-six. Firmly on the shelf. Not much hope of finding relief for your urges in a marriage bed. And you do have urges, don't you?"

Emma hoped that she had not nodded. She would never admit to something as vulgar as *urges*. Yearnings, perhaps, but not urges. Well, maybe some urges. Ever since Charles had kissed her—especially since the interlude in the conservatory—she had felt hot and unsettled. She had definitely had urges to open the door between their rooms.

"Mr. Stockley, I have no idea what you are talking about."

"Allow me to explain, then."

Mr. Stockley employed his mouth, but not for

speaking. His hands closed around her upper arms and pulled her against his body. His lips pressed hers.

She was curious. She admitted it. She had only ever been kissed by Charles. Was kissing an activity that was pleasant in and of itself, or did its agreeableness depend on the skill of the man doing the kissing?

She certainly had no urge to kiss the buffle-headed Marquis of Insolence at the moment. Perhaps Mr. Stockley would be a welcome diversion, even an antidote to her annoying attraction to Lord Blockhead.

He was not.

Mr. Stockley smelled of onions and cabbage and sweat. He gripped her arms too tightly and mashed her lips against her teeth. She felt none of the wonderful, hot feelings she had experienced with Charles. No, she felt bored. Uncomfortable. A strong wish to be somewhere else. She pressed her lips together firmly and hoped he would be finished soon.

"Come to my bedchamber tonight." Mr. Stockley's voice had a peculiar thickness to it. "I'll point it out to you." His hands began to wander. Emma twisted to avoid his fingers, but her movements seemed only to encourage him to greater efforts. She was beginning to become alarmed.

"Emma?"

Mr. Stockley's hands dropped like rocks, and he leapt back.

"Are you in there, Emma?"

"Yes." Emma had to clear her throat and take a deep breath to gather the volume to respond. "Yes, Lord Knightsdale, I'm here with Mr. Stockley."

Charles appeared at the opening to the grotto. His eyes seemed to measure the distance between her and her companion. She swallowed, and cleared her throat once more.

"We were just kis—um, er, *kicking* loose stones away so no one would stumble on them." She looked down to suit action to words, but the ground at her feet was clear of even the tiniest pebble. "Mr. Stockley is very interested in bed—*buildings*. Statuary and, and such. I was urging—um, *helping* him, ah, look for, um, interesting, ah, statues."

She knew her face was as red as one of Lady Beatrice's gowns. Her cheeks certainly felt hot enough to light the darkest corner of this shadowy location.

Charles and Mr. Stockley stared at her. She smiled.

Charles turned to look at Poseidon. "I assume you noticed the sculpture in the middle of the grotto?"

"Yes," Emma said. "We were looking for others."

Charles surveyed the small, clear space. Emma followed his gaze over the rock walls and stone floor. "In here?"

"No, um, of course not. I was talking generally. In the future. Elsewhere."

"Elsewhere, yes." Mr. Stockley bowed. "If you'll excuse me, my lord?"

Charles nodded. Mr. Stockley made his escape.

"Emma," Charles said once they were alone, "would you care to explain what you just said?"

Emma smiled harder. "No."

Something was wrong. Emma looked as nervous as an unbroken horse. What had she and Stockley been doing in here? Surely she could not have been kissing that twiddlepoop?

He stepped closer. She stepped back.

"Are you all right, Emma?"

"Of course I'm all right. Why wouldn't I be all right?"

"I don't know. You seem ill at ease. Did Stockley do something to overset you?"

"*No!*" She took a deep breath, making her lovely breasts swell in an interesting fashion. "No. Indeed not. Mr. Stockley did not overset me in the slightest. I am perfectly fine. What odd notions you have, my lord."

"Hmm. He didn't try to kiss you, did he?"

"*Kiss* me?!"

Charles would swear Emma actually squeaked. He stepped closer. She stepped back again, bringing herself up against the grotto wall.

"I think you've run out of room to retreat, sweetheart."

"Nonsense. I am not retreating."

"No?" He leaned forward, putting a hand on the wall on either side of her head. "I am glad to hear that. We need to talk, love. Why did you slap me?"

Her eyes dropped to study his cravat. "I apologize. That was not well done of me."

"That doesn't answer my question, Emma." He tilted her chin up with the edge of his hand. "I didn't mean to offend you."

"No, of course not." She met his gaze, then dropped her eyes again—he'd swear she was staring at his mouth. Her little pink tongue edged out to moisten her lips. Her voice sounded a hair breathless. "Shouldn't we be getting back to the group? I'm sure Lady Caroline is wondering where you are."

"God, I'm sure she is. In fact, she might be huffing down the path right now, hot on my heels."

Charles could not waste such a lovely opportunity. As Emma pointed out, they could be interrupted at any moment. He let his hand slip from her chin to her jaw. He might have only seconds of privacy. Why waste it in conversation? He could find out later why she had slapped him. He smiled. He might get slapped again, but he would take that risk. He could not have her so close, so private, and not steal a kiss.

He bent to touch his lips to hers. She smelled sweet, clean, of lemons and lavender. Her skin was so soft; the line of her jaw, so delicate. He brushed his lips lightly over hers and she whimpered. Her hands came up to lie on his chest. For an instant he was afraid she meant to push him away, but then her fingers slid up to his neck and tangled in his hair.

He brought her body up against his. The softness of her breasts flattened against his chest. He teased her lips with his, tracing their seam with his tongue. She opened her mouth and he slipped inside.

She had a lovely, small mouth. Warm. Wet. His tongue swept over its roof, followed the length of her tongue. She was too innocent to know yet what to do, but he knew. He would teach her. He stroked into her, and she made a small, needy noise. Her head fell back against his shoulder; her mouth opened wider, giving him more room to explore.

She was so . . . generous.

He had had his share of whores and widows. Those had been pleasant enough encounters—lusty, satisfying couplings—but there had been little generosity involved. Friendship, sometimes. Mutual need, often. But generosity? This innocent giving, this trust he felt in Emma? Never.

It was amazingly erotic.

He moved his mouth to kiss her neck, just below her ear. Could he loosen the blasted neck of her dress? Possibly, but there wasn't time. If anyone asked, Stockley would be sure to tell him—or her—where to find the marquis.

Ah, not enough time at all. He heard the scrape of a foot on the path outside. He straightened.

"Emma."

"Hmm?"

"Emma, love, we are about to have company."

"Company?"

"Yes." He kissed her hard on the lips. "We can continue this very interesting . . . discussion . . . later, but unless you want to scandalize whomever is about to enter this lovely grotto, you had better look less thoroughly kissed."

Her eyes flew wide and she straightened just as Lady Caroline's distinctive voice called his name.

Emma hoped she did not look as disordered as she felt. Lady Caroline did give her a hard stare but then turned her attention to Charles.

"We missed you, my lord."

"You flatter me, Lady Caroline. I could have been out of your sight only a few minutes."

"Every minute without you is an eternity, my lord."

Emma rolled her eyes. She didn't worry that Lady Caroline would take note of her rude behavior; the young lady's attention never left Charles. Emma had ceased to exist as far as she was concerned.

That was a good thing. She needed some moments to get her emotions under control.

Well, she had had her curiosity satisfied. Kissing Mr. Stockley had been as enchanting as emptying chamber pots, but kissing Charles . . .

Oh, my.

She had been anything but bored when Charles's mouth was on hers. Well, her . . . interest had begun the moment he entered the grotto. Just seeing his form sent her brain on holiday with her good sense. He had tried to talk to her, hadn't he? Why hadn't she told him exactly what she thought of his insulting marriage proposal—if one could dignify his suggestion with that term?

Such a rational approach was beyond her. She had seen him, and her stomach had begun to perform odd gymnastic feats. She could think of only one thing to do with her mouth, and it wasn't talking. After Mr. Stockley left and Charles stepped closer, her breathing had become most erratic. And her heart had fluttered like a bird trying to escape a cage. An odd liquid warmth—no, she could not even think of that.

What was the matter with her? She was angry with the man! He had suggested marriage for his convenience, not because he loved her. She was just a handy female, one who would tie up the loose ends of his life very neatly with little effort on his part. One he could get with child easily and leave safely in the country.

Get with child easily—ha! When he'd had his body pressed against hers, he could have asked her to walk backward to London and she would have tried to accommodate him. He must have little doubt that she'd acquiesce with nary a peep of dissent to whatever procedure was required to produce children. Had she no pride?

Apparently not. She looked at him, standing with Lady Caroline and Poseidon, and felt that odd liquid heat pool low in her again. How could she want to slap him silly one moment and the next, wrap her hands around him as if she'd never let go?

She was an idiot—a cabbage-headed, corkbrained idiot.

"Shall we join the others, Lady Caroline?"

Emma's eyes narrowed. If Charles could be charming to that she-serpent, he could be charming to anyone. Even his old playmate. It meant nothing. She must remember that. He was an accomplished flirt—he hadn't learned to kiss in such an expert fashion from studying books or fighting Napoleon. He'd had years of practice.

Well, he could exercise his amatory skills on some other stupid girl.

But not Lady Caroline. Emma couldn't let him marry that harpy. Poor Isabelle and Claire would pay the price. And he couldn't marry Miss Oldston for the same reason. Miss Pelham? Doubtful. Her mother was a gorgon; it was hard to imagine the daughter could be much different. And poor Miss Frampton was as spotty as her brother.

Perhaps Miss Haverford was a candidate. She was prettily behaved. Emma could think of nothing objectionable about her—except she was too young, of course. And perhaps a touch vapid. But she might gain character with age.

"Miss Peterson?"

Charles was looking at her expectantly, as if he had asked the question at least once before. Emma smiled and put her hand on the arm he offered; Lady Caroline was hanging on his other side.

"Don't you miss London, Lord Knightsdale?" Lady Caroline asked. "The theatre, the parties, the balls?" She looked over at Emma. "Oh, I'm sorry—have you been to London, Miss Peterson?"

Emma gritted her teeth. "No, Lady Caroline, I have not had that pleasure."

"No?" Lady Caroline tried to look sympathetic, but her eyes—her hard little piggy eyes—gave her away. They glittered with malice. "What a shame.

But I imagine country life has its benefits, doesn't it? The slow pace. The familiar activities. It must be quite . . . comfortable for, um"—she smiled up at Charles—"for some people," she finished.

For an old maid such as I, Emma thought. Lady Caroline did not say the words, but they hung in the air.

Charles laughed. "I quite like the country, Lady Caroline. I've grown somewhat tired of Town." He smiled at Emma. "However, I'm certain you'd enjoy a visit to London, Miss Peterson. Perhaps it can be arranged soon."

Lady Caroline shot Emma a look that should have killed her, it was so pointed.

"I don't know that a trip to Town is in my future, my lord," Emma said.

"I would wager that it is, Miss Peterson. In fact, I would be willing to lay odds on it."

"Are you taking your nieces up to London, then, my lord?" Lady Caroline bared her teeth at Emma in a formation resembling a smile. "So educational— the museums, the opera, the Tower. You'll enjoy it, Miss Peterson. I imagine it is paradise for a governess such as yourself."

Charles choked. "Yes." He looked at Emma; his eyes were dancing wickedly. "So educational. I might even be able to help you, Miss Peterson. I could teach a few lessons, I believe."

I bet you could, Emma thought, *but what lessons and to whom?* Many more like the one he had just delivered and she would be compelled to wed him— though it would almost be worth it to see the look on dear Lady Caroline's face when their engagement was announced.

Had she lost her mind? Whatever was she thinking?

Lord Knightsdale would most definitely not be teaching her any more lessons.

"I found the bonnet, Isabelle."

"Good. Do you see Miss Peterson's brush?"

Claire looked on Emma's dressing table. "Yes. It's not very fancy."

"That doesn't matter. She'll need it tonight. Come on, let's put it in Uncle Charles's room."

Isabelle led the way to the connecting door. She pushed it open and saw Henderson, Uncle Charles's valet, folding cravats. She backed up quickly and stepped on Claire's toe.

"Ow!"

Henderson looked up. "May I help you, Lady Isabelle?"

"Um." Isabelle stepped into the room. "We were just looking for Uncle Charles."

"Were you now? And what might you be doing with Miss Peterson's bonnet?"

"It's not very pretty," Claire said. She put it on her head. "Don't you think it looks like a bucket?"

Henderson's face twisted as though he smelled something bad. "It's not my place to comment on Miss Peterson's clothing."

"But if it were your place, Mr. Henderson?" Isabelle asked. "Do you think this bonnet is very stylish?"

Henderson appeared to struggle with himself. He sighed. "No, I can't say that bonnet is particularly stylish."

"I think Miss Peterson would be better off without it, don't you?"

"Lady Isabelle . . ."

"We just don't want her to look bad next to those London ladies, Mr. Henderson," Claire said.

"No, I understand. . . ."

"Those London ladies are *mean*."

Isabelle smiled and pushed Claire back toward Miss Peterson's room. "Well, since Uncle Charles isn't here, we'll just be going. Good-bye, Mr. Henderson."

She closed the door and sighed.

"Too bad Mr. Henderson was in Uncle Charles's room."

Claire shrugged. "I put Mama Peterson's brush under the papers on Papa Charles's bureau while you were talking."

Isabelle grinned. "Good job, Claire."

Claire skipped toward the door to the hall, swinging the bonnet by its strings.

"I bet Miss Russell would like this for the scarecrow in her garden."

CHAPTER 8

Emma saw Mrs. Graham the moment she returned from the lake. The woman was standing in the Knightsdale entry hall, laughing up at Papa.

A hard knot formed in her stomach. So Lady Caroline was not the only harpy fluttering about the Knightsdale estate.

"Thank you for the outing, my lord," Lady Caroline said behind her. She turned to see the girl batting her eyelashes at Charles. The hoyden put one hand on her ample chest and the other on Charles's arm. "I am a trifle fatigued from the exertion, I fear. I believe I shall go up and take a nap."

Did she expect Charles to join her?

"Come on, Caro." Miss Oldston sounded almost as impatient with Lady Caroline's posturing as Emma was.

"I shall see you later, my lord." Lady Caroline brushed past Emma and followed Miss Oldston up the stairs.

Emma clenched her hands. She wished she had a few of the burs Chubs and the others had been flinging near the cottage—she'd love to see them arranged on Lady Caroline's ample backside.

She took a deep breath. She was being extremely childish. It was beneath her to feel this way.

She glanced at Mrs. Graham and her temper soared again. The woman had the audacity to smile at her, as if she shared her impatience with stupid Lady Caroline. Emma shared nothing with Mrs. Harriet Graham. Nothing.

Except Papa. He smiled down at Mrs. Graham, and Emma's stomach twisted.

No. He was just being polite. He would not bring that woman into the family. He couldn't.

"Reverend Peterson, just the man I was looking for," Charles said. "And Mrs. Graham. Welcome to Knightsdale. I hope you don't mind if I borrow your escort for a moment? I have a small matter to discuss with him."

"Of course not, my lord." Mrs. Graham smiled at Charles. At least she didn't bat her eyelashes at him.

"Splendid. Lambert," Charles said to the butler, who was hovering in the background, "will you show Mrs. Graham to the blue drawing room?" He smiled back at Mrs. Graham. "We really will be only a few moments, ma'am."

"Please take your time, my lord. I'm in no hurry." Mrs. Graham looked at Emma. Emma ground her teeth. "Would you care to join me, Emma?"

"No."

Emma saw Charles stiffen. Her father frowned. Perhaps she had been a bit abrupt.

"No, thank you. I'm a trifle fatigued." Was she using Lady Caroline's excuse? Lud! She couldn't sink that low. "That is, um . . ."

"That's quite all right," Mrs. Graham said. "I shall do fine by myself."

"I believe Lady Beatrice is in the drawing room with a few of the older ladies, ma'am," Mr. Lambert said.

Charles frowned. "A few of the older ladies, Lambert? You don't mean the Society, do you?"

"Yes, my lord." Mr. Lambert cleared his throat. "I took the liberty of securing the brandy, however."

"Well done."

Emma glanced at her father and saw the reproachful look in his eyes. She struggled with her conscience. She was Papa's daughter—her conscience won.

"I suppose I can stay downstairs a few minutes longer and keep Mrs. Graham company. If you'll excuse me, Papa? My lord?"

Emma focused on her father's grateful smile as she followed Mrs. Graham to the blue drawing room.

"May I offer you some brandy, vicar?" Charles showed Reverend Peterson into his study.

"Do I need it, my lord?"

Charles grinned. "I hope not."

"Then, thank you, I will have a glass."

Charles handed Emma's father the brandy and gestured for him to take a seat. Charles stood by the fireplace. Sudden nerves made sitting impossible.

He had not expected to be nervous.

The vicar sipped his drink. Charles felt his eyes studying him.

"I am not going to quiz you on declensions or conjugations, Lord Knightsdale, nor ask you to translate Caesar."

Charles laughed. "No—and a good thing, too. I don't know that I would acquit myself well."

"Nonsense. You were an excellent scholar—when you wanted to be. I understand you did very well at university."

Charles shrugged. He did not mean to be speaking of Latin. He meant to be speaking of Emma.

"Sir, the reason I asked to speak with you . . . Well, I should like to . . ." Charles cleared his throat and started again. "I would like your permission to . . ."

"Yes? Just say it, boy. It can't be that bad."

"I would like to marry your daughter, sir."

Reverend Peterson sat still, an arrested expression on his face. "Emma?"

"Of course, Emma. Meg is much too young."

"Well, she's not really, but I agree, Emma would be a better choice for you. Meg is not interested in any man as far as I can tell. Emma is, if she will only let herself admit it."

"So I have your permission to pay my addresses?"

"Indeed. Though it will be Emma's choice, of course."

"Of course. And I am not ready to ask her yet."

"Afraid she'll refuse?"

Charles laughed. "Well, to tell the truth, she *has* refused, but with time, I think I can bring her about."

Reverend Peterson nodded. "She's worshiped you for years, you know."

"Well, yes, I did know—though I'll tell you she's not acting so worshipful at the moment."

Reverend Peterson sighed. "Emma is not very happy at the moment, Lord Knightsdale, and I fear it is my fault."

"What do you mean, sir?"

It was the vicar's turn to look uncomfortable. He took a large swallow of brandy.

"You know my wife died within a year of Meg's birth. It was a hard labor, and Catherine never completely recovered. I was devastated, as was Emma, of course. She was only nine years old, but she stepped into her mother's shoes. Took charge of Meg and the household. I should never have let her, but it seemed a good thing at the time. It gave her something to do, a purpose, if you will. And I . . ."

The vicar closed his eyes, his mouth tightening as if a spasm of pain had flashed through him.

"Sir, you don't need to—"

Reverend Peterson held up his hand. "No, my lord, I do." He sighed and put his glass on the table by his chair. He clasped his hands, leaning forward, his forearms on his knees. "I had no interest in taking another wife. Emma kept things running smoothly. I could lose myself in my research, my ancient Greek and Latin texts. I was happy—I thought. And I thought Emma and Meg were happy, too."

"I'm certain they were."

"Perhaps. But life goes on. Things change. Not very profound, I know, but very true. Harriet moved to the village after her husband died—she inherited a small cottage here—and when I saw her after services for the first time . . . well, feelings I thought long dead were resurrected. She volunteered to help with the church—not to be forward, you understand, but because she truly enjoys working with flowers and altar cloths and such. She had been very active at her old church, and she found the activity comforting. We became friends—and then our friendship deepened."

"I understand, sir. You needn't go into details that you would rather not."

The vicar laughed, flushing slightly. "Oh, never fear, I won't." He shook his head. "We have kept to the church teachings—barely. And it is getting harder every day. I'm sure you understand."

Charles grinned. "I believe I do."

The vicar grinned back. "So you don't think I'm too old to . . . no, never mind. The point is, I want to marry Harriet—and she wants to marry me. But I know Emma does not like it. I feel I would be betraying her."

"Well, I do have to say she doesn't overly care for Mrs. Graham."

The vicar snorted. "*That's* an understatement." He ran his hand through his graying hair. "Harriet and I have discussed it, and we really don't understand her reaction. Harriet is as certain as she can be that she never did anything to insult or hurt Emma. In fact, they were friendly—until my interest became apparent."

"How does Meg feel about your marriage? Does she know that you want to wed?"

"Oh, yes. Meg is very different from Emma—well, Meg didn't have to take on all the responsibilities that Emma did. I think Meg doesn't much care, as long as our marriage won't affect her ability to dig in the mud. She's a lot like me in that regard, only my passion is the classics—hers is plants."

Reverend Peterson shifted in his chair. "I've often thought . . . That is, I think . . . Well . . ." Emma's father raised his eyes to stare directly into Charles's. "Now, don't take this the wrong way, young man. I am not advocating you take any liberties with my daughter whatsoever. But I have begun to think

that if Emma had more of an idea of what love between a man and a woman was, she might understand my feelings. If she had experienced an . . .
attraction . . . for a man, perhaps she would understand how marriage is more than . . . Well, maybe she
would understand something about married love.
How the love Harriet and I have for each other
doesn't threaten the love I have for her and her
sister. That I am not betraying her mother or deni-
grating her efforts all these years. That she will
always have a place in my heart as my daughter—she
does not need to continue to run my household."

Charles sat down across from the vicar. "Has Emma
never had a beau, then?"

"No. I did not lie when I said she worshiped you."
The vicar sighed. "Looking back, I should have insisted she have a Season. One of my sisters would
gladly have sponsored her. But Emma didn't want
to leave Meg—and I didn't want my comfortable rou-
tine altered." Bitterness crept into his voice. "I am
paying for my selfishness now."

"Now, sir, no self-recriminations, please. I consider you did me a favor, little as we both realized it.
I believe Emma and I will suit admirably." Charles
grinned. "I just have to convince her of that."

There was really no need for her to be here,
Emma thought as Mr. Lambert opened the door to
the blue drawing room and she followed Mrs.
Graham inside. She would have realized that as
soon as Mr. Lambert had said the Society was here,
if she had not let guilt cloud her thinking.

"Harriet!" Mrs. Begley raised her teacup as Emma
and Mrs. Graham entered the room. "And Miss

Peterson. How lovely. Lady Beatrice, have you met Mrs. Graham?"

Emma surveyed the room as Mrs. Begley made the introductions. Mr. Lambert said he had secreted the brandy, but the ladies were looking suspiciously bright-eyed. The Farthington twins sat together on the settee, giggling, while Miss Russell smiled beatifically at a vase of roses.

"A pleasure to meet you, Mrs. Graham." Lady Beatrice was attired in a Pomona green and puce ensemble with plumes in alternating colors, giving the unfortunate impression of a rotting plum. "Would you ladies care for some tea?"

"Yes, thank you," Mrs. Graham said. "Tea would be very pleasant."

Lady Beatrice poured and then reached into her workbasket. She pulled out a bottle of brandy and grinned. "Shall I add a dollop of French cream?"

Mrs. Graham laughed. "Oh, no. I would be asleep before I got to the bottom of the cup."

Emma frowned as she took her tea, also without brandy. "Mr. Lambert said he had put all that away." She bit her lip as soon as the words were out. It wasn't her place to criticize.

Lady Beatrice shrugged and put the bottle back in her basket. "Mr. Lambert may be an excellent butler, but he is no match for me when it comes to deviousness."

"Come, Miss Peterson, don't frown so," Mrs. Begley said. "It's not as if we indulge every day. Why, we didn't take a drop in our tea yesterday, did we, ladies?"

"Not a drop." Miss Esther Farthington shook her head slowly.

"And we've had barely a drop today." Miss Rachel Farthington sighed.

Miss Russell smiled at the roses.

"You worry too much, Miss Peterson, if I may say so." Mrs. Begley pointed her teacup at Emma while the twins nodded. "You are only twenty-six, not sixty-six. You act like an old lady sometimes."

The twins stopped nodding abruptly and their brows snapped into identical frowns.

"Sixty-six is not old." Miss Esther clicked her cup on the table. "We are seventy, and we are not old, Lavinia."

"Indeed not." Miss Rachel waggled her finger. "Eighty-six, that may be old, but sixty-six—never."

Mrs. Begley threw up her hands, almost upsetting her teacup. "My point is, Miss Peterson, you are still single, marriageable, attractive . . ."

With each adjective, the Farthington twins appeared to puff up like angry wrens, feathers ruffled. Mrs. Begley threw them a harried glance.

"What I *mean* is, you are still *young*—too young to be constantly worried about propriety."

Mrs. Graham chuckled. "I thought it was the young girls who most had to worry about propriety, Lavinia."

"And I am not young," Emma said. This was an exceedingly stupid conversation. "My sister, Meg, is young."

"Your sister Meg is a veritable infant. Children her age need to be chaperoned. You, however . . ." Mrs. Begley paused, tapping her teacup gently against her teeth.

"You are a second-day rosebud," Miss Russell said.

Everyone stared as if one of the chairs had spoken. Miss Russell blinked back at them.

"Whatever do you mean, Blanche?" Mrs. Begley asked.

"Miss Peterson—her petals have unfurled just a little. Relaxed. Opened up."

Lady Beatrice snorted. "Not likely."

"No, I see what Blanche is saying," Miss Rachel said. "She's right."

Miss Esther nodded. "Meg is like a new bud, fresh, tight . . ."

". . . but Emma's been out in the sun longer. Been blown about more."

"Had more bees visit—"

"Miss Esther, I'm not certain where this metaphor is going, but it is beginning to sound quite inappropriate." Mrs. Graham's voice had a distinct edge.

"They are only saying Emma has enough experience to be interesting," Mrs. Begley said. "I quite agree."

Emma sat bolt upright.

"I do not have any experience."

"Not of an intimate nature, of course. At least, I assume . . . ?"

"Lavinia!"

"Well, Harriet, she certainly has more life experience than a seventeen-year-old chit," Mrs. Begley said.

Emma's ears were still burning with the word "intimate." She snorted, trying to act as if the conversation were not galloping away from her. "Oh, yes. Nine years more experience, to be exact."

"And each of those years is important, miss. Not all of marriage occurs in the bedroom, you know. Men do allow one to emerge from the sheets to eat, read the papers, converse. It is vastly more appealing to have a wife with a few interesting thoughts knocking around in her brain box—or his brain box in the case of one's husband, of course."

Sheets? Emma felt a light flush travel up her neck. The image of Lord Knightsdale scantily attired in his bedsheets the night he'd come hunting ghosts in the nursery flashed into her mind.

"You are . . . seasoned, Miss Peterson," Mrs. Begley said. "Much more attractive to a man with a discriminating palate."

"Mrs. Begley," Mrs. Graham said, "you make Emma sound like a beefsteak."

"That could do with a little more seasoning, unless I miss my guess." Lady Beatrice added another splash of brandy to her tea. "Lavinia is correct, Miss Peterson. You worry too much about propriety. You need to take a few risks—have some fun. You are not a girl in her first Season—and yes, I know you've never had a Season, but the concept holds. Society, at least here in the country, will give you a little more freedom than you seem willing to give yourself." She held up her purloined brandy bottle. "A little deviousness is all to the good, Miss Peterson. It's a dull woman who knows only propriety."

"And no man wants a dull woman," Lady Begley said.

"Especially not my nephew."

Emma spewed a mouthful of tea back into her teacup.

"Did I miss something?" Mrs. Graham asked.

"No. There's nothing to miss. Nothing at all. Lady Beatrice has simply imbibed too much spirits. She is befuddled. Bemused. Confused." Emma was horrified. Now all the ladies of the Society knew Lady Beatrice's matrimonial opinion—ladies who had little sense of decorum and tongues that ran on wheels.

"I am not confused, miss. Charles needs an heir; his nieces need a mama. Whom else is he to choose? I mean, look at your competition. Lady Caroline . . ."

Miss Esther oinked.

"Miss Oldston."

Miss Rachel neighed.

Lady Beatrice nodded. "*And* she looks remarkably like a toad as well. Entire family does. Then there's Miss Frampton."

"Spotty." Mrs. Begley wrinkled her nose.

"Miss Pelham."

"Nasty mother."

Everyone stared at Miss Russell again.

"Well, it's true. Miss Pelham has a very nasty mother. I wouldn't want her as a mother-in-law."

"Exactly." Lady Beatrice nodded, sending her plumes bobbing. "That leaves only you."

"And Meg and Lizzie and Miss Haverford, as well as countless ladies of the *ton* not present at this house party."

Lady Beatrice rolled her eyes. "Meg is only interested in weeds, and Lizzie is only interested in the Earl of Westbrooke. Miss Haverford is one of Miss Russell's new rosebuds—too young. I just cannot see Charles offering for her."

"Miss Haverford is not too young," Emma said. "She is seventeen, the same age as Meg and Lizzie. A perfectly acceptable age for marriage."

Lady Beatrice snorted. "Not for Charles. He would be so bored, he'd fall asleep before he could—"

"Lady Beatrice, please." Mrs. Graham scowled at Charles's aunt. "Emma is a gently bred, unmarried lady."

Lady Beatrice scowled back. "And she'll stay that way if she doesn't bestir herself. Charles is a plum waiting to be picked. She can have him if she wants. She just needs to stretch out her hand and pluck him off the bachelor tree."

Mrs. Begley grabbed the brandy bottle. "Gawd, Lady Bea, don't go poetic on us."

"Well, it's true. Part of grabbing a husband is finding one who is ripe. Charles is. The title is sitting heavy on his shoulders. Someone will pick him before the year's out—may as well be Miss Peterson." Lady Beatrice leaned toward Emma. "Go on, girl. Go harvest the man before some other chit beats you to him."

Emma stared back at Lady Beatrice. How did one respond to such a statement? That she wanted something more from marriage?

But what, exactly? Love, of course, but what of the disturbing feelings that flooded her whenever she thought of Charles's body hard against hers?

"Well, I believe we have wandered in matrimonial horticulture long enough," Mrs. Graham said, smiling. "This speculation is groundless until Emma has received an offer from Lord Knightsdale. And I'm certain she would prefer to consider the subject in private, wouldn't you, dear?"

Emma made some noise that Mrs. Graham must have taken as agreement. The older woman directed the conversation into more acceptable channels. It flowed around Emma—gossip of local families, of the London house party guests. Emma was grateful—the first positive feeling she'd had for Mrs. Graham since she realized the woman was more than just another parish lady to her father.

She tried to think clearly, but she could not get the images, the sensations, of her encounter in the grotto with Lord Knightsdale out of her mind. His smell. His taste. The silky-roughness of his tongue filling her mouth.

She felt hot. Melting. At least something was definitely damp.

She stared down at her teacup. Perhaps disgusting Mr. Stockley was correct—perhaps she did have . . . urges. She thought of the door between her bedchamber and Lord Knightsdale's. The door that had no key. The door that was always unlocked.

She waved her hand in front of her face in a vain effort to cool her blood.

"Are you all right, dear?" Mrs. Graham asked softly.

Emma nodded. She hoped none of the other ladies noted her flushed cheeks. What would they say if they knew she *had* received an offer of sorts? Well, doubtless Lady Beatrice would consider Charles's words a full-fledged marriage proposal, but Emma did not. She wanted talk of love, not convenience. Of passion, not practicalities. Was that too much to ask?

Probably. Charles was a marquis, after all. For him, marriage was a necessary duty.

But if she did hear words of love—would she marry him then?

Ridiculous. She would not consider it. She was certain he would speak of love when pigs flew.

She did not expect to see porcine flight in her lifetime.

Lud! Emma stuck her head out of her bedchamber and listened. What in the world was that noise?

"Aaahhh! Mama! Achoo! Aaahhh."

Lady Caroline erupted from her room and flew down the hall, screaming and sneezing. More people poked their heads into the corridor. Emma saw Meg and walked down to her sister's room.

"What's going on, Emma?"

They watched Lady Caroline pound on her mother's door.

"I have no idea."

Lady Dunlee's maid finally answered the banging.
"Yes, m'lady? Oh! Oh, my!" The maid threw her
apron over her face and started wailing.

"Oh, for God's sake, Mary." Lady Dunlee's sharp
voice could be heard over the din. "What is all the
caterwauling about? Can't a body have a moment's
peace—" Lady Dunlee appeared at her door. Her
mouth dropped open, her eyes widened, and then
she started screeching.

Lady Beatrice brushed past Emma, Queen Bess following leisurely behind her. "Lady Dunlee, please,
calm yourself."

"Calm myself? *Calm* myself! I'll calm myself. Look
at my daughter."

Emma looked along with all the other house-
guests in the corridor. Lady Caroline's eyes were
swollen to narrow slits; her face was covered with
raised, red splotches; and her nose was streaming.
She sniffed, sneezed, and scratched.

"I see." Lady Beatrice cleared her throat. "I'm
sorry Lady Caroline is indisposed."

"Indisposed? You call this indisposed? I call this a
disaster."

"Well, it certainly is unfortunate. Perhaps she
would feel better if she lay down?"

Lady Caroline screamed and hid her face in her
mother's shoulder.

"No?" Lady Beatrice rocked back on her heels.
"Precisely what is the problem, Lady Dunlee?"

"That!" Lady Dunlee pointed at Queen Bess, who
had decided to sit by Lady Beatrice's skirts and
clean her hind leg. "That *creature* is the problem."

"Lady Dunlee, do not point at my cat in such a
fashion." Lady Beatrice moved to shield Queen

Bess. "I am sure she did not mean to distress your daughter."

"Ha! I'll have you know that Lady Caroline is very sensitive to cats."

"It was on my pillow, mama. I know it was. I was fine when I lay down to rest."

Lady Dunlee straightened to her full height. "What was your cat doing on my daughter's bed?"

"I have no idea. Queen Bess is not partial to pork."

"Pork?" Lady Dunlee frowned so hard her eyebrows met in a *V* above her nose. "Why are you talking about pork?"

"Just that Bess is a very intelligent animal. I would have thought she'd have taken one look at your daughter and determined there could be nothing of interest in her room."

Lady Dunlee drew a scandalized breath.

"Lady Beatrice, are you comparing my daughter to a . . . a pig?"

"Yes."

Lady Caroline sobbed louder as the assembled onlookers tried unsuccessfully to muffle their laughter.

"Please have my husband and son fetched, and our carriage brought round," Lady Dunlee said. "We are leaving."

Lady Beatrice smiled. "Have a lovely trip."

"Poor Lady Caroline."

Meg snorted. "You don't mean that."

Emma laughed. "No, I don't, but I feel as though I should. She did look so miserable—but all I could think of was how her face now matched her manners. She's a rather miserable young lady."

"She surely is." Meg turned to go back into her room.

"Uh, Meg?"

"Yes?"

Emma fidgeted with her skirt. "I do wonder how Queen Bess got into Lady Caroline's room—I thought the girl was rather careful to keep her door closed."

Meg shrugged. "Perhaps she forgot this time." She stepped farther into her room. Emma remained on the threshold.

"Are you having a good time, Meg? I hardly ever see you."

Meg turned to face Emma. "Emma, do you want to come in?"

"Well, yes, if you'd like me to. I do have a few minutes. It would be nice to chat. I was wondering what you've been up to. You didn't go walking with the rest of the young ladies this afternoon."

"I didn't go walking because walking sedately around the lake is boring. I have walked around that lake before and in better company."

"Better company?"

"My own. Without the nasty, brainless London misses and their idiotic escorts."

"But you are supposed to be getting some social polish, Meg."

"I don't want that kind of social polish. I know not to eat my food with my hands or talk with my mouth full. I don't need to know how to backstab and belittle."

"But . . ." Emma looked around Meg's room for the first time. She blinked. Every horizontal surface but the bed was covered with vegetation. Twigs and flowers were arranged on sheets of paper on the desk. Bits of crockery with green things lined the ledge by the window seat. An assortment of leaves covered the dressing table.

"Meg."

"Don't start, Emma."

"But what are you doing?"

"What does it look like I'm doing? I'm collecting specimens, of course. I don't get over to Knightsdale often, you know. I've found a number of interesting plants here."

Emma surveyed the mess before her but decided for once that she did not want to argue with Meg. She was not Meg's mother.

Sudden tears pricked her eyes. She batted them away.

"Meg, what do you think of Mrs. Graham?"

Meg gave her a sharp look. "What do you mean?"

Emma walked over to examine the greenery by the window seat. "Do you think Papa is going to marry her?"

"Probably."

"Doesn't that bother you? Doesn't it bother you that she's taking Mama's place?"

"Emma . . ." Meg clasped her hands behind her back and sighed. "Would you care to sit down?"

"I can't."

Meg looked around the room. Even the chairs were covered with twigs or leaves. "Oh, yes. I see. Sorry. Um, we could sit on the bed."

"No, I don't mean that." Emma looked at Meg. "I'm too agitated to sit."

"Ah. Well, um, the thing is, Emma, I really don't remember Mama. I wasn't even one year old when she died. You've been all the mother I've known."

"And you don't mind Mrs. Graham taking"— Emma swallowed more tears—"taking my place?"

"Emma." Meg rubbed her forehead. "I haven't needed a mama for years. You're my sister. You will always be my sister. I'm sure you will still feel quite free to tell me what you think of my conduct, my plans, my future. I don't foresee much change in our relationship."

"Really?"

"Really."

Emma sniffed and sat down on Meg's bed. Meg sat on the other side.

"But I do think Mrs. Graham will be good for Papa," Meg said.

"How? How could she be good for Papa?"

"He likes her, Emma. I think he loves her. He smiles more now."

"He smiled before."

"Yes, I know, but this is different. He just seems . . . happier, as if he is excited by something besides his musty old books and translations."

"But he has us." Emma plucked at Meg's counterpane.

"I think he's realizing he won't have us forever. He expects us to marry eventually. Then he'll be all alone."

"No."

"Yes, Emma. Not that I intend to marry soon, but I do think I might marry some day. And you should consider it, too. I know Papa doesn't want you to sacrifice your life for his. You have already done enough."

"I am not sacrificing my life. What a ridiculous notion."

"I know you don't consider it a sacrifice, but think—don't you want a house of your own?"

"I have the vicarage to take care of."

"But what about children? I would think you would want children of your own."

"Perhaps." Emma thought about Meg as a child—and Isabelle and Claire. She did like children. If she stayed home and kept house for her father, she would not have children to raise, that was true. And if her father married Mrs. Graham, she would not have a home to run, either. She would be completely superfluous.

She wrapped her arms around her middle.

"Papa won't marry Mrs. Graham if I don't want him to."

"Perhaps—but you don't want to rule his life like that, do you? Use his love to control him, to limit him? He's never done that to us. He's always let us follow our hearts."

"What do you mean? Where have we followed our hearts? We are still at home, aren't we?"

"That's my point. Papa lets me go off and muck around with my weeds and things. He didn't force you to have a Season—nor did he force me, even though it would have been so easy for him to have sent me to London with Lizzie this spring. He never insisted you marry—and you are certainly past the age where many fathers would have done so."

Emma looked away from Meg. "I never had any offers."

"Because you were never interested in any of the local men."

"What do you mean?" Emma frowned. "I've always danced at the assemblies, haven't I? I have been perfectly polite and pleasant."

"Yes, polite and pleasant. Not passionate."

"Meg! What do you know of passion?"

"Nothing, really. But I have eyes, Emma. I watch, and I am actually quite a skilled observer." Meg chuckled. "Perhaps it comes from noticing subtle differences in similar plants. In any event, I can tell when there is romance in the air. When a girl is interested in a man, she sparkles. Her eyes brighten, her skin flushes, she breathes quickly. She becomes more animated. You always look the same whether you are talking to an elderly chaperone or an extremely eligible young lord."

"Ridiculous. I am sure you are wrong. I believe Papa never pushed either of us to swim in social waters because he was too absorbed in his books to care."

Meg laughed. "Well, there is that. He does prefer to avoid a bother, and up until now—until Mrs. Graham moved to the village—I think he was content to let things stay the way they were. But I don't believe he is content any longer."

"No?" Emma had not noticed any indication that her father was restless. Well, there had been that incident in the study when she had walked in on him and Mrs. Graham. She much preferred not to contemplate that.

"Emma, if Papa truly loves Mrs. Graham, he should marry her."

"Nonsense. He doesn't love her. He's infatuated, that is all. I suppose Mrs. Graham is attractive for a woman her age. She knows how to entice a man. I don't fault her, really. I'm sure the life of a widow can be quite precarious. I just wish she would find another victim to assure her a comfortable future."

"Emma, you don't believe that, do you?"

Emma shrugged. "I don't know what I believe. I do know I can't live in the same house with that woman."

"I don't think you will have to."

"No?" Relief flooded Emma. She smiled. "You think Papa will come to his senses?"

"I don't think it's Papa who needs to see sense."

Emma frowned. "What do you mean?"

"I mean I think you won't be living at the vicarage much longer. I told you I'm quite observant—though in this case, a blind man could read the signs. When you talk to Lord Knightsdale, you do not look as though you are speaking to an elderly chaperone."

"What?"

Meg grinned. "The moment Lord Knightsdale approaches, your eyes brighten, your face flushes, and your bosom heaves."

Emma's eyes widened and her chin dropped to the bedclothes. She stared at Meg. She couldn't mean . . . Surely she wasn't insinuating . . . ? She snapped her mouth closed and glared.

"I'll heave something at you, you miserable excuse for a sister!"

Meg fell back on the bed, laughing, as Emma grabbed the nearest pillow and swung it at her head.

CHAPTER 9

Charles stared at the pile of papers on his desk. He needed a secretary.

No, he needed a wife. Emma. He had been making some interesting progress with his courtship in the grotto. If only Lady Caroline had not come hunting him.

There was a scratching at the door.

"Come."

Mr. Lambert appeared, bearing a large pile of letters. "The post, my lord."

"Put it down on the desk, Lambert."

Lambert blinked at the mountains already occupying the desk's surface.

"Where, my lord?"

Charles sighed. "Good question. Just hand it here, then."

"Very good, my lord. And I presume you have heard the news that Lord Dunlee and his family have departed?"

"Really? That's a bit sudden, isn't it? Did he give any reason?"

"I believe it was Lady Dunlee who insisted on leaving, my lord."

"Lady Dunlee? Why ever would she wish to go? I would have said she was rather intent on the festivities." Intent? She had all the focus of a French officer on a battle line. He had definitely thought she'd meant to take him prisoner for her piggy daughter.

Lambert cleared his throat. "One of the upstairs maids confided to Mrs. Lambert that Lady Beatrice insulted Lady Caroline."

Charles raised his brows. "Odd. Aunt Bea doesn't usually go about savaging young misses."

"I believe Lady Caroline insulted Queen Bess."

"Queen Bess? Why would Aunt Bea get in a pother over British history?"

"Not the monarch, my lord. The feline Queen Bess. Apparently Lady Caroline is sensitive to cats. Lady Beatrice's pet got into the young lady's room, and she was suffering the consequences—Lady Caroline, that is, not Queen Bess. Very . . . spotty, Mrs. Lambert said."

"I see. Thank you for informing me, Lambert."

So, Charles thought as Lambert closed the door behind him, *one less young lady to avoid.* Too bad Aunt hadn't offended Lady Caroline earlier. If she had left before the lake walk, his interlude with Emma in the grotto might have been significantly more satisfying. He might even now be an engaged man.

He needed to plan his campaign carefully. If her response at the grotto was any indication, Emma was not indifferent to him, but she did have some odd bee in her bonnet. She had never explained why she had slapped him. He had only asked her to marry him. He had not even kissed her—that had come

ater, and she had shown no signs of wanting to
slap him then.

No, no signs at all. He shifted in his chair, thinking of her softness and her heat, the way she had melted, had opened to him. God. And it was her fault he had kissed her at all. She had been staring at his lips in a most hungry fashion. It was only polite to give her a taste.

He'd be happy to give her more than a taste. He would dearly love to taste her, every inch, every curve, every secret spot.

"Busy, Charles?"

Charles shook himself free of the sweet lust that had heated his brain. "Not really. Come in, Robbie."

Robbie surveyed his desk as he approached. "Looks like you should be busy."

"I know. I think I've attended to the most pressing business." Charles stared down at the mess before him. "But I'm not entirely certain."

"You need a secretary."

"I know, damn it. I need a lot of things since my brother died and I inherited the blasted title. I can't accomplish everything at once."

"Right." Robbie helped himself to the brandy decanter. "Sounds like you need a drink, too."

"Thank you." Charles took a glass from him. "Your absence this afternoon didn't help matters. I was stuck acting nursemaid to the young misses and singlebrained boys Aunt Bea has collected for this bloody house party."

Robbie grinned, slouching into the chair next to Charles's desk. "Why do you think I was so quick to volunteer to fetch Alvord's sister? I damned well didn't want to be tramping around your lovely lake with that collection of cabbage-heads."

"I thought maybe you wanted some time with luscious Lizzie."

"Lizzie—luscious?" Robbie laughed. "Little Lizzie is like a sister, Charles. You know that. Lovely, charming, but . . . luscious? She's barely out of leading strings."

"Not exactly, Robbie. She's seventeen. She made her come out this Season. Alvord could be receiving offers for her now—he may already have a handful."

Robbie frowned, then shrugged. "No. Lizzie isn't ready to get married—I'm certain of it. James won't force her. In fact—what was that?"

Charles heard the muffled thud also. "I don't know. It doesn't sound like it came from the corridor."

"No, you're right." Robbie got up and poked his head out the study door. "Hall's deserted. Did you look outside?"

"It didn't sound like an outdoor thump," Charles said, but he looked out the window anyway. Nothing. "It sounded like something heavy dropping on wood."

"Perhaps you've got very large rats in your walls."

Charles frowned at the orderly bookcase. "I sincerely hope not."

Emma sat next to Sarah, the Duchess of Alvord, in the drawing room after dinner. She liked the tall, redheaded American instinctively. She guessed she was about her age, perhaps a year or two younger.

"My husband says you are a childhood friend, Miss Peterson."

"Yes, your grace. Well, I'm not certain you could call me a friend, exactly. I was more of a pest, I'm afraid. Lord Knightsdale says the duke and Lord Westbrooke called me 'Shadow.'"

The duchess laughed. "And your sister and Lizzie are of an age, are they not? They are friends as well?"

"Yes." Emma searched the room for her sister. For once Meg had not fled early. She was sitting with Lizzie, and they were laughing about something. "There had been talk of Meg going up to London with Lizzie for the Season, but Meg is not much interested in society balls and parties."

"No?"

"No. She would much rather be out in the fields, looking for new samples for her plant collection."

"I am glad to hear she has such a passion. However, I would not be surprised if she eventually becomes more interested in men and marriage. Most girls do." The duchess laughed. "I taught at a school for young ladies in Philadelphia, so I've spent some time observing young females."

"Ah." Emma nodded, but she was not certain the duchess was correct. Meg had said this afternoon she thought she would marry some day—that was a start. And it was true she did not have an assortment of attractive prospects at this gathering. Chubs—not that he was a prize—had departed with his family. Spots and Toad needed many more years of polishing before they were ready for married life. Lord Westbrooke was a good catch, but Lizzie had been in love with him forever—not that the earl showed any awareness of her interest.

She needed to get Meg to London for a Season, it was as simple as that. Well, simple if she married Charles; not so simple if they had to rely on Papa's sisters.

She was not going to marry Lord Knightsdale.

"And how is the new Lord Knightsdale doing, Miss Peterson?"

"What?" Emma stared at the duchess. "What do you mean?"

"Charles. How is he doing, do you know? When I spoke to him in London, I got the impression he was not eager to inherit the title. Of course at that time there was no reason to suspect he would—his brother was young and healthy. Is Charles adjusting well to being the marquis?"

"Your grace . . ." Charles did not want to be the marquis? He had never said so, had he? Of course he had never expected to inherit. That must be why he was so eager to wed—so he could get the unpleasant business over with and get on with his life. "I really don't know. Lord Knightsdale does not confide in me."

"He doesn't? I was certain James told me . . ." The duchess frowned, then shook her head. "No matter. I must have gotten confused. I do apologize." She blushed. "I'm not entirely myself these days."

Emma smiled. "No need to apologize, your grace. How are you feeling?"

"Fine. I just tire easily, but I have been assured that will pass shortly." The duchess smiled. "I do assume you have heard that I am increasing?"

"Yes. I'm afraid it's no secret."

"Not much is secret in the *ton,* is it?" The duchess laughed. "Not that I wish to hide my condition. I'm just used to living a more private life. Marriage to a British duke has taken some getting used to."

"Yes, life here must be very different." Emma tried to imagine leaving her family and familiar surroundings to cross the Atlantic. "Do you miss your country dreadfully?"

"No." The duchess smoothed her skirts. "Oh, occasionally I will get a little homesick, but I don't really have a home in the United States any longer. My mother died when I was a child; my father died last year—it was his death that caused me to come to England." She looked up and smiled at someone over Emma's shoulder. Emma turned to see the Duke of Alvord leading the men in from their after-dinner port.

"No," Emma heard the duchess say, "my home is in England now."

The duke's eyes found his wife, and a wide smile spread over his face.

It was clear he was madly in love with her, Emma thought as she greeted him and excused herself so he could join his duchess on the settee. She made a point of watching him during the evening. His expression was pleasant but reserved when he spoke to most people, but when he looked at his wife, his face softened and his eyes lit with a special fire.

She would love to have a man look at her in such a way. Would Charles? She snorted. Miss Russell paused in reporting on her gardening woes to give Emma a startled look. Emma smiled and coughed as if clearing her throat.

Charles just wanted a handy breeder and nursemaid. She glanced at him. He was talking with Sir Thomas and Lord Haverford. He caught her eye and smiled.

She looked down at her hands, hoping her heart was not beating so furiously everyone could see it.

She would like to have children. Meg had been right about that. She would like a baby of her own— with Charles's clear blue eyes.

She saw Mr. Stockley looking around the room and she turned quickly. Perhaps if she retreated to the settee in the far corner, she could avoid his annoying attention.

Would Charles be as happy, as proud and protective

of her when she was increasing as the duke was of his duchess? No. He'd be in London, once he was certain his seed had taken root. He might not even bother to come to Knightsdale for the birth. Why should he? Better to stay in London, drinking and whoring. She plucked at her skirt. She probably wouldn't see him again until it was time to start work on the next little Draysmith.

"Miss Peterson, are you all right?"

"What?" Emma looked up to find Charles frowning down at her. "Yes, of course I'm all right. Why do you ask?"

"You were growling again."

"I do not growl."

"No? Hmm. Perhaps it was moaning, then."

Emma flushed. "It was most certainly not moaning."

"No? I should like to make you moan."

You have. Emma slapped her hand over her mouth, but Lord Knightsdale's expression had not changed. She must have only thought the words.

"May I join you?"

"I don't see how I can stop you."

He chuckled, seating himself rather closer to her than necessary. His leg brushed against her skirt. He didn't actually touch her, but she swore she felt the heat from his body all along her side.

Unless it was the heat from her body she was feeling. What if he felt it, too? She tried to move away.

"Now don't be miffy, Miss Peterson."

"I am not miffy." She must have spoken too loudly, because Lady Beatrice looked in their direction and then headed toward them. Emma was relieved— well, mostly relieved—that she would not be having a *tête-à-tête* with Lord Knightsdale.

"Are you annoying Miss Peterson, Charles?" Lady Beatrice settled herself in a chair.

"Of course not, Aunt—am I, Miss Peterson?"

"No." Emma supposed causing one's heart to pound by simple proximity could not be considered annoying. Disturbing—perhaps. Unsettling? Certainly.

"Speaking of annoying, Aunt, I believe you win the prize in that category. Lambert tells me you insulted Lady Caroline to such a degree she and her family fled Knightsdale."

Lady Beatrice shrugged. "She insulted Queen Bess first."

"Good God, Aunt, you sound like Claire. Queen Bess is a *cat*."

"And Lady Caroline is a pig."

Emma muffled a giggle. Lord Knightsdale turned to stare at her. "I take it you agree with Aunt's observation?"

"Um."

"Of course she does. Anyone with eyes would agree with me. And she's a *nasty* pig besides. We are well quit of her." Lady Beatrice smiled, raising her lorgnette to survey the room. "I can think of a few other idiots whose absence would improve this house party." Her glass focused on Spots and Toad, who were sniggering by the door to the garden. "What do you suppose those two are up to?"

"Nothing good, I'm certain. I'll go find out, shall I?"

"Wait a moment. Perhaps it will pass." Lady Beatrice's lorgnette stopped on Mr. Stockley next. "Hmm, there's something familiar about that man."

"He *has* been here since yesterday morning."

"I know that, Charles. No, this bothered me the moment I saw him. Like a word on the tip of my tongue—I just can't quite retrieve the thought. What do you know of him, Miss Peterson?"

"Nothing much, Lady Beatrice. He's renting Mr. Atworthy's house—Mr. Atworthy decided to stay in Town."

"No one stays in Town after the Season, Miss Peterson." Lady Beatrice frowned. "Most unusual."

"You stayed, didn't you, Lady Beatrice?"

"Oh, no. Beastly in London in the summer. Dull as ditch-water, too."

"But I thought you came down from London for the house party?"

"I came *through* London."

Charles smiled. "I stayed in London, Miss Peterson, straightening out my brother's affairs. I am not so opposed to a *ton*less Town as Aunt."

"And who is Mr. Atworthy?" Lady Beatrice was scowling now. "I don't recognize that name."

"Aunt Bea, you'd best move your eyes—you'll set poor Stockley ablaze with the heat of your gaze focused through that magnifying lens."

"That might be a good thing," Lady Beatrice said, but she put her lorgnette down.

"Mr. Atworthy is relatively new to the neighborhood as well," Emma said. "I think he won the house in a card game from the Bannister heir shortly after old Mr. Bannister died."

"Ah, Bannister. Him, I remember. You must, too, Charles. Weren't you of an age with the heir?"

"I believe Bannister was Paul's age."

"Hmm. So where does Stockley get his money?"

"I'm not certain," Emma said. "I haven't interrogated the man."

Lady Beatrice raised an incredulous eyebrow. "Surely you asked a few polite questions?"

Emma shrugged. "I believe he said his family was in shipping."

"Shipping." Lady Beatrice said the word as though it were a curse.

"Perhaps my father knows more."

"I hope so, if he let the fellow run tame at the vicarage."

"Lady Beatrice, Mr. Stockley did not—"

Lord Knightsdale's hand came down on her knee. The shock of his touch stopped Emma mid-sentence.

"You're getting somewhat agitated, Miss Peterson. You might wish to lower your voice."

How dare the man tell her how to behave?

He chuckled. "And, no, don't blast me. Let that breath out slowly. I'll be delighted to let you flay me with your tongue later." He dropped his voice so only she could hear. "Flay or . . . other things."

"Lord Knightsdale!" Emma didn't know what he meant, but she knew that whatever it was, it was not polite.

"Stockley . . . Stockley . . . It will come to me eventually."

"I'm sure it will, Aunt. However, I believe I must go chat with Mr. Frampton and Mr. Oldston before whatever mischief they are planning comes to fruition. If you'll excuse me?"

Lord Knightsdale reached the garden door just in time to capture the piglet Mr. Frampton had intended to introduce into the drawing room.

"Can you believe there are such idiots in the world, Henderson? What were they thinking, to loose a pig in the house?"

"It has been my experience, my lord, that young men the age of Mr. Frampton and Mr. Oldston often don't think at all."

"I wasn't that stupid, was I?"

Henderson coughed into his hand and turned to hang up Charles's coat. "I believe you may have done one or two things that weren't terribly well-considered, my lord. Not dealing with livestock, however."

"Hmm. Perhaps. But—" Charles heard a scratching on the door connecting his room and Emma's. Blood rushed to a variety of bodily locations, not primarily his head. He swallowed and tried to clear his thoughts. "I believe that will be all for tonight, Henderson. I can manage from here."

Henderson cleared his throat. "I'm sure you can, my lord. Please do not do anything stupid."

"Right. I shall try not to. Thank you. Good night." Charles walked toward the connecting door, making a shooing motion with his hand toward Henderson. He paused before he opened the door.

"Good night, Mr. Henderson," he mouthed.

Henderson shrugged, bowed, and departed.

"Well, Emma." Charles had meant to say more, but the sight of Miss Emma Peterson in her nightdress with her curly, dark-blond hair frothing over her shoulders took his breath away—as well as most of his rational thought processes. Add the small detail that she was standing between their bedrooms, and it became very hard to focus on anything besides the part of him that was very hard—and what he would most like to do on either or both of the lovely soft beds at their disposal.

"What, ah, seems to be the problem?"

Emma raised her arms to push back her hair, making her nightgown pull against her breasts.

Charles closed his eyes and prayed for self-restraint. And that he wasn't drooling. He rubbed his hand over his face and swallowed.

"My bonnet is gone, my lord, as well as my hairbrush. I've looked everywhere and I cannot find either."

Her voice was retreating. He opened his eyes to see her walking toward the fire.

God, grant him strength. Her lovely, worn, thin nightdress barely obscured her lush form. The fire behind her outlined her wonderful breasts with their dark nipples. Her slender waist, all the more remarkable, placed as it was between such full breasts and hips. Her hips, her thighs, the lovely, dark shadow covering . . .

A gentleman would tactfully hand the lady her wrapper.

Gentlemen led exceedingly dull lives.

"What is the matter with you?" she whispered sharply. Her hands went to her hips, stretching the fabric tighter, giving him an even better view of her glorious body. "You are standing there like a knock in the cradle."

"Pardon me." Charles averted his eyes from her form—and examined the bed instead. Bad choice. He studied the floor, pausing to ascertain that he was not advertising his attraction too blatantly. Thank God he had put on his dressing gown. Any physical evidence of his admiration was hidden by its generous folds. "My mind has been wanting—um, *wandering*. My apologies. What is the problem?"

"My bonnet—someone has stolen my bonnet." Emma stood in front of her open wardrobe and pointed.

"Are you sure?" Happy to have something to do besides lust after Emma, Charles moved to examine the wardrobe. "Here it is," he said, holding up the bonnet she had worn around the lake.

"Not that one. The other one."

"The other one?"

"The one I wore on our fishing trip."

Charles blinked. "Miss Peterson, no self-respecting thief would steal your fishing bonnet."

"Well, it's not here."

"Perhaps the maid mistakenly thought you had discarded it."

"Why ever would she think that?"

"Because you *should* have discarded it. I believe the most destitute drab in the stews of London would be embarrassed to own that ancient piece of headgear."

"Well, of all the—"

"Miss Peterson, did you really think that bonnet was attractive?"

Emma flushed. Charles could see her struggling between honesty and the honest desire to put him in his place.

"No," she said finally, "but that doesn't mean I like the idea of someone taking my things."

"Well, yes, I can see that would be distressing." Charles tried to think. He could smell her now— a heady mix of lavender and lemon and woman. "Did you say there was something else missing?"

"My hairbrush."

He frowned. "Was *it* valuable?"

"Well, no."

"Could you have misplaced it?"

"Where?" Emma gestured at her dressing table. It was completely bare—no chance of the brush going missing on that clean surface.

"Could it have fallen on the floor?"

Charles knelt to look under the dressing table.

Emma leaned close to peer over his shoulder. At least that is what he assumed she was doing. He felt her nightgown brush against his arm and he turned his head.

Oh . . . God. He was staring directly at the lovely, beautiful, wonderful, unbelievable apex of her legs. Only a thin bit of fabric came between him and the dark, curly hair he could just make out spreading over her . . .

He swallowed. He tried to remember to breathe— and inhaled the musky scent of her secret place. If he just reached out now, he could clasp her soft, round bottom and bring her to his mouth. He could bury his face in her, then bury another part of him there, too.

"I don't see it, do you?" Miss Peterson asked.

"Wha—" Charles sprang out of his crouch and slammed his head against the bottom of the dressing table. He saw stars—and then Emma bent over him and he saw breasts.

"Where did you hit your poor head? Let me see the back of it."

She pulled him toward her. If he pretended to lose his balance right now, he would fall face first between the soft, round globes swaying tantalizingly close to his mouth. He could see her lovely, dark nipples rubbing against her nightgown. He knew they would taste sweet, though not as sweet as . . .

"I'm fine," he croaked, struggling out of her hold. He made certain his dressing gown was firmly closed before he attempted to stand. Frankly, he was surprised that its generous cut was able to cover his tremendous attraction.

"Are you sure? You look a little . . . odd."

"No, no." He cleared his throat. "I'm fine. Truly.

Hard—*barely* a bump, see?" He touched the top of his head and winced.

"See, you *are* hurt." She stretched to touch his head again—that was not the part of him aching the most. He swayed his hips back so as not to impale her on his need. A step or two backward, a careful stumble, and he would land on his back on her bed with her lovely weight on top of him.

"See, you are in so much pain, you are beginning to perspire."

He gripped her shoulders and turned her, pushing her ahead of him toward his room. He had to get away from her bed before he ravaged her like the rutting animal he was.

"I am *fine*, Miss Peterson. Simply splendid. Couldn't be better."

"What are you doing?"

"You need to brush your hair. I am sure I must have a brush you can borrow. In fact, I will even tend to your hair for you."

It might kill him, but having his hands in her hair—the hair on her head—was a much saner idea than any of the others he was currently entertaining.

Lord Knightsdale was behaving most peculiarly. Why was he pushing her toward his room? Did he have dishonorable intentions? She should put her foot down—dig her heels in, literally.

She could not quite bring herself to do so. She really wasn't afraid of him. And she was curious. She wanted to learn what his room looked like—not that it had been his room very long. But still, she wanted to see the place where he was most private. And if she learned one or two other things, well, she was strangely eager to do so. Perhaps Mrs. Begley and Lady Beatrice were right—she worried too much about propriety. She needed to take a few risks.

She paused on the threshold. The dark, heavy furniture and the blue and gold curtains must be his father's or his brother's choices. Still, there were many masculine touches that could only be Charles's— the cravat pins carelessly tossed on the dresser, the clutter of papers on his bureau, the—

"Look!" Emma reached under the papers and pulled out her brush. "How did this get here?"

"I don't know." Charles took the brush from her and examined it. "Pardon me for saying so, but it doesn't look like this would tempt a thief."

"No, but how did it get in your room? Could someone have been looking through your papers?"

"And brushing her hair at the same time? Doubtful." Charles shuffled through the things on his bureau. "Looks like everything is in order."

"In order?"

He chuckled. "I stand corrected. It looks as though everything is here."

"Good. Then I'll just take my brush and go back to my room."

Charles held the brush out of her reach. "I don't think so. I have offered to play your maid, and I am determined to do so."

Emma's heart started to thump in a most unsettling fashion. "That's ridiculous. I can brush my hair myself."

"I'm sure you can." Charles sat her at his dressing table and ran his hands through her hair. "However, I will brush it tonight. It is the price you pay for disturbing my evening in the hunt for your missing possessions."

"I didn't mean to trouble you—"

Charles laughed. "Oh, Miss Peterson, if you only knew." He started the brush moving through her hair.

She closed her eyes the better to feel the long sweep of his strokes. He had just the right mix of gentleness and firmness. The bristles massaged her scalp and pulled through her hair, separating, but not pulling it. His broad hands smoothed it off her forehead, off her ear, her neck.

"You've done this before."

"Perhaps."

"You don't have a sister or a wife."

"You ask too many questions."

So he had brushed the hair of his ladyloves. The thought took a little of the enjoyment from the experience.

"Don't frown, sweetheart." She felt his lips on her forehead, and her eyes flew open. He smiled. "Trust me, I haven't done this quite this way before." His voice was oddly husky. "Mmm. No, not this way at all."

His lips grazed her temple and traveled to her cheek. She made a small sound and instinctively tilted her head. He chuckled and moved to nibble on a sensitive spot just below her ear.

She inhaled sharply. Her breasts felt so odd. Could her nipples actually be doing whatever it was they were doing? They felt like they were . . . pointing. She was afraid to look in the mirror. And there was a definite dampness between her legs.

"My lord . . ."

"Shh, Emma. Don't be afraid. We are only playing. I promise to keep my lips above your shoulders and my hands above your waist, all right?"

"Uh . . ."

All thought left her head as Charles's hands found her breasts.

"Oh!"

"Mmm. Lovely. Your breasts are so beautiful, sweetheart. Perfect."

"But—"

"Shh. Don't worry. Relax. Doesn't this feel good?"

Emma certainly could not deny it felt good. Sinfully good. Charles had his hands on her breasts and was massaging them. He cupped them from below, lifting their weight. His fingers stroked their sides. She let her head fall back against his chest. She arched her back, thrusting her breasts higher.

"That's it, sweetheart. God, you feel so good."

His lips traced her jaw.

"Open your eyes, love. Look in the mirror."

"No . . ." But she did. What she saw was shocking. Her mouth open, her face flushed. His face against hers, the dark stubble of his beard, the brilliant blue of his eyes, heavy now with . . . desire? Was that what the odd light was? And his hands, his fingers, dark against her white nightgown. One finger touched her nipple and she shuddered.

"Emma." He pulled her up into his arms, flattening her breasts against the hard wall of his chest. His hands moved up to cup her jaw, and he opened her lips with his, his tongue surging in to fill her. She had to grab his shoulders or fall. Her body sagged against his.

His hands slid down her back but stopped at her waist. His mouth traveled down her neck but stopped at her collarbone. She wanted his hands on her bottom, his mouth on her breasts.

Had she lost her mind?

She shoved against his shoulders and he loosened his hold.

"What are you doing to me?" My God, she was panting.

So was Charles. "What are you doing to *me*?"

"You tell me," she said. "You're the one who has been this way before."

He laughed. "Not exactly." He took a deep breath and grinned. "We are seducing each other, sweetheart. I would love to pick you up right now and carry you over to that delightful bed behind me to continue our explorations. Would you like to do that, too?"

"No."

"Liar." He kissed her once more quickly and turned her toward her room. "But you are probably right. You should go back to your own bed—alone."

Emma almost ran to the door.

"Do you not trust me, sweetheart? Or is it yourself you doubt?"

"Good night," she said, pulling the door closed behind her, shutting off Charles's soft laughter.

"Sleep well," he whispered through the wood.

Emma touched the door softly, then walked resolutely to her large empty bed.

She was certain she would not sleep a wink.

CHAPTER 10

Charles stared up at the bed canopy and sighed. It was almost dawn. He would go for a swim. Hell, if he'd taken himself off to the lake last night after Emma had closed the connecting door, he might have cooled his blood enough to have gotten some sleep. As it was, he had tossed and turned all night. His body just could not relax. He took his pillow and put it over his least relaxed body part.

Well, he must have slept a little because he'd had some splendid dreams. Could there be anything more exquisite than the feel of Emma's large, soft breasts in his hands, their lovely weight resting in his palms? Mmm. Perhaps the taste of her nipples. She had shivered so nicely when he had touched her there—would she scream when he suckled her?

He closed his eyes, smiling. He'd give anything to cradle those breasts again and to put his face between them. To run his hands over her well-turned ankles, up her shapely legs, her milky thighs to the lovely dark thatch that had tempted him last night. To kiss her there . . .

He shoved the pillow down. It was most definitely time for a trip to the lake.

He swung his legs out of bed and grabbed his breeches. He yanked them on, buttoned them securely, and pulled a shirt over his head.

If only he were not a gentleman, he could have had Emma in his bed last night. It would have been so easy. A few more kisses. A few more touches. If he had let his hands—and his mouth—wander lower. . . . He closed his eyes, imagining her silky wetness, her sweet taste.

He could have brought her fulfillment without taking her virginity. It would have been his pleasure.

And maybe he could have taught her to bring him pleasure.

He hoped the lake was very cold indeed.

He let himself out of his room and moved quietly down the corridor. He didn't want to wake anyone— he didn't want anyone speculating why the marquis was moving about at this ungodly hour, an hour that could have been spent so delightfully in a warm bed with Emma.

Why was she fighting him? She certainly appeared to enjoy his touch. Was she afraid? Was that why she would not agree to wed him?

He would have to coax her out of her virgin nerves.

He would tease her a little. Tempt her. Brush up against her, stand close to her, touch her lightly when they spoke. Make her burn for him so her fears would burn away. He grinned. And he was certain he could misplace any manner of small objects in her room.

How *had* her brush ended up among his papers? He shrugged. It was odd . . . but he wasn't complaining. Not at all. He hoped for many more such odd occurrences.

* * *

Emma pulled her brush through her hair—and remembered Charles's hands doing the same task. Well, it wasn't a task when he did it, it was . . . She didn't know what it was. Indescribable. The feel of his hands tangling in her curls, his broad palms smoothing her skin, his fingers touching her . . . She swallowed.

She put the brush down and hid her burning cheeks in her hands. He had had his fingers on her breasts. On her nip—No, she couldn't even think it. But she could feel it. Her body pulsed with the memory.

At least he had not touched her bare skin. At least she had had her nightgown on.

What if she had not had it on? What *would* his fingers have felt like on her skin?

She tried to take a deep breath as she fanned herself with her hand.

She had spent all night twisting in her sheets. She could not get comfortable. Her body felt too . . . sensitive. She wanted that connecting door to open and Charles to come in and finish what he had begun. Whatever the finish might be.

Mr. Stockley had spoken of urges. Emma giggled with a touch of hysteria. These feelings were more than urges. They were a fever, an illness—a madness. And her cure was just on the other side of the connecting door.

What if she opened that door and said yes, she would marry him, if he would put out the fires he had set in her veins?

She thought he would be happy to oblige.

Would that be so terrible? She suspected that children resulted from such activity. She would like children. He needed an heir. They would both be happy.

And then he would go off to London.

Was a woman impregnated the first time the man did whatever he did? Would they perhaps have to try the procedure more than once? Many times? Maybe if Charles enjoyed the efforts enough, he would stay at Knightsdale, at least for a while. The girls would like that.

But would she?

What of love?

She threw her brush down on the dressing table. She was so confused. She needed to clear her thoughts. She would take Prinny out for an early-morning walk. Then Isabelle could sleep in if she wanted. Emma certainly wasn't sleeping.

She got dressed, took her good bonnet, and quietly made her way down the hall. Prinny had decided he much preferred staying with the girls. Emma suspected Claire was charming Cook out of a few choice bones and smuggling them up to her room.

She found Prinny on Claire's bed.

"Prinny?" she whispered. Prinny's ears twitched and his head popped up.

"Come on, let's go for a walk."

Prinny's toenails clicked over the floor, but Claire didn't stir.

Emma put him on a lead until they were free of the house and he had expended a small portion of his energy. Then she decided she would risk losing him over having her arm dislocated. He tore off ahead of her in pursuit of a squirrel.

Was Meg out on the estate somewhere, collecting specimens? She often got up early to go plant hunting. Emma paused on the broad greensward and looked back at the house. The sun was just lighting its sandstone walls and glinting off the windows. She had always liked its orderly facade best of the great houses in the neighborhood—Westbrooke had been added to so haphazardly over the centuries that it was now an architectural mishmash; Alvord, a castle, gave her a closed-in feeling.

If she married Charles, she would be the mistress of Knightsdale.

She walked down toward the lake. She liked Mrs. Lambert, the housekeeper. She would have no trouble getting along with her. She loved Isabelle and Claire. She would be close to Meg, able to keep an eye on her. And she'd be close to her father.

What was she thinking? The house, the children—none of that really mattered. What was important was Charles. Did he love her—or was she just a simple solution to a pressing problem? Could she stand to enter into a marriage of convenience?

No, not with Charles. Not the way he made her feel. She needed him too much. She knew it. She would hang on him when he was in the country and pine for him when he was in Town. That would not be good for either of them. He would come to resent her—and her heart would break.

She heard Prinny yapping up ahead.

"Prinny!"

The yapping only got louder. Had he found Meg? Did she need help? Emma picked up her skirts and ran down to the lake.

She could hear Prinny, but she couldn't see him. He must be behind the bushes ahead of her. She ducked under a hanging branch and between two overgrown shrubs.

"Pri—"

She skidded to a stop, gaping.

"Good morning, Miss Peterson."

"Uh." She scrunched her eyes tightly closed and then opened them again. The vision had not gone away. The Marquis of Knightsdale was standing under a tree by the lake, bare as the day he was born. Well, not quite so bare. He did have a towel wrapped around his waist—a towel that Prinny was frantically trying to remove.

She swallowed, her mouth suddenly dry. She had gotten a generous look at him the night he had come ghost-hunting in the nursery, but then he'd been partly wrapped in a sheet. Quite a bit more of his glorious body was displayed for her inspection this morning. The strong column of his neck; the broad expanse of his shoulders; the muscles bulging in his upper arms as he clutched the towel; the light brown curls sprinkled over his chest, trailing down to his navel and below—how far below, she couldn't say. The towel blocked her view. Fortunately. Yes. She was very fortunate the towel blocked her view.

Prinny gave another tug on the corner he'd gotten in his mouth and the towel slipped slightly.

"Do you suppose you could call off your dog, sweetheart? Unless you would like to see even more of me than you are currently studying? Not that I object, of course. I am always happy to oblige a lady. I'll just let Prinny have the blasted towel, shall I?"

"No!" Emma leapt to grab Prinny's collar. She reattached his lead and tried to persuade him to release his prize. She struggled to keep her eyes on Prinny's jaws, not Charles's legs. His bare feet. His toes.

"Prinny, bad dog!" she said. Her voice sounded weak to her own ears. *Forget the marquis's toes,* she told herself. "Prinny, let go now!"

Prinny growled. He was not interested in cooperating.

"I'm sorry, my lord," she said, looking up the length of him from where she crouched on the ground with Prinny. "It looks like—oh!" She stared at his towel. There was a very large bulge poking out from his body. "Have you dislocated something?"

"What do you mean?"

"Something is not right, my lord. See?" She reached toward the object.

"Don't touch."

Emma sat back quickly. "There's no need to shout. Are you in much pain?"

His entire body—at least all that she could see—turned bright red.

"Yes. I am in intense pain. I am going to die in about five seconds if you do not turn around and close your eyes this moment."

His voice sounded clipped. She looked all the way up to his face. His mouth was pulled tight.

"Can't I do something to help?"

"Yes, you can. I am positive you can cure my condition, but not today. Today you will turn around, put your hands over your eyes, and keep them there until I tell you to remove them. No peeking. Do you understand?"

"I am not one of your privates, my lord."

"Privates. Oh, God. Just do as you are told, Miss Peterson. Please? I beg of you."

"Oh, very well." Emma did not really want to add to his suffering, but she did not care to be shouted at. Still, she supposed allowances needed to be made for a man in obvious pain. She turned . . . but if she put her hands over her eyes, she'd have to let go of Prinny. "My lord," she said, beginning to turn back.

"Freeze, Miss Peterson."

"But . . . oh!" Emma felt a jerk on the lead and then watched Prinny run off down the lake, dragging Charles's towel in his mouth.

She slapped her hands over her eyes.

Charles struggled to get his breeches on. He looked longingly at the lake. He needed an icy dip even more now. To have Emma examining him in such detail . . . God, it had been slow torture. And she didn't even know what she was doing to him—what she was looking at. He would dearly love to show her. If only he could take her up to his bed now. He could relieve some of his tension. A little relief would make buttoning his bloody breeches easier.

If he didn't marry her soon, he was going to go mad, utterly and completely mad.

"My lord, you should not be out here without your clothing on."

"You sound like a governess, Miss Peterson." He finally got the last button closed. "Are you peeking?"

"No!" she squeaked. "But you should not be out here swimming like that. Anyone could come along."

"Anyone did come along." Charles tugged his shirt over his head.

"Exactly. Meg is probably out here somewhere, looking for specimens. What if she had stumbled on to you? Or Miss Oldston or Miss Pelham or—"

"Or the patronesses of Almack's. Sweetheart, the London ladies will not stir from their beds for hours—and when they do, they are not going to come running outdoors. They will have their chocolate and fiddle with their toilette and maybe make it downstairs by luncheon. I am not worried about encountering any of the London misses by the lake when the sun is barely up."

"Well, what about Meg, then?"

"Meg is—or was when I came out—in the kitchen, talking to Cook. I warned her I was going for a swim."

Charles smiled, remembering Meg's knowing grin. He'd wager Meg had a good idea why he'd felt the need for a morning dip. Certainly more of a clue than her lovely, oblivious sister.

"You can uncover your eyes now, Emma. I'm decent."

Emma spun around. Her eyes immediately fell to the flap on his breeches.

"You are sure you are all right, my lord?" She reached out again as if to touch him. Charles waited, hoping, but no, she stopped and pulled back her hand. "You do look better. There was something clearly amiss with your anatomy earlier. Did you notice?" She flushed and straightened her shoulders. "I know I should not be raising such an intimate topic, but you seemed in such pain. Have you had a surgeon examine you?"

"God have mercy, woman, there is nothing amiss with my anatomy, as I will be delighted to show you once you agree to marry me." He grabbed her and pulled her into his arms. "Perhaps I'll show you sooner, if you continue to torture me in this fashion."

"My lord!"

He had had enough of looking and talking. It was time for touching—past time.

She struggled for an instant and then sagged against him. Her mouth opened readily when his lips touched hers. She was learning.

He tasted her slowly, thoroughly. There was no rush. They were sheltered here by the lake, and it was true that no one else from the house party would be out this early. And if they were, and Miss Peterson were compromised? Well, his intentions were honorable. Completely honorable.

She made a funny little noise in her throat, like a cat purring. He leaned back against the tree trunk, taking her with him, stroking the side of her breast. She whimpered, arching into his hand. He rubbed her nipple with his thumb, and she melted against him. He ran one hand down her back to her bottom, pressing her against his poor, aching anatomy.

He really, really wished there was a nice, soft bed handy.

Emma was melting. Her limbs felt heavy, her knees were useless—she could no longer stand on her own. There was an aching emptiness low in her belly and a disturbing wet throbbing between her legs. Was she ill? She certainly felt fevered. She should move back from Charles. She would, in just a moment. Once she was capable of movement.

Then his finger touched her nipple, and she was no longer capable of thought. Feeling, yes. Lud, she could feel him. She needed to feel him.

His lips grazed her jaw. She turned slightly, tilting her head back against his upper arm, giving his mouth room to roam where he wished. Where she wished.

His lips touched a spot high on her neck, just below her ear. Tendrils of warmth, of need, coiled through her. He moved slowly down her throat, leaving soft, moist kisses, taking her breath away. She moaned.

She felt so warm. Hot. Her breasts felt swollen. She needed him to touch her. She needed to feel his hands on her as she had the night before. She panted, arching, thrusting her breasts higher, begging him silently to touch her.

He did. One hand cradled her jaw, stroked her neck, her shoulders while the other pressed her lower body close. His leg came between hers and she nestled against him. The pressure of his hard, muscled thigh against her ache felt wonderful. She rocked.

"That's it, love. Yes, Emma. Sweet."

His hand loosened the neck of her dress and slipped it down. His fingers—his bare fingers— touched her skin. It was shocking. Or would be shocking if she had any ability to feel shock. She didn't. Her emotions were too occupied with this strange, fevered need that consumed her.

And then his lips touched her breast. She threaded her fingers through his hair, holding him close. His tongue rasped against her nipple. His mouth sucked. His other hand kneaded her bottom, urging her to rock harder against his thigh.

Something was happening to her.

"Charles." Her voice sounded thin and reedy.

"Shh, Emma. It's all right. Come on, sweetheart. You can do it. Come on, love. I'm here. It's all right. I have you. I won't let you go."

Emma felt wild. Wanton. Mad. Desperate.

Something was happening. She was so tense. Charles sucked on one breast and then the other. She felt the cool morning air and the sun on her nipples. She was exposed for the world, for Charles to see. She was beyond caring. She was possessed by need. She panted and writhed against Charles. He grabbed her bottom in both hands, guiding her, helping her rub against him.

It was not enough. Not quite enough. Something was just beyond her grasp.

Charles pulled her tight against him, putting his hand where his thigh had been. He cupped her there, and then his fingers rubbed up against her, against some sensitive small point. . . .

She shattered. His mouth captured the strange sounds she made as something powerful pulsed through her. And then she collapsed against him. She was so limp, she could not lift her head. She let it lie heavy on his chest as her pounding heart gradually slowed to normal.

"Beautiful, Emma," Charles whispered. "So beautiful." His hands kneaded her bottom, stroked her hair. She was draped against his thigh. Small tremors still shivered through her. She closed her eyes. She wanted to stay exactly where she was forever.

By the lake, draped across the Marquis of Knightsdale's body, her gown down around her waist, in full view of any passerby.

Emma yelped, pushed away from Charles, and ran for the house, pulling her dress up as she went.

"What have you done to Emma, Charles?"

"What do you mean, what have I done to Emma, Aunt?" Charles looked up from his papers. This morning Aunt was attired in a violet and apple-green dress. He wondered—not for the first time—how her mantua-maker could bear to perpetrate such crimes against good taste.

"She won't come out of her room. Says she's indisposed."

"Oh? And why must I have anything to do with her indisposition?"

Aunt Beatrice leaned on his desk and skewered him with her eyes. "Because Lavinia Begley said she saw Emma running up from the lake early this morning. It looked as though there was something the matter with her dress. And then, not many minutes later, you came along with Prinny."

Charles was very much afraid he was blushing. "Miss Peterson had an, um, accident with her gown. I brought the dog along so she could return immediately to fix the problem."

Aunt Bea snorted. "Or perhaps she returned to escape the problem. How exactly did this . . . accident . . . happen?"

"I really can't say."

"Can't say? That's rich. Won't say, more like."

"Aunt, I hope you are not insinuating I made inappropriate advances." Inappropriate? Scandalous, more like. He ignored the thought. "I have only honorable intentions."

"Oh, climb off your high horse. I am not complaining. Make all the advances you care to, just slip a ring on the girl's finger before you slip something else between her thighs."

"Aunt!"

"For God's sake, Charles, you ain't a virgin, are you?"

"That is not your affair—but I certainly thought *you* were."

Charles blinked. Aunt Beatrice actually blushed—the color did not go well with her ensemble.

"And that," she said, "is not *your* affair."

"Right. Quite agree. Not my affair." The thought was . . . There *had* been rumors . . . No, he couldn't let his mind contemplate . . . Well, if she had had a paramour, the fellow must have been color-blind. Though one assumes she would have removed— No, he would not think about it.

"Emma, however, *is* a virgin." Aunt paused and raised an eyebrow. "She is, isn't she? I mean, still? You didn't . . . ?"

"No!"

"Good. However, I believe you did *something* to her." She shrugged. "Young girls are so skittish nowadays. You probably only gave her a little too intense a kiss, though there is the matter of her dress . . ."

Aunt looked him over carefully. Charles kept his face expressionless.

"Hmm. Well, whatever happened, it obviously unsettled her. Go upstairs and apologize. Very nicely. Very thoroughly. I want to announce your betrothal at the ball."

Charles acknowledged as he climbed the stairs that he had let his passion outrun his good sense that morning. He was as certain as he could be that the kiss he'd given Emma in his curricle the day he arrived had been her first. And that kiss had been a mere brushing of lips. Well, with Emma nothing was "mere." But still, he should never have taken her so far and so quickly down the road to seduction as he had by the lake.

He knocked on her door. "Emma?"

"Go away."

He looked down the corridor. The Misses Farthington stared interestedly back at him. He bowed and continued on to his room.

He knocked on the connecting door.

"Emma?"

"Go away."

"We need to talk, sweetheart." He pushed on the door. It didn't move. "Have you put something in front of the door, Emma?"

"Yes." Her voice sounded muffled, as though she had been crying.

"Sweetheart, you don't have to be afraid of me. Let me in. I promise we will only talk. I won't touch you or distress you in any way."

Silence greeted this statement. Charles took this as an encouraging sign.

"Emma, you must have questions. Do you understand what happened at the lake?"

"No!" This was delivered in a wailing, teary tone, followed by a definite sniff. He felt the oddest sensation, as if his heart had turned over in his chest.

"Let me come in, Emma. We can talk quietly. You don't want anyone to overhear our conversation, do you?"

"No." This time there was a touch of panic also. He heard her cross the floor and push something out of the way. She opened the door. Her poor eyes were swollen from crying.

"Emma." He broke his promise without a second thought. He squeezed past the small chest she had pushed in front of the door, and drew her gently up against him, holding her close. "Emma, sweetheart, I'm so sorry I upset you. I didn't mean to frighten you."

She sighed and leaned against him.

"Come." He led her back to the big chair by the fire and pulled her down onto his lap. He held her head against his shoulder, stroking her hair as he would Isabelle or Claire.

He loved the feel of her body relaxed and heavy against his. He was amazed he felt no lust. Oh, it was there, of course, but like an orchestra playing in the ballroom when one was standing on the terrace. Wonderful, magical, but in the background.

He felt strangely content. He rested his cheek

against her head, kissing her hair, breathing in her sweet scent.

"What did you do to me?" she whispered against his chest.

How to answer that question?

"I made love to you, sweetheart."

He felt her tense.

"So, am I . . . um . . . Am I . . . p-pregnant?"

He might have found the situation funny, if she hadn't been so distressed.

"No, Emma, you aren't pregnant."

"Are you certain?"

"Completely certain, sweetheart. There is no way you could be increasing."

"But something very . . . odd happened to me."

She was whispering again. He had to hold his breath to hear her.

"I felt so . . . wild. Needy. I ached for you to . . . I don't know . . . *fill* me in some way."

Charles took a deep, shuddering breath. Now he felt lust. It threatened to stampede all his good intentions.

He knew exactly how he could fill her.

"You had your lips on my . . . um . . . you know. Like a baby nursing. And then, I—I . . . shattered. Something inside me pulsed and, and everywhere got hot and flushed and then . . . it all relaxed."

"Uh." God, he was going to explode. "Um, that sounds a little uncomfortable. Did you like it, sweetheart?"

She was silent for a minute, and Charles thought his heart would stop.

"Yes," she whispered finally. "I liked it."

He sighed and hugged her closer. "I'm glad."

"But how do you know I'm not increasing?"

"Because . . ." What could he say? He did not think she was ready for the specifics. "Because something has to happen to me, too, sweetheart, to make a baby. And that thing did not happen today."

"Oh." She looked up at him. "Were you sorry the thing didn't happen?"

God, he had to kiss her. He brushed his lips over her forehead.

"A little sorry, sweetheart, because it feels very nice. But I knew it wasn't the right time."

She dropped her face before he could taste her lips. Her fingers twisted one of his waistcoat buttons.

"So, you've made babies before?"

"No!" At least he was almost certain no children had resulted from his other encounters.

"Then how do you know it feels nice?"

Charles felt desperate. "I just do, Emma. You will have to trust me on that. It's something men know."

"That sounds like humbug to me."

"Well, it's not. Now, do you forgive me for this morning?"

She nodded. "I guess so. But I have one more question."

"Yes?" Charles felt a sinking in his stomach as she dropped her eyes to her hands. Why did he think this was going to be the hardest question?

"You said you made love to me."

"Yes."

"Does that mean you love me?"

Charles felt as if he had just been kicked in the stomach.

Emma had been so frightened and so embarrassed. Embarrassed when she thought of how she had behaved by the lake; frightened when she thought she might be increasing. She was unmarried. How could she care for a child? Where would she live? Hot shame drenched her. Her father, Meg—they would be so shocked, so disappointed.

She could not imagine what her father would say.

She locked the door to the corridor and pushed the chest in front of the connecting door. She did not want to see Charles. She held her hands to her burning cheeks. Oh, God. He had *seen* her breasts. He had had his *mouth* on them, on her nip— She squeezed her eyes tightly closed. He had *touched* her. And she had writhed against him, like, like . . . She didn't know what she had been like. The entire event was beyond her experience.

No, what had happened at the lake didn't bear thinking of, yet she had spent these past hours thinking of nothing else—when she wasn't crying, terrified she was enceinte.

She was possessed by Charles. It was a madness. When she closed her eyes, she saw him as if his image had been burned into her eyelids. She saw him standing in the morning light like a Grecian god, saw his broad shoulders, the muscles of his arms, his chest. Inches and inches of warm skin.

She hugged herself—and felt his hands sliding over her again, over her bottom, her breasts. She felt his lips, his tongue on her skin, his mouth sucking. She felt the wet, throbbing emptiness between her legs. Her skin grew hot and sensitive.

What was the matter with her? This illness was beyond the lust she had felt in the conservatory, beyond the urges Mr. Stockley had warned her of. It truly was a madness.

So when Charles had scratched on her door, she'd

been both afraid to let him in and afraid to keep him out. When she'd seen him standing there, she couldn't say if he were her salvation or damnation. It didn't matter. Whatever he was, she needed him.

She almost cried with relief when his hands touched her and brought her up against his chest. She breathed in his scent, the clean smell of linen and soap and something else, something male.

He was so calm. His hands and voice soothed her. He made the tight knot of fear and shame in her stomach relax.

He was Charles. He was the boy she had idolized as a girl, who had dried her tears when she'd cried all alone by the stream in the woods. He was the young man she had dreamed of when she was putting her girlhood behind her. He was the first man she had kissed, the only man who had touched her.

She let him pull her down to sit on his lap. She felt warm and protected. There was none of the tension and turmoil she'd felt at the lake. Well, perhaps there was some. Just a little. She felt his hard shoulder under her cheek and his hand stroking through her hair. A pulse began to beat low in her middle.

"What did you do to me?" she'd asked.

"I made love to you, sweetheart," he had answered.

She'd tensed. She had heard Mrs. Lambert say those words to a pregnant maid once.

"Oh, he made love to you, did he, girl? He gave you a slip on the shoulder, that's what he did, and you'll be paying for it in a few months' time with a wailing babe."

"So, am I . . . um . . . Am. I . . . p-pregnant?"

"No, Emma, you aren't pregnant."

He'd sounded so certain. He must know. Men were taught these things.

She'd felt immeasurable relief, so she'd told him

how she'd felt by the lake, how she had been over-
come by madness. He had not sounded shocked.
Well, it probably was not shocking to him. He had
done this all before, with other women. It wasn't anything special to him.

That had become painfully apparent when she'd
asked her last question.

"You said you made love to me."

"Yes."

"Does that mean you love me?"

His silence left little doubt as to his answer, so she'd
made her feelings just as clear.

She'd slapped him.

CHAPTER 11

"I think our plan's not working, Isabelle. Mama Peterson and Papa Charles look like they're angry with each other."

Isabelle nodded. She and Claire were sitting on the landing, watching the house party leave for a picnic. Uncle Charles had come up to Miss Peterson more than once, but she had turned away from him every time.

"We have to think of something else, Claire." Isabelle frowned. She had been so certain the hidden hairbrush would bring Uncle Charles and Miss Peterson together. "Is there something else of Miss Peterson's we can put in Uncle Charles's room?"

"What about her nightgown, Isabelle? Let's hide that!"

Isabelle nodded. "She'll definitely need her nightgown. I think she has only one."

"Well, if she has more, we'll hide more." Claire stood up as the last houseguest left the hall. "Let's go. We'll hide them good, so Mama Peterson and Papa Charles will have to look a long time."

* * *

"It doesn't look good, Lavinia."

"I wouldn't give up hope yet, Lady Bea. It's not like there's any competition. Lord Knightsdale is not a fool. He would never pick a widgeon like Lucinda Pelham or Amanda Oldston."

"Miss Haverford is a nice enough girl, I suppose." Lady Beatrice shrugged. "I'm certain she could get the job done."

"Perhaps, but she is too young, as you have said."

Lady Beatrice nodded. She and Mrs. Begley were sitting in the morning room, drinking tea—only tea. "I would like Charles to engage his mind, not just his . . . you know. If he marries simply to procure an heir, I'm afraid he'll stay at Knightsdale only long enough to accomplish that goal. The estate—and the girls—need him here on a more permanent basis."

"Exactly. No, I think Miss Peterson is the only real option."

"So, what can we do to ensure my idiot nephew makes the proper choice?"

"Hmm. I'm not certain. It will take some thought. Perhaps we should enlist the efforts of the Society."

Lady Bea snorted. "I don't suppose it could hurt. Looks like the boy is making micefeet of things by himself."

Emma was furious, and the more she thought about the concluding scene with Charles in her bed-chamber, the angrier she got. Lord Knightsdale had taken incredible liberties with her person, and he didn't know if he loved her? She could have danced a quadrille to his hemming and hawing as she'd hissed him out of her room. He'd barely gotten his backside over the threshold before she'd slammed the door.

She was furious with herself as well. She had stupidly assumed the physical activities they had engaged in reflected more than physical lust on his part. She snorted. She was a pathetic, naive, twenty-six-year-old virgin—did she think men *loved* the whores they frequented? Her stomach lurched. Surely she meant more to Charles than a whore?

She strode up the stairs to the nursery. It had started to rain. Most of the house party guests had decided to move the picnic into the ridiculous replica of the Pantheon Charles's grandfather had had the lunacy to build. Emma had not cared to listen to them "ooh" and "ahh" over the statuary. She had walked back by herself.

"Nanny, where are the girls?" Prinny heard her voice and came dashing out of Claire's room, barking madly. "Shh, sir. You are disturbing the peace."

"Visiting Cook—shush, ye heathen beast!"

Emma frowned. When was the last time Claire and Isabelle had had their lessons? She had been extremely neglectful of her duties. Well, that would change. Tomorrow she would come to the schoolroom first thing in the morning.

"Very well. I'll take Prinny down to the long gallery and let him exercise a little. The house party guests are all picnicking at the Pantheon."

When Emma reached the gallery, she learned that she was mistaken. Mr. Stockley was there before her. He was admiring the long line of Knightsdale ancestors arrayed in artistic splendor on the walls of the gallery. She stopped and bent to grab Prinny's collar. She definitely did not want to repeat her experience with Mr. Stockley in the grotto, especially so soon after her upsetting interlude by the lake with the evil marquis. She started to drag Prinny toward the stairs but stopped to stare at Mr. Stockley's odd behavior.

He was looking *behind* the paintings. She blinked. Yes, he did it again. He carefully lifted the frame away from the wall and peered behind it. Then he stuck his hand into the space and moved it up and down. Whatever was he thinking?

Prinny thought this activity unusual as well. He started barking. Mr. Stockley jumped and almost knocked the bust of Charles's Great-Uncle Randall off its pedestal.

"Miss Peterson. I thought you were at the picnic."

Emma entered the gallery. She didn't really have a choice. Prinny was determined to investigate Mr. Stockley's bizarre behavior. She gave up and let go of his collar. He tore off to sniff Mr. Stockley's boots. The man wrinkled his nose and stepped back.

"Could you call your dog off, Miss Peterson?"

"Prinny's really quite friendly, Mr. Stockley."

"Perhaps. However, the fact remains that I do not care for animals."

"I see." Emma was not surprised. She had decided Mr. Stockley was an unpleasant individual. She bent to grab Prinny's collar, but the dog danced out of her reach.

"Prinny, come here now!"

Prinny sneezed, suddenly losing interest in Mr. Stockley. He went off to sniff the wall behind Great-Uncle Randall.

"I would not say you have much control over your animal, Miss Peterson."

"Prinny is actually my sister's dog."

Mr. Stockley lifted an eyebrow, clearly not believing that statement. "I see." Then a corner of his mouth turned up and his voice got the oily quality it had had at the grotto.

Oh, Lud! He was wiggling his eyebrows at her again.

"I also see we're quite alone. Noticed I'd left the group at the Pantheon, did you?"

"Mr. Stockley!"

He chuckled, putting his hands on her shoulders. She tried to wriggle free. He tightened his hold.

"We were interrupted the last time we had a few moments alone, weren't we? I thought you might find your way to my room." He pulled her closer. "No matter. I'm happy to attend to you now."

"No, please." She almost choked. How could she have kissed this man at the grotto? He obviously did not make regular use of tooth powder. Prinny's breath was better than his.

"Mr. Stockley, I assure you—"

"Now, Miss Peterson—Emma—you are not a young miss. No need for these false protestations."

"They are not false. I wish you to unhand me, sir!"

"You wish me to get a hand under your skirts. I know. I shall be happy to oblige."

Under her skirts! Even Charles had not been under her skirts, though the thought was strangely appealing. But certainly not with this disgusting snake.

"Try it and I'll scream."

"Oh, and who will hear you? Your little dog, perhaps?" Mr. Stockley snorted. "What will he do? Challenge me to a duel? I'm quaking in my boots." He leaned closer, a very nasty light in his eyes. "But thank you for the warning. I'll be sure to cover your mouth before I cover your—"

Emma did not wait for more information. She screamed as loudly as she could, but Mr. Stockley was quick. His mouth slammed down onto hers before she had gotten her lungs more than slightly emptied.

It didn't matter. Someone had heard her. Mr. Stockley let go of her and yelled much louder than she ever could have hoped to. Prinny, her savior, growled.

"You bloody—"

Prinny dropped his mouthful of blue superfine and doeskin and bared his teeth, obviously prepared to take another bite from Mr. Stockley's backside. The man saw reason. He turned and fled, treating Prinny and Emma to glimpses of his snowy-white rump.

"Good morning, Miss Peterson."

"Where's your beau?"

Emma looked up from the book she was reading to stare at the Farthington twins. "Excuse me?"

"They mean Papa Charles, Mama Peterson."

Emma frowned at Claire. "Back to your letters, miss."

The Farthington twins giggled.

"*Papa* Charles," Miss Esther said.

Miss Rachel grinned. "I'd wager Lord Knightsdale would make a very good papa."

"And be very good at earning that title, if you know what I mean," Miss Esther whispered, elbowing her sister in the ribs.

The ladies giggled harder.

"Oh my, yes. Those shoulders . . ."

". . . those legs."

"Mmm. Wears his breeches quite well, don't he?"

"Ladies, please!" Emma felt her cheeks flush. She looked back at Claire. Both she and Isabelle were watching the twins with bright, interested eyes. "Did you come up to the schoolroom for a specific reason?"

"Oh, no."

"Just passing by."

No one "just passed by" the top floor of Knightsdale.

"We'll be going now."

"We'll tell the marquis where he can find you."

"That's quite all right. Please, don't bother."

Emma watched the two elderly ladies leave. She hoped they made it down the stairs safely.

"Now what do you suppose that was about?"

Claire and Isabelle just giggled.

"I just saw Lord Knightsdale go into his study."

Emma centered the tallest red rose in the vase of flowers she was arranging in the drawing room. "Thank you for warning me, Miss Russell."

"No, I'm not warning you, I'm telling you." Miss Russell leaned closer. "He's alone."

"Oh?"

The older lady nodded vigorously. "It would be a perfect time for . . . you know."

Emma straightened her spectacles. "No, I don't know."

"You don't?" Miss Russell frowned. "Lavinia said she'd seen you coming back from the lake with your dress falling—"

"Yes, well, thank you, Miss Russell. I will certainly take note of Lord Knightsdale's whereabouts. So good of you to tell me."

Miss Russell beamed. "I knew you'd want to know. I'll finish up the roses for you."

"Thank you. That would be very kind."

Emma smiled and almost dashed from the room, hurrying to get as far from Lord Knightsdale's study as possible.

* * *

"Miss Peterson—Emma—do you have a moment?"

Emma pulled her head out of the schoolroom cabinet she was inspecting.

"Not you, too, Mrs. Begley."

"I have no idea what you mean." Mrs. Begley looked at Claire and Isabelle. "Girls, why don't you take Prinny for a walk? I have a few words of a private nature to share with Miss Peterson."

"Is it about Uncle Charles?" Isabelle smiled.

Claire grinned. "The Misses Farthington have already told Mama Peterson what a good papa he'd make."

"Have they? Well, yes, I do wish to discuss Lord Knightsdale, so be dears and run off."

"Girls!"

"We'll be back, Mama Peterson."

"I'm sure Prinny does need a walk, Miss Peterson."

Emma watched the children leave and then turned to Mrs. Begley.

"*Mama* Peterson?"

Emma flushed. "Lady Claire would dearly love a mother. It seemed kindest to allow her to call me 'mama,' though she is supposed to do so only when we are alone."

Mrs. Begley nodded and cleared her throat. "So, the Farthington twins stopped by, did they? They can be a pair of ninnyhammers sometimes."

Emma nodded. "Yes, indeed."

"However, in this case they are quite right. Lord Knightsdale *would* make a splendid papa."

"Lady Begley—"

Lady Begley held up her hand. "No, hear me out, Miss Peterson. You don't have a mother to advise you, and I know you and Mrs. Graham are not on the best of terms."

"Mrs. Begley, please . . ."

"You *need* a married lady to speak to, Miss Peterson, about the um . . . married life. About the marriage bed. About conjugal relations."

"Mrs. Begley!" Emma was certain she was going to burst into flames, her cheeks were so hot.

"Now, I know you're almost thirty. . . ."

"I'm *twenty-six*, Mrs. Begley."

"Twenty-six, then. Most girls your age are married with a quiverful of children. But you've lived a sheltered life, and you've had your papa and sister to care for."

"Yes, yes."

"I just don't want you to be afraid of . . . you know."

"No, no, I'm not afraid of . . . of anything."

"Because some girls, they don't like it much. I suppose with the wrong man, it could be uncomfortable, or even unpleasant."

"You really don't need to—"

"But the, um, conjugal act is really quite nice. You do understand what a man and woman do in bed together?"

"Uh . . ."

"No, no one has told you, have they? Well, men, they take their, their . . . *thing*." Mrs. Begley made a vague gesture toward her waist. "And they put it, um, where it goes." Another vague gesture to her waist. "The first time may hurt a bit, but after that it can be quite lovely. And there's usually a bit of kissing and snuggling and . . . and kissing that goes on." Mrs. Begley got an odd, almost dreamy expression on her face. "Squire is very good at it, you know."

"No! No, please, don't feel—" Emma did not want

to think about portly Squire Begley and Mrs. Begley doing anything that involved a bed and . . . *things* located anywhere near a person's waist. Squire Begley didn't even have a waist any longer.

Mrs. Begley grinned. "Very good at it, indeed. Why, just last night . . ." She sighed and shook her head. "Well, that's neither here nor there. The point is, Miss Peterson, that the marriage bed can be a very comfortable place. And I'm quite certain Lord Knightsdale knows how to please a lady. Why, if I didn't have my Squire and if I were a few years younger . . ."

"Yes. Thank you. I'm sure I understand now."

Mrs. Begley leaned forward. "But do you understand this is your best chance? Maybe your only chance? I don't mean to be rude, Miss Peterson, but thirty-year-old women—"

"*Twenty-six!*"

Mrs. Begley waved her hand dismissively. "*Twenty-six*-year-old women, if you will, are quite firmly on the shelf. Few, if any, men are interested in shopping there when they can have their pick of the new crop of fresh, young maidens. I mean, what exactly are you saving yourself for?"

Emma took an agitated turn around the garden. If she saw another member of the Society for the Betterment of Women, she would run away screaming. She turned a corner and spotted Lady Beatrice. Fortunately, Charles's aunt had not seen her. Emma ducked back behind a rose bush.

"Miss Peterson."

She turned to see where the whisper had come from. The voice didn't sound like it belonged to one of the Society ladies.

"Over here, Miss Peterson."

The Duchess of Alvord was sitting on a bench under a tree and waving. She laughed as Emma reached her.

"Whom are you hiding from?"

Emma smiled. "Lady Beatrice."

"Ah. Well, sit here beside me. We shall pretend to be in close conversation. If she comes our way, I'm certain she will be too polite to interrupt."

Emma was not certain of that at all, but, fortunately, Lady Beatrice did not come their way.

"If you don't mind my asking, Miss Peterson, why are you hiding from Lady Beatrice?"

"I'm afraid she is going to tell me why I should marry her nephew." Emma flushed. "I must sound very conceited, but I've had four other ladies corner me today to give me that message, so I expected I would hear the same thing from Lord Knightsdale's aunt."

"Interesting. And you do not want to marry Charles?"

Emma studied the duchess's face. Here was a woman—a young woman—who surely would understand. She was obviously completely in love with her husband—and the duke was wildly enamored of his wife.

"Lord Knightsdale doesn't love me."

"Oh." The duchess blinked. "Has he told you so?"

"No, but it's obvious, isn't it?"

"Not to me. In fact, I do think James said Charles was rather interested in you."

Emma shook her head. "Oh, he wants a wife—he needs one, now that he is the marquis. And I'm convenient. That's all it is."

"Are you certain? I have noticed his eyes follow you when you are in the room with him."

Emma blushed, her heart suddenly pounding. "Surely you imagine it!"

"No, I don't think so." The duchess smiled. "Has he shown you any marked attention? Has he sought you out in private? Has he perhaps kissed you?" She laughed. "Don't feel you need to answer those questions aloud. I am not so bold as to pry into your personal life."

Emma smoothed her dress over her lap. Mr. Stockley had kissed her, and he definitely did not love her. Lusted after her, perhaps, but love? No. Why would Charles's interest be any different?

Well, Charles *had* offered marriage.

This was exceedingly embarrassing, but she desperately needed to get some answers. She forced herself to confide in the duchess.

"Lord Knightsdale has, um, been somewhat particular in his attentions, so much so that I, I . . ." How could she say it? The duchess sat quietly, waiting. Emma reminded herself she needed advice. "I . . . I asked him if he loved me, and he . . ."

". . . he said no?" The duchess sounded appalled. "But you just told me that he had *not* said he didn't love you."

"No! Yes. I don't know. He didn't actually *say* he didn't love me, he just sat there and stared at me, mouth agape like a, a great cod!" Emma sniffed. She was shocked to feel tears trickling down her cheeks. She swiped at them with the back of her hand and bit her lip, but a hiccup escaped anyway.

She wanted to cover her face and wail. She felt as young . . . as lost . . . as if she were Claire's age.

"He said he liked me very much, that of course he cared for me. He went on and on, getting more and more tangled in his words." She swallowed, her face burning. "I think he just . . . lusts for me," she whispered.

"Miss Peterson—Emma." The duchess patted Emma's knee. "Please, it is not so bad. Actually, I think it is quite good. Here, dry your eyes."

Emma took the handkerchief the duchess offered—something had happened to her own—and sat back. She sniffed and hiccupped again.

"Where did this conversation take place?"

Emma blushed. "In my room."

"Your bedchamber?"

"Yes. It's shocking, I know, but . . ."

"No, no. I'm not shocked. It is quite all right." The duchess smiled. "I met my husband in an inn bedchamber. In bed. Naked."

Emma gaped. The duchess *was* an American. Perhaps . . . no, she could not imagine that American customs could be that different.

The duchess laughed. "It was rather a comedy of errors that led to that situation, and it took us quite a while to sort everything out, but I do believe—well, I'm actually happy to say—that James lusted after me from the very first moment he saw me." She blushed. "And he saw quite a lot of me. And I lusted after him, too. A little—or a lot of—lust is a very good thing, as long as it leads to marriage, of course."

"Lust is good?" Emma had never heard her father preach *that* sermon.

"Yes, I believe so, if by lust we mean strong physical attraction. Marriage is a very physical relationship, you know."

"Oh." Emma did not remember her own parents' marriage—she had been too young when her mother died—but Mrs. Begley had alluded to kissing and, and *something* earlier. And certainly her encounters with Charles had been extremely physical. Emma flushed, remembering their highly physical encounter by the lake.

"Yes, indeed. Without the physical component, there would be no babies." The duchess grinned, putting her hand over her stomach. "The thing to keep in mind, Emma, is that men are often uncomfortable with words. They are much better with actions."

"I don't understand."

"Well, what I mean is, men and women are different. Not that I presume to be an expert, of course, but I have given the matter some thought recently."

"I see." Emma swallowed her disappointment. She had hoped to find answers and instead got platitudes.

The duchess laughed. "No, I am not a complete widgeon. Of course men *look* different, but what many women never comprehend is that they really *are* different."

"I still don't understand."

"Of course you don't. It's a difficult concept to grasp. I spent weeks—months—at cross-purposes with James because I didn't understand that." She smiled. "Well, I was also trying to divine the thought processes of an English peer—quite a challenge for an American republican, I assure you. I will never understand the British system of primogeniture or . . . well, that's not the point, is it?"

She leaned closer. "Men don't think the way we do, Emma. For example, suppose another woman ignored you after church. I don't mean she gave you the cut direct—nothing so obvious as that. She just didn't greet you. What would you think?"

Emma frowned. "I suppose I might wonder if I had offended her in some way."

"Exactly. You might think about it and worry about it, wondering what you had done."

"Yes, I suppose I might."

The duchess nodded. "Women analyze every emotion, study every action, always expecting there to be some meaning to deduce. Men don't. I'm convinced of it. If a man ignored James—not that anyone would—the toadying he has to put up with . . ." She sighed and shook her head. "Anyway, if a man ignored James, James would simply assume the fellow hadn't seen him." She smiled. "It's quite refreshing, actually—makes life so much simpler."

Emma frowned. "I'm afraid I still don't see what that has to do with Charles."

"When you asked Charles if he loved you, Emma, you asked him to analyze what he felt for you. He probably didn't know the answer because he had never asked the question. He just knew he wanted you." The duchess grinned. "I assume you weren't just sitting primly in separate chairs having this conversation in your bedchamber?"

Emma blushed furiously. "Well, no . . . but then how can you tell if it's love or lust a man feels for you?"

"Emma, you are still thinking like a woman. There's probably not a difference in Charles's mind at the moment. Once he has satisfied the worst of his lust, he'll be able to realize that he loves you. Right now, he's not thinking with his head so much as"—the duchess blushed—"something else."

"Something else?"

"I am most certain Charles will be delighted to tell you all about that. I am not quite bold enough to attempt it."

"Sarah."

The duchess turned, and a broad smile lit her face.

"Over here, James."

Emma watched the duke approach. He, too, was smiling, and his face had the softened expression it got only when he looked at his duchess. But this time Emma noticed something else as well.

The duke's eyes held a familiar glint. She had seen it in Charles's eyes when he looked at her.

CHAPTER 12

Charles sat in his study, surrounded by mountains of papers. He definitely needed a secretary. He'd swear there were more papers now than the last time he'd sat here. Were they breeding?

Breeding. He sat back in his chair, his hands linked behind his head. How he would love to be busy breeding little Draysmiths with Emma. She had been exquisite by the lake. So responsive. He had almost spilled his seed in his breeches just watching her innocent passion.

He was dying to touch her without layers of clothing between them. To feel her skin against his—everywhere. To put himself inside her . . .

He shifted in his chair. The throbbing anticipation was almost unbearable.

God, when she'd come against his hand—it had been heaven. Well, purgatory, really. Heaven would be coming with her, in her, on a lovely, soft bed.

He had not handled the time in her room well, though. He frowned, rocking forward to put his elbows on his desk, running his hands through his hair. He had done fine until the end, until she had asked if he loved her. He should have anticipated that question, but he had not.

It had been a question he had scrupulously avoided for so many years.

Why did women have to talk of love? When he was younger, many of his bedmates had ended their sessions with that question—did he love them? It had ruined a perfectly satisfactory coupling. He had felt trapped. They all wanted something from him— a promise, a pretty bauble—something. The country girls wanted a few extra coins; the widows, a marriage proposal.

They all wanted to own a piece of him, if only a piece of his heart. He would not give it. He wanted no ties. He liked his freedom too much.

He learned to play only with professionals, women who understood that everything between them was strictly physical—well, and financial, of course. Women who understood the rules. Emotion, beyond satisfaction and perhaps some friendship, did not enter into bed play.

But this wasn't bed play, was it? This was marriage. Family. Children. A line to continue.

Odd. Since he'd taken such a distinct interest in Emma, the title didn't weigh on him anymore. The crushing depression he'd always felt when he thought of being tied to Knightsdale was gone. Instead he felt . . . anticipation.

Because of Emma.

If that anonymous Italian thief had not shot Paul and Cecilia in the Italian Alps, sending their carriage splintering down the mountainside, he would not have come back to Knightsdale and found Emma Peterson all grown up. *That*—not knowing a treasure such as Emma lived in Kent—would have been the tragedy of his life. If his brother appeared on the doorstep today, he would be happy to see him. He would gladly hand back all his duties and leave, but he would take Emma with him, if he could. Well, and he would share with Paul his thoughts concerning the proper upbringing of young girls before he left.

Did he love Emma? If love was this consuming need that hummed through him every moment of the day and night—especially the night—and almost overwhelmed him whenever he was near her—yes, he loved her. He had to have her in his bed—not just once but every day. Several times a day. In several different ways. His lips slid into a slow smile. He would so enjoy teaching her the pleasures of the marriage bed.

And he would learn a few pleasures himself. He could bury himself in her and let his seed flow into her womb with no need for a condom or withdrawal. She was a virgin and fertile. He was supposed to give her children.

He wanted to watch her grow round and heavy with his babes. He wanted to watch them nurse at her breast. He wanted to raise Isabelle and Claire with her. He wanted to wake with her head on the pillow by his every morning. He wanted to grow old and wrinkled with her, to know her body as well or better than his own.

He grinned. Yes, he loved her.

He would tell her, and then he would give her the Knightsdale betrothal ring. He would get it now. It was in the safe here in the study. The thief had not stolen it—it had still been on Cecilia's finger when her body had been returned to England.

He frowned. The solicitor had not been able to tell him what exactly had been stolen, yet the man had insisted an Italian thief had caused the deaths. Paul,

Cecilia, all their servants had been killed. There were no witnesses. Crandt, the solicitor, had relied on Italian investigators who had examined the accident scene. All the baggage had been torn apart as if the thief were searching for something. Even the coaches' seats—those that had survived the fall off the mountain—had been slashed and the padding ripped out.

Why? Had Paul turned smuggler? Was he carrying state secrets? Charles had not been able to discover anything in London. He had given up trying. What was the purpose? Paul was dead.

He opened the safe. All the family jewels were there. Well, maybe not all. He chuckled as he took out the betrothal ring and slipped it in his pocket. The summer he was seven—it was before Emma moved to Knightsdale—Great-Uncle Randall had come to visit. He and Paul had pretended the man was a pirate. They'd spent the summer digging around the estate, searching for hidden jewels and gold doubloons. Great-Uncle Randall had probably laughed himself silly when he'd been sober enough to notice.

He closed the safe. Still, it might have been true. Randall had a raffish quality to him. The sculptor who had fashioned the bust of him that summer had captured it well.

Charles grinned as he left the study. Perhaps he would tell the girls the story. He would wager Claire would love to go treasure hunting.

Every time Emma looked at Charles during dinner, he was looking back at her. It was extremely disconcerting. She pushed a French bean around her plate and tried to listen to Squire Begley discuss his hunting dogs. She couldn't look at him without re-calling his wife's conversation earlier. She couldn't look at his waist without blushing. She kept her attention firmly on his face. His lips. The Squire and Mrs. Begley kissing? And snuggling, whatever that meant. It couldn't mean what Charles had done with her, could it?

Emma scooted her bean under a cabbage leaf. She had quite lost interest in eating.

She turned to address a question to Mr. Frampton on her other side. Mr. Frampton responded enthusiastically, displaying a significant quantity of masticated mutton for her inspection. She returned her attention to her French beans.

Could the Duchess of Alvord be correct? Was it possible that Charles did care for her?

She glanced at him again. He was listening to Lady Haverford, his head tilted politely toward the older woman, but when he noticed Emma looking at him, he gave her a slow smile that caused the most amazing creases in his right cheek.

Oh, my. Emma's eyes retreated to her plate once more. She was eager for the next course, if only so she'd have a change in scenery.

Charles had that glint in his clear blue eyes again. And that . . . focused look, as if there were no one else in the room but her—as if, for that instant, Lady Haverford had ceased to exist.

"Gentlemen," Lady Beatrice said as the sweets were set on the table, "I propose you dispense with your port this evening and join us ladies in the drawing room immediately after dinner for a game of charades."

This announcement was met with groans from all sides of the table.

"Not charades, Lady Bea," the Earl of Westbrooke said. "Have pity, please."

The Duke of Alvord laughed. "Now, Westbrooke, I'd wager there's a frustrated actor somewhere in that soul of yours."

"Well, you'd lose, Alvord. I hate acting, and I hate guessing even more."

"Aunt," Charles said, "our goal is to entertain, not torture our guests."

"Well, I love charades, Lady Beatrice." Miss Pelham leaned forward to address Charles's aunt at the other end of the table. "I'm quite good at them, so I would be happy to be on Lord Westbrooke's team." The young lady batted her eyelashes furiously in Lord Westbrooke's direction.

Lord Westbrooke's face assumed a hunted expression.

Emma glanced at Meg, who rolled her eyes and tilted her head, gesturing up the table to Lady Elizabeth. Lizzie, brows furrowed, mouth in a tight line, was scowling at Miss Pelham.

"We'll play, won't we, Rachel?" Miss Esther Farthington chirped from Mr. Maxwell's left.

"Indeed yes, but only if we are on different teams," Miss Rachel said from Mr. Maxwell's right.

Mr. Maxwell continued working his way through the sweet tray some unwary footman had set within the old man's reach.

"We fight when we are on the same team," Miss Esther confided to the table at large.

"Can't agree on anything."

"Argue terribly."

"Much better to separate us."

The Farthington twins smiled genially—and identically—at the company. The company goggled back.

"Yes, well," Lady Beatrice said, breaking the stupefied

silence, "if everyone is quite finished here, we should adjourn to the drawing room. Mr. Maxwell, *Mr. Maxwell*," Lady Beatrice shouted in an attempt to get the man's attention. "*We are going to do charades now.*"

"Parades? Don't like parades. Do like these little cakes. Got any more?"

"*No.*" Lady Beatrice stood, putting an end to any further discussion, and led the ladies into the drawing room. The men followed, grumbling.

"I shall assign the teams—let's see, how many of us are there?" Lady Beatrice looked around the room.

"Can't count Maxwell," Charles said in Emma's ear. "He'll be snoring the moment he settles into his chair."

"Charles, can't you bring your aunt to heel?" Lord Westbrooke muttered behind them. "Charades— good God!"

"The twins look very happy to be participating," Emma said.

Lord Westbrooke snorted. "They would."

"You heard Miss Pelham, Robbie," Charles said. "She's an expert. She's delighted to give you all the help you need."

"As if that will improve the experience. I think she's decided she can't snaffle you, Charles, so she's set her eyes on me. I've been dodging her all day. Had to enlist Lizzie's aid in defending myself at the Pantheon this afternoon—she and Meg kept me company so dear Miss Pelham couldn't corner me and yell compromise."

"Surely it is not as bad as that, Lord Westbrooke."

"Indeed it is as bad as that, *Miss Peterson*. Why are we so formal these days? You certainly weren't 'my lording' me when Charles here fished you out of the stream that day a few years ago."

"A few years ago? I was only six and you *tripped* me."

"I did not. My foot was perfectly visible—I can't help it if you stumbled over it, can I?"

"Your foot was not perfectly visible until you stuck it in front of my feet."

"Children," Charles said, "you *will* give up this argument some day, won't you? Or will you still be squabbling about it when you are the Farthingtons' age?"

"Oh, I don't know—it's so amusing to ruffle Emma's feathers."

Emma opened her mouth to protest but stopped when she saw the laughter in Robbie's eyes.

"Shall I apologize, finally, Miss Peterson? Shall I say—just to be a gentleman, of course—that it was all my fault?"

He was teasing her. All these years, she had been harboring a grudge, thinking he was doing the same—and he had been teasing her. He enjoyed the verbal sparring. He thought it was fun.

She let her breath out and smiled. Had she been too serious? Perhaps. Arguing over a minor childhood event *was* ridiculous. She grinned.

"Oh, please, don't start now—especially just to be a gentleman."

Robbie pretended to wipe his brow. "Well, that's a relief. I'm certain the strain of being a gentleman would be too much for my poor heart to sustain."

"Definitely too much," Charles said.

"Lord Westbrooke!" Lady Beatrice waved her hand at Robbie. "Stop trying to hide over there. You will be with Mr. Oldston, Miss Rachel Farthington, Miss Margaret Peterson, Lady Elizabeth, Miss Frampton, and Miss Pelham."

"Oh, God," Robbie muttered. "I'm not leaving

this room unless I have Meg on one side and Lizzie on the other. Protection. I need protection."

Emma chuckled. "Are you also in need of protection, Lord Knightsdale? You are a bigger catch than Robbie."

Charles sighed. "Emma, my dear, why do you continue to call me Lord Knightsdale? You were able to say 'Robbie' very nicely. In fact, I have heard my name on your lips before." He dropped his voice and leaned closer. "I think I've tasted my name on your lips."

"We are in a public forum, my lord. Behave yourself."

"So when we are in a private location, I don't need to behave?"

Emma turned red, remembering in exquisite detail their encounter by the lake.

"Hmm," Charles said. "You look a little flushed, sweetheart. Are you perhaps thinking of our encounter this morning? I actually did behave myself then, Emma. Believe me."

"My lord, how can you say so?"

"Because I know exactly what I would have done if I had not behaved. I exerted extreme self-control then, as I did later in your room. We need to talk, *my love.*"

Emma drew in her breath. Did he mean something particular by those words? The glint in his eye was most pronounced.

"Charles, stop whispering in Miss Peterson's ear and come here," Lady Beatrice said.

Emma closed her eyes, wishing when she opened them again, she might find herself alone in her bedchamber. No. When she opened her eyes, Lady Beatrice was gesturing to her.

"Come on. Charles, you and Miss Peterson will join

Mr. Stockley, Mr. Frampton, Miss Esther Farthington, Miss Oldston, and Miss Haverford."

"Why doesn't Alvord have to play?" Robbie had managed to put a settee between him and Miss Pelham.

"I believe us old wedded folk are excused, Westbrooke." The duke grinned, sitting down next to his wife. "Such jollifications are reserved for the unattached."

"That's ridiculous. Squire, what about you? Would you like to join in?"

"No, no, Westbrooke. Quite content to watch. I'll be cheering for you, though."

"And Miss Russell? Surely you would like to participate?"

"Oh, no, my lord. No, thank you, no."

Robbie looked around the room. "Mr. Maxwell?"

A snore was Mr. Maxwell's reply.

"What did I tell you?" Charles murmured to Emma.

"Stop stalling, sir." Lady Beatrice handed Robbie a slip of paper. "You and Miss Pelham—"

Emma covered her mouth to hide her grin at Robbie's expression. To call it a glare would have been too kind. Lady Beatrice appeared to notice, too. She paused and stared at Robbie before she continued.

"And Lady Elizabeth and Mr. Oldston may act it out."

"Shall we sit, Miss Peterson? This may prove to be more entertaining than the best Drury Lane farce."

Emma let Charles lead her over to a settee. Mr. Stockley took his place on one end just before they reached it.

"Please, join me, Miss Peterson." Mr. Stockley patted the place next to him.

To ignore the invitation would be rude. Emma perched on the edge of the seat as far from Mr.

Stockley as she could get, which was not far enough.
It was a very small settee. She was pleased to see the
man wince as the seat shifted under him. Prinny had
left his mark. Mr. Stockley would think twice before
wiggling his eyebrows at her again.

He might also think twice since Charles was glaring at him from an adjoining chair.

Robbie had handed Miss Pelham the slip of paper,
folded his arms, and taken up a spot against the
mantle. Miss Pelham and Mr. Oldston began a
heated whispering exchange; Lizzie listened for a few
minutes and then went to stand with Robbie.

"Ah, Miss Peterson." Mr. Stockley glanced at Charles
as he leaned over to whisper to Emma. "About this
afternoon—ouch."

Emma smiled. "Have you hurt yourself, Mr. Stockley?"

"Slightly. Nothing to be concerned about."

Emma wished Prinny were nearby. She was certain
he could be persuaded to take a larger sampling of
Mr. Stockley's person.

"This afternoon?" Charles's frown caused a deep
furrow between his brows. "Weren't you at the Pantheon this afternoon, Stockley?"

Stockley startled and winced again as his weight
shifted on his injured backside. "Yes, my lord, I was
for a while."

"I encountered Mr. Stockley examining the pictures in the long gallery, my lord." Emma looked at
Mr. Stockley. "Very thoroughly."

"Connoisseur, Stockley?"

"Hardly, my lord. A student, merely. Always *searching* for . . . knowledge."

Emma blinked and examined Mr. Stockley more
closely. The menacing note she had heard in his
voice that afternoon had reappeared.

"Really?" There was an edge to Charles's voice as well. "I'd be extremely careful what sort of knowledge you pursue, especially if it involves Miss Peterson in any way."

Emma blinked again. Charles was almost growling, like a dog with its hackles raised.

"Rape!"

Emma's head swiveled back to the charades players. Miss Rachel Farthington was bouncing on her seat, shouting. Mr. Oldston had his arms around Miss Pelham, who was struggling wildly. Robbie and Lizzie were holding their sides, laughing.

"What the devil . . . ?" Charles started forward, but Mr. Oldston let Miss Pelham go. In fact, both he and she were crouched in front of Miss Rachel, smiling and encouraging her.

Charles frowned at Lady Beatrice. "Aunt, you didn't . . . you never had them act out *The Rape of the Sabine Women?*"

"My lord," Miss Pelham said, clearly annoyed, "you have given it away!"

Emma slipped up to her room as soon as she could. Charades had not been a success. Charles had examined the paper slips to see what other titles his aunt had planned for the company and had declared them all unsuitable. Lady Beatrice had objected, and the two of them had stepped into the hall to discuss the matter. The moment the train on Lady Beatrice's mulberry and orange gown cleared the threshold, the men escaped to the billiard room. By the time Lady Beatrice and Charles returned, the company was severely depleted.

Unfortunately, Mr. Stockley had not left. He kept

hovering near Emma, which enraged Charles. Emma did not like Mr. Stockley, but she found she liked constant argumentation even less. By Charles's fifth cutting remark, she had the beginnings of a headache.

Now she could not find her nightgown. She looked through the wardrobe one more time, not that there was any chance she could have overlooked it. She had little enough clothing—there was no place for an errant nightgown to hide. It was definitely not in the wardrobe.

Well, she was not going to sleep in her dress. She would spend the night in her shift.

At least her hairbrush had not gone wandering again. She sat at her dressing table and began taking her hair down. She glanced at the door connecting her room to Charles's. How had her brush ended up among his papers? Could her nightgown be there now?

The thought made her skin bloom a fiery red. She wouldn't need her nightgown to stay warm tonight. Even her shift was too warm at the moment.

She stared at herself in the mirror, a wicked thought lodged in her mind.

What if she didn't wear her shift tonight? What if she slept with just the bedsheets covering her? No one would ever know.

Her skin began to tingle in a most unusual way.

She was twenty-six years old. A grown woman. If she chose to prance around her bedchamber as bare as the day she was born, who could object? She didn't even have a maid to be scandalized.

She stood and pulled off her shift before she lost her nerve. The night air caused goose bumps to prickle along her arms—and her nipples to harden into little pebbles.

She plopped back into her chair. The silk covering felt cool against her bottom—slightly slippery, smooth but with the barest hint of roughness. She shivered, sitting straighter.

She picked up her brush, concentrating on pulling it through her long, curly hair. At first she looked ahead, staring back into her own eyes, trying to ignore the rest of her reflection as if she would be turned to stone should she let herself look at her own body.

She didn't need to look. She felt. She closed her eyes, concentrating on the new sensations—the fire warming her skin; her hair sliding over her shoulders, caressing her breasts, teasing her nipples; the . . . freedom of her body as it moved though the air unconfined by the slightest touch of cloth.

Her breasts felt larger, more sensitive, their nipples aching. Another part of her was aching, too. The feelings were almost too intense. She gasped, opening her eyes.

She saw curly, dark blond hair and glimpses of skin reflected in her mirror. She gathered the heavy mass of hair in her hands and held it up so she could look at herself. She watched her breasts lift with her arms. They were large, golden in the firelight, nipples round and unbearably hard.

She knew men liked her bosom. She had not grown up in a convent—she had caught more than one fellow eyeing her bodice. She did not care to be ogled. She chose dresses with high necks as befitted the daughter of a vicar. She glanced at the wardrobe. Well, the blue satin ball gown was the one exception, and she had never worn it outside the fitting room. Would she have the courage to wear it to the house party ball?

Would Charles like it? The bodice was so small, it

would take him but a moment to have it down around her waist.

She let her hair fall. She hesitated, then took her breasts in her hands, lifting them, feeling their weight. Charles had done this the night he'd brushed her hair, but she'd had her nightgown on then. He'd had his fingers on her bare skin by the lake. He'd seen her clearly in the morning light. He had put his mouth, his tongue on her nipples.

She felt a wetness between her legs and leapt off the chair. She did not want to stain the beautiful silk seat.

She eyed her discarded shift. She was more than warm enough. She would leave it. She climbed into bed, removed her spectacles, and snuffed the candle.

She could not get comfortable. Where before her breasts had been sensitive, now her entire body was throbbing. If she stretched out on her back, she felt the sheets rub against her nipples and her bottom. She spread her legs, and need pulsed deep between them. A hollowness, a hunger, consumed her. She turned to her side, but the throbbing would not go away. On her stomach was even worse—she wanted to rub herself against the bed. She felt so hot, she was burning. Feverish.

If she touched herself where she most ached, where Charles had touched her, would that cure her?

No. She could not do that. It was too shocking—though how anything could be too shocking to a wanton old maid like herself, writhing naked in her bed, was debatable. Still, she kept her hands safely tucked under her pillow and tried to sleep.

She dozed. She dreamed of Charles naked by the lake. Of his shoulders. The muscles in his upper arms. His chest, the sprinkling of light brown curls trailing down to his navel and the towel just below. And then— She woke up, frustrated. Her imagination could not supply the details of what that towel had hidden.

After the fifth or sixth time she'd jerked awake, she gave up. Perhaps if she put on her shift, she would dampen the fire raging through her.

She was reaching for her spectacles when she heard a creak and then a scraping sound. She sat up, pulling the covers high. Something was moving on the other side of the room. Something white was emerging from the wall. . . .

She tried to drag air into her lungs. She screamed as loudly as she could, which did not sound very loud at all to her. Then she dove under the covers and began her prayers like the good vicar's daughter she once was and promised to be again if only she lived through the night.

CHAPTER 13

Charles put aside his book. He had read the same page at least twenty times. He finally acknowledged that he was not going to make sense of it tonight.

What the hell had Stockley been doing with Emma in the long gallery this afternoon? And he'd been buzzing around her all evening as well. At least Emma had given no indication that she enjoyed the man's attentions.

She'd bloody well better not enjoy them. She was his. He just needed to get her to acknowledge that fact.

He looked at the connecting door again. God, he would love to go in to her now. He needed to see her. To talk to her. To hold her. To . . .

Charles shifted position. He would have to go for another dip in the lake. He would never get any sleep in his current state of arousal. Hell, he wasn't even certain he could get his breeches buttoned. He had to persuade Emma to marry him before a certain organ exploded—and with it all hopes for the continuation of the Draysmith line.

He sat up and swung his legs out of bed, wincing. He had never been in this painful a state. He had to get relief soon. There were accommodating women at the local inn. Nan would take care of him—he had used her before. But he didn't want to visit the Green Man.

In truth, the thought of taking any woman other than Emma to bed was not the least bit tempting. No, it would have to be the lake. Emma had ruined him. If she wouldn't marry him, he was facing a long, uncomfortable life with many nocturnal swims.

He was reaching for his breeches when he heard an odd noise from Emma's room. He froze, heart pounding. He had heard such a muffled noise before, during the war. Women who were too terrified to fill their lungs to scream properly made such a noise.

He surged off his bed, ignoring his breeches and grabbing the candlestick instead. He needed to see the enemy—and the heavy brass candlestick would put a nice dent in a man's head if necessary.

He shoved the connecting door open, holding the candle high. No one. He searched the entire room. He saw no one, not even Emma. He came closer to the bed. There was a large lump in the center under the bedclothes. Cautiously, he grabbed a corner of the blankets and stripped them off in one quick motion.

He had found Emma. She was crouched into a ball, her head buried in her hands, her glorious hair spread around her and her lovely, white, soft, naked bottom in the air.

God, he was panting.

Emma drew in a breath and jerked up, twisting to face him.

He couldn't even pant. He couldn't breathe. He watched her full breasts move with her body, and his mouth went as dry as another part of him grew hard.

He had seen her bosom by the lake, but this was so much better. His eyes traced the long line of her neck, her delicate collarbone, the exquisite sweep of her milky-white breasts, her slender ribs.

"Emma?" he croaked.

"Charles?" She reached for her spectacles. "You're naked."

"Um, so are you, sweetheart."

God, her eyes had dropped from his face. They were staring at the most obviously male part of him. Very obvious, very male at the moment.

"Is *that* what was under the towel this morning?"

"Yes." Charles bit back a slightly hysterical laugh. "I usually carry it with me."

"But how does it fit into your breeches?"

"It collapses for storage." Charles put the candlestick carefully on the bedside table. He swallowed again, his voice shaking slightly. "Would you like to touch it?"

Emma hesitated, clearly curious. "May I?"

"Please."

She cautiously reached out her hand. He watched her small fingers come closer. He closed his eyes for a moment as he felt their butterfly touch. It was heaven, but too fleeting.

"Do all men have such . . . such appendages?"

God, he was going to spill his seed just hearing her talk. "Yes, sweetheart. It's an important part of making babies. Would you like to touch it again? I promise you won't hurt me."

Hurt him, no. Make him insane with lust, definitely.

Her hand came out again. This time she let her fingers explore, tracing the length of him, circling his width, even fondling the sacks that hung between his legs. He moved to give her more room to explore, spreading his legs slightly. He grabbed the bedpost tightly, biting his lip. Sweat trickled down his back. He was going to spontaneously combust, he had no doubt of it. He only hoped he would get the opportunity to bury himself in Emma's body before he did so.

"When I do this, it moves by itself," Emma said, stroking him. He did leap in her palm. He clenched his teeth, savoring the waves of pleasure that rippled from her hand.

"It's so hard and smooth, but the tip is soft and, and damp." Her finger spread his moisture over him and he jerked in her hand again. She giggled, moving her fingers up to the thick nest of curls at his base. "And the hair here is even curlier than the hair on your head."

He grunted and she pulled her hand back.

"Are you sure I'm not hurting you?"

"Yes. I am completely certain." God, did he shudder when he said that? He cleared his throat. "Completely certain."

"Your voice sounds funny."

Because he was mindless with lust. His knees were going to give out. He swore he was going to collapse on the bed—a very good idea—but first there was something he had to get from his room.

"Emma." Charles was delighted his brain was still capable of formulating a coherent thought. "Stay exactly—*exactly*—where you are. Do not move. At all. I will be back in a moment. Swear to me you will not move."

"Well . . ." Emma flushed and reached for the bedclothes. Her hand flopped around on the naked bed. "Where are the blankets?"

"I'll get them—later. You don't need them now.

I promise you. They are totally unnecessary. Super-fluous. Annoying, even. You are perfect the way you are. Don't move. Please."

She let out a short little breath. "Very well."

"Good. Splendid. Wonderful. Stay still."

Charles backed to the door, keeping his eyes on Emma. She did not move. In fact, she kept her eyes on the most prominent part of him. He could feel it becoming yet more prominent. Surely there was a limit to its growth? He was aching almost unbearably already.

He took a quick breath. Aching, yes, but not for much longer. Surely he would find relief tonight. If he didn't, he would die. It was the truth. If he didn't slide into her warm, tight body before another day dawned, he would . . . he would . . . he didn't know what he would do, but it would not be good. At the very least he would cry. More like he would run howling through the halls of Knightsdale completely, utterly mad.

"Remember . . . stay right there," he said as he reached the threshold to his room. "Do not move."

It would take only a second to get the betrothal ring. He knew exactly where it was. He would have it on her finger in a moment. And then he would have his body in hers—but not in a moment. No. It was her first time. He would take many, many moments. He would wait until she begged him to finish it.

If he could wait that long. Sadly, he was not certain of his staying power in this particular instance. He had been able to last as long as necessary in every encounter but his first—it was a point of pride. But tonight . . .

He feared he would be embarrassed tonight. He couldn't—he couldn't fail for Emma's sake, but she affected him so much more than any of the others. It was almost as if he were contemplating an entirely different act, an act he had never performed before.

"Don't move," he said one last time.

She raised her hand to push her hair off her face. Her breasts lifted and swayed with the movement. So beautiful.

"I'll be right back."

He would die, he would literally expire on the spot, if she suddenly remembered she was a proper English miss.

Emma watched Charles back toward the door. The, um, pokey part of him was the oddest thing she had ever seen. It stuck straight out from his body and bobbed a bit as he walked. He had clearly wanted her to touch it, but he had acted like he was in pain when she did.

It had felt so odd—hard and soft, hot and smooth. What could he possibly need in his room?

What was she thinking? He was probably going to get a weapon. He had come in answer to her scream, hadn't he? It was just the shock of seeing her naked . . .

Lud! She grabbed again for the covers. Where were they? She crawled to the bottom of the bed and saw them lying on the floor.

"You promised you wouldn't move."

She jerked her head up. Charles stood in the doorway, just as naked as he'd been when he'd left.

"But I'm not complaining." He smiled. His eyes glowed. "That is a very fetching pose, sweetheart."

Lud, she was up on her hands and knees, every

inch of her exposed for his examination. She flopped flat on the bed. He chuckled and walked closer.

"You still don't have any clothes on," she mumbled into the mattress. The cool sheets felt good against her burning cheeks.

"Correct. I don't foresee a need for clothes in the immediate future. In fact, I'm hoping that they will be very much in the way."

Mercy. She felt his broad hand stroke down her spine from her neck to her bottom. The mattress shifted, then she felt both his hands move down her back. Her front began to throb. She buried her face deeper in the bed. His hands were skirting her sides now, brushing against her breasts, dipping between her thighs. She spread her legs. She had to fight herself to keep from lifting her body up so his hands could slide underneath her.

"Where's your weapon?" She gasped as one of his fingers traced the cleft between her buttocks.

"What weapon?"

She moaned. His hands skimmed her thighs, so close to where she wanted them.

"Am I hurting you, sweetheart?"

She heard the laughter in his voice. "No," she panted. She was not going to let him distract her any longer. "Isn't that why you went back to your room, to get a weapon? You did come in here because I screamed, didn't you?"

"That's right, I did." His hands left her body. She almost cried. The bed shifted again and he appeared before her. His pokey thing was pointing at her, as if it wanted to be petted again. She grabbed the sheets to keep from reaching for it.

"What exactly was I supposed to rescue you from, Emma? I don't see anything threatening."

She lifted her head. She had to admit that there was nothing in the room at the moment. "I saw something over there." She gestured with her chin. "Something white, coming out of that wall."

"Coming out of the wall? Can you be a little more specific?"

Emma flushed. "Well, I didn't have my spectacles on at the time."

"Ah, another ghost like the one Nanny saw."

"No. Well, I'm sure I saw something. . . . " Emma was almost certain—but what could it have been?

"Here?"

Charles had a very nice back. Muscles flexed and rippled as he ran his hands over the wall.

"Is this where you thought you saw your ghost, Emma?"

"Yes." His body tapered from his broad shoulders down to his slim waist and muscled buttocks. She had had her hands on that part of him in the conservatory. He'd had breeches on then. What would his . . . what would *those* feel like without breeches?

"I don't see anything, Emma."

"Um." She was consumed with lust. Her mind was a haze, her entire body throbbed. It was shocking, but she wanted Charles to come back to her bed. She wanted him to show her more of what he had shown her at the lake. She wanted to know everything.

Even if he didn't love her.

It didn't matter. She loved him.

He was the reason she had never felt the slightest interest in any other man. Meg had been right—she had seen eligible lords as no different from elderly chaperones—except for one eligible lord, that is. Charles had spoiled her for all the others.

She had loved him from the moment he had dried

her eyes in the woods when she was six years old, when he had let her shadow him, even though Robbie and James had teased him. He had been her Lancelot then, her Robin Hood.

And when she was older, he had been the hero of all the Minerva Press novels she'd read secretly in her room. He'd frequented her dreams, comforting her when she was tired or discouraged, when raising Meg and keeping house for her father had overwhelmed her. At first he'd just draped his arm around her, kissing her forehead. But after she'd seen him with the anonymous woman on the terrace at his brother's wedding ball, he'd wrapped both arms around her, held her tightly, and kissed her on the lips.

And now? Oh, my. Now her dreams were hot, tantalizing. Frustrating. Some crucial details were still missing.

Well, she would learn them tonight. God help her, if Charles didn't come to bed right now, she was going to cry. She was twenty-six years old. She had never been with a man. As Mrs. Begley had asked, what was she saving herself for?

Even if she had to beg Charles, she was not getting out of this bed a virgin.

He turned, and her eyes dropped to his waist. She smiled. She did not think she would have to beg.

"No sign of any ghost, sweetheart."

"Um."

God, Emma's eyes had fastened on the part of him that most ached for her. He smiled. Perhaps that was not entirely true. His heart ached more. He had never thought such a feeling possible. If Emma wanted him to, he would just hold her tonight.

He fervently hoped that she wanted more of him than that. Much, much more. All of him. Every hot inch of him.

He cleared his throat and tried to clear his mind of his raging need. "I think I'd best stay here with you tonight. To protect you. Don't you think?"

Her eyes traveled slowly from his groin to his face, stopping along the way to examine his stomach, his chest, his throat. When she finally met his gaze, he was delighted to see innocent need reflected there. "Yes." Her tongue peeked out to wet her lips. "Yes, that might be a good idea."

"Sweetheart, trust me—it is a wonderful idea." He sat on the bed. "And I can think of some things we can do to take your mind off ghosts of any sort."

"Really?" Emma whispered. "What might those things be?"

He reached out slowly and stroked the side of one breast. "They involve touching."

"Mmm." Emma's eyes closed, and her tongue slid out again. "Touching is good."

He put a hand on her shoulder and gently turned her so she was on her back instead of her belly.

"Very good." He stroked the other breast, cupped and lifted it. It filled his hand so well, its weight just right. His thumb circled around her nipple, skirting the center.

Emma made a funny little noise in her throat. She arched her back, thrusting her breast farther into his hold.

"God, sweetheart, you are perfect."

"I am . . . I am . . . so . . . hot," she said. He watched her swallow, watched her lovely throat move. "Please. I need you. I need your . . . touch. Everywhere."

He drew his finger along the inside of her breast

up to her neck and rubbed his thumb over the pulse beating there. "Love, you cannot imagine how delighted I am to hear you say so. And I will be even more delighted to accommodate you—in a moment."

"No. Now."

"Ah, sweets. So demanding! I see that I am destined to be your slave—which I will be, willingly, on one condition."

"What?"

"That you marry me." He took the Knightsdale betrothal ring from the night table where he had put it before he'd gone ghost hunting. "I won't lay another finger—or anything else—on you until you agree to wed me."

"All right." Emma reached for the ring. Charles held it away.

"No, no, my impatient little love. This is a choice you are making forever. Think—if you can. Once I slide this ring on your finger, you are committed. You will be my wife, the mother of my children."

Charles paused, listening to his own words. The sapphire in the family ring caught the candlelight. Giving it to Emma was another tie binding him to Knightsdale. He expected to feel a sinking in the pit of his stomach. He expected to feel trapped. He did not. He felt certain. He knew Emma was the woman for him.

And he felt anticipation. Great anticipation. Her lovely body was spread before him, every inch glowing in the candlelight. As soon as he had his ring on her finger . . .

"Say yes, Emma. I need you."

She looked at the ring and then at him. "But do you love me?"

He grinned. "Yes, sweetheart, I believe that I do. I know I feel something for you that I have never felt before. Just thinking about you makes me happy—and other things."

"What other things?"

Charles laughed. "Hot. Hungry. Hard. Insane with desire."

"Oh. That sounds a trifle uncomfortable."

"It is more than a trifle uncomfortable, love. Marriage to you is my only cure, I fear. If you reject me, I shall expire right here in your bed and quite possibly the Draysmith line will die with me. The title will pass to dear Cousin Aubrey, who, according to Aunt Bea, is disinclined or incapable of fathering an heir."

"You are being ridiculous, my lord."

"I am definitely *not* being ridiculous, Miss Peterson. I am being utterly and completely honest. I am in desperate straits. I am in agony. If you don't consent to wed me right here and now, I will go mad. I am certain of it."

"That's not possible."

"It is, sweetheart. Trust me. I feel my sanity slipping as we speak. Say you'll marry me. Please. Say yes."

Emma grinned. "Yes."

Charles laughed. "Yes? That's it?"

"Yes, please."

"I don't suppose you love me?"

"I don't suppose I do."

Charles frowned. He had assumed . . . He had thought if he loved her, she would of course. . . But of course not.

She rolled over on her side, leaning up on her elbow, and reached out to rub the furrow between his brows. "I don't suppose I love you, you looby—I *know* I love you. I have loved you since I was six years old, though it didn't feel quite like this then."

"No, I don't suppose it did." He felt dizzy with relief.

"I tried to deny it, to ignore it, but it wouldn't go away—even when you would not say you loved me."

"I'm sorry. . . ."

Emma put her fingers on his lips. "Enough talking. I, too, find myself on the verge of madness. You said you would touch me if I agreed to marry you. I've agreed, so . . ."

"Ah, yes. So gauche of me to delay. Give me your left hand, sweetheart." He slipped his ring on her finger. "There." He kissed her palm. "Now, I believe you have done your part, haven't you? I can only do mine."

"Yes. Please. Now."

"I am your slave to command. Where would you like to be touched first?"

Emma flushed. "Do I have to say?"

"Hmm, perhaps I can guess. Your nose? Your eyebrows? Your cheek?" Charles let his lips follow his words, kissing each part of Emma's face in turn, slipping off her spectacles and putting them on the night table.

"No. Yes. Oh."

"You are not terribly coherent, Miss Peterson."

She turned as red as a beet and looked him in the eye. "My breasts, Lord Knightsdale. I should like you to touch my breasts."

"Ah, your breasts. What a splendid idea. They are very lovely breasts, aren't they? I should be happy to touch them. Ecstatic."

Charles smiled as Emma arched up when he grazed one of her lovely breasts with the edge of his hand.

He could see it was going to be a splendid night.

* * *

Charles's hands felt *wonderful.* They were large and warm and they were moving over her. This was much better than the time by the lake. Lovemaking was greatly improved by a soft bed and a closed door. And the absence of clothes. Definitely. She ran her fingers over the hard, curved muscles in his upper arms.

There was one problem. His hands were scrupulously avoiding the area she most wanted them to touch. She whimpered and arched up, trying to encourage him. He chuckled.

"So impatient, sweetheart. I will get to every lovely inch of you. We have all night."

"I want you to get to this particular inch *now.*"

"Ah, I see I am betrothed to a shrew. A bossy"—he drew one finger up her breast from her rib cage to just below her nipple—"strong-willed"—he circled her nipple, avoiding the aching center—"termagant." His thumb flicked over the hard nub. She squeaked and her hips lifted off the bed.

"Was that a happy sound?"

"Yes. Lud, yes. Your mouth. Your tongue. I need them there, like at the lake. Please."

"Oh? Like this?"

He bent his head. His tongue rasped over her aching nipple, finally. He sucked, drawing her into his mouth. She felt it all the way to the hot, wet place between her legs. She threaded her fingers through his curls, holding him to her breast. She never wanted him to stop.

He stroked down to her waist and splayed his hand across her stomach. She squirmed. If his hand would just move an inch or two lower . . .

"Sweetheart, you can wriggle all you want—I am not hurrying." He grinned down at her. He sounded so self-satisfied, so confident. She raised her hand and cupped his cheek. He turned his face to kiss her palm.

"It's a game, sweets, a teasing game. Each touch brings you closer to the edge." His thumb brushed over her navel. "Closer and closer, little touch by little touch, until on the last touch, you explode."

"Hmm. So I should touch you, too?" Emma smoothed the curly hair across his chest, explored his nipples, then started the long journey down the intriguing line over his stomach to his . . .

He inhaled, jerking back. He wasn't grinning any longer.

"Don't you want me to touch you?"

"Emma, I would love it . . . next time. This time I wouldn't last a second. And I want this to be good for you." He frowned slightly, bending toward her breast. "As good as it can be, for a first time."

"What—oh!" Emma didn't understand, but she stopped caring the moment Charles's lips touched her nipple. He sucked hard as he dipped one finger into the wet heat at her center.

Her hips lifted off the bed and she gripped his shoulders. She needed something to hold on to in the sensual whirlpool where his mouth and hands had thrown her.

She panted, her hips twisting. She needed to feel Charles's weight.

As if he read her mind, he pulled her tight against him. His finger still played with her, slipping in and out, rubbing her wetness over the hard little nub of sensation hidden there. She had never known . . . never imagined. Her naked breasts were pressed against Charles's bare chest. This was so much better than the time at the lake. This was . . .

. . . unbearable. Her breath caught and she pulsed

against Charles's hand, her nipples peaking and her insides turning to liquid.

"Now, sweetheart," he whispered in her ear, "while you are still wet."

He moved between her legs, putting the pokey thing where his finger had been. He pushed slowly inside her.

"What?"

"Shh. Relax, sweetheart."

He inched farther in. She felt herself stretching.

"I don't think you'll fit, Charles."

"Shh. Don't think. I will . . . fit. Oh, God, Emma, you are so tight."

"Is that good?" He sounded like he might be in pain. She was feeling a little pain herself.

"It . . . is . . . wonderful." He pushed forward until he was fully inside her.

"Ouch." Emma tried to move, but his weight kept her pinned to the bed.

"Don't . . . move." His face was buried in her neck.

Once she got over the shock, she rather liked the feel of him. The pain was easing. She stroked her hands up his sweat-slick back.

"This is how babies are made, love." He lifted himself on his elbows and moved his hips. "I spill my . . . seed"—his hips flexed, pushing him into her—"deep"—he moved in and out again—"inside"—again—"you." He surged forward and held there. Emma felt something warm spurt into her.

"Mmm." Charles relaxed onto her. She threaded her fingers through his hair. She was having a little trouble breathing, but that was all right.

She was having a little trouble thinking. Feeling was about all she could manage . . . the weight of his body on hers, the soreness between her legs. And the fullness. He was still there, still inside her.

Some permanent connection had been forged between them, beyond the obvious physical one. She didn't understand it yet, nor could she explain it, but she knew it had happened.

She felt very married.

"God, Emma."

Charles raised his head to smile down at her, and her heart turned over. His eyes held a look of such . . . possession. No, it was more than that. Acceptance? She felt as if she had just stepped through a door, and now she was with him. Just the two of them. Together. She smiled back.

"Mmm." Apparently lucidity was eluding him as well. He bent his head and kissed her slowly, thoroughly. It was definitely possession this time—she was filled by him. By his tongue and his . . .

"I'm too heavy for you." He lifted himself off her. She felt empty and cold. "And you are probably sore."

"No."

"Yes." He climbed out of bed.

"Where are you going?" Emma did not want to spend the rest of the night alone. "You said you would stay and protect me."

"Don't worry, sweetheart. I am definitely not leaving your bed for long." He vanished through the connecting door. She heard him rummaging in his wardrobe.

"Here we are. I took the precaution of locking my door—don't want to surprise poor Henderson, do we?"

Emma flushed. "No. Definitely not."

He locked her door, too, then came back to the bed. He had something in his hand.

"What's that?"

"An old cravat. Sorry, the water is a bit cold." He reached between her legs.

"What are you doing?" Emma tried to close her thighs, but Charles's hand was already there. She scooted up the bed. "That is cold."

"I know, love. I'm sorry. I'm just cleaning you up."

"Cleaning me up?"

Charles showed her the blood-stained cravat. "Your maidenhead, sweetheart. It's only a little bit of blood, and it will only happen this once."

"Let me do that." Emma was mortified. She hated messes.

"No, love. It is my pleasure. Did I hurt you very much?"

"No. Just a little."

"I am sorry. Trust me, when we do this again, you will have only pleasure."

Charles was still wiping the wet cravat over her. It felt extremely . . . odd, having him do something so intimate. The slight roughness of the linen and the cold of the water made her stomach flutter. And he was actually *looking* at her. He combed his fingers through the hair growing there. Surely that was inappropriate?

"Um." What had Charles been saying? Oh, God, he was running his finger around, um . . . and she could feel him spreading the, um, lips of the, uh . . . "It was very nice in the beginning." She swallowed, trying to close her legs again, but he would not let her. He blew on her, and she shuddered.

"And it will be very nice the next time we do it— in the beginning, the middle, and the end." He dropped the stained cravat and grinned up at her. "You know, I think I should kiss your hurt and make it better."

"What—what do you mean?"

"This."

Emma stared as Charles bent his head. He couldn't mean to . . . No, it wasn't possible. . . .

She felt his warm breath on the secret place between her legs, then the lovely, wet rasp of his tongue.

CHAPTER 14

Charles dreamt a woman's hand was on a very private part of his anatomy.

This was not the confident touch of an experienced whore. No, it was hesitant, glancing, as if the woman were afraid to do what she was doing. *Don't be afraid. Please, God, don't be afraid.* He rolled slowly farther onto his back, spreading his legs, giving the questing fingers plenty of room to work their magic. And magic they were definitely working.

Delicate fingers brushed over him and withdrew. *Come back, come back.* He held his breath, lying still, all his prayers focused on that small hand. God heard him. The fingers came back to trace his length and dip down between his legs. A soft palm held him; fingers lifted and stroked. The touch was too light, too teasing. He needed more. The fingers circled him. He leapt to their touch, and they fled. But they came back. *Thank God.* Hesitantly, cautiously, they slid over him. And then . . . *God Almighty.* He swore he felt the slightest touch of a small, wet tongue, like a kitten's lick, just on his tip.

Sweat pooled on his chest to trickle down his

sides. His groin was on fire. *Please, please, please.* He wanted to feel her mouth on him. He moaned.

"Am I hurting you?"

His eyes flew open. This was no dream. There was a very large, Emma-sized lump under the blankets. He peered underneath to see her wide, worried eyes looking back at him. Her beautiful hand was still holding him.

"No." His voice wavered. He swallowed and cleared his throat. "Not at all. Please, don't let me interrupt you."

Emma smiled and ran her finger up him again. "You do expand in the oddest way. It is quite remarkable. When I first touched you this morning, you were smaller and . . . limper. I could just about cover you with my hand." She rested her hand against him, measuring him from the tips of her fingers to the heel of her palm. "Now you are much longer, and"—she wrapped her fingers around him—"thicker. You are also much, um, stiffer."

"Yes." He was finding this discussion incredibly erotic. "Very, um, true."

"Can I do to you what you did to me last night?"

"Which would be . . . ?" He had done a number of things to her, but not nearly the number he would have liked.

"Kiss you." She stroked him again. "Here."

"Yes. Definitely. Kissing any part of my person is perfectly permissible. Please." He tried to drag air into his lungs. "I would be delighted to have you kiss me there. Or just . . . lick . . . me."

"Like this?"

She ran her tongue up the length of him. His hips lifted off the bed. He grabbed the bedclothes.

"Yes. Definitely. Just. Like. That."

She did it once more, and he knew he could not hold on any longer. He pulled her up beside him.

"I'm not finished."

"Another time, sweetheart. I can't wait."

"Wait for what?"

"This."

He flipped her onto her back. He hoped she wasn't too sore from the nighttime, because he really could not wait. He had never felt this madness with any other woman. He kissed her, stroking her tongue with his as he stroked her below with his fingers. She was already wet. He almost cried with relief.

He loved the taste of her. He loved the feel of her breasts against him. He left her mouth to suckle her nipples. She panted and arched. He licked his way lower. Her legs parted wide. She raised her hips and he tasted her, flicked her hard little nub with his tongue. She moaned, and he surged into her, sliding into the tight passage that was already contracting around him, welcoming the seed he planted in her womb.

It took a few moments for rationality to return.

"That was a lovely way to wake up." He kissed her, keeping himself buried in her. "Are you going to greet me like this every morning?"

She smiled. "Perhaps." A small frown appeared between her brows. "You aren't scandalized?"

He rocked his hips, moving in her again. "Do I feel scandalized?"

She caught her breath. "No."

He kissed the tip of her nose. "I cannot think of a thing you could do in our bed that would scandalize me, sweetheart. My body is yours to explore." Regretfully, he eased out of her. "Just not right now. If we don't make an appearance at the house party soon, we *will* scandalize a significant portion of the *ton*."

"Oh. Yes. Indeed." Even Emma's beautiful breasts blushed. "Lady Oldston . . ."

"Exactly. Lady Oldston or Mrs. Pelham will run all the way to London to spread the interesting word that the new Lord Knightsdale spent the day in bed with the vicar's daughter. I'm certain Lady Dunlee will be an especially interested recipient of the news."

"Ohh." Emma moaned, covering her eyes.

"Don't worry. Marriage will cure all." He caught her left hand, turning it so they both could see the Knightsdale betrothal ring. "We have only antici- pated our wedding vows, sweetheart." He grinned. "As I fear we will anticipate them again several times before your father has finished calling the banns. It doesn't matter. We will be married soon. If I've managed to get you with child, the babe will be only a month or two early." He kissed her finger, just above the betrothal ring. "I hope you didn't have your heart set on an elaborate wedding?"

"Of course not."

"Good." He kissed her one last time and sat up. If he didn't force himself out of bed now, he would try to have her again. He didn't care terribly what the old cats said, but he didn't want to make things un- pleasant for Emma.

"We should tell the girls."

He nodded. "Yes. We'll do that first, shall we? And then Aunt Bea—and Meg, of course. Your father is coming to the ball, so we can tell him tonight."

"Will he be surprised, do you think?"

"No, I don't believe he will." Charles did not want to tell Emma that her father most likely would be relieved. "I've already asked his permission to pay my addresses."

"You have?"

"Of course I have. You don't have to look so surprised. Did you really think I was such a havey-cavey fellow that I would be quite so particular in my attentions without speaking to your father?"

"Well." Emma shrugged, making her naked breasts move in a very entrancing fashion. "I guess I didn't think about it."

Charles grunted and forced himself to stand. If he looked at Emma once more, he swore he'd be on her again. He looked at the floor instead. Something glinted in the morning light. He bent down.

There where Emma had seen her ghost the night before was a very unghostlike watch fob.

"What is it?" Emma scooted over the bed to see what Charles had bent to pick up off the floor.

"A watch fob." He displayed a flat gold disk on his palm. "A Spanish doubloon." He hefted it. "Much too substantial for a specter to sport."

Emma looked at the gold coinlike fob—and the broad palm that held it. The strong forearm, the muscled upper arm, the shoulders, chest . . . "Do you think you could put some clothes on?"

"Hmm?" Charles grinned. "Am I distracting you, sweetheart? Mind wandering to other matters, perhaps?"

Emma sat back on her heels, spreading her knees, and gathered her hair in both hands, pulling it off her shoulders. Charles's face tensed. His eyes focused on her breasts, then dropped to a spot just visible between her parted thighs.

She had become much more knowledgeable in the past few hours. She leaned forward slightly, her eyes looking down to gauge his interest.

"I'd say you were distracted, too, Lord Knightsdale. Greatly distracted."

Charles looked down and grinned. "I see your point. I will go put my breeches on."

"If you can!"

Charles paused. "Are you offering to assist me in seeing that my clothes fit more comfortably?"

Emma slid off the bed and walked toward him. If she let herself think about it, she would be shocked at her boldness—wherever had the vicar's daughter gone, the old maid who worried about propriety? When Lady Beatrice had urged her to take a few risks, she surely had not envisioned this—Emma naked, sauntering toward Lady Bea's equally naked nephew.

"I'll be happy to help you make the necessary adjustments," she said, wrapping her hand around his very large, very interested male appendage.

"Sweetheart." His hands moved over her breasts. "We . . . must . . . get . . . dressed." He shuddered as she rubbed the tip of him with her finger. "Now. Regretfully." Gently, he disengaged her hand. "Very, *very* regretfully. But remember what you were doing. Tonight, after the ball, you can resume your ministrations."

"But we aren't wed yet."

"Love, I will die if we wait to continue our bedroom explorations until your father pronounces us man and wife. Plan on seeing me tonight. Please?"

Emma admitted she did not want to wait a few weeks to experience again the amazing things Charles had done to her. She wasn't certain she could wait a few hours. "Well . . ."

"We are betrothed." Charles kissed her finger that wore the Knightsdale ring. "We will be married very soon . . . but not quite soon enough. I don't want to spend the night in my own bed unless you are there with me, but I will if you insist. If you need to wait, I will . . . try."

Emma laughed. Charles looked almost desperate. "It does seem a pity to waste a perfectly good unlockable door, doesn't it? I mean, if I were supposed to keep you out, the door would have a key, wouldn't it?"

"Indeed it would." He kissed her neck, just below her ear. "You have a wonderful mind as well as a wonderful body. So clever. Of course we should share a bed. How silly of us not to have figured that out earlier."

Emma licked his nipple. "*I* do not care to waste any more time, do you?"

"No. Not another moment. Except we do need to attend to other things at this particular moment." He turned her and swatted her on her naked bottom. They both caught their breaths at the sound and feel of the playful slap.

"Get dressed," Charles said, his voice hoarse. "Now."

Charles tucked in his shirt. Putting clothes on was a very good idea. Clothes definitely were an aid in focusing on the matter at hand, whenever the matter at hand was not Emma. He stopped at the threshold of her room.

"Are you dressed?"

"Yes. It's safe to come in."

Emma still had her hair tumbling over her shoulders, but at least the rest of her beautiful self was confined. He squatted down at the spot he had found the watch fob.

"Can you remember any more about your ghost?" He ran his hand over the rug but found no other clues.

"Well, I did not have my spectacles on, so I didn't get a good look at him—or her. I assume ghosts can be female?"

"Emma."

"Yes, well, I heard a creak and a scrape, rather like a door opening—a door on rusty hinges. And then I saw something white coming out of the wall. And then I, um, screamed and dove under the covers."

"Hmm." Charles stood and turned to look at the wall. "And you think the ghost appeared here?"

"I think so."

Charles studied the surface. "When I was a boy, my Great-Uncle Randall visited one summer—it was before you came to Knightsdale." He ran his fingers over the wall, looking for any odd protrusions or depressions.

"Great-Uncle Randall was the black sheep of the family—my father was extremely annoyed when the man appeared on our doorstep—and even more annoyed when he stayed the whole summer *and* paid a local sculptor to immortalize his unattractive visage in stone."

"I've seen the bust in the long gallery."

"He wasn't the most attractive Draysmith."

"No, nothing to compare to the current marquis."

Charles grinned. "No indeed. Keep that thought, sweetheart. I want your heart to flutter—and other things to, um, respond—when you think of me."

"I shall remain silent so I don't risk feeding your burgeoning sense of importance."

"Please, don't restrain yourself. I shall suffer all the

plaudits you should like to heap on me." Charles
frowned at the wall. He'd be damned if he could find
the tiniest bump or dip in the blasted thing.

"In any event, Great-Uncle Randall spent a good
portion of his stay that summer drinking my father's
brandy and sleeping off its effects. Paul and I thought
he was a pirate—he may even have told us a tale or
two about the high seas, but since he was usually
drunk, we didn't really believe him. Still, searching
for buried treasure was an enjoyable way to spend
a summer, even for Paul, who was usually not very
fond of my company."

"Paul wasn't fond of many people's company."

Charles shrugged. "You barely knew him. It couldn't
have been easy to assume the title at such a young
age—he was only fourteen when our father died."

"No, I suppose you're right."

Charles put his hands on his hips and stared at the
wall. He could kick it, but that probably would not
be a reasonable way to proceed. "Besides telling us
stories of piracy, Great-Uncle Randall told us there
was a maze of passages in the walls of Knightsdale.
We looked one rainy day, but when we didn't find
anything, we decided it was another of Randall's
drunken stories. Now I'm not so certain."

Not certain at all. Nanny's ghost, the fire in Emma's
earlier room, the apparition last night—someone was
moving around Knightsdale at will, and he did not
think it was a spirit. But where the hell was the door
to the bloody passage?

"Hmm. Mr. Stockley was looking behind pictures
in the long gallery yesterday," Emma said, examining a landscape a few feet away.

"He was?" Charles was ready to put his fist through
the wall.

"Yes. And he was behaving oddly in the grotto."
Emma lifted a corner of the painting.

"He wasn't the only one behaving oddly. You definitely looked most peculiar when I came upon you. Almost guilty."

"I don't know what you're talking about. Oh!"

"What is it?"

"There's a little lever or something here. Hold on. I can't . . ."

"Let me see."

"Don't push. It's right there."

Charles followed Emma's fingers. The picture was too heavy to lift off the wall entirely, but they could move it far enough away to get their hands in. Yes, he felt it. Not very far in from the frame—he couldn't have gotten his hand much beyond this point.

"I can't budge it. Does it swing down?" Emma was trying to peer into the dark space behind the painting where his hand was.

"I think so. Yes." He pulled down hard. There was a creaking and . . .

"Look!" Emma spun around, bumping into him.
Part of the wall had swung open.

"Stick something in there, will you, in case it closes up when I let go of the lever."

"All right." Emma looked around and grabbed her hairbrush. "Ready."

He let go. The door stayed open. Emma was already partly inside.

"What are you doing?" He grabbed her arm. "Get out of there. You're as bad as Prinny with a badger hole."

"It's very dusty and dark in here. Go get a candle, Charles."

Charles was rather certain he did not care to be

ordered about in such a manner. "I can see why Meg finds you a trial."

Emma backed out of the passage far enough to glare at him. "What do you mean?"

"I mean I will not get a candle until you have removed yourself from your present location."

Emma frowned and jutted out her chin. "Oh, you won't, will you?"

He waited, his face impassive. He had learned that trick when he was dealing with young privates whose youthful exuberance sometimes led them to inappropriate behavior. Silence was often the most effective rejoinder in such cases.

"Oh, very well, if you are going to be stubborn about it."

"I am."

Emma stepped back. "Don't think you are going to keep me out entirely. You must at least let me look around inside."

"Must I?" Charles lit a candle.

"Yes. Remember, if it were not for me, you would never have figured out how to open the door."

"Oh, I think I would have puzzled it out eventually." He stepped through the opening.

"Charles! I am not going to go scampering off into the bowels of Knightsdale, for goodness' sake. I just want to come in there with you."

"There isn't much room." The passage was very narrow—barely a foot and a half across at a guess. He had to turn sideways to move in either direction. "And it is very dirty."

"I don't mind a little dirt."

Charles looked at the sleeve of his formerly white shirt. "It's significantly more than a little dirt, sweetheart. The maids don't dust in here, you know."

"Of course I know. You are not going to dissuade me, so you may as well stop trying and step aside."

"All right. At least put your hair up and find a cap. You don't want the spiders setting up housekeeping in your curls."

Emma froze. "There are spiders in there?"

"Yes. Lots. Fat black ones and skinny brown ones with long legs . . ."

"You are certain there are spiders?"

Charles shrugged. He should have remembered Emma's spider fears earlier. "And cobwebs. You know how they stick to your hands and face and you can't quite get them off."

"Perhaps I will not . . . Perhaps it would be better if I stayed out here. In case you get stuck in there. I could go for help."

Charles grinned. "Excellent idea."

Emma tucked her hair behind her ear. A futile effort. Her hair was much too thick and curly to stay politely in place without resorting to sturdy hairpins. "How do you plan to proceed, Charles? You can't just hare off into those passages."

"Those spider-filled passages."

Emma shuddered. "Exactly. You need a plan." She bit her lip. "It would be easy to get disoriented."

"True." Emma was right. He would need a plan. He stepped back into her room.

"I hope that isn't your best shirt."

He laughed. "It certainly isn't now."

"Perhaps you should quietly dispose of it when your explorations are completed. You would not want to give Mr. Henderson an apoplexy."

"Perhaps." Charles made an attempt to brush the worst of the dust off his clothes. "Oh, look, here's one of those spiders now."

Emma squeaked and stepped back. "Kill it."

"So bloodthirsty. Are you certain?"

"Yes."

He laughed and brushed the poor spider onto the ground, dispatching it with the sole of his shoe. "And here I thought you were a softhearted, gentle soul."

"I am. It's just spiders I can't abide." Emma examined the splotch on the floor.

"It's quite dead, sweetheart." He grinned. "You don't have to be afraid. I'm happy to protect you from the evil spiders of the world."

Emma frowned at him. "I'm sure. Now, where do you think this passage goes? Do you suppose it's possible to get into every room in the house through a secret door?"

"Doubtful. I imagine it goes from the lord and lady's rooms to a hidden exterior exit."

"What about the ghost Nanny saw in the nursery?"

"Yes, there is that. I have also wondered how the fire occurred that necessitated your move here."

Emma blushed. "I didn't *have* to move into this room. I could have moved in with Meg."

"You could not have moved in with Meg. She has a very small room with one very small bed and, if I understand the maids' whisperings correctly, an overabundance of vegetative matter."

"Well . . ."

"*And* if you were billeted with your sister, my love, I would not have found it nearly so convenient."

"Which would have been a very good thing!" Emma turned an even brighter shade of red.

"Which would definitely *not* have been a very good thing." To have missed last night's—and this morning's—activities would have been a tragedy he didn't care to contemplate.

"Yes. Well. Hmm. Getting back to the question at hand . . . what was the question at hand?"

"Passages, sweetheart." Charles grinned, thinking of Emma's lovely tight passage. "Passages of the architectural variety, unfortunately."

Emma flushed and frowned at him. She opened her mouth, then closed it. Obviously she had thought better of her question.

"It does look as if there must be more entrances," Charles said. "I think the only way to discover the answer is for me to do some exploring."

"Are you certain you can get out again?"

"I'll examine the fastening here to see how it operates."

Emma opened the door wide, casting a nervous glance at the spider-laden darkness. "I don't see anything here."

"It's probably on the wall inside. I doubt if the latch is hidden—what would be the point? I imagine you want the person in the passage to be able to find the release."

"Unless you're afraid someone will sneak in that way."

"True." Charles raised the candle to shine more light on the problem. Whoever was opening the door probably would not be taller than he, so he did not think the door release would be very high on the wall. It also should not be too far from the door itself—the passage was too narrow to allow much maneuvering. That left a limited area—but he still could not find the release.

"Close the door, and let's see if I can open it."

"Definitely not."

"How else am I to figure out the mechanism?"

"I don't know—I just know this door is staying

open. If I close it and you cannot open it . . . no, that does not bear thinking of."

"But, Emma—"

"No. Save your breath, my lord. I'm not risking entombing you in the walls of Knightsdale."

"You are a very stubborn woman."

"I have been called that, yes."

Charles glared at Emma. Emma glared back. It was clear she was not going to compromise on this issue.

"So what do you propose?" Charles almost snarled the words.

"Why don't you see if you can find your way up to the nursery? There must be a door there, because that's where Nanny saw her ghost. I will go up and get Isabelle, Claire, and Prinny to make noise. That should help you locate the entrance, shouldn't it?"

"I suppose so."

"And this door will stay open. In fact, we'll have Mr. Henderson guard it, so no one can come along behind us and lock you in."

"I doubt that will happen."

Emma grabbed his arms. "How can you say that? Something very odd is going on, and we don't know who is behind it."

"We don't? My bet is definitely on Stockley. In fact, I believe I'll put one of the footmen on duty watching him. I disliked the man from the moment I saw him."

"But Mr. Stockley is new to the neighborhood. How could he know about these secret passages?"

"That is an interesting question, isn't it? I suspect it has an interesting answer. Now if you'll excuse me?"

Emma hung on to his arm. "Get Mr. Henderson first."

"Emma."

"Get Mr. Henderson first or I will scream and drum my heels against the floor."

Charles grinned. He could not picture Emma having a tantrum, but she did look deadly serious.

"Get Mr. Henderson, Charles."

"Oh, all right. If you insist."

CHAPTER 15

Emma watched Charles disappear into the opening. "You'll be certain no one touches this door, won't you, Mr. Henderson?" she asked for the fifth time.

"Yes, Miss Peterson."

She checked the area for spiders, then stuck her head inside the dark passage. Charles had not made much progress.

"Be careful."

He glanced back and grinned. "I will. It's too narrow to move very quickly."

"You won't get stuck?"

"No. Will you come rescue me if I do? Brave the spiders?"

"I will definitely send someone after you." Emma did not like the thought of Charles stuck in the walls of Knightsdale. It brought up gothic images of skeletons and ghosts. "Try banging on the wall."

"Why?"

"Just do it."

"Very well. There's not enough room in here to do much more than knock politely." Charles tapped.

"That's enough. We can hear you. If you get stuck

or lost, knock and we'll find you. I'll have the men tear the wall down to get to you, if need be."

"I don't know, Emma. Knightsdale is hundreds of years old. I'm not certain we should be tearing out a wall."

"Stop teasing, my lord. I am certain. Now hurry along as best you can. Mr. Henderson is here standing guard—I'm going off to await you in the nursery. Do not get lost."

"Yes, ma'am. I shall do my best not to."

Emma backed out of the opening and dusted herself gingerly for spiders.

"You will be certain no one closes this door, Mr. Henderson?"

"Yes, Miss Peterson. You do not need to worry. No one will close the door."

"Odd things have been happening, Mr. Henderson. You cannot be too alert."

"Miss Peterson, please. I will not let anything happen to his lordship."

"No, no, of course you won't." Emma took a deep breath. She was letting her imagination run away with her. "I'm just a little nervous. It is not every day one discovers a secret passage in one's room."

Mr. Henderson smiled broadly. "You're right there, miss. Now, if I may, I suggest you go on to the nursery to meet his lordship."

"Yes. Yes, I'll be on my way."

"And please encourage him to return to his room immediately," Mr. Henderson called after her. "I am afraid his clothing will need some attention."

Emma hurried down the hall. Where was Charles? How far had he progressed? He would not get stuck, would he? No, certainly not. She was silly to worry. Whoever had been using the passages had not gotten wedged in them, so there was no reason to think Charles would. It was not as if he were portly like Squire Begley.

Prinny greeted her at the nursery door with his usual frenetic barking.

"I've taken him for his walk this morning, Miss Peterson."

"Thank you, Isabelle. I'm sorry Prinny's care has fallen to you. It is most remiss of me."

"That's all right. I like walking him."

Emma looked up from patting Prinny to see Isabelle and Claire staring at her with more than their usual interest.

"Did you sleep well last night, Mama Peterson?"

Isabelle elbowed Claire. Emma flushed. Certainly the girls could know nothing of her nighttime activities? Well, she could not answer that innocent question without looking exceedingly guilty, so she ignored it.

"Girls, do you remember the night Nanny thought she saw a ghost? Can you help me find the spot where she thought she saw it?"

"Over here, Mama Peterson, in the schoolroom. I'm sure it was here, by the shelf with my dolls."

"I think you're right, Claire." Emma banged on the wall and then listened. Nothing.

"What are you doing, Miss Peterson?"

"Your uncle discovered some passages in the walls, Isabelle. He is exploring. We think there might be a door up here."

"Secret passages!" Claire hopped up and down and clapped her hands.

"You are not to put one speck of one toenail inside one, Lady Claire," Emma said. "They are dark and dirty and full of spiders."

"I like spiders."

Emma's jaw dropped. "You do?"

Claire nodded enthusiastically. "Yes, I—oh, look at Prinny."

Prinny had been sniffing vigorously for several minutes at the base of the wall. Suddenly he started barking and scrabbling with his front paws as if he wanted to dig through the paneling.

"What is it, Prinny?" Claire bent down and tried to get an answer from the dog.

Emma tried to get an answer from the wall. "Charles!" She banged on the paneling so hard she feared she might break it. "Charles, are you there? Quiet, Prinny! I can't hear a thing. Charles!"

"Miss Peterson," Isabelle said, "if Uncle Charles wants to get out of the wall, I think we had better move to give him room."

Emma took a deep breath. "Yes. You are probably right." She stepped back. "Claire, can you move Prinny also?"

There was now plenty of room for the door to swing open. Emma waited. Nothing. Prinny barked and tried to lunge forward, but Claire kept him restrained.

"Don't you think something should have happened by now?" Emma asked no one in particular.

"It hasn't been that long, Mama Peterson."

It has been forever, Emma wanted to say, but she held her tongue. It did no good to snap at the child.

"Well, be sure you have a tight hold on Prinny. If—*when*—the door opens, we don't want him dashing through. We'd never get him out of the walls."

"Very true," a male voice said.

"Charles!" A portion of the wall had swung open and Charles was standing there grinning, smears of dirt on his face and cobwebs in his hair. He looked wonderful. Emma wanted to throw herself at him and hug him.

He must have seen the look in her eyes. His grin widened and he opened his arms. "What, Emma, no kiss? Are you going to let a little dirt and the fear of a spider or two deter you?"

"Charles! I mean, Lord Knightsdale . . ." Emma gestured at Isabelle and Claire, whose eyes had grown huge at his banter.

"Are you going to kiss Miss Peterson, Uncle?"

"Yes, indeed."

"Definitely not!"

"But you *want* to kiss him, don't you, Mama Peterson?"

Emma opened her mouth, but she could not lie. She felt a hot flush bloom over her face.

"It worked!" Claire jumped up, letting go of Prinny. "Isabelle, it worked!"

"Prinny!" Emma lunged for the dog, but Charles caught his hind leg before he disappeared into the walls.

"I guess I should have closed this earlier." Charles pushed the door firmly shut. "What worked, Claire?"

"Claire," Isabelle said, "perhaps it would be best if you didn't—"

But Claire would not be stopped. She was dancing with excitement. "Isabelle is so smart. She said we had to get you alone together, so we hid Mama Peterson's brush in your room, Papa Charles. But that didn't work, so then we hid Mama Peterson's nightgown. And that did work! You are getting married."

"Claire, just because Uncle Charles wants to kiss Miss Peterson doesn't mean they are getting married."

"Well, Isabelle," Charles said, "I hope you do not intend to kiss men you are not going to marry."

"No, but . . ." Isabelle pushed her wispy white-blond hair behind her ear. "*Are* you going to marry Miss Peterson, Uncle?"

"Yes, I am. And you and Claire will live here with us and be the first of our children. Would you like that?"

Isabelle nodded. She bit her lip, blinked, then threw her arms around Charles's neck. "Yes," she sobbed. "Yes, Papa, I would like that very much."

Charles made the girls promise to keep the secret of his betrothal to Emma until the next day. He didn't want the entire household to know before he told Aunt Bea and Emma's father. They would make the formal announcement at tonight's ball. First, though, he needed to get cleaned up. He was covered in dust and spiderwebs—and probably a few spiders.

"It took forever for you to come out of the wall," Emma said. They were walking back to their rooms from the nursery. "You must have been there—Prinny scented you. He was barking."

"Yes, I heard him. It took me a few minutes to figure out the release. It's a lever, but it was lower on the wall than I expected, and you push it up, not down. It was also well oiled."

Emma darted a glance at him. "I noticed the door did not creak like the one in my room."

"Yes. I suspect having you, Nanny, and the girls sleep downstairs invited our mysterious visitor to make the nursery floor his nocturnal base of operations."

"I'm very glad you pushed that heavy chair in front of the door, then—but how many other doors are there?"

"I don't know. I am definitely assigning one of the brawnier footmen to watch Stockley."

"But what if he's not the culprit? And even if he is, what could he possibly want?"

"I don't know. At least we don't have much longer to worry. Once we announce our betrothal, most of my guests will pack their portmanteaux and find other fields to hunt. The fox here has been caught."

"Good morning, Charles. Miss Peterson." Aunt Bea chose this moment to step out of her room. "What is this about foxes being caught?"

Charles saw Aunt Bea focus on Emma's left hand. He'd wager she could spot the Knightsdale betrothal ring from the far side of a ballroom.

"Aunt, you are just the person we wanted to speak to. Do you have a moment?"

"My time is completely at your disposal, Charles. Please, step into my sitting room."

"Splendid." Charles let the women precede him, then stepped over the threshold and shut the door firmly behind him.

Aunt Bea's sitting room was decorated in pleasant shades of green, accented by a large, orange cat on the window seat. Queen Bess yawned, stretched, and returned to napping. Aunt Bea eyed Emma's hand again.

"As you may have noted, Aunt, Emma is wearing the Knightsdale betrothal ring."

Aunt Bea beamed. "Yes, I did notice. This is perfect. I am so happy." She hugged Emma and then Charles and then Queen Bess. Her majesty was not delighted to have her sleep disturbed. She jumped down from the window seat and stalked into the other room.

"When shall we make the announcement?" Aunt Bea asked. "At the ball tonight, I presume?"

"That would be best. Reverend Peterson will be here for dinner beforehand. I had his permission to pay my addresses, of course—Emma and I will let him know tonight that she has accepted my suit."

"Splendid! And you'll be married next year in St. George's, Hanover Square." Aunt gave a little skip reminiscent of Claire. "It will be the event of the Season."

"I am sorry to disappoint you, Aunt, but that will not be possible. We will be married at Knightsdale as soon as the banns are read."

Aunt Bea paused in her waltz around her sitting room. "You can't be married so soon. People will talk."

"They are welcome to do so."

Aunt Bea turned to Emma. "Miss Peterson—Emma—surely you want a big London wedding?"

"Actually, Lady Beatrice, I would be much happier being married by my father at Knightsdale. I have never been to London. I would be overwhelmed."

"Well, yes, I see your point. But to be married so soon . . ."

"I am twenty-six. There is no point in delaying."

"Yes, well." Aunt shot Charles a look. He raised an eyebrow and clasped his hands behind his back. She hesitated but then soldiered on. "Emma, I know you don't have a mother to counsel you, so you do not understand the repercussions of such a hasty wedding. The point is, dear, if you are married in such a hurry, people will assume you have anticipated your marriage vows."

Emma turned as red as Aunt Bea's morning gown.

Aunt Bea looked at Charles again. "Ah. Yes. Well, then. I guess we'll have a wedding within the month."

Charles grinned back at her. "I do think that would be best." He moved away from the door. "On a different topic, Aunt, have you remembered anything about Mr. Stockley? You were saying the other evening that there was something familiar about him."

Aunt nodded. "Please, sit down." She chose the large upholstered chair; Charles and Emma sat together on the settee. "I confess my mind has been on other matters"—she smiled broadly at them—"which have been resolved to my great satisfaction. Now, as to Mr. Stockley"—Aunt Bea frowned at a large floral painting on the wall—"I think he has some connection to Uncle Randall."

"My Great-Uncle Randall?" Charles leaned forward, resting his elbows on his knees. He had never discussed Randall with anyone except Paul when they were playing pirate. He might have tried once, but his father's abrupt reaction to his simplest questions discouraged him from pursuing the topic. "Is it true Randall was a pirate?"

"I believe he would prefer the term 'privateer,' Charles, but yes, I think so. Randall went off to sea when he was a boy—you never met him, did you, Emma?"

"No, I don't believe I did."

"You wouldn't have," Charles said. "The last time Randall visited was the year I turned seven. He died shortly afterward. Had a few too many glasses of blue ruin one night and walked off the end of a pier."

Aunt Bea snorted. "That's your father's story."

"Was there another? I never heard it."

"Nor did I." Aunt Bea shrugged. "I just never believed it. Randall drank, of course—sometimes heavily. But he could hold his liquor. I do not think it possible he was so drunk he didn't know where he was. I think he was helped into the harbor."

"You think Randall was murdered?" Charles couldn't keep the shock from his voice. "Did you tell my father your suspicions?"

"Of course I did—George just laughed at me. He

was happy to have Randall removed from his list of responsibilities." Aunt Bea turned to Emma. "My brother and uncle did not get along. We all grew up together—Randall was the same age as George. Father died when I was two and George four, so Grandfather raised us. Mother wasn't happy about the arrangement, either. Grandfather's second wife— Randall's mother—was a year or two younger than she. It was an awkward situation all the way around."

Queen Bess wandered back into the room and jumped into Aunt Bea's lap. Aunt Bea absently stroked her ears.

"Randall insisted George call him 'Uncle Randall,' I suppose because it made George angry. Randall was always joking, and my brother had no sense of humor. When George inherited the title, it was even worse. Randall would not give George the respect he thought his due. I loved Randall, but it was almost a relief when he left to go to sea."

"Hmm. I knew Father wasn't delighted by Randall's visit," Charles said, "but I didn't think anything about it. Delight was not an emotion with which my father was familiar."

"Exactly. George was a dry old stick," Aunt Bea said. "An angry, dry old stick. I often wished Randall, not George, was my brother."

"Still, I can't see my father being pleased someone murdered his uncle, no matter how much he may have disliked the man."

"No indeed. George would have investigated thoroughly if he'd thought Randall had been murdered— murder was not an appropriate end for a Draysmith. But a tragic accident—that could happen to anyone, even someone from such an exalted family as the

Draysmiths of Knightsdale. George accepted the easy, obvious explanation."

"But you did not," Emma said.

"No." Aunt Bea shook her head so that her gray sausage curls bounced. "No, indeed." She stroked Queen Bess for a few minutes in silence.

"Randall was worried when he was last home," she said finally. "I'd swear to it. He was drinking a lot."

"He was drunk most of the time," Charles said.

Aunt Bea sighed. "True. That was unusual. Something was bothering him." She bit her lip. "He even joked about dying. Well, I thought he was joking, but then he had that odd little sculptor make a bust of him. Said he wouldn't live forever, and he wanted to be certain his place in the Draysmith line was recorded for posterity."

Aunt Bea's voice had grown slightly shrill.

"Aunt, there's no need to tell us this, especially if it stirs up unhappy memories."

Aunt Bea blotted her eyes with her handkerchief. For once she looked all of her sixty years. "No, I want to tell you, Charles. I don't think of Randall often, but when I do, I feel so sad. It's the uncertainty that bothers me the most. I feel an injustice has been done, that Randall's ghost has not been appeased."

"Surely you don't think his spirit walks the halls of Knightsdale?"

Charles was happy Emma asked the question. He hoped Aunt Bea wasn't so addled she thought Knightsdale actually was haunted.

"Of course not, dear. I was speaking figuratively." She smiled and shook her head. "If any spirit is walking the halls of Knightsdale, it must be George's. He was livid over that bust. It did not suit his sense of propriety to have some unknown local artist do the work. If Randall was determined to add to the effigies in the long gallery, George wanted to have a well-regarded artist in from London. He most certainly did not want inferior work displayed at Knightsdale. But he lost that battle—he always lost when he argued with Randall. It did not improve his temper."

Charles decided it was time to bring the conversation back to the main point. "But Stockley, Aunt?"

"That is what is so frustrating. I'm almost certain Randall said something about the man the last time he was home, but I just cannot remember what. I have racked my brain, I promise you."

"But, Lady Beatrice, Mr. Stockley is not old enough to have had anything to do with Lord Randall's death."

"No, of course not—I did not mean this Mr. Stockley. I imagine it was his father whom Randall knew."

"But how would they have met?" Charles snorted. "I can't imagine Stockley is a member of the *ton*."

"Randall didn't frequent *ton* events, Charles. He left for the sea as a boy, remember." Aunt Bea laughed. "I can no more picture him at Almack's than I can picture George at a . . . a common brothel. An uncommon brothel, well, perhaps. But no, George preferred to visit Mrs. Borden for those needs."

Charles stared at his aunt. Mrs. Borden? The nice old lady who had lived in the cottage by the big oak tree and given him lemon drops?

"I do think Mr. Stockley said his family was in shipping," Emma said. "Perhaps Lord Randall worked on one of the Stockley family ships?"

"Pshaw! I doubt Stockley's family ever owned any ships. He does not look like a man who comes from money—and ship owning requires money."

"And I'm certain I've never run into our Mr. Stockley before." Charles shook off the unsettling image of his father and Mrs. Borden. He focused on Stockley. He'd have remembered the annoying twiddlepoop if he'd met him in Town. "I should have crossed paths with him at some point if he moves among the *ton.*"

"Very true." Aunt Bea frowned and stopped stroking Queen Bess. Her highness protested the neglect, meowing and butting her head against Aunt Bea's hand. Aunt Bea gave her one long stroke from her nose to the tip of her tail. "I *wish* I could remember."

"I wish I could boot Stockley out the door." Charles did not care to have a suspicious character under his roof, especially one who showed any interest in Emma. Especially if he had access to her room at night. Well, that would not be too much of a problem. If Stockley decided to haunt Emma's bedchamber, he was in for a surprise. Charles did not intend to let Emma sleep alone again.

"Lady Beatrice," Emma said, "did you know there were secret passages in the walls of Knightsdale?"

"Hmm?" Aunt Bea's mind obviously was still on the Stockley problem. "Secret passages? I thought George had them nailed shut when he inherited the title."

"So you did know about them?"

"Of course, Charles. They really weren't secret— we used them often enough to escape our lessons."

"*I* knew nothing about them. I thought they were just another of Randall's drunken tales."

Aunt Bea shrugged. "As I said, I thought George had them all nailed shut. I suppose hidden passages did not sit well with his notions of propriety, either. Guests could—and did—get up to all kinds of immoral behavior. Why do you ask?"

"Because someone is using them again."

CHAPTER 16

Who was using the hidden passages? Emma pondered the question while Betty, Lady Elizabeth's maid, dressed her hair for the ball. Charles was certain it was Mr. Stockley, but he did not like the man. Well, she did not like him either, but that did not mean he was sneaking through the walls of Knightsdale. Of course, she had seen him engage in some odd activities. Looking behind pictures was not a normal occupation for a guest. Nor was examining the statuary and stone construction of the grotto quite so thoroughly. It was almost as if he were looking for something. But what?

If only Lady Beatrice could remember what Lord Randall had said so many years ago. Emma sighed.

"Do ye not like yer hair, miss?"

"Oh, no, Betty. It's quite nice." Emma actually looked at herself in the mirror then and gasped. "Oh. Oh, my. It is more than nice, Betty—it is wonderful."

"Well, I thought so."

Emma barely heard the maid's words. She was staring at her reflection. Lady Beatrice had kindly offered to loan her Claudette. Fortunately, Lizzie had been standing nearby and had seen Emma's expression. She'd insisted on sending Betty instead. Thank God! Not only did Emma find Claudette intimidating, she did not want to go to her first ball looking like Lady Beatrice. But she never thought she could look like this.

"I have to go, miss. I still have to do Miss Margaret and Lady Elizabeth."

"Go ahead, Betty. You have worked your magic here. Thank you."

Emma kept staring at herself as Betty left. The girl must think her a complete pea-goose, but she didn't care.

She looked . . . well, as close to beautiful as she could ever hope to come. Closer than she'd dreamt possible. Betty had tamed her wild curls so they looked elegant and . . . alluring. As if they were casually caught up on her head, just waiting for a man to come and pluck a few pins, sending them tumbling over her breasts.

She flushed. She knew which man she hoped would do just that.

And the blue satin ball gown might be four years old, but it looked as good—better—than she remembered it. Would Charles like it?

Would he be tempted to see what was barely hidden by the dress's low neck?

She closed her eyes. She hoped so. She definitely hoped so. She would love to feel his hands on her shoulders, her breasts. She imagined his fingers sliding over her, his lips following, tracing a line down to . . .

Her nipples hardened, and her body began to throb.

"What a lovely way to greet me, sweetheart."

She felt Charles's breath skim her collarbone and his fingers dip beneath her bodice to tease her nipples. She wanted his mouth there. She arched back, turned her head. His breeches were right by her cheek—his tight, revealing breeches. She smiled and put her hand over him.

He inhaled and jerked his hips back.

"So bold, Emma."

"I'm sor—"

"Don't be, sweetheart. I love your boldness—unfortunately, at the moment we cannot see where it might lead us. We must attend this ball, and we must look presentable while doing so. No suspicious wrinkles or stains." He grinned down at her. "But after the ball, please feel free to be as bold as you can imagine. And if your imagination falters, I shall be delighted to make some suggestions." He nibbled her earlobe. "Will you come to my room tonight, Emma? Make love with me in the Draysmith ancestral bed?"

"Oh, yes." Lust surged through her again, making coherent thought difficult. "Why do we have to go to the ball tonight?"

"Because it is your betrothal ball. Because people will be scandalized if I, the host, don't appear. And because we need to tell your father we are getting married. I suspect he would like to know."

"Yes." Emma took a deep breath, trying to think of something other than Charles and the lovely, magical thing he had hidden in his breeches.

"Emma."

"Hmm?" She heard the serious note in his voice.

"Mrs. Graham will be there, too."

"Oh." Emma waited for the confused mix of emotions that always flooded her at the mention of Mrs. Graham.

Lust apparently left room for no other strong feelings.

"Mrs. Graham. Yes." Still nothing. She did remember how Mrs. Graham had tried to protect her when she had felt besieged by the Society in the blue drawing room.

"It would be much appreciated by your father, I'm sure, if you could manage to be pleasant to Mrs. Graham. I do think he would like your blessing, or at least your acquiescence, in their marriage."

Emma expected to bristle at the word "marriage," but again, she felt little—except a spurt of excitement at the thought of her own marriage.

"All right." She wondered if the anger and hurt would bubble up in her again once she saw Mrs. Graham.

Charles would have much preferred to strip Emma of her lovely gown, lay her on the bed, and sheath himself deep inside her. He might have done it, if he had not known the scandal would be immense. And he did want to see her father and get the banns read as soon as possible. His betrothal ring on her finger was enough in his mind to make their bedroom activities acceptable, but he would rather have his wedding ring on her finger before he had his heir growing in her womb. If possible. He wasn't prepared to sleep alone to ensure that outcome. An "eight-month" babe was fine with him.

God, she was lovely tonight. When he'd walked in and seen her eyes closed, her head back, her breasts high, her lovely nipples pebbling clearly against the satin . . . And then she'd put her small hand on him. It was almost more than he could bear without bearing her directly to bed. That blue gown was obscene. It didn't leave much to the imagination—or, rather, it prompted a man to imagine everything. No man had best do so tonight.

Charles dragged his mind away from bedsheets and bare skin.

"Emma, I actually came here with a purpose." He reached into his pocket and pulled out the necklace he'd deposited there when he'd seen more enjoyable activities for his fingers. "This goes with your ring. There's a bracelet and tiara, too, but I think this will be enough for tonight."

He looped the sapphires around her neck and fastened the clasp.

"Oh, Charles." Emma put her fingers on the stones. She shook her head. "They are beautiful, but I can't accept them."

"Of course you can. You are going to be my wife, my marchioness." If anyone had told him in London he'd ever say "wife" and "marchioness" without cursing, he'd have called the man a liar. Amazing how things could change in such a short time. "If it's any consolation, I'm not really giving them to you. They go with the title. I believe you'll have to give them up to our son's wife eventually."

Emma blinked at him. "That sentence has too many new concepts for me to absorb."

"Then don't—just smile and wear the necklace." He pulled her up into his arms, careful not to crush her dress, and brushed her lips with his. "Let's go see if your father has arrived."

Emma discovered that she did have room for feelings other than lust. She stood outside the study door and gripped Charles's arm. Excitement, worry, embarrassment, contrition, and love all churned in her stomach.

"Thank you for putting Papa in your study. I could not have borne telling him in front of anyone else."

"Mrs. Graham may be with him. Would you like me to ask her to step out?"

"Yes. No. Oh, I don't know." She chewed on her lip. "I don't know what I feel anymore."

"No? Well, I suggest we just go in, then. I believe your father will grant you the luxury of any feeling that presents itself. I know I will—unless you decide to feel a strong aversion to my presence."

"Impossible."

"Good. Then after you, Miss Peterson."

Emma put her hand out quickly, stopping Charles. "You don't think . . . ? I mean, they wouldn't . . . Should we knock first?"

Charles grinned. "I doubt your father will be doing anything in my study except examining my book collection, Emma."

"Are you certain? The door is closed."

"True. And I would guess Mrs. Graham doesn't have a chaperone in there with her."

"Exactly!"

"And they are awaiting our arrival—I do not think they will be in an especially amorous mood. But the thought does have possibilities. Are you hinting that I need to guard my virtue any time we find ourselves alone behind a closed door?"

"Of course not!"

"How disappointing."

Charles opened the door and Emma stepped into the study. Her father was alone, standing by the desk, hands in his pockets. He looked . . . lonely and a little sad. Older. His shoulders were a bit stooped. She noticed that his hair was gray—surely it hadn't just turned color in the few days she'd been at Knightsdale?

When was the last time she had really looked at him? Had she ever?

"Papa."

He turned and smiled. "Emma—and Lord Knightsdale."

"Please—Charles, sir. You are going to be my papa-in-law, you know. Can't have you 'my lording' me all the time."

Emma watched her father's face light up. He looked at her.

"Emma? Are you going to marry Charles?"

"Yes, Papa, I am." Why were her feet glued to the floor? She should be flying into her father's arms. He certainly expected it. "Where's Mrs. Graham?"

"She is waiting in another room. She thought . . . well, she's not part of our family, really."

"She should be."

Papa's face grew very still. "What?"

"I said she should be. Mrs. Graham should be part of our family, Papa, if you love her. Do you love her?"

"Um." Papa took a deep breath. "Yes, I love her, but neither of us wanted . . . You are my daughter, Emma. My first loyalty should be to you."

"No." Emma was shocked to realize she believed what she was saying. She wasn't just voicing words to set her father free. "No, I think your first loyalty should be to yourself, Papa. At least in this case. And to Mrs. Graham—Harriet." Emma took a deep, shuddering breath. "Meg thinks you should marry Harriet. She saw it first—that you smile more now. That you're happier."

"Emma—"

"That you're excited by something besides your old books and translations. I think she's right. I should have seen it, too, but I was too selfish and I'm sorry. I never meant to keep you from following your heart."

Tears streamed down Emma's face. The knot in her stomach loosened. When her father opened his arms, her feet moved at last. She flew to him, opening her own arms, hugging him hard.

She looked up and saw that he was crying, too.

"What . . . interesting news, Miss Peterson." Lady Oldston choked on her words, like Queen Bess coughing up a hairball.

"Indeed." Mrs. Pelham sniffed. "I never would have imagined . . . but, then, you are a childhood friend, are you not?"

"Yes. An *old* friend." Lady Oldston smiled when she emphasized *old*. "There is something comforting in familiarity, I suppose."

The Misses Oldston and Pelham simply glared. Emma tried to smile.

At least the Society ladies were happy about her betrothal. They clustered around her after the London ladies had left.

"Well done," Mrs. Begley said. "Glad to see you took my advice."

"We'll be looking for an heir in nine months' time," Miss Rachel Farthington said.

"Or sooner!" Miss Esther elbowed Miss Rachel, and they giggled.

"I see you spent your time in the study well," Miss Russell whispered. She looked up, then ducked her head again. "He's coming."

"A little decorum, ladies, if you please," Mrs. Begley said. They looked at Charles and smiled. His eyebrows rose, but he smiled back.

"Good evening, ladies. If you'll excuse Emma, she and I are supposed to open the ball."

"Certainly."

"Go right ahead."

"Oh my, yes."

"He *does* wear his breeches well." Miss Esther's comment carried across the ballroom in the hush before the orchestra struck its opening note.

"I believe I am blushing," Charles said, leading Emma into the dance.

"Well, it's true." Emma flushed. The image of what exactly his breeches covered flashed into her mind.

"Hmm." Charles's voice dropped lower. "You have turned a lovely shade of pink, sweetheart. I do wonder what thought caused you to color up so nicely. Will you tell me?"

"No. I couldn't possibly." She was certain lightning would strike her if she did. Or worse, one of those harpies, Lady Oldston or Mrs. Pelham, would hear her.

"I know what I'm thinking." Charles swung her through a turn. "I'm thinking how beautiful you look in that dress—but how you will look even more beautiful without it."

"Charles!"

"I'm imagining you spread naked on my bed tonight."

"Charles!" She must have squeaked louder. The Duke of Alvord glanced at her, and his duchess smiled.

"Your creamy skin against my sheets, your beautiful hair spread over my pillow . . ."

"Charles!" Emma glanced around. No one appeared to be overhearing Charles's scandalous words.

". . . your glorious, soft breasts, their nipples hard, begging for my mouth . . ."

Emma felt her knees wobble and the hot, wet throbbing start in her center.

". . . your waist, your hips, the lovely nest of curls between your thighs—and those thighs! Those smooth, white thighs spread wide, welcoming, beckoning . . ."

"Charles." Emma whispered. She could barely get his name past her lips. To hear him say such things on the ballroom floor, where anyone might overhear . . .

"I want to bury my face between your thighs, to smell you, taste you—"

"Charles, if you don't stop right this minute, I will . . . I will . . . Well, I don't know what I will do, but it will be highly improper and extremely embarrassing."

"Really? That sounds promising."

"Charles . . ."

"Oh, all right. I will behave—until later, when I have you in my bed." He put his lips by her ear as the music drew to a close. "Then I promise to misbehave more than you can possibly imagine."

"Oh." Emma hoped her face was not as red as it felt.

She danced with the Earl of Westbrooke and the Duke of Alvord. Squire Begley had a dance, as did her father. Then Mr. Stockley found her.

"Congratulations, Miss Peterson. You won the grand prize, didn't you?"

"Excuse me?"

"Now I know why you never found my room—you were too busy in Lord Knightsdale's chamber."

"Mr. Stockley, you are insulting."

Mr. Stockley shrugged. "Your pardon. No insult intended. We all must have an eye to the main chance, mustn't we?" His eyes dropped to her throat. "Interesting necklace." He stared so intently, it would have been embarrassing except it was clear it was the jewels and not her person that attracted his attention.

"Thank you."

"Betrothal gift?"

"It is part of the Knightsdale set, yes."

"Hmm."

The music began. Every time the steps brought her back to Mr. Stockley, his eyes were on the Knightsdale sapphires. It was most peculiar. She was delighted when the music finally drew to a close. She was beginning to feel like a museum display, though she doubted even the most interesting artifact got the undivided attention Mr. Stockley was lavishing on the Knightsdale necklace.

She was fanning herself by one of the windows to the garden later when a servant brought her a note.

"Thank you." She took the folded paper from the tray he offered. She didn't recognize the man—he was one of the temporary help brought on expressly for the ball.

She didn't recognize the handwriting, either, but she wasn't focusing on that as she read the short message.

Claire needs you in the nursery. Come quickly.

Why the nursery? Claire shouldn't be in the nursery this late. What could be the matter? Where was Nanny?

Emma tapped the paper against her hand. It didn't matter—if Claire wanted her, she would go. Perhaps the little girl just needed some attention, a good-night kiss. Emma would slip out and see what was amiss. She'd be gone only a moment. No one would miss her.

She hurried up the stairs.

"Claire? Claire, it's Mama Peterson. Where are you?"

The nursery was dark and quiet. Too quiet. Something was wrong. She caught her breath. She was quite alone. She should have told Charles where she was going. She should have had him come with her. At least she should have stopped by Nanny's room on her way up the stairs. She turned to leave.

"I don't think so." Mr. Stockley's hand slapped over her mouth and his arm pulled her back tight against his body. For a small man, he was very strong.

"I have a knife, Miss Peterson."

Emma felt something sharp prick her side, right under her left breast.

"I will stick you if you make the slightest noise. Nod if you understand me."

Emma nodded.

"Good." He released her but kept his knife against her side. "Now, very carefully, remove that lovely necklace."

Emma fumbled with the clasp. "Are you the one who has been using the secret passages, Mr. Stockley?"

"Yes, not that they have proven at all helpful. Hurry up."

"I am trying. It is not easy." Emma's fingers were shaking too much to work the clasp free. "Is Claire here?"

"Claire?"

"I got a message—"

"That was just to get you up here. As far as I know, your little Claire is sleeping soundly in her bed. Hurry up with that necklace."

Emma felt Mr. Stockley's knife pressing harder into

her side. She took a deep breath, closed her eyes, and concentrated. Finally she felt the clasp come free. Mr. Stockley grabbed the necklace.

"Tell me where Knightsdale got this." He punctuated his question with another stab of his knife. "Where's his safe?"

"I don't know. He had the necklace in his pocket. I never saw a safe."

"Hmm. I guess I'll just have to ask him myself." He grabbed her right hand and twisted it behind her back, keeping his knife under her breast. "I believe that's a conversation I shall enjoy."

Emma tried to keep from panicking. "I don't understand. If you are just a thief—" Emma sucked in her breath as Mr. Stockley jerked her arm higher.

"I am not just a thief. I am not a thief at all. This belongs to me."

"The necklace?"

"No." He pushed her farther into the nursery. "Not this necklace. Others. Necklaces and earbobs and stickpins. Rings. Tiaras. I can't find them. I've looked. Bloody hell, I've looked. I know they're here somewhere. I'll get Knightsdale to tell me. I'll show him your necklace and tell him he won't see you again if he doesn't give me the jewels. I think he'll talk quickly. I've seen the way he looks at you."

Emma tried to slow their progress. Where was Mr. Stockley taking her? "I still don't understand. There are jewels hidden at Knightsdale?"

"Yes. Randall stole them from my father."

"Are you certain—" Emma eyed the candlestick by the schoolroom shelves. Could she . . . ?

He jerked her arm again. "Don't even think about it. I'd rather not kill you, but I will if I have to. I've killed before, so don't think I haven't the stomach for it."

Mr. Stockley shoved the heavy chair away from the door to the hidden passage.

"You couldn't have killed Lord Randall—you were too young."

He pushed Emma against the wall, holding her there with the weight of his body while he reached up with his left hand and felt along one of the high shelves.

"Of course I didn't kill him—that was my father."

"William?" Emma felt sick. Had Mr. Stockley killed the man Charles had assigned to watch him?

"The footman? No, I just knocked him out. Men, especially big brawny idiots like your William, underestimate my quickness and strength. He's trussed up safely in my wardrobe. Ah."

The door swung open. Emma stared at the dirty, dark, spider-filled passage. Mr. Stockley was not going to make her go in there, was he?

"I killed the present marquis's brother, of course— and his wife and servants. I paid Atworthy well to spy on them—he told me they had taken the jewels to Italy. I tore that carriage apart, went through all their bloody belongings. Atworthy lied. He meant to steal the jewels himself. He admitted it before I skewered him."

Mr. Stockley's knife pricked Emma again. This time she was certain it had drawn blood.

"I see."

"Not for long."

Mr. Stockley shoved her in the small of her back. She stumbled into the passage.

"I hope you don't mind the dark, Miss Peterson. I neglected to leave you a candle."

"But, you can't—"

"Ah, but I can."

He slammed the door in her face. She heard the scrape of the heavy chair being pushed back into place.

She bit her lip. She would not give Mr. Stockley the satisfaction of hearing her scream.

CHAPTER 17

Where the hell was Emma? Charles looked over the ballroom again. Could he have missed her? She *was* short.

"Aunt, have you seen Emma?"

"Hmm. Now that you mention it, no, I haven't. Perhaps she's in the ladies' retiring room. I'm sure she'll be back shortly."

Charles nodded and went off to play host, asking Miss Russell to dance. He'd already partnered each of the Farthington twins. At least he hoped he had danced with each one and not just one twice. They had dressed exactly alike tonight, even down to the same color ribbon in their hair.

Miss Russell was too intimidated by his presence or too polite to object when he spent most of their dance scanning the ballroom for Emma. He did not see her. Surely no woman could spend thirty minutes or more in the retiring room?

He hadn't seen Stockley, either. Damn. He was glad he'd put William to watching the man. The footman was an amateur pugilist. He should be able to handle Stockley. Still, he'd be happier if he saw Stockley's ugly face in the ballroom.

He deposited Miss Russell with the Farthington twins at the end of their set and went in search of the Duchess of Alvord. He'd ask Sarah to look for Emma.

He found her with her husband and Robbie.

"Ah, the newly betrothed." James grinned. "Congratulations, Charles. I highly recommend the married state."

Robbie rolled his eyes. "I'm going to have to find new friends. You are both becoming as dull as ditch-water."

"Perhaps you should consider joining us." James grinned.

Robbie shook his head. "Not I. I'm too young for parson's mousetrap." He laughed. "Where is Emma, Charles? I'm surprised she's not at your side."

"I was wondering the same thing. Have any of you seen her?"

"No, I don't think so." Sarah frowned. "Would you like me to check the retiring room?"

"Please."

"Are you worried something has happened to Emma, Charles?" James asked as Sarah hurried out of the room.

"No. Well, yes. I don't see Stockley either." Charles reminded himself William was shadowing Stockley, but the thought did little to settle his churning stomach.

"Surely you can't think Emma would prefer Stockley to you?" Robbie took another glass of champagne from a passing servant. "She's not so jingle-brained."

"No, I don't think that."

"You think Stockley poses some danger?" James's tone was sharp.

"Perhaps." Charles could tell James was thinking of his cousin, Richard, who had kidnapped and almost raped Sarah in the spring. "I'm certain it's nothing like you faced. I just don't like the man." Where *was* Emma? He looked around the ballroom again. Surely she should be back now.

"And?" Robbie asked.

"And?"

"There is obviously something else you are not telling us."

Charles shrugged. "Well, there have been some odd occurrences."

"Odd occurrences?" James's eyebrows shot up.

"Yes. Someone has been using Knightsdale's hidden passages."

Robbie choked on his champagne. "I didn't know Knightsdale *had* hidden passages."

"Neither did I, so whoever is prowling the estate knows more about it than I do."

"Well, that's not a surprise." Robbie took another sip. "Both your father and your brother kept you in the dark there."

"To be fair, I wasn't much interested in Knightsdale affairs." He felt a tap on his arm and turned to see Sarah. She did not have Emma with her.

"I'm sorry, Charles. I couldn't find her. I did ask a servant. He said she'd received a note and left a half hour or more ago."

"Damn. Uh, your pardon, Sarah." Charles did not like having Emma and Stockley both missing. Who would have sent Emma a note?

He felt James's hand on his shoulder. "Can we help, Charles? Robbie and I will be happy to look for Emma."

"Or Stockley," Robbie said.

"No. It is probably only a coincidence that they are both absent. Most likely one of my nieces wanted Emma. I'll just go upstairs to check. I'm sure there's nothing to worry about."

"All right," James said. "But if you're not back in half an hour, Robbie and I are coming after you."

"I'll be back—but yes, if I'm not, I'll be happy for your assistance."

Charles tried to walk sedately through the ballroom— no need to give Lady Oldston, Mrs. Pelham, or the other society tabbies any tidbit of gossip to chew on. Once he cleared the door, he picked up his pace. By the time he reached the staircase, he was running, taking the stairs two at a time.

He reached the long gallery and stopped. There was a pistol pointed at the center of his chest.

Mr. Stockley smiled. "Just the man I was looking for," he said.

Emma counted slowly to ten, then fumbled in the dark for the lever Charles had said was there. She wished now she had asked more questions—she wished she had asked to see the lever. He had said it was lower on the wall than he expected, but he was taller than she. Where was it?

Something crawled across her hand. She screamed, jumping back, bumping into the passage's back wall. Something filmy brushed her face.

Dear God. Spiders. She could not think of spiders. She would not. The real spider was Stockley. If she did not keep her wits about her, Stockley would entrap Charles in his web. The man was mad. And a murderer. There was no time for a fit of the vapors.

She stepped up to the door again and carefully felt

all around it. There, on the right side—the lever. Charles said to push it up, not down. It moved easily. The door opened—barely. Emma shoved as hard as she could.

It was hopeless. The door would not move another inch. It was securely blocked by the heavy chair Charles and then Mr. Stockley had pushed in front of it.

No one—certainly not she—was going to get out of the passage this way.

She could try shouting, but there was no one on this floor—no one to hear her until Nanny and the girls came upstairs in the morning. By then it would be too late. Mr. Stockley would be gone and Charles—she wouldn't think about Charles.

She would just have to find another door. She would have to make her way along this black, dirty, spider-filled passage.

She had the sinking feeling Charles's life depended on it.

She ran her hands carefully around this door so she could recognize an opening by feel alone. There was no hope of seeing anything in this stygian dark.

She wished again she had asked Charles more questions. Were there other doors on this level? If the passages had been built to help the family escape, it was unlikely. There were no other family rooms up here. Which meant she would have to descend to the next floor, probably not by staircase. She had best plan on doing some climbing.

She was happy the neck of her beautiful ball gown was so low—it made wiggling out of it somewhat easier. The thought that this exposed more of her person to spiders was one she firmly shoved aside.

She would worry about spiders after she had warned Charles of Stockley's madness.

She put her hand on the wall and shuffled toward the main hall. She hoped. It would be so easy to get lost in the dark.

She shoved that thought away also.

She wanted to move faster, but she forced herself to be patient. Somewhere ahead was the way down to the next floor—she would not do Charles any good if she took it flying head first.

In a moment, she was glad of her caution. Her lead foot slid into air. She pulled it back quickly, leaning heavily against the wall, heart pounding.

Once her legs stopped trembling, she stooped and ran her hands over the ground. There was a ladder. She grasped it tightly and carefully climbed down deeper into the darkness. When her foot touched the ground, she sighed, relief making her weak. She clung to the ladder for a moment, giving her heart time to slow its wild beating. Then she turned.

And walked straight into a huge spiderweb.

Charles swore he heard Emma screaming some-where, though Stockley showed no signs he'd heard anything. Perhaps it was his imagination. The mind did odd things when faced with a loaded gun.

"Where is Emma?"

Stockley shrugged. "Upstairs. I haven't hurt her . . . yet. Cooperate and I won't have to."

Charles tried to control his anger. "What do you want?" If he could keep the man talking for thirty minutes, Robbie and James would come charging up the stairs. They were men of their word.

"I want the jewels Randall stole from my father."

"Jewels? Stockley, I don't know what you are talking about."

"Don't lie."

Charles did not care for the way Stockley's gun jumped when he was angry. He hoped this pistol did not have a hair trigger.

"I'm not. I really do not know what you are talking about. I was only seven years old when Randall died— he was my great-uncle and at sea most of his life." Charles moved casually away from Stockley's gun. "You know far more about Knightsdale than I do. The hidden passages, for instance. I did not know they really existed; you, on the other hand, appear to be intimately familiar with them. How is that?"

Stockley shrugged, following him toward the marble Draysmiths. Charles hoped to lure him close enough to knock one of the busts on to him. It wasn't a brilliant plan, but he didn't have much to work with.

"My father had a diagram in his papers. He and Randall were partners." Stockley snorted. "Da was a fool to think he could trust one of Randall's kind. They were supposed to share the jewels. Randall took them. Thought his aristocratic nephew would protect him. Well, his fancy nephew wasn't there to catch him when he stumbled into the harbor, was he?"

"I wonder if poor Randall had a little help into the water."

"Bloody right he did. If my da had had an ounce of sense, he'd have snaffled the jewels before he bashed Randall on the head."

"Hmm. That was more than twenty years ago, however. I find your sudden interest somewhat peculiar." Stockley was standing next to Great-Uncle Randall's bust. It would be fitting if that was the

Draysmith sculpture to take him down. Charles stepped closer.

"Move back." Stockley motioned with his pistol.

Charles moved back. It was unwise to argue with an armed man.

"It ain't so sudden. My da died in the spring. Surprised he lived that long." Stockley frowned. "God, what we could have done with those jewels! If I'd known about them, you can be sure I'd have been here sooner. But I didn't know. I only found out about them when I found Da's papers in a box under his bed."

His voice dropped to a mutter, but he kept his gun up and pointed at Charles.

"Bloody hell. I thought your brother had the jewels with him. Went to Italy, tore that damn carriage apart looking for them. Knightsdale tried to be a hero; his wife screamed like a banshee—shot her first to shut her up. Had to kill the servants, too. And then the bloody jewels weren't there."

He waved his gun at Charles.

"They have to be here, damn it. They have to. Why can't I find them?"

Charles moved closer to Great-Uncle Randall's bust.

"I said move back, you bastard." Stockley's gun pointed squarely at Charles's chest. "If you want to live, tell me where I can find the bloody jewels."

Charles measured the distance between him and the bust. Stockley was standing right next to it, but that did Charles little good. Unless Stockley was an abysmal shot, Charles would be dead before he could get a finger on Great-Uncle Randall. Apparently thirty minutes had not yet elapsed—he did not hear Robbie and James pounding up the stairs to his rescue.

"Talk, damn it."

Charles took a deep breath. "I'm afraid we have a minor problem, Mr. Stockley. I truly have no idea where these jewels are."

"Liar. Goddamned liar."

Stockley raised his pistol and pointed it directly between Charles's eyes.

"You've told your last lie, Knightsdale."

Sanity came back to Emma gradually. She shuddered, clasping her hands together tightly to stop the trembling. She had gotten the last strand of sticky web off her face. She was certain of it, but she still felt its horrible, nasty touch.

Were there still threads of it in her hair—threads and . . . spiders?

The madness threatened to swallow her again. She could not let it. She had to get out of there. She had to find Charles.

But where was she? She had completely lost any sense of direction when she walked into that web. Dear God, when she had felt the sticky threads all over her face, she had turned into a mindless animal. She had screamed and jumped and spun as if she could shake herself free. She'd scrubbed her face with her hands, then rubbed her hands against the corridor walls trying to get any hint of spiderweb off. She shuddered.

She would pick a direction. Any direction. She would go as far as she could, then she would try another way. Panicking did no good.

She edged along the wall. Almost immediately

she heard men's voices. She slid her feet a little faster over the floor. There was no guarantee that she would find a door by these men, but perhaps she could bang on the wall and get their attention. She could tell them about Mr. Stockley. They could warn Charles.

The voices were getting louder. Thank God. She was going in the right direction. She shuffled faster and her fingers bumped against an upright piece of wood. It was the edge of a door. She sagged against it in relief.

And heard shouting. She pressed her ear flat on the wall. It was Mr. Stockley. He was close, just on the other side of the wall. She could almost make out his words. They sounded angry, threatening. She heard Charles's calm response. Mr. Stockley shouted back.

She was certain that in a few minutes something very bad was going to happen.

She scrambled for the door, her fingers flying down to find the latch. It wasn't there. Panic surged through her. She forced herself to concentrate only on the door. There. The catch was just a little farther to the right. She pulled up on it. Nothing happened. This door had not been opened in years.

Stockley shouted again. This time she could make out the words.

"You've told your last lie, Knightsdale."

She had run out of time. Desperate, she yanked up on the latch and flung herself against the door. This time, it gave, swinging open. She heard a crash and then an explosion as she tumbled out of the passage and onto the floor.

Charles looked down the barrel of Stockley's gun. He knew he could not stall any longer. He hoped for a miracle and readied himself to dive to the side when the man pulled the trigger.

A miracle arrived. Part of the wall behind Stockley flew open, knocking Great-Uncle Randall's bust into Stockley's arm just as Stockley fired. The gun discharged harmlessly into the portrait of the first marquis.

Charles tackled Stockley, shoving him on to his stomach and twisting his arm up behind his back.

"Damn. We missed all the fun, Robbie." The Duke of Alvord appeared at the top of the stairs.

"I told you your watch was slow, James." Robbie turned to Charles. "If he'd listened to me, we'd have been here five minutes ago. But no, the Duke of Alvord could not possibly have an imperfect timepiece."

"I was wondering what was keeping you." Charles jerked up on Stockley's arm as the man bucked under him. "Would you care to come help me deal with this fellow?"

"Be delighted to, wouldn't we, James? What exactly happened?"

"I'm not certain. If you'll take charge of Stockley . . ."

". . . you can clean up the mess." James nodded. "I quite understand. So untidy to have emeralds and diamonds lying about, isn't it, Miss Peterson?"

Charles twisted around. Emma sat on the floor, covered in dirt and cobwebs, her hair flying all about her face. She looked beautiful.

"Emma!"

James grabbed Stockley as Charles scrambled to his feet.

"Watch your step," James said.

Charles finally looked somewhere other than into Emma's eyes. On the floor scattered around her were tiaras, bracelets, necklaces, and rings. Gold and jewels. Great-Uncle Randall had split in two, spilling all his secrets.

"Well," he said, "it looks like we have found Mr. Stockley's treasure."

CHAPTER 18

"That was an interesting end to the house party."
Emma sat by the fire, drying her hair. She'd come
upstairs as soon as Charles had picked her out of the
rubble. He'd given her a thorough kiss and sent her
off to her room before he took Stockley downstairs
and dealt with his curious guests. She'd heard a
few of the men, drawn by the sound of the gunshot,
coming up the stairs as she left.

She'd had a long, warm bath, washing away every
last wisp of spiderweb. If the water hadn't started to
cool, she might still be in the tub. Then she'd waited
for Charles to come upstairs. It hadn't been very
long. She'd heard him in the other room, talking to
Mr. Henderson. Then he'd sent his valet away and
come in to her.

She had wanted to go to him immediately, but she
had hesitated. He'd had such a remote look on his
face. He sat in the chair next to hers and stared at the
fire, his hands in the pockets of his dressing gown.

"What did you do with Mr. Stockley?"

"James is taking charge of him. He'll stand trial for
killing my brother. I have no doubt he'll swing."

She brushed her hair and studied his profile. His lips were pulled into a hard, thin line.

"It was bad enough having Paul die, but to learn now he was murdered . . ."

She leaned over and put a hand on his knee. "Don't think about it. There's nothing you can do to change what happened."

Charles slumped lower in his chair. "I should have asked more questions. I should have insisted someone investigate as soon as I got the news."

"Why? An investigation would not have brought anyone back to life."

"It might have turned up Stockley. Then you wouldn't have had that unpleasant time with the spiders."

"And *you* would not have had that unpleasant time looking down the barrel of Mr. Stockley's gun."

Charles shrugged. He stared at the fire for a while. Emma stared at him. When he spoke again, his voice was low.

"I was just so angry when they told me Paul was dead. I hardly considered Paul. I could only think about what his death had done to me. How I was trapped."

"Charles, we can't control what we feel, just how we act. You did all that was proper. No one thought Paul's death was anything but a random crime." She sat back, twisting her fingers in her wrapper. "If anyone should feel guilty about their feelings, it is I. I tried to keep my father from finding happiness with Mrs. Graham."

Charles's frown deepened. He looked away from the fire to her. "Your feelings were natural—"

"My feelings were childish and selfish. I see that now. But I can't go back and change them, much as

I would like to. Just as you cannot go back and change how you reacted to Paul's death. We can only go forward."

He hunched a shoulder. "I don't know . . ."

"*I* do. And much as I dislike saying anything critical of the dead, especially your brother and his wife, I think the girls will be better off with you as their papa. And the estate will be better as well—you do intend to stay here, don't you?"

"For part of the year, yes."

"Only part of the year?"

He finally smiled. "Well, I guess I should take this peer business seriously. Take my place in Lords. And you should see London during the Season. The girls might enjoy Astley's Circus and Hyde Park. I think leaving Knightsdale for part of the year is acceptable, don't you?"

"Yes." Emma smiled back. "You can leave Knightsdale as long as you don't leave us."

"No danger of that, sweetheart." His smile widened to a grin. He leered at her. "I have to get an heir, don't I? I believe we determined I cannot accomplish that goal with you in Kent and me in London."

Emma felt the throbbing start low in her stomach. She certainly understood that concept now.

He leaned closer. "What? You aren't going to throw something at me this time? No china canines to shatter?"

"No." She still saw sadness lurking in his expression. She smiled. She believed she knew a way to chase the darkness from his eyes. "I was angry with you then. I am not feeling anger now."

"No?"

"No. I am, however, feeling a number of other strong emotions."

"Really? That sounds promising."

"Exactly. You made a promise to me this evening that you have not yet kept."

Charles's eyebrows rose. "I did? What did I promise?"

Emma stood, turning to face him. She let her wrapper slide down her arms to pool at her feet so she stood naked in the firelight. She smiled, noting how lust and love burned the last shadows from Charles's face. "You promised to misbehave more than I could possibly imagine."

He reached out to cup her breasts, trace her hips, stroke her thighs. She felt wet heat, and spread her legs slightly.

"I warn you," she said, "I've recently developed a very vivid imagination."

He couldn't talk. He could barely think. He stared at the sweet white of her thighs, her dark silky hair. He breathed in the heat of her. He ran his hands over her smooth hips. She parted her legs wider and he dipped his finger inside.

"Emma."

She put her hands on the chair arms and leaned forward to kiss him. Her tongue licked over his lips and then darted inside. He put his hands on her full breasts, swaying in front of him. He stroked them, kneaded them, felt their nipples harden. Emma moaned softly in the back of her throat and spread her legs wider, sitting on his lap, putting her wet center exactly where he most wanted it. She spread the top of his dressing gown and slid her hands inside, skimming over his heated skin.

He did not want to take her in this chair. He wanted her in his bed. In the Draysmith bed. He needed her there to free him from the last of his ghosts.

He put his hands on her face and drew back from her lips.

"I thought I was the one who was supposed to misbehave," he said.

"What?"

"You said I had promised to misbehave more than you could imagine, but you are definitely the one misbehaving now, Miss Peterson. More than *I* could imagine."

The minx gave him what looked like a very self-satisfied smile. He spanked her lovely bottom very lightly, and she laughed and stuck out her tongue. He sucked on it gently.

"I am not going to let you seduce me here, my love." He lifted her off his lap, setting her on her feet. "Some day, but not today." He shrugged out of his dressing gown. She grinned and reached for the most prominent part of him, but he caught her wrists.

"Behave yourself, my dear."

"Make me."

"With pleasure." He scooped her up and carried her into his room, dropping her into the center of his bed. She laughed and held out her arms to him.

When he felt them wrap around him, he knew he had finally come home.

Don't miss this sneak peek at
THE NAKED EARL,
coming in 2007 from Kensington . . .

Robert Hamilton, Earl of Westbrooke, was a light sleeper. His eyes opened the moment his mattress shifted. He turned to see what had caused the disturbance.

Two very large, very naked breasts were right in front of his nose. Damn! He looked up to see to whom they belonged. Lady Felicity Brookton. She gave him an arch look as she drew in her breath to scream.

Bloody hell.

He bolted from the bed and leapt for the window. There was no time for such niceties as breeches or shoes. Once Lady Felicity started her caterwauling, the entire house party would be banging on his door. He'd be securely caught in parson's mousetrap, condemned to face Lady Felicity at the breakfast table every morning for the rest of his life.

Could there be a more succinct description of hell?

He swung his leg over the sill and dropped down onto the roof of the portico as she emitted her first screech. The sharp surface cut into his bare feet, but the pain was nothing compared to the panic raging in his chest.

He had to get away.

Thank God he had scrutinized the view from his window when he'd arrived at Tynweith's house party. He'd made a habit of looking for escape routes since the ladies of the *ton* had gotten so persistent. If they only knew . . . Well, if he was forced to flee naked from his bed perhaps it was time to do something. A discreet rumor judiciously planted should deter most marriage-minded maidens. He glanced back at his window. Or perhaps they would be happy to have his money and title without having to pay for them in his bed.

He shivered as an early spring breeze rushed over the portico. He couldn't stand here like a nodcock. At any moment one of Tynweith's guests would respond to Felicity's screams, look out the window, and wonder what the Earl of Westbrooke was doing standing naked in the night. He snorted. Hell, all of Tynweith's guests would assume they knew exactly what he had been doing, and he'd be as securely caught as if he'd stayed between his sheets.

It was much too long a distance to the ground to consider jumping. He had not quite reached that point of desperation.

Felicity screeched again. Someone shouted. He scanned the other windows that faced the portico. There, at the end—flickering candlelight showed an open window. He sprinted for it, hoping the room's occupant was male.

Lady Elizabeth Runyon stood naked in front of her mirror, hands on hips, and frowned at her breasts. She tilted her head, squinting at them through her right eye and then her left. Bah! They were small, puny little lemons next to Lady Felicity's lush, ripe melons. No corset in England could make them more impressive.

She turned sideways, grabbing the bedpost to steady herself. Perhaps this angle was more complimentary?

No.

A gust of cool air blew in from her open window, sliding over her skin, causing her nipples to tighten. She covered them with her hands, trying to push them back into place.

She had an odd tingly feeling, as if a vibrating harp string ran from her breasts to her . . . her . . .

She took her hands off her body as if burned. She should put her nightgown back on and climb into bed. Pull the covers up to her chin, close her eyes, and go to sleep. She would if the room didn't swirl so unpleasantly when she did so. She grabbed for the bedpost again.

That last glass of ratafia had definitely been a mistake. She wouldn't have taken it if she hadn't been so bored. If she had to listen to Mr. Dodsworth drone on about his stables one more time . . . It was drink or scream. The man hadn't had an original thought—or any thought that did not involve prime bits of blood—since her come out three years ago.

She leaned against the bedpost. How was she going to survive another Season? Seeing the same people, hearing the same conversation, tittering over the same gossip. It had been exciting when she was seventeen, but now . . .

Was it possible to die of ennui?

And Meg was no help. Lud! She'd finally persuaded her friend to leave the weeds of Kent for the wonders of London, and Meg turned out to be as big a bore as Dodsworth. Her topic of verbal tor-

ture was horticulture. Shrubbery. Damn shrubbery. If Meg had her way, she'd spend every
moment in the shrubbery—and not with a gentleman bent on seduction.

Lizzie scowled at the bedpost. She should have
poured that last glass of ratafia over Robbie's head.
That would have livened things up. Ha! She pictured
the looks of horror that would have adorned the assembled *ton* if Lady Elizabeth Runyon, sister of the
Duke of Alvord, pattern card of respectability, had
caused such a scene.

At least she would have gotten Robbie's attention.
She'd wager next quarter's pin-money on that.

She looked at her mirror again. It was very daring
standing here naked. She straightened, letting go of
the bedpost. Perhaps she should be daring this
Season. Wanton, even. Playing by the rules hadn't
gotten her what she wanted—*whom* she wanted—so
she'd break them.

She put her hands back on her breasts. She sighed.
The poor little things barely filled her palms—they
would be lost in Robbie's larger hands.

Mmm. She half-closed her eyes, biting her bottom
lip. Robbie's hands. His long fingers, his broad palms.
On her skin.

She felt very daring indeed. More than daring—
hot. She rubbed her thumbs over her nipples. The
harp string started vibrating again. She licked her
lips, arching her hips, spreading her legs slightly so
the breeze might find and cool her where she most
needed cooling.

What would it feel like if Robbie touched her *there*?
Her hand slid down her body.

"My God!"

A male voice, hoarse and strained. Her eyes flew

open. Robbie's reflection was staring at her in the mirror. Robbie's very naked reflection.

She spun to face him, grabbing the bedpost to keep from falling. The room shifted unpleasantly, then righted. She blinked. Yes, Robbie was still there, still naked, standing just inside her window.

She had never seen a naked man before, except in paintings or statues. She stared.

Art did not do reality justice. Not at all.

Then again, perhaps no artist had ever had a model quite as splendid as Robbie.

He looked so different from the civilized London lord she had left downstairs. He was larger. Well, obviously, he could not have grown simply by shedding his clothes, but it certainly seemed as if he had. And he was so . . . different. His neck, freed from yards of muffling cravat and concealing collar, was a study in angles and shadows. And his shoulders . . . How had they fit into his coat?

She never would have guessed he had hair sprinkled across his chest. Golden red hair dusting down to his flat stomach, then spreading out below his navel around . . .

Oh, my.

She'd never seen *that* in any art work. The . . . appendage was long and thick and stuck straight out.

How did he hide it in his pantaloons?

Lizzie looked back at Robbie's face. It was far redder than his hair. Could he be injured? The blacksmith's thumb had swollen to twice its size when he'd hit it with his hammer. Had Robbie bumped this part of his anatomy climbing in the window?

"Are you in pain?" She glanced at her bed. "Lie down. I'll get a wet compress."

He made a short noise that sounded like a cross

between a laugh and a moan and jerked around to slam her window shut, pulling the curtains tight.

"No, I'm not in pain. Where's your nightgown?"

"Are you certain?" His back was almost as beautiful as his front. She studied his tight buttocks. She would love to touch them. "You sound like you are in pain."

"Just tell me where your blood—blasted nightgown is." He turned back to her, jaw clenched, eyes focused on her face. "Better yet, just put it on. Now."

Lizzie did not care for the note of command in his voice.

"No, I don't want to. I'm hot." She flushed. "Very hot." Uncomfortably hot. And damp. Wet, really. She moved her hand down to be certain she wasn't dripping.

"God, no." He caught her before she reached her stomach. His fingers—thick, warm—encircled her wrist. She needed them somewhere else. Her breasts ached; her nipples had tightened into hard pebbles.

He shook her arm slightly. "Put on your nightgown." He sounded a bit desperate.

She shook her head. She could smell him now. She inhaled deeply. He smelled of Robbie. She giggled. Silly, but true. It was a musky, spicy scent, stronger now that it wasn't muffled by layers of clothing.

His eyes kept darting looks at her breasts. She felt them swell with his attention. She needed to rub them against the hair on his chest.

Who cared about a nightgown? She didn't want a nightgown. She wanted his body against hers. His skin on hers. Everywhere. She panted slightly. She was certain a puddle of need was forming at her feet.

She reached for him.

"Lizzie!" He grabbed her other hand, holding both wrists in a firm grip.

"Let me go." She jerked back. His grasp was gentle but unbreakable. Well, she knew how to get free. She had an older brother. She wasn't above telling a small lie if necessary. "You're hurting me."

He released her at once.

"Ah!"

She lunged, but he caught her by the shoulders.

"Lizzie, you're bosky."

"N-no, I'm not. I just want to touch you. Please? Just let me touch you." His arms were too long. No matter how much she stretched, she could not reach his body.

"I don't think that would be a good idea. Now put on your nightgown."

"*I* think it would be a splendid idea." She lunged again. No luck. "Why won't you let me touch you?"

"Because besides the fact that you appear to be thoroughly foxed, I'm certain there are going to be people at your door and quite possibly your window any moment now. You don't want them to find us like this, do you?"

She hiccupped. "Yes, I do." She lurched toward him again. If she didn't feel his body against hers soon, she would cry.

Robbie gave an odd little growl. "You wouldn't say that if you were sober."

"Yes, I would." She stopped fighting and touched him where she could reach. The muscles in his arms were warm rocks. She could barely get her fingers around his forearm. She stroked his wrist with her thumb and saw sweat bead on his upper lip. She wanted to lick it off.

"I love you, Robbie. I've loved you forever."

His jaw tensed. "No, you haven't."

"Yes, I have."

He shook his head. "Hero worship. Calf love."

"No. Kiss me. You'll see."

He rubbed his face on his arm, wiping off the sweat. "There's no time for that, Lizzie."

"Yes, there is. Kiss me."

"Lizzie." His hands clenched on her shoulders, but gentled when she drew in a sharp breath. "Lizzie, please. If I'm found here, the scandal will be beyond belief. James will kill me."

"No, he won't. You're his friend."

Robbie snorted. "You're his sister. Trust me. He will kill me if he finds out."

"I don't see why. He met Sarah naked, didn't he? How can he complain?"

"That's different."

"No, it's not."

"Yes, it is, and if you weren't so foxed you would see that. Now put your nightgown on."

"All right, but you'll have to let me go. I can't put it on with your hands in the way."

"True. Just don't—"

Robbie loosened his grip too soon. Lizzie ducked, closing the distance between them in one step and throwing her arms around his waist.

"Lizzie!" He moved almost as quickly, dropping his hands to her hips, pushing them back.

She had forgotten about his swollen part. She didn't want to hurt him, but she so ached to feel his entire body against hers. Well, what she could feel felt very, very good. Her hands played over his back, running up and down his warm, smooth skin. She pressed her cheek against his chest and heard his heart pounding. She found a drop of sweat trickling down between his nipples and licked it, running her tongue up the trail to his neck.

"Lizzie!"

"Mmm?" His hands on her hips were wonderful,

but they were too still. She tried to wiggle, to encourage his fingers to roam. Perhaps she could show him the way. She slipped her own hands over his buttocks and around to his stomach, careful not to touch . . .

"Lizzie!" Robbie leapt back as if scalded.

"Did I hurt you? I'm so sorry. I didn't mean to." She glanced down and smiled in relief. "No, see—you're better. The stiffness and swelling are almost gone. You should be able to tuck your . . . um, well, you should be able to tuck *it* into your pantaloons now."

"*God,* Lizzie."

Lizzie frowned, looking up. Robbie's mouth was so tight a muscle jumped in his cheek. His eyes looked . . . haunted.

"Robbie, I—"

She jumped. Someone was banging on her door—and someone else was banging on her window.

"What . . . ?"

"Your company has arrived." Robbie grabbed her shoulders, turned her, and pushed her toward the bed. "Get your nightgown on."

Damn. Bloody hell. Lizzie was not moving quickly enough. And she was clearly half-seas over. Did she grasp the seriousness of the situation? No. She was sitting on her bed, staring at him. Staring at a particular part of him.

At least she had stopped grabbing him.

More banging. Whoever was hitting the window might manage to break it if Lizzie didn't get her nightgown on soon.

He snuffed out the candle, leaving the room lit only by the banked fire in the hearth. Perhaps darkness would help her concentrate on the matter at hand.

"Put on your nightgown."

"Hmm?"

"Lizzie, you need to put on your nightgown *now*. You have to answer the door." He reached to help her—and encountered a soft breast.

"Mmm."

Good God, the girl was purring. If only . . . No, he wouldn't think of it. It was impossible. Completely im—

"Lizzie!" He tried to keep his voice down, though with all the door and window pounding, he could have shouted and not been heard over the din. "Lizzie—oh, no!"

He grabbed her wrist and pulled her fingers away from where they had wandered.

"Did I hurt you? You're swollen again."

"Lizzie, just put your nightgown on and get the door. Please?"

She huffed and the small puff of air tickled over his stomach.

"All right. Will you touch me again after they are all gone? It felt so good."

Damn. He balled his hands into fists. He really would like to hit something. He tried to keep his voice calm.

"We'll see. Now be a good girl and put on your nightgown." Louder banging on the door and some muffled shouts. At least James wasn't here; he was at Alvord, awaiting the birth of his second child. "Hurry, the door first. Try to look as if you've just woken up. And remember, I'm not here."

"Not here. Right."

He watched her take her first steps toward the door, then jumped onto the bed, pulling the curtains closed.

Betty, Lizzie's maid, must sleep like the dead, he

thought. Hell, she must *be* dead if this racket hadn't woken her. Of course, that was assuming she was in her bed at all. More likely she was with his valet somewhere. It was no secret those two would like to make a match of it. Collins had certainly hinted about it enough. Robbie was beginning to fear for his life when the man shaved him each morning.

Betty and Collins would be merry as grigs if Robbie married Lizzie. Well, he would be, too, but it would never happen. He would never curse Lizzie with a half-man like himself. He sighed. When he had seen her, standing naked in front of her mirror, the candlelight making her skin glow, her hand sliding down her curves to exactly the place he most wanted to be . . .

He buried his face in the pillow. A mistake. He inhaled her scent and grew even harder.

He stifled a moan.

The door swung open. Light and the babble of voices, some shouting flooded the room. God, only a miracle would keep him from detection.

He prayed for a miracle.

"He's here, isn't he? I know he's here." Lady Felicity Brookton, clad in a pistachio-colored dressing-gown, pushed Lizzie aside and stepped into her room, holding a candle high. "Where are you hiding him?"

"Um." Lizzie blinked, staring out her door. Half the house party had assembled in the corridor.

"Someone is knocking at the window." Lady Caroline, the daughter of the Earl of Dunlee, maneuvered her ample bulk across the room and opened the curtains. "Oh, look! It's Lord Peter."

"Let him in." Lady Felicity peered inside Lizzie's wardrobe.

"Um." Lizzie wished she could think. That last glass of ratafia had definitely been ill-advised. Her head felt as if it were stuffed with cotton wool.

She couldn't let them find Robbie: he didn't want to be found. She watched Lady Felicity light all the available candles. How was she going to stop them? There were only so many places to look.

Lord Peter, dressed in his shirt sleeves and pantaloons, climbed in the window. "Saw him vault in here." He chuckled. "Hard to miss his lily-white as—" Lord Peter coughed. "Ankles. His lily-white ankles. Hard to miss them in the dark."

"So where is he, Lady Elizabeth?" Lady Felicity glared at her.

"Um, he who?"

"Lord Westbrooke, of course. Didn't he just climb in your window?"

"Uh . . ." Lizzie's mind went blank.

"Lady Felicity, surely you cannot be suggesting that Lord Westbrooke would behave in such an inappropriate manner?"

Lizzie turned to see Lady Beatrice, her nominal chaperone for the Season. Thank God! Lady Bea would deal with this mess in short order.

Lady Felicity lifted her chin. "I only know what I saw."

Lady Bea lifted an eyebrow. "And what exactly did you see, miss?"

"I saw Lord Westbrooke leap naked out the window."

"I thought you said he came *in* the window."

"Not this window."

"Ah, the window in your room then? Correct me if I am wrong, miss, but any man exiting your window would end as a rather unsightly corpse on the terrace. Or have you changed rooms recently? I thought your bedchamber was just a few doors down the hall from mine on the other side of the corridor."

Lady Felicity turned red. She opened her mouth as if to speak, but no words issued forth.

"Let's look in the bed, Felicity." Lord Peter left the window and reached for the bed curtains. "I'll wager Westbrooke is hiding between the sheets."

"Lord Peter!"

Everyone turned to stare at the petite woman who'd managed to push to the fore of the crowd. The Duchess of Hartford—Lady Charlotte Wickford before her marriage to the elderly duke—was not someone Lizzie would ever have imagined coming to her rescue. Charlotte hated her. Well, she really hated James, but James spent most of his time in Kent these days. Lizzie was a much more convenient target.

"What, your grace?" Lord Peter stood back, gesturing to the bed curtains. "Would you like to do the honors?"

Charlotte stared at him. He flushed and dropped his arm.

"If you won't do it, *I* will." Felicity grabbed a handful of cloth.

"Lady Felicity." Charlotte's tone stopped Felicity's hand before it had moved an inch. "Surely you do not mean to imply that Lady Elizabeth would entertain a man in her bedroom?"

Felicity looked at Lizzie's small bosom. Lizzie crossed her arms over it.

"Entertain? No, however—"

"However, if Lord Westbrooke should be so bold as to visit Lady Elizabeth in her room at night—if he were found in her bed—I assume he would do the gentlemanly thing and offer for her." Charlotte shrugged. "Her brother, the duke, would insist, wouldn't you say?"

Felicity paused, an arrested expression on her face.

"In fact, I imagine if Lord Westbrooke were indeed hiding behind those bed curtains, he'd be wed to Lady Elizabeth before the week was out." Charlotte smiled. "I'm certain you would want to dance at that wedding, hmm, Lady Felicity?"

Lady Felicity's hand fell to her side. "Ah, yes. You're right. Of course. Lord Westbrooke would never invade Lady Elizabeth's room. I don't know what I was thinking."

"I know what you were thinking. You told me—"

"Lord Peter!"

Lord Peter frowned and turned to Charlotte.

"I believe we intrude on Lady Elizabeth's privacy." Charlotte smiled up at him as she ran her fingers over his shirt cuff. "It's time you went to . . . bed, don't you think?"

It was Lord Peter's turn to have an arrested expression. He stared down at Charlotte for a moment and then grinned.

"I believe you are correct, your grace."

"Of course I am." Charlotte glanced at Felicity. "I imagine you dreamt the event, Lady Felicity. Sometimes our dreams are so vivid, they appear real, do they not?"

Felicity tore her eyes off the bed curtains. "Yes. Yes, I'm certain you are right, your grace." She glanced back at the bed. "Sometimes my dreams do seem real."

"Exactly." Charlotte moved toward the door, Lord Peter at her side. "So sorry to disturb you, Lady Elizabeth." Her eyes drifted to the bed also. "I'm certain you are eager to get back to"—Charlotte smiled slightly—"sleep." She inclined her head. "You have depths I never suspected."

Lizzie watched the crowd disperse. Lady Beatrice

was the last to leave; she looked at the bed and raised her eyebrows.

"Anything you would like to tell me, Lizzie?"

Lizzie looked at the bed, too. "Um, no."

"You're certain?"

"Yes." Lizzie nodded. She was definitely certain. She did not want to discuss the evening's bizarre events with anyone. She was of half a mind that she, too, was the victim of a very vivid dream. "I'm a trifle out of curl. I think I will just go to bed."

"I see." Lady Beatrice addressed the bed in a very stern voice. "Well, I am more than certain the duke would eviscerate any man who played fast and loose with his sister's reputation—or harmed her in *any* way."

"Yes, I'm sure. Thank you. Good night."

Lizzie ushered Lady Bea out the door and closed it firmly behind her. Then she sagged against the solid wooden surface, puffed out her cheeks, and eyed the bed.

Could she have dreamt the entire sequence of events? Was it possible the evening was simply the product of overindulgence?

There was only one way to find out. She pushed away from the door and stepped toward the bed.

About the Author

A native Washingtonian, Sally MacKenzie still lives in suburban Maryland with her transplanted upstate New Yorker husband and four Washingtonian sons. She's written federal regulations, school newsletters, auction programs, class plays, and swim league guidance, but it wasn't until her nest started to empty that she tried her hand at romance. Her first novel, *The Naked Duke*, was released by Kensington Books in February 2005. She can be reached by email at writesally@comcast.net or by snail mail at P. O. Box 2453, Kensington, MD 20891. Please visit her home in cyberspace at www.sallymackenzie.net.

More Historical Romance From
Jo Ann Ferguson